PRAISE FOR AL HESS

"Al managed to balance cozy small town mystery with retro-future scifi horror and a incredibly sweet romance arc."
Sunyi Dean, the Sunday Times bestselling author of *The Book Eaters*

"Al Hess serves up a moving story of found love, found family, and hard-won self-acceptance, all wrapped in one of the most intriguing alien invasion stories I've read.
Nathan Tavares, author of *A Fractured Infinity* and *Welcome to Forever*

"Hess handles the otherworldly proceedings with a deft touch in this compulsively readable tale, and balances apocalyptic devastation with well-drawn characters and emotionally resonant relationships. A motley crew, aliens, and pie. What's not to love?"
Khan Wong, author of *The Circus Infinite*

"Utterly charming and delightful. A story of kind yet socially excluded people learning their true courage in the face of a UFO invasion."
Jen Charlton, @thecaseofbooks

"Unabashed in its exploration of neurodiversity and tender in its exploration of romance and found family, Key Lime Sky is nothing short of delightful, combining surrealism with wit, and adding in a dash of eldritch horror in an unforgettable adventure fueled by tangerine nightmares, key lime skies, and hazy, iridescent photographs."
Melissa, Space Between Pages

"A cozy, queer alien invasion adven. and the benefits of th
@thespineofmoth(

Al Hess

KEY LIME SKY

ANGRY
ROBOT

ANGRY ROBOT
An imprint of Watkins Media Ltd

Unit 11, Shepperton House
89 Shepperton Road
London N1 3DF
UK

angryrobotbooks.com
twitter.com/angryrobotbooks
Everybody wants a slice.

An Angry Robot paperback original, 2024

ISBN 978 1 91599 812 5
Ebook ISBN 978 1 91599 813 2

Printed and bound in the United Kingdom by CPI Group (UK) Ltd, Croydon CR0 4YY.

9 8 7 6 5 4 3 2 1

For seven year-old me

Denver

Ezra

Molly

Iridescent ichor quivers on my lashes; it streaks my hair, coats my lips. A heavy ozone scent with top notes of decomposing tuna challenges me to keep down the pie in my stomach. Key lime.

The air in this pocket is thin. Black stars dance in my vision, my lungs burning as I pull in a rattling gasp. Watery, kaleidoscopic color refracts endlessly through translucent tissue like a funhouse of cosmic horror. I jab my open hand through the flesh in front of me, and it splits apart like gelatin. Hot gore gushes over my arm. The surrounding walls clench, pressing against my body, and a pained moan rumbles from somewhere deep below.

Webs of veins brush my cheeks and catch in my hair as I squeeze through the gap, and I concentrate as hard as I can on the creamy tartness of lime pie. If I don't, if I think too much about the tuna smell, the sticky fluid coating my face, and the dizzying light, I'm going to stop, shut down, and be absorbed by this monstrosity.

My fist tears through membrane. The flesh cocooning me clenches harder, muscle squeezing, trying to expel me like a splinter.

Key lime.

Peanut butter.

Bourbon pecan.

Cherry.

Keep going.

Don't stop.

1

LAST FRIDAY

The cherry pie at *Lynn's Diner* off of Highway 287 was abysmal, and I said it much louder than intended.

The waitress turned to me. Her foundation was two shades darker than her skin tone, making her head seem like it had been popped off of a different body and twisted onto this one. "Suppose I'll be taking this away then, huh?" She reached for the plate of pie.

I jerked it toward myself, and the fork clattered onto the counter. "I'm not finished."

"But you said it's awful."

"It is." Watery pink juice ran into the creases of the plate, and bits of anemic pastry clung to the fork. I captured a few more contact lens photos with a flick of my eyelids, then carved into the slab and pushed another bite into my mouth. The waitress watched – maybe she thought I'd change my mind.

She folded her arms over her pinstriped uniform. "Well? What's wrong with it?"

It wasn't sensational. It wasn't even palatable. I stretched out the display on my phone, then propped it on the counter and hit record, not bothering to keep my voice down since she *had* asked. "The crust leaves a greasy film on the roof of my mouth and has the consistency of stale crackers. It's hard to imagine these cherries as ever being anything other than the congealed, indeterminate mass they are now. Metallic and overly sweet mush that makes my tongue unhappy. This tastes like broken dreams. Two stars."

Frown lines cut into the waitress' cakey makeup. "You a food critic?"

"Something like that. You probably saw my article about *The Lounge*'s delicious alphabet pie back in November."

Everyone had seen it. The post had gone viral. My blog itself was a failure, and I'd never managed to recreate the popularity of someone resurrecting a bizarre 1940s recipe that involved cinnamon red hots and alphabet noodles. There was still enough traffic to that post to generate a bit of income, but anything I wrote about this cherry pie wasn't going to help me pay my rent next week.

The waitress cocked her manicured eyebrow. "You wrote that, huh?"

"Yes. And I hate to say this, but I was expecting much better from this place." I supposed that's what I got for taking the word of a couple of random truckers. What a waste.

Dishes clattered into a busser's tub, and I flinched and nearly knocked over my phone. There were only a couple of other diners in a booth by the window, the conversation so sparse that I hadn't needed to use my earplugs, but the shriek of ceramic on ceramic made me stuff my hand in my pocket and squeeze the rubber plugs, ensuring they were there in case it happened again.

"We aren't really known for our pie, hon. It's not homemade. The regulars come for our burgers. Want one?" This time, when the waitress reached for my plate, I didn't stop her. I wondered if it was a prerequisite when applying for a serving job that you called people *hon*.

"No, thank you. You know, I don't know what brand that is" – I pointed at the pie – "but Southern Tree makes a great one. Flaky crust with tart, whole cherries and the slightest hint of almond. Just egg wash the top and dust it with sugar and you'd have a six- or seven-star pie. You could be known for burgers *and* pie."

She pulled in a measured breath the way everyone did when I started giving my opinion too much. "I'll pass your suggestion on to Lynn."

"Are you insulted? It wasn't my intention. I'm judging the pie's character alone. And it's about as respectable as Muddy Gap's last mayor."

It was supposed to be a joke, but the waitress' scowl deepened. The neon scrollwork behind her head gave her hair a hellish pink outline. "Do us all a favor and don't come back, huh?"

"You didn't actually *like* the last mayor, did you?"

"No one liked the last mayor."

"Then why–"

She turned away with my plate, disappearing into the back of the kitchen.

Sighing, I dug out some ones and tucked them under my coffee cup. I scrawled on the back of a napkin that finding the right shade of foundation was a simple matter of testing it on one's inner wrist, and some blending sponges would make the application look better at the jawline.

The vinyl stool groaned as I slid off with my backpack, and I wedged on my felt boater. Hesitating, I turned back and crumpled up the napkin note. Someone needed to tell the waitress, but she'd already taken personal offense to my observations once. Pointing out her makeup skills wasn't going to make her evening better.

I hit record on the phone, absently squeezing the display into a stick. "Despite the secret ingredient of the pie being disappointment, the coffee was fresh and the diner's atmosphere pleasant." Framed prints hung above empty butter yellow booths; all of them depicting barns in various seasonal settings. They looked like they may have been pulled from a wall calendar. I blinked a few photos and received no error messages in return. These little places didn't employ privacy fields the way bigger restaurants did. "The decor is dust-free and follows a themed, if somewhat uninspired, setting. I'm told *Lynn's* is well-known for their burgers, so if you find yourself in the area, give them a try and let me know what you think."

If I used an earbud and eye commands to dictate instead of a phone, it would likely garner me less irritated glares. I only needed to whisper for an earbud to hear my voice. But it also picked up me chewing, which had sounded so obscene on the playback that I hadn't attempted it again. And despite contact technology coming a long way in the past decade, many of the features still caused eye strain and headaches. A phone would have to do, unless I wanted to walk around with a notepad full of chicken scratch like some old-timey journalist.

A brusque wind hit me as I pushed through the door, whipping long strands of hair across my face. I pressed my hat firmly onto my head and hunched into my coat. Gravel squeaked beneath my cowboy boots. The first stars glinted above in the clear dark. My little Ford sat lonely in the parking lot, bathed in the jaundiced glow of an arc sodium light.

Maybe writing up a post about this place was unwise. It wouldn't make the diner look good, and even though there were blogs that thrived on roasting restaurants with bad food, I had never wanted to be one of those. I gave an honest opinion, that was all. But my honest opinions weren't paying the bills.

I slid into the truck and pushed the starter, my nose pressed against the scratchy wool lapels of my coat. It was late April and the snow seemed to finally be gone, but that chilly wind never let up. Once the cab grew marginally more toasty, I turned onto the highway, heading back for Muddy Gap.

Writing for online magazines used to be my bread and butter. I was a regular contributor to several popular sites, and when that wasn't quite enough, I'd supplement it with freelance gigs. But the opportunities were coming more and more infrequently. It was hard to say whether they were scarce or the magazines no longer liked my writing enough to hand me new projects. In an attempt to put a little more padding in my bank account, I'd subscribed to a service that would ship items to me from different companies to review. The money was more dependable, but it wasn't enough to survive on. I'd been asked to select a gender upon signing up so they could tailor products to me, but their site was woefully behind the times and didn't have an option for non-binary. They also seemed to conflate gender with sex. This sometimes caused issues with what I was asked to try. Vitamin supplements, lipsticks, cologne samples, and hair removal cream were all fine. But when I didn't possess the specific anatomy or functions needed to use something, I had to pay postage to send it back. I could have told someone in customer service the issue, but their only contact information was a phone number.

I tried unboxings. The appeal of watching someone else open a package and pull the shrink wrap off of a white noise machine was beyond me, but it was popular and seemed easy enough.

I hadn't anticipated that I would freeze up as badly on a video as I did on the phone. I became so frustrated and flustered that I lay on the floor, the phone still recording, with the unopened package and an X-Acto knife sitting on the table.

Trying to get a nine-to-five job had done nothing but reinforce that I am not, by any stretch of the imagination, a people person.

My landlady, Mrs Mumford, had no sympathy for my money problems, and I'd already borrowed too much from Cousin Billie last month to make ends meet.

Zagging static suddenly exploded from the radio, and I jerked the wheel in surprise. The truck swerved past the edge line and onto the rumble strip, the combined noise becoming an awful crunch that filled the cab. I slammed on the brakes, heart hammering, then punched the audio button off. I'd never had it selected for radio – who listened to the radio?

The hard-edged thumps of tires over the rumble strip still echoed in my ears. I pulled in a slow breath, trying to let sanitizing silence back in. There were times I'd had pie so good I thought I could die happy, but after that cherry abomination back at the diner, crashing and expiring in a ditch was *not* how I wanted things to end.

Something caught my eye beyond the windshield. A bright light rolled across the sky like a loose pearl on velvet. It veered off course so quickly it took me a moment to find it again. I mashed the hazards and hopped out of the truck. The wind threatened to carry away my hat.

Muddy Gap was still quite a few miles away, only a faint light huddled against the horizon gave any indication that it was ahead. The object drifted over town, then grew in size, flaring into an aggressive brilliance. Sour green bled from the central point, fingers of color chasing away the dark. An explosion?

I blinked half a dozen photos, a white half-moon from the flare still ghosting in my vision. The chartreuse iris of sky grew magenta at the edges, then shrank as the night swallowed it.

Goosebumps erupted on my skin, and I wrenched my jacket around me, unsure if I was cold or just disturbed. That was not a plane. Bringing up a search engine in my contacts, I looked for probable causes but only found unhelpful suggestions of meteorites, space junk, or the wink of a satellite as it rotated. Considering how quickly the thing had changed directions, that wasn't possible. Ball lightning and earthquake plasma discharge sounded interesting, but if there was an earthquake, I probably would have felt it.

I slid back into the truck and pulled onto the road. There was always the classic go-to of "alien spacecraft". My inner child squealed at the prospect. So many hours on the school bus, nose buried in a book, squinting at grainy photos of mysterious saucer shapes.

But if aliens had stopped over Muddy Gap, surely they were lost.

Trees and ranches flew by on both sides of the highway. I slowed, coming around the curve that took me into town. I still wasn't used to the new gateway sign arching over Main Street. *Muddy Gap, Wyoming* was cut out of a copper oval, framed by silhouettes of mountains and horses, looking like a freshly minted penny against the rustic backdrop of false-front saloons and feed stores. The squat brick of Gem's Market looked less Old West than the buildings welcoming people to town, though I wasn't sure there was anything more Wyoming than taxidermy in the produce aisle.

It was tempting to stop at the tiny restaurant across from Gem's and ask if anyone had seen the UFO, but I wasn't well-received there after comparing their peppermint chiffon to a tin of chalky breath mints.

Darkness shrouded the parking lot in front of my complex, none of the lights on. I parked and picked my way past silhouetted bushes, stumbling twice on parking chocks. Trevor, my new downstairs neighbor, stood outside his open door, smoking. "Hey Professor Pie."

I stopped as he exhaled his lungful of cancer, a halo of smoke curling around his head. He had one of those generic white frat-boy faces that I couldn't pick out of a lineup if I tried, but at least I knew his name. "My name is Denver. I introduced myself to you last week. We had an argument about skim milk." Skim was nothing but white water, but Trevor had disagreed.

"I remember."

"Okay, well..." What point was I trying to make exactly? The nickname didn't bother me in principle, but my name was unique enough that it should have been easy to recall. "Did you see that flash in the sky?"

He looked up like it might still be there. "No. I'm watching the game, but I'm only half-invested. What was it?"

"I don't know." I peered beyond his open curtains at the whisper-thin screen mounted on the wall. A tiny NO SIGNAL

announcement drifted across a blue background. "Your signal
is out."

He turned. "Huh."

I was close enough to my own apartment for wi-fi to have
kicked on, but an urgent exclamation point sat over the icon.
I glanced at the NO SERVICE indicator on my phone, then
I coiled a lock of hair around my finger and tugged on it.
Would ball lightning knock out TV and phone signals? Or a
radio signal? Maybe there *were* none and the truck had always
played static.

"What radio stations do we get here?"

"Who listens to the radio?" Trevor stubbed out his cigarette
and walked back inside.

I stared at the dying embers in his ashtray, then climbed
the stairs and fought against my obstinate front door lock.
The overwhelming scent of *Vanilla Escape* bombarded me as I
entered. The little air freshener was only supposed to perfume
the bathroom, but even at the lowest setting, it permeated the
entire apartment. The issue would definitely be going in my
product review.

Fractal light played across the wall from the fish tank. I pulled
off my jacket and hat and peered through the glass. Neon tetras
and zebra danios darted by. One of the African dwarf frogs sat
with its head buried in a plastic plant, legs in the air.

"Goofybutt."

Dropping onto the bed, I sent all the photos from my contact
lenses to my laptop, then opened the folder. I tried clicking the
first one and an error box appeared. FILE SYSTEM ERROR
0x2309729525.

That was new. I clicked on the next one and was met with
the same error.

"Damn." I hadn't expected the pictures to be great, as the
contact camera didn't work well at night and at long distances,
but even with internet and phone signals out, the images
should have at least come up.

I tried opening all of the files, then paused. Where were the photos from the diner? The pie and the calendar prints of barns in the fall?

Cycling back, I hovered over the time stamps. The last six were taken at eight fourteen, when I'd been driving home. Then seven forty-three, when I'd been looking at the wall prints. Seven thirty-five. Seven twenty, when the waitress had set my plate on the counter.

I tried to imagine the pie with its sickly crust and watery filling instead of the little error box.

A heavy, ominous dread sank into my stomach, though I wasn't quite certain why. I slid out my phone and hit play on the recording, expecting to hear: *The cherry pie at* Lynn's Diner *off of Highway 287 is abysmal.*

A lattice of crackles and hisses blasted from the speaker, and I turned down the volume. The progress bar slid from one end to the other, seconds rolling over.

One minute and three seconds of nothing but static.

Certainly not a handmade affair, the blob of red sandwiched between a limp, insipid crust looked more like a special effect from a horror movie than anything that should be on a diner's plate.

I rubbed my gritty eyes. Without my dictation, I couldn't remember any of the details of what the pie tasted like, other than *bad.* And maybe that line was unnecessarily cruel. I had trouble determining things like that, but previous experience told me that often when I thought I was being honest, I was, in reality, being mean.

I sipped the dregs of my chamomile tea and picked a soggy bit of leaf from the side of the cup.

Trying again, I wrote: *Focused on the pride of their diner – hamburgers that their regulars can't get enough of – it's clear that pie is an afterthought. An accoutrement poorly chosen and not in high enough demand for a suitable replacement to be purchased. This*

pastry is better off in the back of the freezer where it came from than
on anyone's plate. Order a burger instead.

I thudded my head against the desk. I could gush at length
about the buttery, melt-in-your-mouth phyllo on the chocolate
silk at *Goat's Inn*, or the creamy texture and bright notes of
clove in the deep dish pumpkin from *Elm's Bakery*. After the
internet came back, I figured I should get my thoughts down
in a post before they evaporated, but it was too late. It was
1am, I couldn't remember shit, and the only thing on my mind
was the notion that a UFO had exploded over Muddy Gap and
corrupted all my pictures and voice notes.

Maybe I should delete the blog and end this exercise in futility.
No more Professor Pie. Hoping to go viral again, to have people
notice me and care about my opinions, was foolish. What went
viral and boosted someone's popularity was unpredictable, and
it was clear the revenue from my dutiful reviews of diner and
bakery fare wasn't sustainable.

But voicing my thoughts during my daily life always ended
in trouble. In the past, when I'd shopped for groceries in
person, the manager hadn't cared that she could be ordering
Rose Bush brand ice cream instead of that crap they had in the
cooler. And when I mentioned my concern about Mrs White's
beer-purchasing habits, the cashier only became irritated.

I needed the blog. At least there I could have opinions
without people getting upset.

After reading over my brief review, I added that I had
no photos to share and explained why. Putting down my
experience and questions about the event in the sky was
useless to tack on, but I wanted to tell someone.

The more I wrote, the more that part of me – the kid who
had been so absorbed with aliens and the paranormal – started
to push its way to the front. I'd checked out the same books
from the library over and over, to the point that the librarian
not-so-subtly tried to guide my attention to something else
every time our class arrived. The classic saucer shapes were

fun, but the photos always looked like something I could easily fake at home with the toss of a Frisbee. Cigars were weird and light formations kind of boring, but the black triangles had given me chills.

My first experience with something possibly extraterrestrial had been so far away that I couldn't tell the craft's shape, which was too bad. But if I'd been in town, I would have missed it entirely. At least the trip to the diner was worth it in that respect.

I hit publish on the post, then closed down the laptop and crawled beneath the covers. Cocooned in warmth, it was easy to relax, but my mind wouldn't turn off. Could magnetic discharge have wiped my photos and notes and disrupted TV and radio signals?

Maybe it wasn't an alien craft, but a secret government jet on its way to Groom Lake.

Or maybe those teens who liked to hang out at the park had shot off illegal out-of-state fireworks.

I snatched a fidget toy from the desk and clicked a button on the side continuously until my harried thoughts quelled. Amethyst light from the fish tank danced on the ceiling, water burbled from the filter. My sleep must have been deep and dreamless, because when I opened my eyes to the sun streaming through the curtains, it felt like no time had passed.

With a steaming cup of coffee and a slice of salted caramel apple pie, I sat at the laptop and checked the Rawlins city news, scrolling past new game and fish laws, a child abuse arrest, and the herd health of migrating mule deer. A tiny sun shimmered on the screen beside a projected high of forty-seven degrees.

Hmm. Well, even though Rawlins was closest, it wasn't huge, and anyone in Muddy Gap who'd seen the UFO likely called Casper news stations instead.

I pulled up the *Oil City Tribune* and carved into the pie. Starbursts of salt and soft spiced apple overwhelmed my mouth as I took a bite. I sagged into the chair with a sigh. Now *this* was worthy of writing a blog post about. Unfortunately, I already had, and at great length. If it got Duran's Bakery any additional traffic, no one ever mentioned it when I showed up and ordered more.

Caramel stuck to my lips, and I wiped it away, scrolling down the front page. A high-speed chase ended in a crash into the side of Greater Lending Bank on the west side of Casper. Ongoing construction on E 2nd Street near the hospital. A high of forty-nine degrees, partly cloudy.

Still nothing?

I typed into the search bar, *explosion over Muddy Gap, Wyoming*. Photos of a fiery truck collision appeared on screen. Typing in *meteorite, ball lightning,* and *strange lights* yielded nothing relevant.

Scooping up stray bits of apple and gooey sauce, I clicked on a photo of UFOs seen north of Muddy Gap three years previous. The little specks of light looked more like gnats stuck to a windshield.

There should have been bold headlines screaming about blinding flashes that disrupted television signals, and high-resolution photos of the kind I had failed to capture. Certainly, I couldn't have been the only one to have noticed. There'd been people in the supermarket parking lot and cars driving through town.

Good pie remedied bad, but if search results didn't reveal answers or even evidence of what I saw, my curiosity wasn't going to leave me alone.

I opened a new tab and checked my email. Twelve messages waited, all of them with the same headline: *You have a new comment on* "Lynn's …

When my post about the alphabet pie at *The Lounge* went viral, I woke up to six hundred new comments and a lot of gripes on Push Pin about the blog crashing because so many people were trying to visit at once.

I'd foolishly increased my bandwidth after that, thinking the traffic would remain steady.

This was nothing close to that, but still more comments than any of my other posts received.

A small thrill lightninged through me as I opened the blog and scrolled to the bottom.

sherryb13: So what was it?
> **food_dood**: maybe there's a crater in your town with a chunk of satellite in it.
>> **мороженое_12**: And maybe it hit a radio tower on the way down!!

heyo234093: The answer is always ALIENS
> **catfever0808**: if Denver gets probed, I want pictures

coffeerings: Did not expect mysterious intrigue from a pie blog. 😄 Seriously tho, what was it?

burnt_nugget: The government has been doing secret experimentation on small towns like yours for years. This is right out of their playbook.

hippie69: Don't leave us hanging! I love your witty posts and excellent photography. You can't share something even juicier than pie and not let us seeeee.
> **mammas_apple**: tell us Denver
> **mammas_apple**: Denver tell us
> **mammas_apple**: i live in casper and if the military is doing experiments i wanna know
> **mammas_apple**: btw ive eaten the pie at many of the places on your blog and your critiques are always spot on

Not only were there comments, but several people had gone through my archive, liking all of the posts from alphabet to zucchini. Opening a new tab, I checked my ad revenue. My fork slipped from my fingers and clattered against the desk. On an average day, I made *maybe* twenty-five dollars, and nearly all of that came from the alphabet pie post. *$106* stared back at me from the screen, and I clicked the date to be certain the parameters were only set for today.

Shares on Push Pin had driven more people to the blog than would have ever visited organically. Clicking the links inundated me with more mentions of my snappy writing, people's favorite types of pies, and how beautiful my hair was.

My pulse pounded in my temples, and I had to seize back control of my excited hands to even scroll down the page. I was popular again. People liked my opinions, and my hair, and me. Not only that, I was making money.

My cheeks ached from how hard I was grinning, but I couldn't sit here all day, enticing as it was. The attention was wonderful, but too much of it would make me overwhelmed; I'd be compelled to delete the post and hide under the sheets.

Just five more minutes. I clicked a new comments thread. More stories about pie. More people referring to me by name. And of course, everyone asking what the hell flew over town and did I have pictures?

Well, I needed them now. Without convincing evidence or someone to corroborate the story, the attention would fizzle and my ad revenue would drop back to double digits.

I couldn't let that happen.

2

Molly stared, parentheses forming around her frowning mouth like I'd insisted she have one of my breath mints. I'd done that once, but only out of concern. If *my* breath smelled awful, I'd want someone to tell me.

She was around my age – thirty-something – with a perpetually irritated expression, but the similarities stopped there. Her hair was an unusual shade of strawberry blonde, skin so light the overhead fluorescents might give her a sunburn, and she didn't seem fond of makeup or jewelry. I had always been tempted to tell her that her hair was pretty, but something flippant or nasty always came out of her mouth and I'd change my mind. It looked like today wouldn't be the day I'd be giving her that compliment either.

After scanning my packages, she slid them across the counter. "Nothing flew over town last night. Someone would be talking about it."

"*I'm* talking about it. Were you even here?"

"No."

"Then don't call me a liar." I slapped my mail on top of the packages and scooped them up.

"You're holding up the line. Danny is waiting."

An older Japanese man in a ten-gallon hat stood behind me, concentrating on his phone with a small box under one arm. "His name is Danno. Not Danny." He'd already waved me in front of him and looked like he might be content to stand there all day.

I stepped out of the way anyway. When he didn't move forward, Molly cleared her throat.

Danno rubbed his wrinkled forehead and tapped his phone. "I'm trying to look up a damn address. If Professor Pie wants to yak, I'm not going to stop him. Her. Them." He looked up. "Is that one right? Them?"

"Any are fine," I said.

"Well, I just said like three of them so choose your favorite."

Molly huffed and disappeared into the back.

Danno watched her go, then set his package on the counter. He picked up a pen and clicked the end.

"Did you happen to see the UFO?" I asked.

He tried writing on the package, but no ink came out of the pen. "These damn things. The price of postage goes up every year, but I can't have a pen that works."

I slung my backpack off my shoulder and found one, which he accepted with a grunt. "I take it you didn't see it then. The UFO. I'm hoping someone here in town saw it explode, because I was so far away that there was no way for me to tell where wreckage may have fallen."

Danno scrawled an address, then looked pointedly at me. "Molly doesn't like you."

"I gathered that."

"Okay. I know you're" – he waved his hand – "autistic or whatever, so I wasn't sure how much of that you pick up on."

"I'm socially cognizant enough to know when people are upset with me." Though that didn't seem to help me prevent it from happening in the first place.

"It's easy to get on her bad side, so don't take it to heart."

I was used to it. But having a conversation with someone who *wasn't* angry with me felt pretty good, even if he was avoiding the subject of aliens. "My name is Denver, by the way."

He mumbled a distracted acknowledgement as he wrote a return address on his box, his letters wobbly.

"They don't like it when you wrap your packages in paper like that."

"Molly has never said anything to me about it."

"And if you use one of the universal weight boxes, it'll be cheaper."

He sighed and smacked the pen down on the counter. "I'm fine, Professor. You want to talk about stargazing, ask Sam at Gem's. He uses his telescope quite often... Just don't tell him how to bag the groceries."

I shoved through the post office door and strode outside. Danno could remember that I was autistic, but still didn't address me by name. Holding me at arm's length like everyone else. Maybe he didn't care when people called him "Danny" – it wasn't the first time I'd heard someone call him that and he didn't correct them. And it wasn't that I cared necessarily about being called "Professor Pie". I cared about being called it exclusively. I should have asked Aunt Georgina to rename me *Pie* and I wouldn't have this problem.

As I stepped off the sidewalk, a mustachioed Latino man slammed into me, and our combined mail fell into a confusion on the asphalt. He gripped my arms, steadying me.

"I am so sorry," he said. "I wasn't looking."

I drew in a breath of his honeyed cologne and readjusted my backpack. There was something vaguely familiar about his dramatic waxed mustache and the ample chest hair curling out of his V-neck tee, but if I'd met him before, surely I would have remembered. I bent to collect my envelopes. "It's alright."

He squatted, peered at the front of a letter, then handed it to me. I traded him for one of his, then recognition clicked in my mind and sudden heat flared in my cheeks.

"You look like a porn star," I blurted.

His gaze snapped to me, and he frowned. "What's that supposed to mean?"

I stood and clutched the mail to my chest, my attention snagged on his long black lashes and the caramel flecks in his dark eyes. "Like Julio Manhammer."

"I have no idea who that is." He smoothed his shirt over his belly, then strode away. "Sorry again."

Fuck. What was wrong with me?

I hurried down the street, slipping through a pocket of residential houses on my way to the market.

I was a failure at romantic relationships, but that had to be a new record of screwing up even the prospect of interacting with a cute guy. I needed a timer in my contacts. If I talked to someone for longer than ten seconds, it would flash and I'd know to wrap it up before I said something offensive. Better yet would be an app that told me when a conversation was going off the rails. Big red letters that spelled out *STOP TALKING, STUPID*.

Mr White stood in his driveway, spraying dirt from his car and sipping a beer. Several empty cans lay in the grass. I didn't know how he could stand living in this new subdivision with its cut-and-paste houses and perfect postage stamp lawns, marching into the distance like some horrible liminal space. Maybe the drinking helped.

Even tiny towns of eight hundred people had to expand, but there were far better aesthetics than this cookie-cutter version of suburbia. The older houses had more character with their log cabin siding and lawns staked with solar pathway lights. My apartment complex was rather nondescript, but the rustic charm of the town as a whole – even if it was mostly veneer since the majority of the buildings weren't more than twenty years old – had drawn me in when I'd first moved here. Muddy Gap had fewer amenities than a bigger city, but it had also promised more simplicity and peace. I wasn't sure it was delivering.

I headed past the subdivision, nearing the Mormon church. Vehicles lined the street, and a woman stepped over the curb carrying a tray of rice crispy squares.

Only a few cars sat in the supermarket parking lot. Perfect. Asking questions would be hard if it was too crowded for me to concentrate, and hearing answers would be impossible with my earplugs in. I could be in and out without taxing myself further, hopefully with corroboration or a new lead.

Sagging banners hung from the brick exterior, advertising sales on Diet Pepsi and rotisserie chicken. Fluorescents flickered in the store's vestibule, adding to gaudy lights throbbing from a 3D candy printer beside the door. The smell of spoiled dairy hit me, resurrecting memories of my ill-fated encounter with "slap jack", which was probably good – like flan or custard – when cooked all the way through and not made with expired cream.

Despite the place being practically unoccupied, someone still managed to ram their shopping cart into another. The crash ricocheted through my head, and I cringed and searched my pocket for my earplugs. Even with my eyes squeezed shut, the strobing lights pressed against my eyelids, but I was too busy holding a hand over my nose to cover my eyes. My stomach was revolting, vomit rising in my throat, but the tightness in my chest insisted I needed a deeper breath of the tainted air.

My backpack slid off my shoulder and hit the floor. I hunched against the sensory hell. Where the hell were my earplugs? Loud whispers drifted: "What's wrong with Professor Pie?"

Someone pushed my pack back into my arms, and a gravelly voice said, "You shouldn't be here."

"The fluorescents are flashing."

"I hadn't noticed."

"It reeks like rotten milk in this place. I'm gonna be sick." I yanked the collar of my shirt over my nose. The lights carved harsh shadows into Charla's gaunt cheeks and smoker's lips.

She led me out the door. "You should place an order online for delivery like you always do."

Her powdery perfume and the notes of road tar from the parking lot weren't ideal, but still better than inside. I drew in a deep breath and shook out my hands. "I didn't come to shop. I wanted to talk to Sam."

"Sam?" She pulled out a pack of cigarettes, but something in my face must have made her reconsider, because she tucked them back into her pocket. Her teased bottle-blonde hair held resolutely against the breeze. "He's not here. At the church."

Half the town was there, and just walking into the store had drained so much of my energy that entering the church was out of the question. "Damn. I wanted to ask him if he saw anything interesting with his telescope yesterday evening."

"Was there something to see? He'll be sorry he missed it." She cocked her penciled eyebrow. "Hopefully not too sorry, though. He was with me."

"Ah. I'm assuming your attention wasn't on the sky around eight o'clock, then."

"You assume correct. Though there were some heavenly bodies involved." She rasped a laugh.

I forced a smile, trying not to picture Charla and Sam naked. "Congrats. It was a UFO. Maybe you can keep your ears open and let me know if anyone mentions seeing it?"

"I'll tell Sam to look up pictures of what he missed. That milk smell has been in the rugs all month, and we've tried cleaning it twice. Just place your orders online."

Before I could tell her there *were* no pictures, she turned and headed back inside.

What a bust. How could I have been the only one in town to witness the UFO? And the only one to care? Sometimes the hivemind of the internet sensationalized things unnecessarily, but in this case, the reactions to my blog post seemed much more appropriate than the casual ease with which the subject was brushed off here in Muddy Gap.

It was me. Anything that came out of my mouth was

discredited or played down. I was just Professor Pie, and everyone in town would prefer that I kept my opinions to myself and went back to my apartment where no one could see me.

I could probably tell people Godzilla was outside, and they wouldn't bother to look out the window.

Normally I kept notifications off in my contacts. It became too distracting when I was trying to write or run an errand. But knowing there were people out there who cared about what I had to say balmed the sting of the brush-off I got in town.

Two new comments popped up in my vision.

grandmaZ: Bless you, honey, for trying so many terrible pies. I think you ought to make them yourself. It's clear you have good taste. I bet your recipes would be fantastic.

jerseydevil6: New to your blog, but I love me some pie with a side of UFOs! I'm hungry for some answers here.

I walked toward the library with renewed vigor, my hat crushed under one arm so the sun could warm my face. After checking out a couple of neglected books on alien craft and paranormal activity, I headed home. But the small high from internet comments didn't hold up in the face of my dim apartment. No one here in person to talk about pie, or UFOs, or... anything.

A dirty plate still sat on the desk, and the only sound was the faint gurgle from the fish tank. Bubbles streamed from the air stone in the back, and tetras zoomed by like a shower of sparks. One of the dwarf frogs stood on its hind legs, pale belly pressed to the glass. The other hid in the synthetic cave, toes poking from the shadows.

Maybe if I gave them all names, it would add to their sentimentality and dispel some of the conscious weight of my solitude.

Hey Daisy, hey Pickle, I'm home.

Were those good frog names? Did it matter?

I pointed at the one with its stomach against the tank. "You're Pickle." To the one in the cave, I said, "You're Daisy. I expect you to remember that because I can't tell you two apart."

There were too many fish to name individually. I could call them The Board of Directors. The Collective. The Cult.

I tossed my mail on the counter and turned on the TV, half-expecting the signal to still be out. A local RV dealership commercial splashed across the screen. A drag queen in a rhinestone cowboy hat stepped out of a behemoth of a motorhome and kicked her leg like she was performing cabaret.

The background chatter filled the silence, so I left it on, then opened the laptop to check the news. The only change to the *Oil City Tribune*'s front page was the weather bar in the corner.

Reading more comments on my blog and Push Pin was tempting, but the little burst of serotonin from the last ones wasn't enough to boost my mood for a prolonged period, and even semi-critical ones mixed in with the good were going to hurt me more than I could handle. Instead, I cracked open one of the library books, inundated with images of lenticular saucers, conical hats, and boomerang craft. It didn't seem to matter how recent, every picture of a UFO was the same grainy, squint-and-you-can-totally-see-it photo people had been taking for over a hundred years.

Childhood nostalgia flooded me. I could almost smell the dirt and the vinyl seats of the school bus, feel the rumble from the road and the unwieldiness of a hardback book with smashed corners, too big to zip closed in my backpack.

I flipped through the pages, tracing photo spreads of mysterious lights piercing pine trees, and foo fighters racing alongside Allied aircraft.

And with it there was that familiar ache for something not of this world, for the desire to be whisked away to a place I would better fit in. That feeling wasn't something cultivated during my time here in town. It had been with me for as long as I could remember.

I realized I was staring at a crumb on the desk, the library book forgotten in my lap. Opening my laptop, I clicked on Porchswing, and navigated to Aunt Georgina's page. Her profile photo was a shot of her and Uncle Joe at some outdoor concert they'd gone to years ago. I didn't use Porchswing very often – commenting on people's posts always turned into misunderstandings, which turned into unfriendings – but my cousins had threatened to start calling me on the phone if I deleted my account.

How long had it been since I talked to Aunt Georgina? Months, easily. She was going to chew me out, but thinking about childhood memories of bus rides and library books made me ache for one of her enveloping hugs that always smelled like that three-dollar aerosol perfume from the drugstore.

In the message box, I typed *Hi Auntie.*

After waiting a moment, I moved my cursor to the close button, but a large red telephone icon flashed on the screen. My heart filled my throat, and I squeezed the edges of the desk. No no. No video calls. I was going to freeze up and have nothing to say, or stim too much and say *too many* things. But she'd been the one to change my diapers, kiss my scraped knees, and dry my tears. She wasn't even my aunt, but it was the closest thing she ever let me call her to "Mom", and I needed to see her face even if I had nothing to say.

I clicked the accept button with a numb finger, and she appeared in low quality resolution, glasses perched on her nose and a wooden spoon in one hand.

"Denver! You should have heard me shriek when I saw your message pop up. Woke Joe from his nap on the couch. I'm just making supper. Meatloaf." She set down the spoon and leaned her elbows on the counter. On the wall behind her was a gnome doll that had terrified me as a kid.

"I haven't heard from you in forever," she said. "How you doing, honey?"

All I could manage was a shrug, because I was certain if I opened my mouth I'd start crying, and I wasn't sure why.

She stared into the screen, and her glasses slipped down her nose. "Having a rough day? You don't need to talk. I'm just glad to see your face. And I'm glad you answered my call. I didn't think you would."

Uncle Joe's voice drifted. "It's Denver? Tell the kid I say 'hi'."

"You get off your ass and tell him yourself." She looked back at the screen and rolled her eyes with a smile like we were sharing an inside joke.

It reminded me of so many times as a kid when I would climb onto one of the high-backed counter stools while she made supper, needing to tell her something but being unsure how to begin. She'd dice an onion or bread chicken thighs, enduring my silent fidgeting with patience until I figured out how to form my feelings into words.

I swallowed hard, my nose stinging. "I don't know why I sent you a message. Was just thinking of home, I guess, and things have been strange here lately."

"You should move back. You're welcome to stay with us until you can find a place of your own in town. Or at least come for a visit. Your cousins miss you. Do you talk to them?"

"Billie, sometimes. She sends me pictures of chunky turquoise jewelry or sundresses she thinks I'd look good in."

"She hasn't stopped playing fashion show with you."

Abraham had always refused, but Elizabeth and I were Billie's "models" for years as kids. We'd make a catwalk path between couch cushions and swagger across it in Billie's avant-garde outfits. *Sashay your hips, Denver! Pout your lips!*

The stuff Billie suggested was always nice and fit my style but came with a hefty price tag. Whenever I pointed that out, she'd insist I remind her of my dress and pant sizes so she could buy things for me. I didn't mind gifts, but she offered too often. It was only desperation that drove me to ask for a hundred dollars last month. She'd sent me two.

Auntie was still talking. "Beth is going to have her baby any day now–"

"She's pregnant?"

She gave me a look that said I'd know that if I kept in better contact. I rubbed my eyes and let her ramble about ultrasounds and nursery remodeling until she said, "How's that boy you've been seeing online? Have you met in person yet?"

"We broke up."

Her lips bunched. "Is there someone new at least?"

"No." I sighed. "It's just me, Auntie, in my little studio with my tank of fish, scaring away all the neighbors and cute guys with my off-putting personality."

"You aren't off-putting."

"You raised me. You're obligated to say that."

"Oh! That reminds me. I was talking to your mom and she–"

"No."

"–really wants to see you. She's trying hard to make an effort and–"

"No."

"–thought you might let me give her your contact inform–"

"No!"

Auntie flinched. "I know you resent her, but she's clean. She has a good job. Children – two brothers you've never met."

"That's good." A tightness filled my chest as I pushed down the memory of my ninth birthday. That wasn't a part of childhood I wanted to think about. "She has some other family. She doesn't need anything to do with me."

"All she wants is a phone call."

I smashed the crumbs on the desk into powder. "If she knew anything about me, she'd know I can't do phone calls. I'm sure you told her."

Auntie took off her glasses and massaged the bridge of her nose. "A letter then, maybe? An email?"

"No. What about my dad?"

"What about him?"

"Does my mom know where he lives or his middle name or anything? I tried to do some family history a while back, but I wasn't sure I had the right James Bryant." I'd followed our shared name through branches, squinting at delicate cursive on Dawes Rolls spreadsheets, copies of land deeds, and sepia-toned photos of men with long braids and three-piece suits, but after searching I felt more hollow than when I started.

"That would be a great question to ask your mom when you talk to her," Auntie said.

I ground my teeth. "I should go."

"I'm not trying to make your day worse. I'm sorry."

"Don't you hate her? This estranged foster sister of Uncle Joe's who dumped me in your arms when you already had kids of your own to take care of? And she promised to come back and be a mom–"

"She came back when you were nine."

"And that was worse!" My voice broke and tears spilled down my face. "It was worse, and you know it."

Lines formed between her brows. "You were never a burden to me, honey. Never ever."

I let out a sob and slammed the laptop closed.

In the sandy depths between awake and dreaming, something pinged against the window. My eyes flew open, struggling to adjust.

Another tap became two, then a dozen. Each hard *snik* was like a tiny electric shock on my soul. Wincing, I threw off the sheets and wedged in a pair of earplugs. It muffled the sound but only to a marginally tolerable level. Beyond the parted curtains, hail poured from the black sky, dashing against the pane and bouncing off the grass far below.

The tone wasn't right. It filled the apartment, the sound of an entire bag of popcorn kernels being spilled on a tile floor. I pulled on some sweats and opened the front door. Bitter wind flung my hair across my face. The white pellets drummed against the stairs, some of them careening erratically. The tiny impacts against my neck and ears were like hard flicks from an annoying cousin.

The beads collected in my open palm. Irregularly shaped, lighter than I expected, and not cold. In fact, they were *warm*. Heat sank into my skin like they were tiny pebbles plucked from a sunny beach.

Waking dreams had happened to me before, but only when I'd been sick with a fever. And if this was really a dream, I wouldn't be questioning it.

Whatever it was, the hail hurt and so did my ears. I hurried back inside, then crawled into bed and pressed the pillow over my head until the sound faded enough to sleep.

When I next opened my eyes, light danced across the wall. I rolled over and one of the earplugs clung to my cheek. The reminder of the hail propelled me out of bed to the window. Two magpies hopped in the grass, pecking at bugs, and Mrs Baker's dog was taking a shit directly onto the sidewalk.

I rolled my eyes. Disgusting, but normal.

But what did I expect? It was morning. The hail had melted. Or I dreamed the whole thing, which is what I got after a strange event I still didn't have an answer for.

Even without pictures or concrete evidence, my initial blog post had exploded compared to the activity my posts normally received. It was still a far cry from being viral, but if I couldn't find answers, talking to people in town would at least turn into more questions, and hopefully be enough fuel to keep up engagement.

There had to be someone here who'd seen something. Maybe my whole approach was wrong. In those contrived detective shows, there was always evidence that pointed them in the right direction. But my photo files had only opened to error messages. Maybe my fans were right and there was a chunk of satellite or spacecraft in a person's backyard.

Radio stations were working fine again, just like the TV and internet, as I'd gotten an earful of dreadful gospel music and cardboard political commentary when I spun through the frequencies in the truck.

I left the apartment and clanked down the stairs. The air held the heavy scent of petrichor, grass and sidewalk damp, but there was a stinging top note to the smell, like fertilizer.

The piercing voice of the landlady drifted from the first-floor office. On the next block, a boy slowly pedaled his bike down the sidewalk, pausing every few moments to push with his feet instead.

He waved. "Hello."

"Hey."

"What's your name?"

"Denver."

"I like your hat."

"Thanks." I stuffed my hands in my jean pockets. "Do you play outside in the evening?"

"Yeah. I go to Arthur's and jump on his trampoline. But tomorrow... no, yesterday, his dog jumped up too and fell on me. Look." The boy lifted his shirt, revealing long pink scratches stretching across his belly.

"Sorry to hear that. Were you outside the day before yesterday, when it was dark? There was a big flash in the sky. Some kind of UFO."

The boy's eyes bloomed. "I told Arthur we needed to hide under the trampoline so the aliens didn't know we were there."

"Really?" A surge ran through my heart. The account of a kid wasn't the best evidence, but it at least confirmed that someone else had seen it. "Did you see it before the flash? Was it a disk? A triangle?"

"Uh-huh. And *big*. It stopped right over the trampoline, and

I knowed the aliens might still find us because the trampoline is see-through, you know."

I squatted in front of him and nodded. "How many lights did it have?"

"Like a lot! And I didn't want the aliens to get us, so I pulled out my laser gun and shot – *PEW PEW* – and then the UFO was all" – he put his hands together, then yanked them apart and made an explosion noise, spit flying from his mouth – "and one of the aliens fell on the trampoline."

I pressed my lips together and stood. This is what I got for asking a five year-old. "Okay."

"It was real gross. His blood was green, and his guts were hanging out."

"Yep." I side-stepped the bike and continued down the sidewalk. "Great job saving Muddy Gap from the alien menace, kid. The mayor should give you an award."

"Yeah!"

I probably sounded as ridiculous to everyone I met as that kid did to me. Probably to my readers too. Talking about UFOs and aliens and explosions in earnest. The compulsion to delete the blog rose in me again. Just shut the whole thing down and never talk about it. Eat pie in the sanctity of my own home, no obligation to venture to a noisy diner and risk getting a slice of something disappointing. I'd save money on eating out and paying to charge the truck. Unless I had to commute to Casper, since I'd need a real job – well, I'd need a real job even more than I did now.

But the idea of giving up my small adventures in pie tasting and the readers who looked forward to my posts formed a hard lump in my throat.

The UPS truck rumbled toward me, then slowed to a stop. A bald white man in sunglasses – Mick – leaned out the open door. "Hey Professor Pie! Got a package for you. Wanna take it now and save me a trip?"

Mick knew my name – of course he did. It wasn't like I had mail addressed to "Professor Pie".

I shrugged. "Sure. Can I ask you something? Were you in town Friday night, around eight?"

He rummaged through the back for so long I was certain he'd forgotten my question. Appearing with a small box, he held it out to me. I stared at my name on the address label.

"Friday night? Nah, I was at home in Casper." He lifted his sunglasses and pointed to my package. "Is that product review company worth it? You like doing it?"

"Sometimes. Doesn't pay much, and the cabinet below my bathroom sink is overflowing with sample creams, oils, soaps, and cosmetics. Maybe if I mix them all together and take a bath in them it will make me immortal."

Mick laughed. "You figure out the recipe, you let me know." He hopped into the driver's seat and pulled away from the curb.

The tape on the package shredded as I tried to peel it off. I wedged my fingers inside and ripped off one of the flaps. Beneath the bubble wrap were two silver tubes and a package of nutrition bars. I dumped the empty box in a trash can, then pulled off the lid of the first tube and twisted the bottom. A pleasant shade of peachy pink appeared, shimmering in the sun. The review company sent me lipsticks quite often, but I didn't have this shade.

Ensuring there were enough nearby reflective surfaces to stitch together a composite image, I flipped to mirror-mode on my contacts, no longer looking at a line of cars against the curb, but myself. My hat threw the top half of my face into shadow, long nose and prominent cheekbones painted in dappled light from the trees above. I tried to imagine what features I shared with my dad. Raw sienna eyes, deep umber hair. The faint waviness came from my mom, and so did my fair, freckled skin.

When I was a kid, people who didn't know I was adopted would say I had Auntie's nose, Uncle Joe's chin, that I looked similar enough to Elizabeth to be her fraternal twin the way

Bram and Billie were. But it wasn't remotely true no matter how much I wanted it to be.

I'd asked Auntie one day why I couldn't call her "Mom".

Because I'm not your mom. You already have one. The way she'd said it – like I was asking for another toy or an ice cream – made me want to smash something. If my mom was a toy, she was a broken one. If she was an ice cream, she was one that had long since fallen off the cone and become a gooey mess on a hot sidewalk.

I'd tried to contain my hurt to the inside, because if I was bad, Auntie would want me even less. She'd sensed my distress though, because she said, *I've been your Auntie since you were a baby. It would be weird to change that now. But that doesn't mean I love you less than a mother would. You're still my boy.*

I'm not!

You are, honey. I promise.

I'm not a boy! As soon as I screamed out this truth, I slapped my hands over my mouth, wishing I could take it back.

She stared at me for a long moment. *You know, even when you were very small, I had the feeling that one day when you were older you'd come home with a boyfriend. But... you like wearing Billie's dresses. You're a girl?*

There'd been tears in my eyes as I'd avoided her gaze. *No. That doesn't feel right either. I guess I'm just nothing.*

Aunt Georgina had swooped around the side of the counter and hauled me into her arms. *You're not nothing. You're my child, even if you're not a boy. And even if I'm not your mom.*

I realized I was still staring at myself in mirror mode, the lipstick growing sweaty in my grip. Clearing my throat, I applied the lipstick, which was tricky because though the image looked like me, my movements were delayed and slightly off. I wiped a streak of peach from my chin, then pouted my lips.

One of the questions when reviewing lipstick was how long it endured when kissing. The company didn't seem to know how single I was.

I switched off mirror-mode and blinked hard at the change in view. After tucking the peach lipstick into my pocket, I tried twisting off the cap of the other tube.

It vibrated loudly and I nearly dropped it. "Shit." I switched it off and crammed it into my pocket before someone told the cops a pervert was hanging around their house.

Maybe the company *did* know how single I was.

Hurrying past, I cut down a residential side street. The ringing slap of a basketball on pavement echoed from down the block. Something crunched under my boots. I stopped and lifted my sole. White bits clung to the tread. Scattered across the sidewalk and filling the seams were the same hail-like beads from last night. They dotted the grass and a driveway, oddly confined to this one yard.

Not a dream. My heartbeat thumped in my ears as I picked one up. Not warm like before, but not cold or melting either.

"They're strange, aren't they?" The man who'd slammed into me at the post office leaned against the railing of his porch, a coffee mug in one hand. The top of his robe hung open, exposing dark chest hair and a hint of a tattoo. Great.

I straightened and squeezed the pebble between my fingers.

Recognition flashed on the man's face, then his brows knit. "Ah, it's you."

The urge to flee bubbled up inside me, but I said, "Did you see these things fall last night?"

"Didn't see it. I was at work in Casper. Nearly crashed into my own recycling can when I was pulling in because my tires had no traction on them. Saw the rain, though. They came from the sky?"

I took off my hat and raked a hand through my hair, wishing for that hypothetical conversation warning in my contacts. "Yes. But I didn't understand what I was looking at. Thought I might be dreaming."

"Weirder things have fallen." The man sipped from his mug.

"Frogs. Fish. Golf balls. Pebbles are hardly a scandal. Though I'm not quite sure that's what they are."

"Did you see a UFO night before last? Around eight?" Why in God's name was I asking him that? He already thought I was an asshole. Now he was going to think I was a deranged asshole.

"UFO?"

As I explained what I saw, the man's gaze on me grew more intent. I bent down and plucked pebbles from the sidewalk seam to avoid concentrating on the curve of his lips and the way the sun kissed his fawn skin.

"That is... very peculiar." The man stroked the dramatic waxed end of his mustache. "You'd think the news would have some coverage on it."

"You don't know how refreshing it is to hear you say that." I stopped at the porch stairs and gave a little wave. "By the way, I'm Denver Bryant. Any pronouns. I like xe/xem, but it seems to be hard for people to conjugate. And I'm sorry for telling you that you look like Julio Manhammer. It's the mustache, mostly. I didn't mean it as an insult."

"He a favorite of yours or something?"

I was suddenly aware of the vibrator in my pocket and didn't need to turn on mirror-mode to know my face was a brilliant shade of crimson. "I–I was paid to write an article on Julio once. That's how I know who he is." I wasn't going to add that I'd bookmarked some of his videos on my phone for later viewing. "What's your name?"

"Ezra Gómez Miramontes, he/him." He stepped off the porch and the rich scent of hazelnut coffee wafted from his mug. Toeing at the pebbles on the sidewalk, he said, "I swear there were a lot more of these last night."

"There were. They seem to be exclusively in your yard now." I tapped one of the beads against my front tooth. "They sound hollow. Or porous. And crushed easily under my shoes. I suppose the wind could have blown the rest of them away."

How long had I been talking to Ezra? He hadn't sighed loudly, brushed off my description of events, or tried to end our conversation. I probably needed to stop talking if I wanted to keep it that way. Or at least stop mentioning porn stars.

A new notification from my blog appeared in my vision:

vintagecatmemes: My god, your HAIR. 😍 I've been staring at your profile pic for like five minutes. What shampoo do you use?

I swiped the comment away and wound a long lock around my finger.

"I dumped a handful of those pebbles into a bowl in my kitchen," Ezra said. "I was planning to look at them through my microscope anyway, but I'm more intrigued now that you say they're hollow."

A microscope! The pictures captured from that view would be excellent. "Can I look with you?"

Ezra's mouth pulled into a tight line, and he glanced back at his house like the fact that it was there was supposed to be a secret. "I mean, I just woke up. I'm not dressed and I'm only on my first cup of coffee."

"Oh." Shit. Shit. I was ruining this. "I'm being rude again, huh?"

"Not rude. A little too forward maybe."

"I'm sorry. I'm trying to compile evidence and got excited."

"Evidence of what?"

"Not sure. But my gut says something isn't right around here."

Ezra's fingers drummed against his coffee cup. "You going to call the news?"

"I would if I had something to present. I'll be writing an article for my blog. My readers are very interested in what's going on."

"Can I be in the article?"

He probably thought I was popular and had a huge following. But with any luck, that would happen with tangible evidence I could present to my fans. "Sure. I'll depict you as my handsome neighbor, Not-Julio Manhammer, who cracked the mystery wide open with his microscope skills."

Ezra laughed. "Then it'll be fiction."

"Only the being neighbors part, though I live just a block away."

"Do you usually embellish your stories like that?"

"Not at all. Normally I blog about pie."

"So I've heard. Tell you what... Come back in an hour with your favorite kind, and we can look through my microscope. I'll provide the canned whipped cream."

"Blasphemy. If you have to have whipped cream, it should be made from scratch. Are you allergic to anything?"

"No."

"Alright. It's a date. I mean – no, not really. Turn of phrase."

The corners of his eyes creased in a smile. "See you then, Denver."

3

After an hour spent agonizing over the pie choices in my freezer, making a batch of whipped cream, and checking my ad revenue, I walked back to Ezra's with a fluttering stomach.

A new comment appeared in my vision:

pierat369135: I'm in Wyoming too. I saw a UFO when I was a kid, and my dad spanked me for "telling lies". Been looking for proof ever since. Not for my dad's sake, but for mine.

I blinked it away. The steadiness of comments cheered me, but I had too much on my mind to reply right now.

Just don't talk. It was that simple. Dish out the pie, peer through the microscope and go *hmm, interesting*. Take some photos for the blog. Don't mention Ezra's mustache, or his taste in curtains, or what kind of milk he had in the fridge.

Water splashed beneath my feet. I looked down. A stream ran across the sidewalk, teeming with white pebbles from the night before. They floated on the surface, running into the gutter and down the street. I followed the source of the water to a nearby yard, where an elderly Black woman stood with a hose, her gaze unfocused. "Ms Pierce?"

There were so many pebbles in the grass that it looked like a beanbag had burst. Aside from Ezra's, this seemed to be the only other location that still had them. Where did the rest of them go?

I took a step, and my boot squished in the soggy earth. The water had risen beyond Ms Pierce's crocs, up to her veiny ankles.

I shifted my backpack of pie and whipped cream to my other shoulder. "You leave that hose on any longer and you're going to need a boat."

She didn't blink, her attention still vaguely directed at the Silvas' house across the way. Windchimes tinkled from the eaves of her little ranch house. A cat sat in the window, its tail swishing.

"Hello?"

She was probably in her seventies, but if she was having cognitive issues it hadn't been juicy enough gossip to get around to me. I sidestepped the lake forming beneath her and walked to the house, then turned off the water.

Grass squelched under my feet. A dribble ran from the end of the hose, making a tiny patter. I waved my hand in front of Ms Pierce's face. Maybe I needed to tell someone. She had family in town, but I couldn't remember where they lived.

"Hey, what's your daughter's name? Emily? Ellen? Something that doesn't start with an E?"

I grabbed the hose in her hand and pulled. Her gaze locked onto me. She shrieked and swung her arm. The hose whipped through the air, and the metal end snapped across my cheek. I stumbled back in shock and clutched my stinging face. My ankle caved beneath me, and I tripped and fell. Something in my backpack crunched, and water soaked into the ass of my jeans.

"How dare you!" Ms Pierce shook her hose and took several steps back. "Get out of my yard, Professor Pie, before I have you arrested for assault!"

I scrambled up, heart hammering and my cheek throbbing. Water filled my socks, and glass rattled inside my bag, something clearly broken. Ms Pierce's admonishments chased me down the street. I fished my earplugs from my pocket with a shaky hand and crammed them into my ears.

A comment appeared:

mammas_apple: Denver what did you find out

The log siding of Ezra's house peeked between high juniper bushes, but I wasn't sure I could make it there. Adrenaline fizzed through my limbs and turned my stomach, my throat tight and cheek throbbing. I pulled in a shallow breath and leaned against the warm metal of a transformer box on the corner.

Suddenly, fingers grazed my arm. I gasped and pulled back, staring into Ezra's face. He'd changed out of his robe and into a V-neck tee with an even deeper plunge than the one he'd worn the day before. His mouth was moving, but with my racing heart and the earplugs, I couldn't understand any of it.

I pulled them out and dug my nail into the rubber. "What?"

"You're bleeding."

"Ms Pierce hit me with her hose."

Ezra's eyebrows shot up. "The little church lady who makes quilts for the homeless hit you. Why? What did you do?"

I scoffed and gently prodded my wet cheek. "Nothing that warranted an attack! Is she senile? She was overwatering her grass so I–"

"Her grass." Ezra looked beyond me, then jerked his head toward his house. "C'mon. I have bandages. And steriglue."

"Is it that bad? Jesus." I pulled the bag containing the pie from my backpack, wondering if there were shards of glass in the whipped cream.

I struggled to keep up with Ezra's pace. When we reached his porch, he lightly took my arm and ushered me inside. The musk of leather and aged wood enveloped me, with top notes of coffee. Bookshelves spanned the walls of the front room, peppered here and there with antique cameras. Two heavy umber armchairs crowded a small coffee table, and a polished globe made of different kinds of stone sat as the centerpiece.

"Stay right there," Ezra muttered, disappearing down a hall.

He probably thought I'd sit in one of those leather chairs with my wet pants or leave bloody fingerprints on the walls.

I shook out my tingling fingers, shifting from one foot to the other, but there was too much nauseous energy inside me wanting to get out. Wiggling my toes in my wet socks was a regrettable decision because the sensation was awful, and once I started, I couldn't stop. The best idea right now was taking off my boots and socks and walking barefoot back home, but I was already here, and Ezra wanted to help me. He likely had better first aid supplies than I did, and besides, if I left, he might get busy with something else and not want me to come back today.

He returned with several squeeze tubes and a sheaf of paper bandages. After taking my bag and setting it on the floor, he wiped at my cheek with a cloth. I winced and sucked air through my teeth.

"People talk about you," he said.

"It's a small town. People talk about everyone."

"True, but I've heard stories about *you* in particular." He folded the cloth, exposing a clean side, then dabbed at my face again. "Now, I only met you briefly yesterday, so I didn't want to make judgments based on rumors. People deserve to make their own impressions. But I'm going to have to join the town consensus that you need to mind your business."

I pulled away. "Excuse me?"

He leaned forward, eyes narrowed. "I hope this leaves an impression on you for the next time you decide to tell a random person that they look like a porn star – who they *clearly* don't look like – or they drink too much or they're overwatering their grass."

mammas_apple: don't leave me hanging

Waving my hands, I backed into the wall, my throat closing and chest so tight a rebuttal dried up in my mouth. I had perfectly good reasons for saying the things I did. I worried about people. I was trying to help. If I just explained how strangely Ms Pierce was acting. If I just explained that it seemed like Mrs White was buying beer for her alcoholic husband because he forced her to. If I just explained that Ezra was handsome and made me flustered.

mammas_apple: you need to answer me

Damn it! How was I supposed to get the correct string of words out of my mouth with these messages popping up?

Ezra's dark gaze bored a hole straight through me. My throat worked, trying to produce some semblance of speech. I flapped my hands instead and whirled for the door. This whole thing was a mistake. Microscope pictures were out of the question now, but going home was far more appealing than getting chewed out in a stranger's living room in my wet socks.

I stomped down the porch steps and dropped my bag on the sidewalk. "Enjoy the pie. It's glass-flavored."

mammas_apple: i know you read these comments
mammas_apple: don't be a dick

"Fuck!" I pressed my fingers into my eyes until error codes flashed. I wanted to rip out the contacts, but I needed them for blog pictures. Everything was going to shit.

Ezra gripped my elbow, and I wrestled away. "Get off me!"

He put up his hands and stepped back. I tried pulling in a steady breath, but the tight band around my chest wouldn't let me–

mammas_apple: why do you reply to other people and never me
    vintagecatmemes: You need to chill out, Karen. And use some punctuation for God's sake.

mammas_apple: DONT TELL ME TO CHILL OUT

How the hell did I shut off these notifications?

Warm concrete pressed against my cheek, and I realized I was on the sidewalk. My hat slid off, and I hugged my knees to my chest. The cut on my face pulsed in time with my heart.

Hard ground beneath me helped wrestle back my spiraling thoughts. Sun bathed my skin, the scent of dirt and lipstick filling my senses. My bones were vibrating, but a bit of the tension bled away from me.

Ezra's shoes crunched on white pebbles. He dropped his voice. "Do I need to get someone?"

"Who?"

"I... I don't know. An ambulance?"

"No."

He sat next to me and rested his elbows on his knees. Birds chirped, and the soft whisk of bicycle spokes grew near. The tires scraped on the asphalt and someone said, "¿Se encuentra ella bien?"

"Eso creo," Ezra said.

"What happened to her face?"

He replied with a question in a mixture of Spanish and English that included Ms Pierce's name.

"Oh my god. Her yard is soaked. Like, *soaked*. Looks like a water main burst or something. And she was all wet. I tried to ask her what happened, but she screamed and threw one of her crocs at me. I called Elaine to go deal with her. Está loca." The spokes on the bike clicked, heading away.

Ezra pinched the bridge of his nose, eyes squeezed shut. He sat that way for a moment before saying, "I'm a complete douche."

An orange spider mite sped across the ground. It paused at a lock of my hair, then veered in another direction. Every breath I took was shaky with adrenaline, and I forced my concentration on the sidewalk beneath me before my thoughts tried to run away again.

Ezra flicked a bit of grass from his tennis shoe. "I mean it. I'm so sorry. I shouldn't have jumped to conclusions. Do you want to come inside? I'll finish patching up your cheek. Though I won't blame you if you just want to slug me."

"You should get as far away from me as possible, so my pariah essence doesn't rub off on you. I'm sure people are staring."

He left my side, and I pressed my brow harder against the concrete. I had instant glue at home and a box of plasticky adhesive bandages that had been thrown into one of my grocery orders by mistake. They were for kids, white with cartoon kitty faces. I'd probably need two or three of them. They would have to do, because I couldn't afford a trip to the doctor.

I expected the slam of Ezra's front door, but he sat back down with my bag and peeked inside. "What kind of pie did you bring?"

"Bourbon pecan. Is it smashed?"

"Your pie server broke, but everything else looks intact. I have one we could use."

I sat up. In the house across the street, a woman clutched her open curtains, face pressed against the windowpane. A man stood in his driveway, one leg inside his car but his body twisted toward me. He pushed his glasses up the bridge of his nose and stared.

A tiny river ran down the sidewalk gutter, carrying away white pebbles and bits of leaves. Ezra tugged at his mustache, a blotchy flush mottling his cheeks, and it was hard to tell if his embarrassment stemmed from misjudging me or the scene I just made. Probably the latter.

I followed him back inside, gripping the straps of my backpack like a lifeline. He gathered his medical supplies and led me into the kitchen. A microscope sat on the table beside an empty coffee cup and a shallow bowl of white pebbles.

I perched myself on the edge of a chair and pointed to the

open box of glass slides. "Did you look at them yet?" My voice came out unsteady, and my body felt like an overinflated balloon that only needed one prick before popping.

"No. I was waiting for you." He uncapped a tiny tube, then pinched my cheek wound and squeezed glue onto it. The cloying scent of his cologne and the way he bit his lip as he concentrated distracted me from the pain. When he unwrapped a bandage and smoothed it over the top, all I felt were his fingers on my skin.

His gaze lingered on me. "How often does that happen?"

He didn't need to specify what *that* was. "Only when I'm overwhelmed. It's like everything inside me is suddenly too big for my skin and if I don't do something about it, I'm going to explode. I sometimes slap myself. Pull my hair. But lying on the ground helps drain out that energy. I don't know why, but it works."

"I'm glad."

"Are you? I made a scene."

"It's my fault."

"No." I sighed. "It's everything. UFOs and Ms Pierce and internet weirdos calling me a dick."

"I looked up pictures of Julio Manhammer after you left earlier." Ezra's jaw clenched, and he looked away. "I don't resemble him at all."

The handlebar mustache, the chest hair, the dark eyes. Their eyebrows arched the same at the corners and they both had pillowy mauve lips. "But you do."

"*No.* I don't. I–" He pulled a deep breath through his nose, then let it out and gave me a tight smile. "But being cranky isn't a good reason for me to lash out at you, and I'm sorry I did. My hang-ups aren't your fault."

There was something here I was missing. "Is this about dick size? Because those standards are impossibly high."

He sighed. "No. Maybe a little. It's mostly…" He made a vague gesture toward his body.

"What?"

He flapped his arms harder in the direction of his stomach.

I frowned. "I'm really bad at charades. You need to spell it out."

"My weight."

"Oh." I cocked my head. "You're right. Your body types are definitely different. He looks like he spends every moment in the gym and greases up his body like it's a baking sheet. You're cuddlier looking than he is. And you have a better ass."

Ezra's mouth hung open. He blinked at me and finally said, "You mean that?"

"Yeah. I give honest assessments. Usually of pie, but I can rate asses too."

He barked a laugh. "Well, I'm not going to go against the word of a professional critic. And I'm sorry I upset you so badly. So what should I do if you melt down again? I wanted to stop you from hurting yourself, but I didn't know how. Grabbing your arms seemed like a bad idea."

That he was asking at all was touching, but an embarrassed heat crawled into my cheeks. "Help me on the ground, I guess. Don't restrain me. Don't yell."

"Okay." He headed into the kitchen and washed his hands, then pulled plates from the cabinet.

Dishes clinked, and I dug my nail into one of the earplugs in my pocket. This had gone as horribly as an impression could, but for some reason I was still here, and Ezra wanted to eat pie. "That shirt elongates your neck. And your mustache is almost Dali-esque. A very bold choice."

"You just tell it like it is, huh?"

Damn it. I told myself I wasn't going to bring it up. The nervous energy was coming out of my mouth now, and I wasn't sure how to shut it off. "I like the mustache. But to keep from looking weirdly eccentric, I'd avoid spearing flowers on the ends... Um, your living room is nice. Looks like it was lifted straight from a library."

"Would you believe I'm a bartender?" He rummaged through a drawer and pulled out a pie server.

"Bartenders aren't illiterate that I'm aware of."

"No, but people who know I bartend walk into my house and accuse me of stealing all my furniture from a country club."

"There's no country club in Muddy Gap." If he was trying to connect with me over people making assumptions about him too, he was going to have to do better than his friends surprised by his leather armchairs. "What bar do you work at in Casper?"

"A little dive called *Uneven Pavement*. No pie there, but I swipe their cans of whipped cream."

I wrinkled my nose. "Homemade is easy. All you need is heavy cream, powdered sugar, and vanilla."

"Not as convenient to squirt on your lover, though."

I pondered that for a moment. "You could get a piping bag. And the cans make that horrible *whoosh* noise when you use them. That's not sexy."

Ezra chuckled. He set the pie on the counter and pulled the lid off the whipped cream. After dishing us both a slice, he dug into his and took a bite. He moaned and sagged against the counter. "Oh my god. Where has this been all my life?"

I brought up a search in my contacts and found the location of *Uneven Pavement*. "About two blocks from your bar."

"Seriously?" He stuffed another forkful in his mouth. "Aren't you going to have yours?"

A sourness still sat in my stomach, nerves vibrating. "Maybe in a moment."

"This is a breakfast of champions, that's for sure. You have other kinds at your place too?"

"Sure. Salted caramel apple, honey-lavender, and I think I still have a slice or two of pistachio in the fridge."

Ezra popped a pecan in his mouth, then brushed his hands on his pants. "I don't know what honey-lavender is, but if you like it, I'm guessing it's good."

At least my credibility in pie wasn't challenged today. I opened my mouth to tell him about the flavors and texture, but he picked up a pair of tweezers, carefully plucked one of the white pebbles from the bowl beside the microscope, then placed it on a glass slide. I dug into my slice of pie, mostly to keep my hands and mouth occupied. The pecans made a satisfying crunch between my teeth.

One eye squeezed shut, Ezra bent over the microscope's eyepiece and turned a wheel on the side. In elementary school, we'd been given a box of slides with specimens already sandwiched between the glass – leaf sections and mushrooms. But of course it was more fun to find our own things. Hair follicles, a dead fly from the window, Jimmy's papercut.

Ezra made a *hmm*, then straightened and blinked.

"What is it?"

"Take a look."

Gathering my hair away from my face, I peered into the eyepiece. Magnified, it was much easier to see why the bead felt irregular and hollow. Not a pebble, but a shell. A delicate whorl unspooled from the center, and translucent bands striped the iridescent sides.

I blinked a handful of photos. What in the hell had caused a hail of mini seashells over Wyoming? Ezra would say a waterspout sucked them up like it could with frogs or fish, but the ocean was over a thousand miles away. A tornado would never carry something so far.

"I don't know how this would be connected to the UFO I saw."

"Neither do I," Ezra said. "Unless it was carrying two tons of micro shells when it exploded. But you think it *is* connected?"

"I'm not sure." It was hard to know what my gut felt when it was full of pecan pie and leftover adrenaline. But I didn't need definitive answers this very second. Just engagement. And it was a certainty that my readers would be excited to speculate what caused it.

I pulled up the photos I'd taken so I could attach them to a new blog post. A dark, blurry spot sat in the center of the first photo; the only indication that it was a photo of something at all was a pale vignette showing part of the glass slide. Maybe my contacts couldn't handle a photo taken through an eyepiece. Blinking hard, I cycled through the other photos, but they were all some flavor of sunspot.

That deflated some of the intrigue, but maybe if I magnified photos taken with my naked eye, it would be enough to see the spiral on the shells. I snapped a few shots of them in the bowl, but when I viewed them, the center of each image was just as dark as the previous ones.

"Everything okay?" Ezra asked.

"These things are malfunctioning."

His face pinched. "You, uh, jammed your fingers into your eyes pretty hard when we were out on the sidewalk. Maybe you broke the camera."

That wasn't good. "Do you have contacts in? Want to try?"

After blinking through the eyepiece, then at the bowl beside it, Ezra tilted his face toward the ceiling, his eyes unfocused and flicking rapidly. "Huh. There's a black blob on all of them." His gaze snapped to me and he blinked. "Pictures of you are coming out fine."

I thought of questioning why he was testing his contacts on me instead of any number of other subjects available in the kitchen. Instead, I took a picture of him.

The image caught him in a candid half-turn as he reached for his pie, the arm of his T-shirt stretching over a softly defined bicep. His side-parted curls were slightly mussed, and a dollop of whipped cream clung to his chest hair.

"Oh, you have, um." I pointed to his chest and curled my toes in my wet socks.

He looked down, then wiped away the cream and sucked it off his thumb.

I wrangled my thoughts back from the pit they were sliding into. "Will you pick up that bowl of shells?"

"And do what with it?"

"Hold it while I take a photo."

He took the bowl and struck a campy pose. I smiled, but tension crowded behind my lips. After blinking a pic, I pulled it up. My pulse pounded in my ears. Ezra came out as crisp as the last shot, but a black hole sat in the place of the bowl.

Goosebumps erupted on my arms and the back of my neck. "This is... I don't like this."

"Too gay? Or not gay enough?" Ezra adopted a new posture. "You tell me when I look hot enough to include in your article. Want me to hold the microscope?"

Shaking my head, I took the bowl from him and held it over my face, commanding my hands to stay steady. "Take one of me."

"Okay, but you don't want one where..." The playful tone fell out of his voice. "I see now what you were doing. This is, ah... What's happening?"

"I wish I knew." I set down the bowl and pushed it away with a trembling hand. "Or maybe I don't."

These photos would be great for the blog. *The mysterious hailshells defied both my photographic efforts and the laws of reality!* But it was hard to make that a priority when there was something very wrong with this situation.

I pushed out of my chair, overcome with sudden nausea. "May I use your bathroom? The pie isn't sitting well on my stomach."

4

The wall of Ezra's bathroom was textured and cool against my cheek. The sour sickness in my gut had refused to come up, but I gripped the fuzzy bath rug and tried to force my pulse to slow down.

A soft knock came at the door. "You okay?"

"I don't have enough bandwidth for this shit."

"Do you want to lie down?"

Oh, yes, that was going to calm my racing heart. "I'm not going to crawl into a strange man's bed."

There was a pause, and Ezra's shadow shuffled beneath the door. "Not like that. I was thinking of the living room. My bathroom floor probably isn't the best place. Although it might be better than a sidewalk."

I stood, a hand to my stomach, and opened the door. "I'm not having another meltdown. I'm just... disturbed."

Ezra tugged on the corner of his mustache, and his wide eyes said he wasn't unfazed by what we'd seen. "Okay. But if you need to, my floor can be a place for you... That sounds degrading. All I'm trying to say is I feel really bad about what happened before, and in the future if you're in the area and you need a safe space to decompress, you can come in."

"Do you feel sorry for me? Because I don't want pity."

"No, I..." He rubbed his forehead and looked away.

Why was I questioning his kindness? He called me by my name and had been patient and understanding in a way I hadn't encountered from anyone else here. Even if it was only because he felt guilty for the way he acted earlier, it would be nice to have an ally. "Thank you. I appreciate that."

He shrugged. "I can drive you home if you want, but I kind of want to talk about what we saw in those pictures. Or rather, what we *didn't* see."

"Yeah." I headed down the hall and sat in one of the armchairs in the front room. The leather groaned, stiff and slick like it was brand new.

He sat across from me and held out a plastic contacts container. "I took mine out. I think you should do the same."

"I don't think the contacts are the problem."

"Whatever you saw over town the other night, and whatever these little pebbles are, the government doesn't want us to know." He set the container on the coffee table and pushed it toward me. "That's all I can think of. It's some kind of experiment and our contacts have a program to keep us from capturing proof. It's like our photos are automatically redacted."

That was more logical than what I'd been dwelling on while staring into Ezra's toilet, but this was wholly different than a privacy field set up in a space that didn't allow photography.

He continued, "When contact tech came out, even with the finicky eye commands and no internet capabilities, it was still lightyears ahead of other things being developed. You know the government had to be working on it in secret for a long time before it was actually unveiled. I don't think it's outrageous to believe they did it for a specific reason."

"It was just a pissing contest between the US and China. And the pebbles don't look like tech to me. They look like seashells. Organic things."

"Either way, I'm going to spray all of them off my driveway. I don't need tiny cameras or mind-control devices or whatever they are surrounding my house."

It sounded silly, but so did my idea. Ezra wasn't mad at me

anymore and probably wouldn't mind if I turned the globe sitting on the coffee table, but I stuck my hand in my pocket and dug my thumb into an earplug instead. "Ms Pierce's yard was full of them. And she acted so strange. I'd agree that they could be affecting people in some way, except that I stood outside and let them beat down on my head and nothing happened to me. What about the ones in the kitchen? We should keep some as evidence."

"I put them in the freezer."

"I guess they can't cause problems there. Only spy on your bags of peas. I want to try something else with the shells."

He scooted closer. His gaze drifted down my neck, then back up to my face. "Something I can help with?"

"Yeah." I pointed to the antique cameras on the shelf behind him. "Do those still work?"

"A couple of them, but I don't have any film. I've found some for one of the Polaroids at the thrift store before."

"I've been thinking about this book I read. I was one of those weird kids who was big on stories about unexplainable stuff. Ghosts, aliens, cryptozoology."

"Not pie?"

I smiled. "That has different roots. Anyway, this one story stuck with me about a family dealing with a haunting. They couldn't see anything strange with their own eyes, but managed to capture images of what they believed were ghosts by using an instant camera. The photos would appear with smoky silhouettes or strange streaks of light."

Ezra stood and pulled a Polaroid from the bookshelf. He wiped dust from the lens. "If our contacts have some kind of redacting technology, it makes sense that we'd be able to take actual photos of the shells through something vintage."

"And if they're otherworldly, maybe it will show us something other than just shells."

He raised his eyebrows, then wagged a finger. "Extradimensional hermit crabs."

"What?"

"Convergent evolution. Nature has tried to make crabs at least five independent times. Makes sense that if we met an alien, it would be crab-shaped."

"You're making fun of me."

"No. I'm trying to find a little humor in this, because if I don't, my mind is going to start spiraling into government conspiracies. If something sinister is going on, we need evidence, and I like your Polaroid idea. I can go to the thrift store and see if they have film." He picked up my hat from the coffee table and held it out. "Want to come?"

"You're inviting me somewhere with you?"

He shrugged. "Yeah."

I tucked my hands under my thighs to keep from fidgeting further. "Is it crowded?" I'd never been to the thrift store, and the last thing I needed was another sensory experience that spiked my anxiety.

"Only with junk. I don't think I've seen more than two people in there at a time."

"Does it smell bad?"

"Not that I can remember. I'm surprised you've never been. You look like you shop there." He waved his hands. "That came out wrong. I'm putting my foot in my mouth a lot today. Sorry. You look like the kind of person who's into cool vintage clothing."

It was hard to tell if Ezra was flustered because of the whole situation or if it directly had to do with me. With my reputation for having opinions, he probably thought I'd jump down his throat every time he misspoke. "It's okay. I'm not offended. I do like vintage clothes, but I do most of my shopping online." Maybe the thrift store had socks. Ones still new in their packaging or novelty Christmas ones the recipient had never worn. It didn't matter as long as they weren't wet.

As we walked down the driveway, early afternoon on Orchid Street was deceptively cheery. Dappled light played on the grass, a poodle chased a ball, and the laughter of children drifted. White shells littered the ground, and I imagined them as my contacts saw them, as empty, undefined holes swallowing the driveway and sidewalk. Dark matter. Negative energy. Something existing partially in another dimension. What if an instant photo could see through the hole to the other side, at something so unfathomable you'd lose your mind simply by looking at it?

Ezra was right; without a solid answer, it would be easy to get lost in a spiral of fear. As I slid in the passenger's seat of his sedan, I said, "Tiny space crabs wouldn't be so bad. What color do you think they are?"

He climbed in and started the engine. "I think their color changes depending on what angle you're looking at."

"That sounds pretty. I could add them to my fish tank."

"Gotta be careful, though." Ezra backed out of the drive and headed for Main. "If you stick them in water, they'll grow to the size of a cat."

"That's bad news for Ms Pierce."

He snorted, then put a fist to his mouth, his chest hitching. It wasn't that funny, but it was infectious.

I giggled and clutched my smarting cheek. Putting on my best news anchor voice, I said, "'Residents of Muddy Gap, Wyoming were shocked to find their sleepy town overrun by disturbingly large crabs, which commandeered dumpsters, toilet bowls, and the baseball field. Where did they come from? The southernmost star in the Cancer constellation, of course. Townsfolk are asking for donations of butter and lemon'."

Ezra laughed harder, his cheeks flushed. "You better get on that recipe for Space Crab Pie. We're going to need it."

"That sounds delicious. Buttery pastry, some leeks, cream cheese."

"Do you write about savory pies on your blog?"

"Yes."

"Do you eat things *besides* pie?"

"Of course." I side-eyed him. "Sometimes I have cobbler and cheesecake."

"Oh, well, as long as you're getting a varied diet."

"My diet is mainly bologna sandwiches, actually."

"Too lazy to cook? I'm not judging, I do the same thing."

"I try occasionally, but that isn't really it." If a food didn't have a familiar enough element – a shape or texture I was certain I'd like – I wouldn't eat it. If someone tried to serve me crab salad, no, absolutely not. But if they put it in a pie shell, I'd try it.

Air vents hummed, and an evergreen-shaped air freshener long past its usefulness wavered in the current.

Ezra slowed as he pulled onto Main, passing barber shops and saloons with their quaint *howdy, partner* false fronts, a car charging station, and the hardware store, which was missing half the letters off of its marquee. "We could have supper sometime. You know, when we're not solving space crab mysteries."

The expression on my face must not have been what he expected, because he said, "Or not. It's cool."

"I don't understand. I've made a horrible impression today, and your neighbors will be talking about me – and *you* – for weeks. And..." My chest tightened. "I'm the resident weirdo. People don't tell me their house can be a safe space for me to decompress or ask me out on dates. Why are you?"

He pulled up to the curb beside the thrift shop and shut off the engine. The air freshener did a lazy spin.

"Because you're incredibly perceptive. You're witty." His tongue poked through his lips. "And you're so pretty. Can I call you that?"

I swallowed. "Sure."

"Something bizarre is going on in town and you're the only one clever enough to have noticed."

"I saw an exploding UFO. Not sure what cleverness has to do with it."

"I'm angry at myself for buying into the rumors about you because you seem like a smart, cool–"

"They're true, though. I say things to people all the time that come off as mean-spirited. And my intention doesn't matter if it hurts someone. I know this, but it still happens. Like me comparing you to Julio Manhammer. I didn't know that would make you self-conscious of your weight. And it shouldn't. Different doesn't mean *worse*."

"Thanks. Don't worry about my neighbors talking. You think they don't already whisper about the guy who has a degree but can't get a good job so he bartends at a shitty dive in Casper?"

"Why can't you get a job with your degree?"

He slumped in the seat, staring out the windshield. "Did you know bartending pays better than working as a real estate agent? 'Bartender' doesn't have the same suburban air to it that these people expect, though. I'm no longer classy Ezra with the Christmas parties that everyone wants to attend. Now I'm trashy Ezra who stole his living room furniture and wouldn't my parole officer like to know about that?"

"People actually say that to you?"

"Just one. But at least when *you're* saying hurtful things to people, it's the naked truth, not gross fabrications about a person's character and morals."

"There's nothing wrong with working at a bar if it pays the bills. I have to try out a vibrator and write up my thoughts on a product review website if I want to get paid."

"You say that like it's a bad thing." He climbed out of the car and I followed. Stopping beside me on the sidewalk, he said, "Anyway, you don't want to have supper with me, that's fine. But don't let it be because you think you don't deserve someone's attention."

A small smear of whipped cream still stuck to Ezra's chest above his scandalously deep V-neck. Noon sun danced across his black lashes, and his proximity and scent were

almost enough to push worries about disturbing photos out
of my mind. "Have you been to *The Lounge*?"

"Yeah. Their steaks are excellent."

"So is their pie. I'd love to go there with you sometime."

"Great. I'm looking forward to it."

I flapped my hands before I could stop myself, then pressed
my fists into my sides and looked away. "Sorry. I'm kind of
excited."

He smiled. "Don't apologize for being yourself. C'mon."
He turned toward the thrift shop and opened the door. A
cluster of sleigh bells jingled, and the scent of aged plastic
and decades of dust hit me. Ropes of black power cables,
yellowed appliances, scummy glass vases, and chipped dinner
plates crowded the shelves. A sad-looking Christmas tree
with sparse faux needles sat askew, straggly tinsel dripping
from the branches. Racks of pilly shirts and kids' pajamas
that looked like they'd shrunk in the wash sat beside a sofa I
wouldn't sit on if someone paid me.

Well, it would depend on the amount.

A pair of bright green socks with a repeating pattern of *KISS
ME I'M IRISH* hung from an endcap. They still had their plastic
fasteners attached and a strip of cardboard taped around the
center. The tag said fifty cents. A small price to pay for dry
socks, even if I wasn't Irish.

Ezra's ample ass swayed as he veered past milk crates of
stuffed animals and precariously placed eggbeaters. The
thought of going to *The Lounge* with him on a slow night, sitting
in the dim lighting of one of the velvet-flocked back booths
while we had steak and alphabet pie flipped my stomach, but
in a good way.

Some of the butterflies in my gut shriveled and died as I
remembered why we were here. I followed Ezra down an
aisle. He pawed through little point-and-clicks with missing
battery compartment lids and waterproof disposables with
tangled charging cables.

Pulling out a dented cardboard package with fuzzy corners, he shook it and smiled. "Last box."

And a step closer, maybe, to knowing what was going on. I poked at the cameras. A box tumbled off the shelf, and I caught it before it hit the floor. It was a tiny instant deal that spat out half photos, according to the faded image under the title. Not the best piece of equipment, and I'd have to take a picture of the picture to load it to the blog, but having two cameras might be better than one. The gummy orange label said five dollars.

I tucked the box under my arm and held out my hand for the Polaroid film. "Let me have it. I'll go pay."

He frowned. "You don't need to do that."

"I know. But this is my idea. And had I not walked by your house earlier, you'd be doing something ten times more fun than stressing over mind-control conspiracies."

"You already brought a pie over, and I'm sure that cost more than this film."

"Just give it to me."

Sighing, he offered me the package, then caught my hand and pressed a five into it.

My nostrils flared. "Dammit. I didn't mean–"

"Are we going to fight over who pays for supper too?"

"Yes. I'm not a fan of the sexist subtext that comes with being chivalrous."

"It doesn't have anything to do with the way I view you. I figured I'd pay for supper because I invited you. If you'd asked me out, I'd assume you'd pay. Or we could split it. We can still do that."

I let out a breathy chuckle. "We're arguing about paying for supper and we haven't even gone on the date yet. Sorry. Just don't pull out chairs for me or something."

"No chair pulling." His gaze made a circuit around my face. "But to be honest, thinking about going on a date with you is taking my mind off of whatever is happening on those photos we took."

"Same here." I shifted and something poked me in the leg, then clattered on the floor. It was a net with an aluminum handle, the loose-knit mesh tangled and broken on one side. "Here we go. Perfect for catching cat-sized crabs. Should we get it?"

"Looks like one already escaped out of it. Better pass."

I carried the camera and film up to the counter. Cloudy knickknacks sat to one side of the register, and water-warped signs written in marker declared that cryptocurrency wasn't accepted. The tiny backroom beyond the counter was unoccupied aside from a computer desk and a vinyl chair with a split down the middle of the seat.

"Hello?" I popped open the flap on the camera box and shook it out, expecting an accompanying packet of film and folded instructions, but it was clear by the scuffed edges of the camera that it was used and probably already loaded.

I held it up to the light, trying to figure out which tiny window indicated the film count. If I opened it, would it expose the film and ruin it? Was that how it worked? Ezra would know, but he was still back beyond the shelves. Maybe debating on whether to add another camera to his collection, though none of them had looked nearly as old as the ones in his house. Muddy Gap probably wasn't the best place to shop for antiques.

Squinting through the camera's viewer shrank the cluttered store down to a distorted miniature. When I pressed the button on top, a loud click followed. The camera whirred and a small rectangle rolled from the slot in the front.

A groan came from the other side of the counter. Hesitantly, I peered over the top. An older white man lay on the floor. Scrapes covered the side of his face and orange sand stuck to the wounds. Blood ran down his neck, pooling in the collar of his flannel shirt.

"Good god!"

He struggled to sit up and sand cascaded onto the floor.

"Ezra!" I rounded the counter and put an arm around the man, helping him up. Ezra stopped short, eyes wide. He helped me lift the man into the vinyl chair in the office.

"S-sand." The shop owner moaned and touched his face.

"I see that. What happened? Do you need medical attention?"

Ezra pulled out his phone and tapped the screen. He held it to his ear. "Hi, yes, I need medical services to Davis' Thrift on Main in Muddy Gap."

Small dunes of orange sand covered the floor behind the counter, punctuated with translucent shards. Maybe a fish tank or decorative bowl had fallen on the shop owner's head.

He blinked hard, then looked around his office with glassy eyes. His gaze landed on the camera in my hand. "Hey!"

His voice was so jarringly forceful that my finger spasmed against the capture button. The camera whirred and ejected another photo.

"Give that to me right now, you shit." He lunged from the chair, but Ezra shoved him back in. The man thrashed as Ezra pinned him down. His hand shot out, and he tried to slap my camera away. The shutter clicked.

Blood oozed from the raw skin at the shop owner's temple, and sand fell from his hair and shoulders. "You punks don't even know what a goddamn corded phone is." Spit flew from his mouth, his eyes bulging and bloodshot. "And you come in here and think you can mess with everything and play dress-up with the clothes!"

"Whoa, calm down." Ezra's attempt at a soothing voice was at odds with his pinched face. "We came in here as customers with every intention of paying for our purchases. But that hardly seems like something you should worry about at the moment. You're injured."

The man snatched the camera, and the roll of photos tore off in my hand. He growled. "Professor Pie. Touching my stuff."

My shoulders sagged. I didn't even know this man's name – couldn't remember seeing him around town – but he sure as hell knew who I was. I brushed past Ezra. "I can order Polaroid film online. We'll have to pause our alien investigation for a couple days while we wait for it, but maybe it's best for me to stop going places where I'm not wanted."

Ezra took my arm. "Now hold on–"

The shop owner smashed the camera against the doorframe and shards of plastic exploded, bouncing off the counter and skittering away. One struck Ezra's chest, another nicking my neck. The man slammed the little instant against the wood repeatedly, until it was pulverized. Chunks of casing gouged his palm and blood ran down his arm.

"What the hell!" Ezra yanked the man back into his chair. "What are you doing? Stop it!"

The sleigh bells on the front door shrieked, and two police officers rushed inside. One said, "We were across the street. What– Shit, Davis, what happened?"

Voices mashed together. I cupped my ears and pushed through the front doors. My chest heaved, tinny music drifting from the bar across the street. The neon of the Miller High Life sign in the window blurred in my vision until I could no longer make out the letters. I wasn't sure how long I stood there, breath whistling through my nose, before Ezra touched my elbow.

The roll of photos I'd dropped hung limply from his hand. "Let's get out of here, huh? Those guys in there are handling it. This is the second time today that someone has acted totally bananas and lashed out."

"Lashed out at *me*. Because they don't want me around. Didn't you hear him? Same with Ms Pierce screaming, 'Get out of my yard, Professor Pie'."

Ezra glanced over his shoulder at the closed front door, then led me to the car. "That teen on the bike said Ms Pierce yelled at him too. There's nothing wrong with you."

I slid into the car and sighed. "I never said there was. Will you drive me home?"

Air wheezed from the vents as Ezra started the engine and pulled away from the curb. The car rumbled softly across uneven asphalt. "Want to stop by my place first so you can get your pecan pie?"

"Keep it."

"I can order the Polaroid film. Should I get a little disposable camera too, like the one you were going to buy?"

"I don't know." I wiped my hands down my face. "I can't think now. I just want to go home." I directed him to my apartment complex.

He stopped in a parking space and stared ahead. "I don't like any of this."

"The landscaping definitely leaves something to be desired."

"No, I meant–" He let out a brittle laugh. "You really are witty."

"I'm tired."

"Okay. I won't keep you. But I'd like to talk about" – he gestured vaguely, which somehow managed to encompass all of the weirdness of the past couple days – "this, when you're feeling up to it. Where the hell did all that sand come from? Maybe– No. Later. If I give you my number, will you call me?"

"Not unless you want to hear five seconds of heavy breathing before I hang up."

"Sounds sexy."

I side-eyed him. "I'll text you. Tomorrow." Concerns about the shop owner, the hailshells, and my blog crowded my mind, but I pushed them away. I was going to sleep and worry about it all later.

After punching Ezra's number into my phone, I undid the seatbelt and turned to him.

His jaw was tight with tension, a knot of worry between his brows. "You'll be okay?"

"Yeah. Thank you for the ride. And for the date invitation. And for" – I shrugged – "being nice."

"It's nothing."

"Not nothing. I appreciate it."

I climbed the steps to my apartment, the hollow clang of my shoes on metal too much for my raw nerves. Ezra's car still sat in the parking lot. I gave him a small wave and walked inside.

5

The groan of my stomach pulled me to consciousness. I threw off the covers and staggered to the bathroom. An awful film coated my teeth, and my breath was so bad I could taste it. After relieving myself, I brushed my teeth and inspected the bandages on my cheek. They were stiff with blood, and the wound underneath, though closed with steriglue, was long and inflamed at the edges. Beside it were thin scratches from the threaded end of the hose, and the whole area was tinged a plum purple.

My joints ached and sweat stuck hair to my brow. After a quick shower, I rummaged through the fridge for the milk then paused, staring at 4:13 on the microwave. Ezra dropped me off around three, and I'd fallen right to sleep. It sure felt like I'd slept longer than an hour.

The tetras and danios darted across the tank at my approach, and the frogs perked up, pressing against the glass. I checked my phone and blinked hard. It was 4am. No wonder I was hungry. And so were my pets.

"Sheesh. Sorry guys." I sprinkled in a pinch of fish food and some pellets for the frogs.

After making myself a sandwich, I sat on the bed and opened my phone. Writing messages that way was slower, but too much typing with my contacts strained my eyes.

A stream of email notifications appeared. I swiped them away. Keeping the blog updated and engaged with evidence of what was going on was still a priority, but the unsettling occurrences deflated a lot of the excitement of being popular and making money.

Six unread texts blinked on the screen. I opened the first one, which was dated yesterday at 4:35pm.

<I keep staring at these pictures. I don't understand what I'm looking at.>

Why was Ezra still looking at the contact pictures? Maybe he'd changed his mind about them being "redacted" and was now considering the cosmic horror ideas that I was.

The next text was stamped 4:42pm. *<I want to send them to you to see. I want to talk about this with someone. It's creeping me out. But I know you're upset and need to unwind.>*

"We already looked at them and talked about them." Unless those weren't the pictures he was referring to. I'd snapped some in the thrift store and vaguely remembered the curling ream of them hanging out of the camera, but I hadn't brought them home with me. I must have left them in his car.

5:12pm: *<I'm sorry for all these texts. I wanted to tell you that I work tonight but I'll be off at 2. 3am probably isn't the best time to get together, but I'll be up if you want to talk. Otherwise, maybe tomorrow?>*

5:20pm: *<Just look at these two photos. You can see the rest later.>*

My finger hovered over the next message. Ezra freaking out about instant photos from the thrift store didn't bode well for whatever I was about to see. It couldn't be worse than the store owner raging with his bloody, sand-coated face, which is what I *thought* I'd captured.

I opened the first picture message, and a mixture of relief and confusion washed over me. It was the first photo I'd taken to test out the camera. The image was a bit dark, colors not as vivid or crisp as I'd get from a contact photo, but the cluttered shelves of the thrift store were clear. A smeary vignette of rainbow light bent across the shot, but that could have been due to the film's age or even a normal detail of instant cameras for all I knew.

Squinting, I held the phone closer to my face. Maybe I was missing something. A ghostly face in a reflection, or more voids of darkness where there should have been objects.

Aside from one slightly suspicious shadow below a stack of dinner plates, there was nothing there.

I texted Ezra. *<I looked at the first pic. What are you seeing?>*

When I opened the next picture message, it took me a moment to piece together what I was looking at. Rainbow light fractured through the image in front of what might have been Ezra's hand and part of the vinyl office chair. I clucked my tongue and typed out a text. *<You really had me scared for a moment. But that camera was preowned. It was old. Either the film or camera was faulty and producing artifacts.>*

Ezra's reply was immediate: *<You sure?>*

<Yeah, it's just a light flare.>

<Don't they have those in your ghost books?

Never mind, I feel stupid now. I'm sure you're right. When I saw those pictures and thought of the ones we took with the black spots, I tried putting 2 and 2 together I guess. And the way Davis acted freaked me out.>

I typed back. *<Not stupid. You're right - our brains have been trying to make connections of things that are unrelated. The simplest answers are usually correct, right? And I think the shop owner fell in the parking lot and hit his head.>*

The drifts of sand on the floor had been a vivid orange. That occurred naturally on certain beaches, but anything blowing in from outside wouldn't match that color. Foreign then, or artificially dyed. There'd also been chunks of clear glass or stone. Had there been hailshells in the mess? It was too hard to remember.

My gut nagged that all these things weren't unrelated, but I couldn't make them fit. *<Maybe something crashed down on him. There were clear chunks of glass or stone mixed in with the sand. That thrift store was a fire hazard. He was in shock.>*

Dropping onto the bed, I shut my eyes and blew out a

breath. The phone vibrated on my chest. Ezra said, <*I bet you're right. I'm going to follow up with the police station to make sure Davis is okay, but I feel so much better now after talking to you. Hopefully I can get some decent sleep. How are you feeling today? Good, I hope.*>

<*Better, yeah. I slept forever. Going to work on my blog and get organized about how to approach this. We should get the news involved, like you said. Maybe the authorities too. Send me the photos you took of the shells and of me yesterday when you get the chance, please.*>

<*Great idea,*> he said. <*I called in to work last night because I couldn't focus on anything but those stupid pictures, then spent half the night staring at the ceiling thinking about it. I even tried lying on the floor like you do, but it didn't help calm me down.*>

Image messages appeared: views through the microscope of black voids; my face blotted out as I held up the bowl of shells; a shot focusing on my fingers as I touched my neck, my gaze distant. Maybe he hadn't meant to send me that one.

A final text bookended his images. <*Shoot me a message later with an update. I'm going back to bed.*>

The desk chair creaked as I sat down. I typed "sweet dreams", then brought up emojis, hesitating over a sparkly heart. Before I could change my mind, I tapped the heart and hit send, then closed out of my phone and stuck it in a desk drawer.

Calm settled over me as I wrote out a to-do list and organized the tasks. Write a new blog post with the redacted photos. Email the *Oil City Tribune* with the same pictures and an account of the UFO and hailshells. Put in a shopping order at Gem's Market because there was nothing left in the kitchen but one slice of bologna and some bread heels.

Ad revenue for yesterday had amounted to $98. Today was only at $51, but it would be nice to see it uptick with the traffic to my newly published post.

Hundreds of blog comments inundated me. I worked my way through, responding to each one, even the handful of nasty ones. Even though my fans and visitors didn't know any more about my situation than I did, it was almost like they were investigating with me.

I kept a separate tab open on my newly published post, watching comments about the redacted photos appear even as I was still trying to reply to the ones on my previous post. By the time I finished answering questions about the noodles in alphabet pie and the probability of alien radiation, then added laugh emojis to all of the tired jokes about me getting probed, an hour and a half had passed.

I peeked at my phone. There was an unread text from Ezra. He'd replied to my *sweet dreams* 🥰 with: <*I hope they are* 😳>

My heart fluttered.

Everything was crossed off my list, but where the hell were my groceries? I'd placed the order a little after eight. It was ten now. Normally the groceries were at my door within forty-five minutes. I checked the site, but the delivery progress bar hadn't advanced from "Order Received" to "Order Processed".

I walked into the kitchen, the number for the market punched into my phone and sweat breaking out on my upper lip. I squeezed the display down into a stick, then stretched it back out again.

Phone call, or braving the flashing lights and rotten milk smell of being there in person.

My finger hovered over the call button, adrenaline racing through my limbs. It would only take thirty seconds tops.

Why hasn't my order been processed?

Sorry Professor Pie, Sam got backed up with a large order, but yours is next.

That was it. That was all it would take. Sam had never been backed up with a large order before, but sometimes things were added into my order by mistake. The kitty bandages, a novelty flavor of potato chips, nail polish. Maybe someone had yelled at Sam to take his time packing things so the right items were consistently delivered to the right people.

I swallowed, staring at the tiny green *Call* icon. Talking to people in person was easy. Texting was easy. Replying with overly cheery responses to rude blog comments was easy. And I'd managed to answer Aunt Georgina's video call.

Just press the button. *Hi. It's Denver Bryant. Where's my order? Hi. It's Denver Bryant. Where's my order? Hi. It's—*

The phone slipped from my clammy grip and clattered across the linoleum.

"Fuck!" I snatched my wallet and keys, picked up the phone, and rooted through the clothes drawers beneath the bed until I found a handkerchief. After wedging on my hat, I left the apartment and stomped down to the truck.

"I hate myself."

Trevor stood on his balcony, the wind ruffling his carob-colored hair. He took a drag from his cigarette, gaze unfocused like the only thing rattling around in his head was a stray penny and some lint. I didn't crave that kind of sublime ignorance, but I often wondered what it was like for neurotypical people to just... exist, without the skin-itching anxiety of crowds and phone calls and knowing you weren't going to get a conversation right because everyone had the manual for social navigation but you.

What it must be like to go anywhere, no matter how noisy or bright or populated with smells, without feeling like someone touched your soul with a live wire.

I threw open the truck door and drove to Gem's. The tiny parking lot was peppered with cars. Monday morning likely wasn't their busiest time, but I'd still have to navigate past clattering shopping carts and the insect whine of gossiping neighbors to reach someone who could help me with my order.

Leaving the truck in a sparse area toward the edge of the lot, I tied the handkerchief over my nose and mouth and wedged in my earplugs. I probably looked like I was going to whip out a couple of six-shooters and demand all the market's pie be put in a bag for me.

The doors slid open. I hunched my shoulders and pulled down the brim of my hat to shield myself from the lights of the candy printer. A faint whiff of spoilage hit me, and I pressed the handkerchief against my nostrils.

Something crunched underfoot. Little orange grains that looked like decorative sugar winked in the flickering fluorescents. Great. Some other broken-open grocery to add to the sedimentary layers in the rugs.

I looked up. The bank of checkout counters stretched to my left, half of them self-service. A cart sat askew beside the first one, bags of groceries in the basket and the rest waiting to be scanned. A box of cereal sat neglected on the scanner.

The lamps above the human-operated counters gave off a welcoming glow, but no one stood in line or behind the registers. Apparently all of the cashiers had decided to take a smoke break at the same time.

Another half-scanned cart was parked at a checkout. Bags of dog food sat on the belt, and a carton of weeping French vanilla ice cream made a puddle on the black rubber. That brand was terrible, so it was no great loss, but it had clearly been sitting there for a while.

Hairs prickled on my neck. Tentatively, I pulled out one of the earplugs. The candy printer beeped and beckoned, and an electronic voice said, *"Please remove your item from the scanner and place it in a bag."*

Breath whistled through my nose. I looped the last checkout and strode the other way, glancing down each unoccupied aisle. Taxidermal pronghorns and bison heads mounted to the wall stared down at me with menacing glass gazes. Skiffs of orange sanded the floor, dotted with white shells. They burst beneath my shoes. This was just like the thrift store.

"Please remove your item from the scanner and place it in a bag."

The flickering lights were driving a screw of pain into the center of my brain, but I pushed it away and detoured down the frozen foods section. A door stood open, condensation fogging the glass.

"Please remove your item from the scanner and place it in a bag."

Shaking out my tingling fingers, I stopped at the abandoned cart and pulled the box of cereal off the scanner.

"Please place the item in a bag."

"Hello?" I clutched the box to my chest and turned in a circle.

"Please wait. An attendant has been called."

My stomach clenched into a knot. "Hello!"

Dread increased with every step. Past the islands of potatoes and onions, where more of the shimmery orange sand had collected, the deli lay vacant, water dribbling from a faucet. In the garden area, the back door stood open, a light wind knocking it into the wall. I pushed open the scuffed swinging doors to a storage bay, but it was just as empty as the market.

No one was here, like they'd all been vaporized *War of the Worlds* style while trying to decide what brand of paper towels to buy.

And I was stupidly standing in the middle of the target zone.

I strode down an aisle toward the front of the store and tried to hit the text button for Ezra, but fumbled the phone. It slammed onto the floor, spraying huffs of orange sand.

Tiny shells rolled away as I scooped up the phone. A faint *"Hello?"* came from the speaker, and I nearly dropped it again.

Seconds rolled over on the screen, recording the call time. I stared, a battle inside me waging over whether to say something or hang up.

"Denver?"

"There's no one in the market," I whispered.

"I can't hear you. There's no one where?"

"In Gem's." I straightened and hurried down the aisle. My hip jostled a cart full of pasta sauce and spaghetti noodles.

"Good day to go shopping then?"

"No." I explained what I found, wondering why I was so

damn breathless just walking through a store, and equally bewildered that I was talking to Ezra on the phone. But his voice grounded me enough to reel in my thoughts and make a beeline for the exit.

"Hang tight. I'm coming to check it out."

"Wait, what? No, no. I don't think we should be anywhere near here."

"I'm at the police station. I'll be right there."

"The sand, Ezra. It's all over the place. The sand and the shells." The doors slid open and I hurried outside, squinting in the sunlight. A gust of wind caught the brim of my hat, and I held it down.

"It's too bad we didn't get any film so we can get photo evidence."

He wasn't wrong, but that wasn't the biggest concern on my mind at the moment. "I don't want to get raptured."

There were dozens of cars in the parking lot. Dozens of people who were just... gone now. Were they coming back? Maybe in an hour or a week they'd reappear, moaning on the ground with oozing wounds like the thrift shop owner.

That was a classic alien abduction scenario, and meant that, exploded UFO or not, the extraterrestrial influence was still here in town. Maybe I'd drive around the back of the store to see shoppers and cashiers standing rigid, their faces tilted to the sky in unison.

I shuddered.

Rustling and the slamming of a car door came through my phone. Ezra said, *"On my way. Don't go anywhere."*

"What if I don't have a choice?"

"I'm not above running over a group of little green men to save you."

I stood on the sidewalk for what seemed like ages, every *whap* of the sales banner against the side of Gem's setting my nerves on edge. This was a terrible idea, but I wasn't going to leave with Ezra already on his way. Finally, his sedan whipped around a corner, and he came to a crooked stop near the front entrance. I waved my arms as he climbed out. "I don't think we should go back in. How do you protect yourself when you don't even know what the danger is?"

He strode past me, his phone hanging limply at his side. "Give me five minutes."

"We shouldn't be here. I don't want something to happen to you."

"But you're right. We need to piece together what's going on and protect ourselves in the meantime."

I'd been down every aisle of the store, but Ezra might spot a clue I didn't, and that could be worth the risk. "Three minutes. Then I'm hauling you bodily out of there."

I half expected him to say, "Sounds sexy", but he gave me a thumbs up and crept into the store like it was a forest in enemy territory.

"I'm serious," I called. "I'm setting a timer in my contacts."

The numbers rolled over in my peripheral vision. I paced and tugged at my hair. What if a car pulled up? Some woman with a shopping list in her pocket and a toddler on her hip. If I tried to explain to her what was going on, she wouldn't believe me. Not when the words were coming from Professor Pie.

Police could wrap caution tape around Gem's, but that wouldn't prevent abductions somewhere else. In all of those alien movies, the cops never stood a chance. They'd point their little peashooters at some tentacled monstrosity and be torn in half like tissue paper.

2:00 flashed in my contacts. I rocked on my heels. This was too big for just me. The authorities and news would certainly pay attention with so many people missing. But if we compiled evidence that made a strong case, it could cause mass hysteria. Maybe the government would send in scientists in hazmat suits to quarantine the town. That could be someone else's problem. It wasn't my job to try to evacuate an entire town.

1:00. Ezra believed me when no one else had and was trying to help. It made my heart skip. Without him, I'd be stuck in a pit of my own thoughts, with only internet fans to use as a sounding board, which would absolutely feed into more paranoid speculation instead of making it better.

Sand stuck between the webbing of my fingers. I made a noise in my throat and wiped it away. If proximity to the sand and shells was evidence of an imminent abduction, it should have happened to me. I'd stood outside and let the hail beat on my head.

At least now I had a good idea of why Ms Pierce and the thrift shop owner had acted so disoriented.

The clatter of a shopping cart from within the store grew louder, then Ezra pushed it out the entrance. It was the one I'd knocked into in the pasta aisle, but in addition to jars of sauce and noodles, it now overflowed with canned goods, toilet paper, tortillas, dried beans, and oatmeal.

"What are you doing?" I said. "You can't steal all that food. And I *know* you didn't have time to scan it all."

Ezra threw open the trunk of his car and started tossing things inside. "We don't know if anyone is coming back. Who's going to place orders to have shelves restocked? Where will we get our groceries?"

"Casper is only an hour away. There are like twenty grocery stores there."

"I got you six different pies and some bologna."

"Ezra! What about the rest of the town? We can't think only of ourselves."

He dumped in an armful of shampoo bottles and bags of rice. "I guarantee that everyone else here would do exactly what I'm doing, and they wouldn't give one thought about you or me."

"That still doesn't make it right." I *had* already paid for an order online, which was never delivered, so Gem's did owe me food. But it was nowhere near the quantity that Ezra had grabbed.

I rummaged through my backpack for my wallet, knowing it was pointless to pull it out. Even if I could afford to pay for two hundred dollars' worth of groceries, I wasn't going to go back in there and scan them all.

"I went to the police station to check up on Davis. I told them about Ms Pierce, the shells, the redacted photos. Everything." Ezra pushed two bottles of vodka between the packs of toilet paper, his cheeks blotchy. "They laughed their asses off at me."

I clutched my elbows and bit the inside of my cheek. If no one believed Ezra, they certainly weren't going to believe me.

There was an edge to his voice. "Cops don't believe me. Again. Fine. This is turning into everyone for themselves, so I'm stealing the goddamn bologna."

"But we have a mass abduction as evidence now."

"I'd rather not get laughed at again when I have a serious situation to report."

"Something like that happen before?"

Ezra jammed a box of cereal into the trunk so hard the cardboard dented.

I didn't like the anger bristling off of him, so I filled the space with words. "We can try calling the Casper station. Different town. They have no reason to–"

"Tried it. Couldn't get through."

I stared at the Red Barn brand peanut butter pie with chocolate crust Ezra set in the trunk. Holing up with stolen food and waiting for this to either blow over or turn into a scene out of *Mad Max* couldn't be our only option, but seeing more food in Ezra's trunk than was ever in my kitchen at one time did quell a little of the tumult inside me.

"You're really lucky Gem's is still old school and doesn't have RFID tags on everything." If he'd tried this in the city, he'd get charged as soon as he pushed the cart out the door, abandoned supermarket or not. Scooping up jars of salsa and tomato sauce and adding them to the pile in the car, I said,

"I don't know if I'm okay with this, but I'm not going to stop you and I'm not going to say no to that pie, as long as you do something for me."

He tossed in bags of instant mashed potatoes. "What?"

"We drive to Casper. Just... leave town. Get away from this before it gets worse." I checked my notifications. "The *Oil City Tribune* hasn't replied to my email, but I still have activity trickling in from my blog. Some of my fans mentioned living in Casper, but none of their new comments corroborate anything that I've detailed happening here. What's going on is likely exclusive to Muddy Gap. We can go to the Casper news station, to the police–"

"*You* can talk to the police next time."

"Okay. We'll let them figure it out. This is too big for just us. We'll stay in a hotel room or..." I couldn't afford more than one night in a dumpy motel, but sleeping in a car while the authorities handled this problem hardly felt like a dealbreaker.

He slammed the trunk. "That's a great idea. I won't unload any of this stuff at home then. Let's go pack and I'll meet you at your place."

I nodded. "Okay."

"And if Casper is tainted too, we just keep driving. Go to Cheyenne. Or" – a faint smile crossed his face – "to Denver."

"Denver does Denver. I'll pack as quickly as I can."

6

People passed me on the way home and stood in their yards, pulling dandelions and bathing their dogs. They were going about their business like nothing was wrong, but word would get out about Gem's. More people would bombard the police station, and it was doubtful they'd be laughed at.

Ezra and I could be in Casper in an hour and have more authorities and news stations paying attention. Someone would figure out what to do.

After pulling into a parking space and shutting off the engine, I stared at my apartment complex. The blinds in the office were open, the wraithlike silhouette of Mrs Mumford drifting past the window. Trevor stood outside the door; he crushed a cigarette under his shoe and walked back inside the office.

I couldn't warn the entire town, but telling at least a couple of people might be enough to save them should more abductions happen before I reached Casper.

Hurrying across the parking lot, I hopped over parking chocks and pushed open the office door. A high-pitched whine from the fluorescents dug into my brain, and I cringed. I squeezed my fist around my earplugs, but didn't take them out of my pocket.

Mrs Mumford looked up from her desk, her expression of irritation deepening. "No, Professor Pie, we haven't replaced the card reader on your favorite dryer. Just use a different one."

"That's not–"

"And I got your text about the lights in the parking lot not turning on at the correct time. The timer isn't working. Maintenance is looking into it."

I opened my mouth, but she pointed to the chairs beside the door; one was occupied by Trevor. "Trevor's water heater is leaking and has bubbled up the linoleum, and I've gotta take care of it. He should have told me weeks ago."

"Trevor only moved in last week," I said. "If it's been neglected that long, it's your fault for not noticing it during inspection."

"That's what I said!" Trevor pocketed his phone and stood. He was wearing a shirt that read, *I enjoy romantic walks to the taco truck.* "I don't want my deposit eaten up on something that isn't my fault."

Mrs Mumford glared at me, then at Trevor. She shut a drawer in her desk, then headed for the door. "I need to get maintenance up there."

"Hang on." The buzz from the lights made my eyes water, and the band of pain wrapping my head cinched tighter as the door slammed closed.

"Thanks for sticking up for me." Trevor glanced at foiled wrapped chocolates in a bowl on a corner of the desk, then grabbed all of them.

"Those candies have that waxy white look chocolate gets when it's really old. I wouldn't eat them."

"Oh." He dumped them back in the bowl.

"Trevor." I leveled my gaze at him for as long as I could stand. I was wrong in deciding his dime-a-dozen features were unmemorable. They conveyed so much expression that his emotions might as well be written on his forehead in Sharpie. And right now, he was looking at me like I was his battle partner in the war against greedy landladies. "I need to tell you something. It's serious."

His eyebrows rose. "Okay."

"Something really bad is happening here. I think you need to leave. We all do."

"Yeah, Mumford is a bitch, huh? I don't want to lose my deposit."

"No, I mean leave town. Remember that flash in the sky I told you about? It was a UFO. Whatever came out of it is abducting people and we could be next. I'm packing and leaving town. You should too."

He broke his gaze, the previous intensity of his face fading back to bland indifference. After plucking one of the chocolates from the dish, he peeled back the foil, and scraped his nail across the white film. "Nah. If maintenance is fixing my water heater, I need to be there. I don't trust them. They'll steal my Xbox."

I blinked at him. "Did you hear me? There are *aliens* in town. Everyone in Gem's is gone. Snatched away. We need to leave. This is not a joke."

"They'll steal my Xbox." He dropped the chocolate back on the desk and walked through the door.

What the hell? Maybe that was a technique people employed when dealing with someone they thought was delusional. Don't argue with them. Just deflect. I was probably lucky he didn't laugh in my face instead.

With a sigh, I shoved through the door and took the steps two at a time to my apartment. I tossed my hat on the bed and snatched my backpack. After slipping my laptop inside, I stuffed clothes and toiletries around it as a cushion, then hefted it over my shoulder.

Tranquil light from the fish tank rippled on the wall. Shit. How was I going to–

I gasped. All the little neon tetras and zebra danios floated at the surface, belly up. Daisy and Pickle lay at the bottom, their legs stiff and one of them tangled in a plant.

I squeezed my eyes shut and put a hand over my mouth. Goddamn it. Fish, especially in a smaller tank, were sensitive to any changes in temperature or PH balance. Whatever was happening in town had affected them too.

Their little corpses bobbed in the current, eyes wide and staring. They were all I had.

A knock came at the door. I opened it numbly and walked back to the bed, barely able to see with the blear in my eyes.

Ezra stepped inside. "What's wrong? I mean, besides everything?"

My mouth wavered, and I pulled a wet breath through my nose. "My fish and frogs died."

He turned to the tank and put his hands on his thighs, peering through the glass. "Damn. I'm sorry."

I reached for my hat, but he gripped my wrist and pulled me against him. Startling, I stiffened as he hugged me, but the honeyed scent of his cologne and his strong arms enveloping me erased my tension. I relaxed and melted into him. His skin warmed my cheek, firm chest expanding against mine. I stayed that way for as long as I dared, fighting back tears.

Pulling away, I wedged on my hat and shut off the lights on the fish tank. "Let's go."

We clanked down the steps as I wiped my eyes. Ezra's car idled at the curb. We slid inside and he turned onto the road.

"I don't know what I expected to do with the fish anyway. Not like I could keep them alive in a car or a hotel room for very long." I pressed my forehead to the cold window. Houses and a coffee shop slipped out of view.

"That doesn't mean you aren't allowed to feel upset about it."

The church and Gem's Market rolled by. The same cars still sat in the parking lot, no one new pulling in or pushing a cart out the doors. We rounded the curve, taking us out of town, and as soon as we passed below the arch of the new gateway sign something inside me lifted despite the hurt in my heart. We could escape this before it got worse, and I'd be somewhere new, somewhere I wasn't yet known as town eccentric.

"Go faster," I whispered. "Get us the hell out of here."

Ezra pressed the accelerator harder, and Muddy Gap shrank in the side mirror. I'd called it home for over ten years, and it had been good to me in many respects. Rent was cheap, the neighbors were quiet, and anywhere I'd needed to go was within walking distance. But I didn't belong there anymore than I'd belonged in South Dakota.

"Do you have family in Muddy Gap?" I asked.

"No. Mostly in California and Mexico." He popped the lid off a glass bottle of iced coffee and drained half of it before setting it back in the cup holder. "But a couple of them live in Rawlins. There's another coffee there for you."

"Thanks." I clutched the chilly bottle. Foothills rolled by beyond the window. "My aunt and uncle live in Rapid City. I'm not very good at keeping in contact."

"It happens. I call my mom on her birthday every year, and half the call is her lecturing me about how I need to call more often. But we're friends on social media, and we chat there. It's not the same thing to her, I guess. What about yours? Does she nag you for not calling since you're allergic to phone calls?"

I let out a humorless laugh. "I only met my mom once. I wasn't impressed."

"Wow." He glanced at me, then finished his coffee.

"Sorry." I was still messing up our conversations. Why the hell was I talking about a woman I never thought about, who'd shoved me back at Auntie like a piece of garbage? "Maybe we can talk about aliens turning us inside out instead."

"You don't need to apologize. It's your mom we're talking about now, not mine."

I'd inadvertently brought this up, but I wasn't going to carry this subject for an hour-long car ride. I pulled up a blank spreadsheet in my contacts and started to fill in events and their dates and times. "I saw the UFO Friday night. It interfered with radio, TV, phone, and internet signals, and wiped out my photos and voice recording. Saturday night was hailshells. Sunday was Ms Pierce and the thrift shop owner–"

"Davis." If Ezra found my topic shift abrupt, he didn't show it. "Both of whom attacked you unprovoked. Was there sand in Ms Pierce's yard?"

"Not that I can remember, though her hose could have washed most of it away. The shells were everywhere. Floating in it. Today, we have sand and shells in the grocery store, with everyone gone. And my fish." I slumped and the seatbelt dug into my neck.

Lining up each event in a neat column made them easier to process in a distant, surreal way, but it was going to take a while for it all to sink in. Cocooned in fresh sheets in the safety of a Casper hotel room later seemed like the perfect place to break down. I just needed to hold on for another hour.

Ezra's voice pulled me from my thoughts. "What does it mean that today, instead of angry, illogical people, they're gone entirely? That things are getting worse or that we didn't wait around long enough for them to come back?"

"I think Ms Pierce and Davis were abducted then brought back. Probably the shoppers too. Honestly, I'm glad I wasn't in there when they came back – *if* they're coming back. No way I could handle a crowded store full of noisy, violent people."

"We may have left town at exactly the right time; it might have broken out into chaos. But that also means Casper could be dangerous too. At least we know what signs to look for." He frowned and adjusted the rearview mirror, disturbing the faded air freshener. "Did we pass the Bucklin Reservoirs already?"

"I don't know. I wasn't paying attention." Heavy clouds sat against tawny hills, nothing on both sides but prairie. A little green mile marker appeared next to a lone traffic cone, and I strained to see the number. "Mile three. Bucklin is up ahead."

"Feels like we should have passed it already, but I think that about every point of interest from here to Casper. I get sick of this drive. What I want to know" – he jabbed a finger in the air – "is why seashells? Why sand?"

I popped the lid from my iced coffee and took a sip. It was much sweeter than I normally took my coffee and I had to stop myself from chugging it. "Budget cuts."

Ezra's nose wrinkled in amusement. "What?"

"Clearly this experiment was intended for some resort town with sandy beaches where their tech would blend in. Not enough money in the budget for Hawaii, though, so they had to settle for butt-fucking Wyoming."

His laugh filled the car, heaving his chest so hard I thought he might run off the road. He wiped his eye. "You know, I bet you're right. They've gotta be disappointed."

"Who wouldn't be?"

"I know I am. If this happened somewhere else, it wouldn't be my problem. But I am glad for one thing."

"What's that?"

"It helped me meet you."

I huffed. "I'm not worth it. Besides, odds are I would have insulted you at the post office on a different day regardless."

Fingers looped through mine, and I startled. I folded my hand into Ezra's, the heat of his skin a contrast to the chilly bottle of coffee in my other. I leaned back and shut my eyes, running my thumb across the meat of his palm. I had two instances of prolonged human touch today, which was two hundred percent more than I got on any other day. It was something I'd grown used to going without. The last relationship I'd been in was strictly online and dirty pictures weren't the same thing as being with someone in person. The one before that had started online, but we'd eventually met up. He'd been as handsome as his photos, and it was easy to picture him on his phone in bed, typing out our late-night chats. But he couldn't say the same for me. Even though I'd told him upfront that I was autistic, my online eloquence wasn't something that translated to real life, apparently. He found my quirks off-putting. That didn't stop him from sleeping with me, but once I went home to Muddy Gap, he didn't message me anymore.

I glanced at Ezra, who squinted out the window then at his odometer. "I really like you."

His concentration broke and he gave me a preoccupied smile. "I like you too."

"A lot of times people don't– What's wrong?"

He let go of my hand and rubbed his forehead. "We should have passed Bucklin by now."

The high grasses on both sides of the embankment obscured the water, and it would be easily missed by someone not looking for it, but Ezra had been. Another mile marker came into view. Ice sleeted through me as I saw the number.

"Mile one?"

"What?" Ezra hit the brakes and pulled onto the shoulder, nearly slamming into the marker. "You said we were at mile three."

"We were."

"Maybe you saw wrong." His furrowed brow and the bright whites of his eyes said he didn't believe it.

A million thoughts spilled into my head, but I dammed them up. "Keep going. We'll see what the next one says."

A mile never took so long, our ragged breath filling the cab as foothills streaked by. When the new marker appeared, I pressed my forehead to the glass, straining to see. Tension in my shoulders relaxed. "Mile four. And there're the reservoirs." Pale blue water sat beyond a weathered wooden fence, surrounded in shaggy sedges and pussytoes.

"Is this another instance of me getting worked up over nothing?" he asked. "And you'll have some genius explanation for it that I should have figured out already?"

"Afraid not." I checked GPS, but it gave me an error, stating it couldn't determine location.

The reservoirs passed from view. A white cross stood at an angle near the fence, adorned in sun-bleached faux roses and glittery picture frames. "Have we passed any cars, going either way?"

Ezra's grip on the wheel tightened, his knuckles whitening. "No."

A new marker appeared, and a plea ran through my head: *Say five. Say five. Say five. Say five. Say–*

A reflective white *2* mocked my prayer. "Shit."

Ezra floored the accelerator, as though whatever hold this warped reality had on us could be outrun if he went fast enough. The car roared down the road and jars clinked in the trunk.

Mile one again.

Mile four, the reservoirs streaking by.

Mile three, with its lone traffic cone.

Mile two.

Mile one.

I stared at the crooked DMV sign. "Turn around."

"No."

"Turn around, Ezra. We're stuck on a damn treadmill. You're going to run out of charge."

"I have plenty."

After another twenty minutes, I stopped looking at the markers. There wasn't enough room for my usual stims, and energy bubbled in my limbs. Lowering the seat back, I pressed my face into it and hugged the headrest. Testing GPS and the internet yielded no connection, and my phone had zero bars. For some reason, the knowledge that I couldn't access my blog turned the anxiety in my core into a rolling boil.

"Six!" Ezra gripped my knee and laughed. "We made it to six!"

I pressed my nose harder into the seat, my breath whistling. "Casper is seventy miles away. If it takes us twenty minutes to jump to the next mile, we'll have to drive for twenty-four hours to get there. We have enough food, but not near enough charge."

"We went two miles in one jump. Four to six. And for all we know the next leap might be thirty miles."

"Or it will take us back to mile one. I don't want to be stranded."

"No, we're getting the hell out of here." He squeezed my leg. "Promise."

I wanted to believe it. I wanted to pretend. To have this guy in the driver's seat who was probably much sweeter than Julio Manhammer be the hero and rescue us from this hell. But neither of us had any idea what was happening, and being unable to see a possible solution beyond trial and error frayed my nerves and sank heavy dread into the pit of my stomach.

I twisted a lock of hair around my finger and yanked until pain prickled along my scalp. This was like that vintage video game. *The Legend of Zelda*. If you didn't walk through the forest in a certain direction, you'd keep going forever, every new section of the screen an exact copy. If you gave up and turned around, you'd be back where you started.

For some reason, that idea calmed me, and I let go of my hair. We didn't know the answer to the puzzle, but we could flip the car around, and Muddy Gap would be on the horizon.

Ezra shook my shoulder, and I sat up, my eyes gritty and sweat sticking my shirt collar to my neck. He stared ahead, tendons in his jaw straining. The traffic cone sat beside mile marker three, loose reflection tape fluttering in the breeze. "How long?"

"Over an hour. I don't know how you can sleep." He shook his head. "It keeps jumping back to one, to four, to two. Can't even get to six again. You're right. We're never making it to Casper. I'm going to turn around and pray we can get back."

"Okay. I have to pee, and I'm hungry. Let's go back to your place and make a new game plan. We'll write everything down. Every event and effect, potential causes, and what we can do. I already have that spreadsheet started."

He blinked hard, then looked up at the headliner fabric. Obviously the idea of data sheets and lists didn't calm him as much as it did me. He flipped the car around and sped back toward Muddy Gap. I gripped the armrest, expecting the DMV, outlying houses, and the shiny copper gateway sign welcoming us back as the highway curved into town.

Instead, the back of the white cross appeared, reservoirs sparkled beyond in the afternoon light.

"Oh, come on!" I slammed my head back against the seat, the comforting idea of video game puzzles dissolving into an image of us as desiccated corpses by the bank of Bucklin.

The car lurched forward as Ezra mashed the accelerator. He hunched over the wheel, eyes glossy and jaw set. He plowed into the 4 mile marker and it disappeared under the tires. The car skated on loose gravel, fishtailing, then flew down the road. After ten minutes of mile two, mile three, mile one, we arrived at the reservoir again. For some reason, I expected the mile marker to have reset, back in its proper place, but it was still flattened. Ezra parked, shut off the engine, and put his face in his hands.

I unbuckled my seat belt and pulled him to me, cupping his head against my chest and fighting back the urge to scream. "I want to take back what I said about stealing food being a bad idea. It was really smart. More than I can say about trying to get to Casper."

"We can't leave and we can't get back," he moaned.

"We'll go down to the water and take up new lives as ducks." I laughed, too loud, wound too tight. Throwing open the door, I stepped onto the road and shook out my anxious limbs. Dirt scraped beneath my heels as I swiveled and stumbled through weeds to the bank of the reservoir. I pissed into the grass, watching heavy clouds drift. Our journey had been so seamless, no obvious sign that anything was repeating until we spied a landmark.

I wrote the event into my spreadsheet as I washed my hands in the water, but it did nothing to reassure me, only adding to the evidence that things were building up. After all, Ezra had been able to go to work the night before– No, he'd called in and never left town. This could have been happening since the hailshells. Ezra didn't see them fall, but he'd come back from work only a few hours afterward, apparently not enough time for any kind of *Legend of Zelda* puzzle effect to yet be established.

Marching back up to the car, it occurred to me again that if the sand and shells were evidence of imminent abduction, it should have happened to me.

Ezra sat against the bumper, morosely crunching chips loaded with salsa. "I can't get any reception. Not sure who I'd call for help at this point anyway."

"I checked too." I took a chip from the bag and dipped it into the jar. Heat overloaded my mouth as I took a bite. I gasped, then snatched another iced coffee from the trunk and drained it.

A small smile appeared on his face. "Too spicy for your white ass?"

"I'm part Cherokee. Not sure how much. From my dad, whoever he is. My mom gave me his last name."

"Bryant is a Cherokee name?"

"Cherokees often have English names that were imposed upon their ancestors by the government. '*Rayetayah* is too hard to pronounce. Your name is Christopher Columbus now'." I shook my head and pulled the peanut butter pie from the trunk. "I want to do one of those DNA tests that tell you your ancestry, but they're expensive and their Indigenous results are often inaccurate because they don't have enough data to go on. Not sure what I'm looking to get out of one anyway."

"Belonging? Some connection to family you don't have?"

I shouldn't have yelled at Aunt Georgina. Should have insisted that Uncle Joe got off his ass to say hi to me. Should have packed up when I had the chance and driven to Rapid City. "I guess. I'm white-passing, obviously, and wouldn't ever claim myself as a person of color no matter what my DNA said. I don't know why I'm talking about this again."

"You don't have to." He snapped a chip in half to fit it into the jar. "Sitting here, stuck in this... hiccup in reality. I really wish I would have called my mom more often, though."

"We have time to figure this out before we're in real trouble. I'm not giving up."

Some of the whipped cream stuck to the lid of the pie box, but everything was more or less intact, and it would taste good regardless. Ezra hadn't grabbed any utensils on his supermarket sweep, so I dug my fingers under the crust and broke off a chunk. Crumbs rained onto my shirt as I took a bite. Creamy peanut butter slicked my mouth.

"I'm part Spanish and part indigenous Mexican," Ezra offered.

"We're kind of the same then. European and Native. Only not really because you have a family and traditions."

"You have an aunt and uncle."

"I shouldn't complain. I always felt like an outsider, like I didn't deserve them, but that isn't their fault. I found excuses to think otherwise when I was younger, though. My cousins' names are Wilhelmina, Abraham, and Elizabeth – Billie, Bram, and Beth. When I came out as non-binary, I asked my aunt to give me a new name. I wanted something gender neutral, but my other motive was having a name my aunt chose, not my mom. I was hoping that she'd give me a name that would have a 'B' nickname, like my cousins. *Then*, I thought, I'd be one of them."

Ezra's mouth twitched, voice so low I barely heard him. "But she named you Denver."

"She named me Denver. Yeah. And even after I found out that she'd never been a fan of the all 'B' nickname thing – that was Uncle Joe's doing – and that she loved the Red Rocks Park near Denver, Colorado, I clung to that resentment for a long time." And if I was being honest with myself, I'd never really outgrown that assumption that people wouldn't welcome me, that they'd immediately sense that I was different from them in some fundamental way, even when I had evidence to the contrary. But I wasn't going to do that with Ezra.

"Anyway, I'm rambling," I said. "My family is good to me and have always insisted that I'm a part of it with them. My aunt is the reason I love pie." I took a bite and licked chocolate crumbs off my lips. "Do you think we're stuck in a dream?"

"Hang on, don't change the subject again. If you don't want to talk about your mom, that's cool, but I want to hear this pie origin story. I'd like to have a few minutes where things feel normal and okay and I'm not worried about government mind control with stolen alien technology."

"Oh, we're combining theories now. That's good."

"I'm serious. Did your aunt bake the best pies, or what?"

"If I critiqued them on my blog, they probably wouldn't get great reviews compared to others I've had. She didn't bake them. Store bought. I can't stand frosting. Even when I was little, it made me sick. I never wanted a cake for my birthday. I remember asking for bread and butter one year instead." I brushed crumbs from my front. "My aunt said she couldn't stick candles in a slice of bread. So she bought me a pie. Banana cream. The next year it was pumpkin. Then apple. Do you know how excited I got when I realized I could eat pie on days *other* than my birthday? I thought it had to be a special occasion."

"I love that."

"Pie reminds me of home. Of family. The shitty thing though, is I can't really tell this story *without* thinking about my mom. She showed up at my ninth birthday. I'd never met her, but I'd seen pictures."

"You don't have to talk about it."

"I had chocolate cream pie that year. Same brand as this one." I nodded to the box in my lap. "We were sitting in the backyard at one of those long plastic tables with the foldable legs, and my aunt had taped a disposable tablecloth over it. It was patterned in... UFOs."

Ezra snorted.

I could still see little curls of chocolate scattered across that tablecloth. Above the UFOs stretched bright pink letters that said *OUTTA THIS WORLD*. "My mom walked through the gate with a huge cake, some loser boyfriend trailing behind her."

I pulled in a slow breath. I wasn't sure if I was telling Ezra this because I needed someone else to assure me that my feelings were justified, or so that I could expel them all into some pocket of reality that might not be here tomorrow.

He screwed the lid on his jar of salsa and tucked the bag of chips away, then turned his attention back to me.

"The cake was the kind you always see in supermarket bakeries. Sheet cake with a stenciled cartoon character and so much blue food dye in the frosting that it's practically black. She pushed my plate of pie away and plopped the whole cake in front of me. I gagged just looking at it. My aunt rushed up and tried to talk to my mom, but my mom shoved her away. I didn't know it at the time, but she was high on something. She squatted next to me and told me she was taking me home with her."

Ezra cringed. He scooted closer and slipped his arm around my back. I instinctively leaned in, his strength and softness insulation enough for me to keep talking.

"She started rambling about all these great toys she was going to buy me, how she had a bed waiting and she had the cartoon channel and cereal and whatever. All my cousins were gaping. My aunt couldn't pull my mom away, so she ran to get my uncle." I couldn't tell if it was tears or anger welling in my throat, but I swallowed it down and leaned further against Ezra. "My mom started singing 'Happy Birthday'. The cake and the attention and the song, and the idea that I had to leave with this strange woman who knew nothing about me – it was too much. I *screamed*. I don't remember a lot after that." My face had hurt like it always did after I hit myself during a meltdown, and there'd been blue frosting under my nails and in the webbing of my fingers. "Later, I was sitting on the couch with one of my presents. A book on 'totally true' ghost stories. My mom stormed into the room, yanked me up by my shoulders, and flung me at my aunt. She said, 'This *creature* isn't my kid. It's your burden forever'."

Ezra's nostrils flared, a tendon in his jaw jumping. "She called you *it*?"

I tried to ignore the constriction in my chest and focus instead on the solidness of his thick fingers wrapped around my side. The way his soft belly pressed against me. I inhaled the earthy musk of his skin beneath the cologne. If I let myself – if *he* let me – I could get lost in the scent of him.

Clearing my throat, I tried to pick up the dropped thread of the conversation. "My mom wants to get in touch with me now, and my aunt thinks–"

"No. Fuck that. What kind of mom says that about their own child?"

"She's clean now. I'm probably supposed to feel guilty that I don't want to see her, but I don't care."

"You don't owe her anything."

The breath I drew in was easier, some of the weight of that memory eased from around my neck. The look on Ezra's face suggested I gave some of it to him.

I took a bite of pie. "Don't be upset about it. It was a long time ago."

"But it's still affecting you. You're carrying it around."

Crumbs stuck to my chin, and I wiped them away. "I feel better now actually." I shouted at the empty highway. "You're not my mom!"

"Yeah, screw you. You're not Denver's mom!"

"She probably doesn't even know my name is Denver now." Wind ripe with the scent of marsh plants drifted, and a duck took to the sky. I studied the curls of chocolate scattered over the top of the peanut butter pie. "Thanks for letting me talk about that."

"You're welcome."

I scuffed my foot against the gravel, the sound jarringly loud in the lull of our conversation. Ezra's arm still hung loosely around my waist. I leaned closer to him, and his hold on me tightened, his thumb rubbing against my side. I took another bite of pie to keep my mouth occupied before I said something that would ruin this.

I'd kept my family trauma bottled up for so long – my cousins knew, Uncle Joe knew, Aunt Georgina knew. But they didn't *know*, not in the way I did. Ezra couldn't either, but I'd felt comfortable enough with him to share, even though I'd convinced myself it wasn't something I ever wanted to speak out loud.

That sense of ease – even laced with the always-underlying trepidation that I would misstep in this social dance – was something I hadn't felt in ages. And having someone who was safe, who didn't judge me for being myself, was the sexiest possible thing I could think of.

His gaze dropped to my lips. "You've got a little whipped cream. Right there."

Blood pounded in my temples. "You going to do something about it?"

Slipping his fingers through my hair, he gave me a soft kiss. His tongue slid across my upper lip. I let out a moan and kissed deeper. An eager noise rumbled in his throat, and his teeth clicked against mine. My mouth tingled with serrano and jalapeno.

"Your kisses are spicy," I breathed.

"And you taste like peanut butter." He pushed the pie off my lap and it hit the ground, smashing against the side of the box. His hand slipped up my thigh and squeezed. I leaned back; a package of toilet paper crinkled.

"I want to touch you, but my hands are sticky," I said. He took my wrist, then wrapped his lips around my finger and sucked off the whipped cream. My cock throbbed, straining against my jeans. "Oh my god. Into the car with you. I don't want to get it on in a pile of groceries."

"You don't want to make use of this pie?" He swiped up some whipped cream and smeared it on my neck. He sucked hard at my flesh as he kissed it off.

My nerves lit up under the press of his lips and the scratch of his mustache. "I'm not going to have sex with it. I love pie but not like that."

He chuckled, then pulled me to my feet and ushered me into the back of the car. Taking a pillow from the floor, he wedged it behind my head, then opened my belt. I fought the zipper with clumsy fingers, then pushed down my jeans and briefs.

Ezra's mouth parted, his chest heaving. When he took me into his mouth, I gasped and squeezed my eyes shut, certain I would come right then. I dug my fingers into his hair and thrust in time with his movements. His stubble scraped sensitive skin and I squirmed, but he growled and gripped my ass, holding me in place as he pulled me closer to ecstasy.

What the hell were we doing? We were stranded in a place that would turn deadly once we ran out of food, which was only marginally worse than trying to stay safe in a town where people were randomly disappearing. There was no telling when some new and more horrifying thing would crop up, and we had no hope of finding the outside world.

We'd have to solve this thing ourselves, with very little to go on, but instead of melting down and lying on the asphalt, I was clutching Ezra's hair for dear life, sweat breaking out on my brow and my breath fogging the window.

If this was the definition of seizing a few minutes where everything felt normal and okay, I could get behind it.

"Wait," I gasped. "Stop, please."

He pulled back, his lips wet and reddened. "What's wrong?"

"I don't want this to be over yet."

I undid his pants and pulled him out. He sucked in a breath and said, "I was thinking about this earlier. After you texted me 'sweet dreams'. Thinking about your hands on me."

I probably would have been thinking about him the same way if I hadn't been so wrapped up in where my grocery order was. I maneuvered his hips closer to mine, then took us both in my hand and stroked us together, coaxing whimpers from Ezra. "Like this?"

"No… This is even better."

It wasn't something I'd tried before, and I wasn't about to tell him I'd seen it in a porn video. But his reaction was encouraging, and it thrilled me in a way watching a tiny screen in the dark never could.

His long lashes fluttered, the flecks in his eyes like captured amber. I sucked his earlobe as he slid his hand under my shirt.

"You're so beautiful. Your freckles and your hair and–" He caught my lip with his teeth. My mouth worked against his, and I squeezed his ass. He pressed his nose into the crook of my neck. "I don't want to die out here."

"This HG Wells shit isn't going to get the best of us. We're going to figure it out. Now shut up while I make you feel good."

He moaned. I pushed my tongue into his mouth and stroked faster. His hips bucked, thighs clenching against mine as he came, and I let go of everything wound up inside me. I shuddered and gasped his name. My foot kicked the window, and I dug my fingers into his back.

No matter how lost we were in a maze where the exits were really dead ends, for a moment, we were both free.

7

Wind whipped hair across my neck, carrying the scent of wet earth and vegetation. My boots sank in marsh grass. I splashed water on my torso and sweat-sticky face.

I imagined the highway between Muddy Gap and Casper like an accordioned map, but with sections folded back in on themselves. If we drove parallel to the road instead, heading west through one of the creases, maybe we could get back on 287 and reach Jeffrey City. Or maybe it accordioned both ways and we'd be stuck without even a road.

It was tempting to find a jug for the reservoir water, even though Ezra had several jugs from the market in the trunk. We could get trapped in some other hiccup. Mile six could replace mile four, and this water we were so tired of seeing might not appear again.

Ezra stood beside the trunk, cleaning his stomach with a car detailing wipe.

"Is that safe?" I asked.

"It's just an alcohol wipe. And you're the one washing yourself with water fish have peed in."

I picked up the container and turned it over. " *'Great for your car's dash, vinyl, fabric...'* and bellies with the perfect amount of squish." Setting down the container, I pinched Ezra's fuzzy gut and leaned in for a kiss. "I want to drive for a while."

"Sure." He drew me tightly against him and pressed his lips

hard against mine. After pulling on a shirt, he rounded the passenger's side of the car.

I mourned the smashed peanut butter pie, watching the lid of the box waver in the breeze. A very untimely and undignified demise for something so delicious, but I could hardly complain when considering what had happened afterward. I made a bologna sandwich and held the corner in my mouth as I found a clean shirt from my backpack.

After starting the engine, I pulled back onto the highway, speeding in the direction of town. "You said you hate this drive. Seeing it randomly repeat, getting farther away the longer you go, must be a new kind of hell."

"I don't need the reminder." Ezra leaned the seat back and threw an arm over his face.

Checking my notifications in my contacts while driving wasn't exactly safe, even though I could still see the road, but it wasn't like there was anyone to crash into. It wasn't surprising that I didn't have new messages, since the internet still wasn't working.

My contacts couldn't store video, but I could stream it to my blog's files section. I blinked, starting a recording, and took extra care to look at each mile marker as they passed.

Mile two.

Mile three.

Mile one.

Mile two.

Mile three.

Mile four. The box of peanut butter pie sat at the shoulder, the lid flapping in the breeze.

I wasn't sure if I was doing this as evidence for authorities or for my fans. Neither seemed to matter much anymore. There was a good chance the video would end up "redacted" anyway.

The car's charge meter indicated sixty-one percent. We could drive for hours still, but the monotony of it almost made me wish for a cosmic horror to appear just to break up the scenery.

Ezra's chest rose and fell. He'd chosen a shirt with a disappointingly modest crew neck. Stubble dusted his jaw, his curls hanging messily across his forehead. I hadn't expected kissing him to turn into fogging up the sedan's windows so quickly. Maybe he thought we were going to die and wanted one last fuck before it happened. It wouldn't be the first time someone decided to make use of me just because I happened to be there and not because they actually liked me.

"Was what happened back there between us a one off?" I asked.

Ezra sat up and rubbed his face. "Why are you asking that? Did I do something to indicate that I don't want to do it again?"

"No. But I've only had sex two other times and both guys decided they–"

"Hang on. What?" He blinked at me. "How old are you?"

"Thirty-four."

He stared at the dash, smoothing out the ends of his mustache. "Not having sex is a valid choice, but... do you wish you had more?"

"God, yes." I tightened my grip on the wheel, unsure if I was angry at his questions or at myself. "Autistic people often have a hard time making connections with neurotypical people, okay? That doesn't make me pathetic."

"I didn't say you were. It sucks to be lonely, and–" He made an exasperated noise. "I wish you would have told me that."

"Why does it matter?"

"We went from zero to sixty back there. Or I should say, *I* did. I should have taken it slower."

"I'm not a virgin. And I get half the credit for what we did."

The orange traffic cone zipped by at marker three, and Ezra stared out the window like there would be something else to see. A flush tinted his cheeks. He rubbed his eyebrow and blew a noisy breath through his nose.

My nails bit into the steering wheel, the high from our frenzied lovemaking dipping into something that felt a lot like shame. "Why are you mad at me?"

He kept his attention fixed on the scenery. "I'm not mad. But I don't feel right about it now. It was a mistake."

I clenched my jaw. We'd both needed it for some physical and emotional comfort, and I thought Ezra and I had been on the same page. Clearly I'd screwed up this song and dance again. He didn't want someone so inexperienced, and somehow I was supposed to know that beforehand. It was unfair that my past poor experiences with relationships were now coming back to haunt this one.

For once I didn't feel like sharing my opinion. This was the worst road trip ever.

My excursions to diners and bakeries to sample new pies was fun, but nothing compared to being safe at home, away from noise and smells and crowds. I now had no safety to go back to even if we made it, and Ezra wasn't interested in me anymore.

He pulled the pillow from the back and tucked it under his head, then rolled over. Prepared for a long haul.

We reached the reservoir again. The box of pie appeared, and I slowed and threw the car in park. Hopping out, I picked it up and assessed the damage. The contents had slid to one corner, chocolate crust pulverized and whipped cream melting into the peanut butter, but no gravel or bits of leaves dusted the top.

Screw it. I picked up the box and climbed back in. After turning on cruise control, I dug a chunk of pie out and pushed it in my mouth. I couldn't click my red slippers together and warp to Kansas, but eating pie and pondering what my blog readers would think was a tiny scrap of home.

After turning on my phone and hitting record, I wedged it into the door.

"I wish I could say eating smashed pie from the road was a new low for me, but nothing will compare to that mock apple from Suzy B's that tasted so strongly of vinegar that I threw up in my napkin." I broke off another chunk and sampled it, my nerves stilling as I sank into the dictation. "Despite this pie having endured both a devastating fall as my travel partner pushed it off my lap in an apparent misguided bout of hunger for something other than baked goods, *and* several hours wilting in the heat of a hiccup in this plane of reality for which there might be no escape, the velvety texture of peanut butter custard and hearty crunch of chocolate crust is enough to satisfy a cultured sweet tooth during even the most trying of times. If you find yourself ensnared in a dimensional accordion fold, I highly recommend Red Barn brand. Ten stars."

I crammed another bite in my mouth, my nose stinging and eyes wet with tears I was not planning to shed. "Peanut butter road pie is delicious. A perfect salve for despair and rejection. Serve it smashed with no utensils."

I hit save on the dictation and transferred it to my blog files along with the video to complete the illusion of normality.

"Are you going to post that?" Ezra asked.

"No network connection."

"I'm not mad at you. I'm mad at myself."

"Because you realized I'm a mistake. Just like the last guys did."

"I'm sor–"

A gust of wind suddenly rocked the car, and my heart leapt into my throat. I fought to correct course. Sand blasted against the windshield, and something thundered the roof, the sound like swift punches to my skull. I cringed and reached for my earplugs. The car swerved and Ezra grabbed the wheel. Throwing it in park, I jammed in the earplugs and cupped my ears.

A torrent of orange dust blotted out the sun and consumed the car. It lurched, buffeted by a violent gust, and chunks of clear stone slammed into the windshield. Pain flared in my head, and I balled myself into the seat. The sound of each impact smashed against my nerves like a meat tenderizer and drained what little emotional resilience I had left. I hummed as loudly as I could to block it out, but it didn't help much. Ezra's hands closed over mine, and somehow that made it worse, because he was shielding my ears in lieu of his own. And sensory sensitivities or not, that sound would hurt anyone.

I gritted my teeth and rocked in place, tears squeezing from my eyes. The sound was turning me inside out, and just when I wondered if a noise could kill me, everything hushed, one final *thump* against the roof punctuating the end of it. I sat up. Chunks of clear stone and glittery orange granules – like the thrift shop, like the market – coated the windshield. Pits and cracks marred the glass from impacts, and the side mirror had been obliterated.

Ezra leaned over and pushed the wiper fluid. The wipers crunched and squealed, and I winced. The semi-clean path they left revealed a tangerine haze from the settling sand.

He snapped closed all the air vents and turned off the A/C.

I removed my earplugs. "What are you doing?"

"I don't know if you have to breathe this stuff in for it to get a hold on you, or actually touch it, but I'm not going to take any chances. I know why Davis' face looked so bad, though. Shit."

Whipped cream and custard stuck to the front of my shirt. I peeled it off and stuffed it and the pie into the back. "It won't affect us. I already exposed myself to a massive amount of the shells. I touched the sand in Gem's."

"That's no reason to take a chance."

"I don't think it's mind control. I don't think the sand or shells do anything at all. They show up when... when the aliens do. Some byproduct."

Ezra's gaze dashed to the window, and his voice came out tight. "Well that's a whole lot better. Let's get the hell out of here before we get abducted." He pushed the wiper fluid button again. The wipers whined, dragging sand and a wedge of clear stone away from the windshield.

"And go where?" But I didn't want to hang around any longer either. I pressed the brake and shifted into drive.

"What if the storm blew across every mile we've been to?" he asked. "There's no way to escape an abduction if one follows the appearance of the sand. We're screwed."

My stomach dropped. Trapped in this cramped car that smelled like peanut butter and regrettable sex, my underarms already growing damp from the lack of circulating air, and the jugs of water were in the trunk. "Then we'll have to hope it's only this mile."

I slammed my foot on the accelerator and the car jerked forward. The side mirror dangled by electrical wiring and thumped against the door. The wipers made another vain attempt at cleaning the pocked window. It was hard to see through the haze, but it didn't matter because I'd already memorized the terrain. The outcropping that looked like a sheep's head. A cottonwood tree with a zagging branch, burdened by a bird's nest. A speed limit sign.

How did the pattern for that video game puzzle go? North. East. South. East. Mile markers flew by. North. East. South – I sat up straight and sucked in a breath. "They're repeating."

"No shit," Ezra moaned. He put a hand over his eyes and drew in a watery breath.

"I mean it's a pattern." I stopped the car, turning the miles over in my mind.

Ezra started to say something, but I shushed him – probably a little too forcefully – and said, "Hang on. I'm thinking. What was the first mile we were at after leaving town? Was it really mile one?"

"Yeah. We passed the DMV sign. I wasn't looking at it per se, but I remember seeing it out the window while I was checking you out."

"Okay. I wasn't paying attention to the miles until I noticed marker three. That took us to one, then to four, then to two."

"Then it was one again." Ezra's brow furrowed. "Then four."

I wrote down what we could remember in my contacts' spreadsheet, then kept it pinned in my lower vision so I could reference it. "It's a long number. Because two doesn't always come after four. Sometimes it's three. And we're going the opposite direction now, so the pattern is backward from what I have noted."

Ezra read the mile markers as I drove, and I kept track of them in the spreadsheet until it was a confirmed pattern: 132431421432. One of those numbers was occasionally a six, but that had only happened once, so I wasn't going to factor it in.

I scrubbed my clammy hand against my jeans. "Now we need to test it."

Slowing at mile four, I made note of where we were in the pattern. Backing up, I flipped the car around and headed toward Casper. Mile two came into view. Blood pounded in my temples.

"Good. If I'm right, we need to get back to mile one from mile three, then go *back* the other way."

Ezra's mouth pulled tight. His eyes were glossy with unshed tears, but he nodded. "Okay."

If I was wrong, or I messed it up, he would lose the last of his resolve and I was going to fall apart with him. This had to work.

I slowed, less to see through the orange haze than to make sure I was following the correct pattern. It was like a combination lock; go a little bit too far before turning the other way, and it wouldn't open.

If there was an intelligent being behind this, I was going to personally strangle them for making me use so much left-brain power to solve this.

Mile marker one appeared. I dug my nails into the steering wheel. Ezra stared out the window, muscles working in his jaw. I probably should have said something reassuring in case I got this wrong and we ended up right back where we started, but instead, I flipped around and pressed the accelerator.

Silhouettes formed in the distance, and the *Muddy Gap, Wyoming* gateway sign appeared so suddenly that I gasped and fought the wheel to keep from driving off the curve that led into town. Ezra braced himself against the dash, eyes wide.

My heart kicked against my ribs, my mind screaming *HOME*. I didn't slow, afraid it would disappear again before we got there.

"We're back." Ezra's mouth hung open, then he laughed and shook my shoulder. "Denver! You're a genius!"

The air cleared enough for me to spot the church as we rolled by, and the restaurant across the street. A trashcan had blown over, pizza boxes and potato peelings strewn in the road. Chunks of stone and skiffs of sand coated sidewalks and yards.

There was no activity, which was both comforting and disturbing. Nothing nefarious, but it was too hard to tell if people were in their houses, taking shelter from the sandstorm, or if every home was as empty as the supermarket.

A sudden ream of notifications popped up in my contacts as they found a signal, but I flicked them away and turned the alerts off. I was far too tired to look at them now. I pulled into Ezra's driveway in a daze and shut off the engine. We were here. We'd made it.

"Do we get out?" Ezra curled his fingers around the door handle. "Maybe one of us should stay behind in case we're affected by the air or the sand."

"I'm not sitting in here any longer. I'm gonna walk home and shower." I stuffed my phone in my pocket and reached for my backpack, but Ezra snatched my hand.

"Don't leave. I don't want you walking back. It's not safe."

"I'll be fine. I'm sure of it." I wasn't sure. Solving the conundrum of how to get back to town was a boost to confidence in my theories, but there was no guarantee we couldn't be snatched up by a tractor beam or just... vanish. I couldn't hang around in Ezra's house after he'd decided it was wrong to sleep with me, though.

Sand rained down on my hair and bare shoulders as I popped open the door. "I'm going to go home, cry, and take a nap."

"Denver."

I didn't look back. "Text me if something weird happens. Actually, text me later even if it doesn't. I don't want to worry about you."

Weariness ached in my bones, and I wanted nothing more than to fall asleep and wake up to realize this had all been a dream, but the thought of shutting my eyes and letting my guard down crimped my stomach.

The bright sun of late afternoon cut beams through the settling haze and threw long shadows across driveways and streets. Sand crunched under my cowboy boots, and I nudged a chunk of glass out of my path. Hesitantly, I picked it up. Broken and irregular as it was, it was hard to tell if it was a naturally formed stone or actual glass that had been dashed off of something larger. If it was, did that mean it was a piece of something intelligently designed? Some kind of alien tech? Tiny rainbows of light warped through the clear center as I tilted it. Perhaps it was part of the exploded UFO, but I didn't want to think about it now. I stuffed it in my backpack and hurried on.

Ezra's house was far enough behind to be obscured by the orange gloam, my own complex too far ahead, suspending me in a hazy limbo as reminiscent and desolate as Mars.

By now, word would have gotten around about Gem's, but my mind stalled, too overburdened and burnt out to chew over possible plans and outcomes. When my complex appeared, I sighed and broke into a jog, nearly twisting my ankle on more clear stones.

The sign in the office window was flipped to closed, bursts of light from a nearby pop machine igniting the floating dust in crimson and cyan. Someone's TV played canned laughter, and a noxious bouquet of laundry soap and boiled chicken drifted.

I made it inside and slammed the door behind me, dumping my pack and hurrying into the bathroom. I started the shower and climbed under the hot stream. Shutting my eyes, I braced myself against the tile, likely to disintegrate and spiral down the drain with as much tension as it washed away.

Ezra's steriglue was still holding together the gash on my cheek, but after I showered, I applied fresh bandages. The cheery kitty designs were at odds with my haggard face.

I pulled on my favorite pajamas – pink cotton, butter soft from so many washings, the unicorns faded – then stopped before the fish tank. The dead eyes of neon tetras stared back at me. Emotionally drained as I was, I couldn't go to sleep with them there. I scooped them up in a net, but I had to detangle one of the frogs from a plant by hand. After pouring them en masse into the toilet, I pressed the handle and stared as they swirled down the drain.

Tears burned in my eyes. I tossed the wet net on the floor, climbed into bed, and sobbed into my pillow.

8

A distant beeping pulled me to consciousness. Something told me it had been going on for some time, though I couldn't remember it in my dream. Stupid things like the heater clicking on or someone slamming a door in the parking lot were always waking me up. It had taken forever for me to fall asleep. Once I'd finished crying about the dead fish, I cried about Ezra.

Rolling over, I checked my phone for texts, but he hadn't sent me a message. It was 3am, but he worked nights, so it wasn't unlikely that he was awake. I typed: *Did you die?* then hit send.

So many email notifications crowded my alert bar that when I tried to expand them, the phone crashed and restarted. Pushing out of bed, I opened my laptop and winced in the sudden surge of light.

My email loaded, an entire page of bolded messages titled, *You have a new comment on "Peanut...*

Ice flooded my veins. That dictation I'd made in the car about eating pie off the road was published? I hopped onto the blog, met with my post titled *Peanut Butter Road Pie and Accordion Fold Reality.*

"Oh my god." Instead of my usual typed posts with tastefully filtered photographs, there was a little bar for my audio file, and beneath it, a video. I hadn't meant to hit publish. The post must have sat in queue until we arrived back in town and found a satellite signal.

I pushed play on the audio. My voice, tight and on the cliff's-edge of tears, came from the speakers. *"I wish I could say eating smashed pie from the road was a new low for me, but nothing will compare to that mock apple from Suzy B's that tasted so strongly of vinegar that I threw up in my napkin."* The rumble of the road and sound of chewing filled the silence. *"Despite this pie having endured both a devastating fall as my travel partner pushed it off my lap in an apparent misguided bout of hunger for something other than baked goods,* and *several hours wilting in the heat of a hiccup in this plane of reality for which there might be no escape–"*

I sounded deranged. But the audio actually went through. Maybe the video would too.

Leaning in, I pressed play. An image of the highway splashed across the screen, and my heart leapt. The reservoirs passed by, my hands white-knuckled on the steering wheel. My recorded gaze focused on the mile marker, then flitted to the passenger's seat, lingering much too long on Ezra.

Working in tandem with my phone, the recording had captured audio as well as video, and the hum of air vents and cadence of my breathing momentarily garbled. The screen distorted like vision through crossed eyes. Then my gaze was back on the mile markers, watching each one streak by. Another ripple – two images of reality overlaid on top of each other, askew only enough to sense something was wrong – then the orange traffic cone flew past.

Blood pounded in my ears. The video worked. It was clear evidence that backed up my outrageous audio recording. Except... what did it matter anymore? Even if the entire outside world believed me, no one could leave town. We were stuck here. And anyone who tried to enter might become entangled in the same reality hiccup. Muddy Gap was the new Bermuda Triangle.

But surely scientists or the government would find a way to help. They might not care about the deaths of eight hundred people in a miniscule Wyoming town, but if there was an indication that the effect was *spreading* and might consume bigger cities, then they'd pay attention. I could twist the truth enough in an email to get someone in a position of power to take notice.

If I even needed to. I scrolled down. Six hundred plus comments on this post alone. It might have gone viral. With any luck, a think tank was already hard at work saving Muddy Gap.

I laughed. Our excursion out of town hadn't been pointless after all.

My voice came from the video, and my smile fell away.

"Was what happened back there between us a one off?"

"Why are you asking that? Did I do something to indicate that I don't want to do it again?"

"No. But I've only had sex two other times and both guys decided they—"

"Hang on—"

Oh. Oh, God. I'd recorded that? My cheeks throbbed with heat, and I pounded the stop button. *I* didn't even want to hear that conversation again. With one eye squeezed shut, I checked the count on the video, then let out a squeak. Twenty-six thousand, eight hundred and six views.

Masochism kept my finger on the scroll key, and I stopped on the comments.

> **pierat369135**: HOLY SHIT. I've got chills. This is messed up.
>> **dankdog**: nah bro photoshopped
>>> **seeker06**: It's not. Contact recordings are notoriously fiddly to alter due to ethical safeguards meshed into the software. And anyone can look up the raw source data to check integrity. The video was uploaded twenty seconds after it was recorded. It's legit.

Twenty seconds? It took much longer than that to get home. Either my contacts had found a satellite signal while out on the highway, or time slowed down while we were driving, which wouldn't be the wildest thing to have happened lately.

I skimmed comments about government cover ups, the Manhattan Project, the possibility of Cthulhu coming out of the Bucklin reservoirs, and news stations and social media going wild.

Before I opened a tab to check the developments, a new thread of comments caught my eye.

grandmaZ: Aw, Denver, honey. I'm sad for you. 😢 He's a cute boy. I hope you two make up.

> **food_dood**: omg he was a hit and run except he's still stuck in the car with the guy. AWKWARD.

>> **ziggyb**: like, stuck forever? Do you think they got out or are they still driving?

>>> **verymary**: worst Twilight Zone episode ever

>>>> **excellent_taste3**: BEST twilight zone episode ever

>>>>> **hippie69**: This isn't a joke! Denver! Are you okay? I called the police, but they didn't believe me. I wish I could send you a care package. Do you have a 3D printer? I'll design you some stim toys.

>> **notabot2097239070**: Dump his ass. Ur hot. I'll help you fight aliens if he won't.

> **mammas_apple**: Denver are you ok

> **mammas_apple**: Denver are you ok

> **mammas_apple**: Denver are you ok

I sat back and wiped my hands down my face. There were hundreds more comments on everything from the pattern of the mile markers to how heartbroken I sounded as I ate pie off the road.

My life had become a bizarre science-fiction soap opera.

I could be embarrassed later. I opened a new tab and searched for the news stations mentioned, but a *Whoops, no internet* page appeared. The blog tried to refresh, then gave me the same page. Shit.

My phone refused to establish a connection, and my text to Ezra hadn't gone through.

Since my last – accidental – post had published as soon as it found a connection, I could at least do that again.

Bringing up a cached blog page, I wrote out everything I could think of. How we'd made it back to town, the sandstorm, our abduction theories, and that we needed help as soon as possible. I asked someone to paste in developments from news sites since I couldn't access them.

I refrained from mentioning the mess with Ezra, but I did thank them for caring about me. At least someone did. In light of everything, my ad revenue was the least of my worries, but I still wished I could check it to see what it was up to for the day.

What in the hell was that beeping sound?

The chair squeaked as I swiveled. The fridge hummed. My heart pulsed. A trickle came from the water heater.

Beep. Beep. Beep.

I did a circuit around the kitchen, then stopped and pressed my ear to the carpet near the bed.

BEEP. BEEP. BEEP.

Smoke alarm, coming from Trevor's place downstairs.

I jumped up and hurried outside. A chilly breeze licked at my arms, rain dotted the sidewalk below, and a sharp chemical smell wound through the petrichor. Hearing the smoke alarm from a neighbor's apartment wasn't unusual, and I never judged anyone for it since I was a terrible cook myself, but it had been going on for a half an hour at least.

Metal steps iced my feet as I walked to Trevor's door. Light glowed through the curtains, but it was too hard to tell if there was smoke. I slapped the doorknob; it was as cold as the stairs.

Knocking, I leaned toward the door. "Trevor?"

His ashtray on the tiny patio table was empty of butts. The tenor of some dramatic movie soundtrack coming from an adjacent apartment added to the cacophony of the smoke alarm. I should have grabbed my earplugs.

"Trevor!"

I knocked again, then tested the doorknob. It turned, and I pushed open the door. A wave of acrid smoke billowed out, and I coughed and pulled my pajama top over my nose. The smoke alarm shrieked from the kitchen. His studio set up was the same as mine, and I veered past his bed, reaching the alarm above the sink. I gritted my teeth, the piercing beeps lancing my brain, and yanked the case off the wall and pulled out the battery.

Opening the front door had dispelled much of the smoke, but a cloudy haze hung in the air, and the stench of burnt plastic filled the room. A bag of bread sat open on the counter, and beside it, a toaster so jammed full of slices it was a wonder the fire had died instead of spreading. Scorch marks licked the sides, and the top of the plastic casing was melted and sagging. A thread of smoke spiraled from the charred toast, and it looked like Trevor had tried to stuff fresh pieces of bread in around the burnt hunks.

I yanked out the cord, wrapped a towel around the toaster, and dumped the thing outside.

"Trevor?"

Water soaked the carpet of the tiny hallway, and stepping across it reminded me of Ms Pierce and her hose. I clenched my jaw. The last thing I needed was to be assaulted with shaving cream and toilet brushes.

The bathroom door stood slightly ajar. I tapped on it. "Hello?"

It creaked open, and Trevor peered out. His gaze struggled to focus on me. "Oh, hey Professor Pie."

"You okay?" I leaned around him. The bathtub overflowed, scummy water running down the sides. The legs of Trevor's drawstring pants were soaked up to his knees.

He looked around the room. "Yeah, I was just…"

His unfinished sentence hung between us. I gently took his wrist and turned his hand over, unsure what a sign of abduction would look like.

Pulling away, he mumbled, "I'm not gay."

"Don't flatter yourself. What's the last thing you remember?"

"Making toast."

"Uh-huh. Before that."

His eyes scrunched closed and he put his fingers to his temples like the effort pained him. "Watching a movie. TV's not working."

I brushed past him, plunged my hand into the icy tub water, and pulled out the stopper.

Why had Trevor been abducted and not me? Not Ezra? I thought of Trevor smoking outside his apartment, unconcerned about the flash in the sky. And when I'd told him about aliens his eyes had glazed over, the only thing on his mind that maintenance would steal his Xbox.

The pieces clicked.

Neither Ezra nor I had been in town when the UFO exploded. And of everyone in town I'd asked about the event, only Ezra had been interested enough to be concerned. I thought it was simply because he was kinder than everyone else, but maybe the UFO affected people to a greater extent than I'd surmised. Maybe *that* was why all my readers were going wild – rightly so – when no one here gave a shit that their TVs went out or that there were tiny seashells all over their yards.

I imagined the burst of light from the UFO like a net, draping across the town, reality bent and crumpled at the edges. Something – radiation, parasitic particles, nanotechnology – had come out and settled as Ms Pierce walked around in her crocs, Trevor watched football, and Charla and Sam had sex. I'd been miles away and so had Ezra.

That nasty cherry pie at *Lynn's Diner* had saved me.

This was good. It was great. It meant we couldn't be

abducted – we wouldn't be complacent – which is what seemed to have happened to Trevor and everyone else. There could be other people who entered town during the pocket of time before the highway folded up who hadn't succumbed to the effects. I could band together with them and figure this out. Any little green men who appeared wouldn't be expecting us to fight back.

My immediate urge was to share the revelation with Ezra. It clenched my gut. I wasn't sure I could with the bristling energy between us. But no matter how strained things were now, he needed to know. There were a lot of things to worry about, but being affected by the UFO was one he could cross off the list.

Trevor drifted out of the bathroom, his feet squelching on soaked carpet. I followed behind him, trying to decide if a written letter taped to Ezra's door seemed callous.

Stopping at the kitchen counter, Trevor picked up the bag of bread, then looked around in confusion.

"I put your toaster out to pasture."

His bottom lip jutted out. "Hungry."

The idea of letting him putter through my kitchen, turning on water faucets and stove burners constricted my throat, but he couldn't stay here alone with whatever was going on in his affected brain. I'd have to keep an eye on him.

I took a stick of butter off the counter and retrieved a half-empty carton of eggs from the fridge. "I have a toaster. Bring that bread with you."

Though I expected more of his protests of "no homo", he followed me outside and up the stairs to my apartment. He walked in without comment, then sat on my bed, picked up the remote, and hit the power button. A blue light washed over him; NO SIGNAL floated across the screen.

I popped bread into the toaster and set a pan on the stove for the eggs. Who, besides Ezra, hadn't been in town Friday evening? Some of the people in the complex worked in Casper, but I didn't know their schedules. Sarah Perkins refused to shop at Gem's and drove to Rawlins once a week for groceries. Mick, the UPS guy, drove in every day but said he hadn't been here Friday night – he'd probably tried to leave since I saw him last and got stuck out on the repeating highway.

My heart sank. He'd been nice.

Trevor stared at the blank TV screen, eyes half closed, but he perked up when the toast popped. I cracked eggs into the pan and slathered butter on the toast.

He devoured the plate of food I handed him. When he was finished, I traded the dirty dish for a glass of milk.

"It's whole. Skim is disgusting."

Trevor took a sip. "That's a weird hill to die on, you know."

"I have a lot of hills. Ask anyone in town." I carried the plate to the sink. "Assuming there's anyone left to ask."

"Where did they go?" His clear gaze focused on me, brow furrowed. Maybe the effect was wearing off.

"Not sure. I think you might have gone with them but came back. It has to do with the aliens I told you about. Remember?"

He turned to the blank TV. "I don't like runny eggs, but I was starving."

Hmm. Deflected the topic again. "What game are you playing on the Xbox right now?"

"That new FPS everyone's been talking about. It sucks, honestly. Not nearly as good as Red Blaze 2 because–"

"Muddy Gap is being invaded by aliens."

"–single player and I was promised nudity, but it turns out it's just some dude's bare ass in a cutscene."

"Do you know why your pants are wet?"

"I should go home."

"You can't. Uh, maintenance is fixing your water heater."

He pulled at his soaking pant legs, and that evidence must have been enough to convince him, even though it was three-thirty in the morning. "I'm crashing here?"

"For the moment. Are you tired? I can put clean sheets on–"

He peeled off his pants and climbed under the comforter.

I watched for a moment, even though that was probably creepy, then pulled a blanket from the closet and wrapped up on the floor beside the bed. If he decided to jam forks into the light sockets, he'd have to step directly on me to get up.

My mind was in overdrive, but I must have dozed off at some point, because a knock on the door startled me awake. Trevor's arm dangled over the mattress, the covers kicked off and bunched on the floor.

Someone at the door meant Ezra, or not Ezra, and both came with implications I hadn't yet prepared myself for. It was tempting to pull the blanket over my head until the person went away, but if it was Ezra and I didn't answer, he'd worry that something had happened to me.

I got up and crossed to the door. He needed to know about my realization. Telling him in person was better than a note on his door, even if he did smash my heart worse than that Red Barn peanut butter pie.

Hopefully I could say what I needed to with adrenaline coursing through me and the shudder in my chest. I unlocked the door and swung it open. The honeyed scent of Ezra's cologne wafted in. He stood on the mat, a small cluster of white daisies in one hand.

His voice was barely a whisper. "Hi."

"Hi." Tension radiated between us like an electric charge, and I desperately wanted to say something to dispel it, but I couldn't figure out how to arrange the jumble of words in my head. I combed my fingers through snarls in my hair instead.

"Is it too early?" His gaze drifted over my pink pajamas, then he pointed to my cheek. "Cute bandages."

"Sam's always putting random things into my grocery orders."

"Ah. I tried texting, but it didn't go through."

"I tried texting you too. We should definitely talk, but–"

A snort came from the front room and Trevor mumbled. "Want some toast."

Ezra's eyes widened as he peered past my shoulder. His face fell. The tips of his ears grew red. He hurled the daisies at my feet and stomped away.

I stared at the scattered petals as Ezra's shoes clanged against the stairs. His anger seemed directed at Trevor, but the guy hadn't lived in Muddy Gap long enough to piss someone off to that extent. And what was the point of the daisies if Ezra wasn't interested in me?

I vacillated in the doorway. Trevor was rousing, hungry, and I didn't want my apartment catching fire. But I needed to talk to Ezra.

"Shit." I shut the door and hurried down the stairs. Ezra stalked down the sidewalk, pace swift and fists balled.

"Hey! What did I do this time?" I reached for his arm, and he whirled on me.

His eyes were wet and blazing, nostrils flared. "I wanted to– I thought–" He growled and viciously wiped at his face. "I'm stupid, huh? I'm stupid for my guilt, and for wanting something romantic. And stupid for thinking you cared. Clearly you were right when you said you don't need to take things slow, since you're actively trying to make up for all the sex you haven't had!"

"What?" I thought of Trevor, asleep in his underwear, the sheets kicked off onto the floor. "Wait. You can't possibly think I had sex with that airheaded dudebro in my bed."

"Don't insult my intelligence."

"Don't insult my taste!" I flapped my hands and scowled. "Even with his brain a hardboiled egg, when I touched him, he managed to tell me how very not-gay he is."

Ezra's face crumpled.

"I didn't mean touch him like *that*."

"Sam's into you too, huh? Throwing little gifts into your orders?" A vein twitched at his temple, his voice rising. "I didn't realize I'd be competing with the whole town for your affections."

"*Affections*?" I gaped at him. "Are you shitting me? This entire town hates me! None of them remember my damn name, and they don't want me in the grocery store, or the post office, or the restaurants. And they certainly don't want my affections! Neither do you, and I don't know why the hell you're here." Shallow breath whistled through my nose, my words coming too fast. My voice was too high; I sounded hysterical. "I'm trying to take care of my post-abduction neighbor so he doesn't drown himself in the toilet or burn down the complex, and he's still back there and he's going to ruin my fucking toaster and you brought me flowers and you're yelling at me. I am *so confused* right now."

The whites of his eyes flashed, and he reached for me. "Take a breath."

"Don't touch me!" I yanked on my hair until pain bloomed across my scalp. This was a complete mess and I couldn't get enough air and my life was every bit the pathetic sci-fi soap opera my followers thought it was.

Ezra's hands hovered over me like I was a bomb he didn't know how to disarm. "I'm sorry for getting you worked up. Why don't you lie down."

"I'm fine!"

"No, you aren't. Sit down."

I thought of him cupping his hands over my ears during the storm on the highway, and my heart ached. I folded onto the sidewalk and pressed my brow to the concrete.

My mind was trying to shut down, but I focused on physical sensations: the grit of sand against my forehead, the cramp in my thigh from my awkward prostration, the scent of faded rain and Ezra's cologne.

He sat next to me. "That guy up there was abducted? Has he been lashing out like the others?"

"The only one lashing out is you."

"You have to know what it looks like."

"Forgive me for having completely benign intentions for my

neighbor and assuming your belief would be the same. And it's a wild leap of imagination to think Sam's hitting on me by mixing up my grocery order."

Footsteps thumped down the complex stairs, and Trevor's voice drifted. "What are you two yelling about?"

Ezra stiffened. "Stay right there. You're okay."

At first I thought he was talking to me, but he jumped up and ripped off his shirt, then jogged toward Trevor. I stood and brushed hair from my face. Blood ran down Trevor's arm, spattering against the sidewalk.

I sucked in a breath. It had been a bad idea to leave him alone, and I knew that and did it anyway.

Ezra wrapped his shirt around Trevor's arm. Trevor ignored him, staring pointedly at me. "How come there aren't fish in your fish tank?"

"Stay here. I'll get first aid." I ran past them, then stopped. Two people walked down the street carrying makeshift weapons. Molly, from the post office, stood in the lead, wearing bicycle knee pads and gardening gloves. She rested the end of a baseball bat against the street and leaned on it. Long nails had been driven through the wood.

Her face crimped like she tasted something sour. "You know, Professor Pie, I figured if aliens actually arrived in Muddy Gap, they'd be here to take you home."

9

My apartment was a crime scene. Glass from the shattered fish tank glittered on the floor, the carpet soaked. Decorative plants and dribbles of blood covered the blanket I'd been sleeping with. The little cave the fish had liked to hide in sat on my mattress in a puddle. The urge to clean up the mess pulled at me, but I had bigger problems.

I ran into the bathroom and retrieved my bandages, a half of a roll of gauze, and some instant glue. This crap would never do. Maybe Trevor had better supplies in his place. I tripped over the UFO books from the library on my way out the door.

Strained voices drifted from the parking lot – Molly, Ezra, and Trevor. Having people find *us* was a start, and they were armed to the teeth with weapons. Maybe they knew something I didn't. There could be wreckage from the craft somewhere in town and surviving aliens. We could catch them unaware and take them out before this place descended further into madness.

I didn't have a lot of experience with fights, other than a couple scuffles in high school, but you didn't always need brawn to defeat an enemy.

Floss and condom boxes rained out of Trevor's bathroom cabinet as I pawed through, my feet chilling on the wet floor. I snatched a package of large fabric bandages, antibiotic ointment, and some towels, then took the complex's stairs two at a time to the ground level.

Ezra stood on the sidewalk, gripping Trevor's arm, his shirt compress damp. I wrapped a towel around Trevor's injury and guided him to the stairs. He was the definition of disinterested, face expressionless as he sat down.

"I don't think it's as bad as it looks." Ezra's bare belly was streaked in blood, his fingertips red.

Molly stood nearby, watching with disapproval. "You shouldn't bother. When they get this way, it's only a matter of time before they disappear."

That conclusion was the opposite of my theory, but regardless, her flippancy grated on me. "Even if that's true, that's no reason not to help him now. What am I going to do, let him bleed out in the road?"

She shrugged.

I picked up a rock and flicked it at her shoe. "Have you killed any aliens?"

"Killed… aliens. No, I'm afraid I haven't had the pleasure."

"But your weapons–"

"Something is happening, and there's not many survivors. That's what I know."

I gritted my teeth, thinking of Gem's empty of shoppers, ice cream cartons sweating on the conveyor belt. "How many survivors is 'not many?'"

She thumbed to the person beside her. Her companion was a Black person with a side-parted afro and multiple nose piercings that somehow looked elegant instead of excessive. Their denim jacket was burdened with colorful enamel pins, which *was* excessive but also clearly the point. If I were closer I likely would have gotten distracted admiring them all. Molly said, "Including the two of us, there were seven who could still think clearly. The rest either try to hurt themselves or lash out at us."

"*Seven*?" That was a sobering number, and I tucked it away to turn over after the rest of my questions were answered. "How many of the others whose brains are affected?"

"I wasn't counting. What does it matter?"

Molly's companion shook their head and walked into the street, tucking their hands in their pockets as they peered at the sky. They clearly knew a pointless conversation with Molly when they heard it, but I wasn't ready to cave that easily.

"Because maybe there's a way to reverse it," I said. "And having concrete facts and numbers about something could be useful in the future."

"If they disappear, that number is useless. Not sure what you two" – she glanced at Ezra – "have been doing, but I spent the past day looking for people after that first sandstorm."

"There was more than one?"

"Where have you been?"

"It's a long story."

She scraped her bat across the ground and one of the nails screeched. "Mm-hm. I bet you were the ones who raided Gem's and the hardware store while everyone else was forming a rescue party. Ezra probably has the entire potato chip aisle in his bedroom closet."

He glared at Molly. "We were out looking for help too. And don't tell me you saw Gem's empty but didn't take anything. Everyone here probably did."

"Sure, but we haven't made a career of it."

"I haven't–"

"You should share that food. Judging by all the weight you've put on, you could stand to part with some."

His brows pushed up, hurt in his eyes, and he pressed his hands to his naked stomach.

"That's incredibly rude," I barked.

"And so are you. So I guess we're even," she said.

"No, no." I wanted to stand and face her, but didn't dare take my hand from Trevor's arm. I jabbed a finger at her instead. "We're not even at all. I'm not the one body shaming Ezra or suggesting Trevor can die in the street. You think I'm rude? You haven't seen anything yet. Wait till I'm an asshole on purpose."

Her nostrils flared. "I'm not sticking around for that."

"Good. Because you're cordially invited to fuck off."

She scoffed and stomped away. I shook my head; so much for working together.

Ezra bent toward my ear. "Do you mind if I get a new shirt from your place? You have a tee that might fit me?"

Trevor tried to pull the towel off his arm, and I clamped down and scowled at him. "Leave it on." Many of my shirts were flamboyantly bohemian, and likely tight enough that Ezra would feel worse about his weight if he wore them, but I did have a drawer of clothes I didn't wear for various reasons. I turned to him. "The far-right box under my bed has some that might work. Just be mindful of the broken glass on the floor."

Molly's companion watched us from the street. Since they hadn't flounced away, I waved. "Hi. I'm Denver. Any pronouns."

"I–I know." They strode over and tugged at the hem of their jacket, their voice quiet. "I mean, I know *of* you. I only recently moved here, but I've seen you around."

Oh, my reputation preceding me again, even with people brand new to Muddy Gap. Great. I gave them a tight smile. "What's your name?"

"Taisha. She/her."

"Well, you're really pretty. Not in an 'I'm hitting on you' way. I just mean I like your hair and your lipstick. And your jacket is very badass."

She looked more startled than if I'd told her that her style belonged in a dumpster. She said, "Thanks. You're pretty too. I've wanted to tell you that I love your outfits."

I raised my eyebrows. "Why didn't you?" But the look on her face told me why. She thought I'd cut her down, say something to offend her just like I did with Ezra and everyone else.

But before I could take back my question, she said, "I haven't... been out very long, and I feel like I don't really know what I'm doing."

"That would be more reason to talk to me, not less, don't you think?"

Some of the tension left her shoulders, and she stopped fussing with her jacket. "Yeah, I guess so."

"I'm not trans femme, though. I don't–" I glanced at Trevor. He still looked fairly out of it, but having a conversation with Taisha about hormone replacement therapy or anything else was probably best left until later. "I don't know how to get symmetrical wings with liquid eyeliner."

She let out a surprised laugh. "If that's the requirement, then I'm in trouble too. Maybe we can figure it out together when things aren't so... y'know."

Now it was my turn to be surprised. It felt surreal to talk about this with everything that was going on, but I wondered how long it would have taken for her to introduce herself under normal circumstances. Maybe she never would have. "Yeah. I'd like that."

Afraid if I kept talking I'd ruin something, I turned my attention to Trevor. Carefully, I peeled the towel from his injuries and peeked beneath. Long gashes ran up his arm, but the bleeding had mostly stopped, and none of the wounds were gaping. I cleaned them with a washrag, then applied ointment and bandages. "You get kitty bandages for this last one, sorry."

There was no way Sam was attracted to me. It wasn't like he slipped handwritten love poems into my grocery bags. And he and Charla were an item, or at least coworkers with benefits. I did talk to him occasionally, and once he'd offered me a beer and a view of Saturn through his telescope... Now that I thought about that, it made my exclamation to Ezra that the entire town hated me seem like an exaggeration. But that didn't mean Sam was attracted to me.

Trevor stared at his arm. "Seems like it should hurt, but it doesn't."

"You're a good friend," Taisha said to me. "It's sweet that you're taking care of him."

I thought of the shock on Ezra's face when he spotted Trevor in my bed. "We're not really friends. Just neighbors."

Trevor picked at the kitty bandage, then looked up. "Thanks for having my back. I don't feel well."

"In what way? Physically? Mentally? Emotionally?"

"My head hurts. I keep trying to think about things, but get confused, then do it all over again. Reminds me of that time at my brother's wedding when I accidentally got super stoned and couldn't remember how to put on my coat."

"Hmm."

Ezra stepped around me, and my heart throbbed. How long had he been standing there? He probably thought me being sweet to Trevor meant we really had slept together.

He'd found a faded black tee emblazoned with "Cheyenne Pie Fight" and the date of the competition. A lone daisy dangled from his hand, and I half-expected him to throw it at me.

Taisha leaned against the wall, arms folded. "Sorry about Molly. I know we're all scared, but that's no excuse to be such a jerk. I don't like the way she's gone about some things, but I didn't want to be alone. Although I'm not sure what help she's going to be if my mind starts becoming affected like your friend here." She nodded at Trevor, then wrinkled her nose. "She'll probably leave me for dead."

"Were you in town Friday evening around eight?" I asked.

"No. Wasn't here. At a friend's in Casper. I drove back the next morning. Molly said she and her two brothers weren't here either. They're at the rec center right now."

"That's what I thought. You won't be affected like Trevor then. I wasn't here – a few miles out of town when I saw the UFO – and neither was Ezra."

Ezra and Taisha sat down as I explained my theory about how people were being affected, and Molly lingered in my peripheral vision, leaning on her baseball bat. Trevor's eyes glazed over again as soon as I mentioned UFOs, and I wondered if there were certain keywords that jammed up his brain, and how an extraterrestrial entity would know to use them.

"So you're saying there's no chance of any of us ending up like Trevor? Or like that old lady who was screaming in her yard yesterday, then disappeared?" Taisha cringed and glanced at Molly. "She was freaking over nothing. I tried to help her, but she lashed out at us. Molly insisted we leave her. When we came back by later, she was gone. Not in her house or anywhere nearby."

"Was it Ms Pierce?" I asked. "And do you mean 'gone' like abducted?"

"I don't know. And I guess us not being able to find her doesn't mean she *disappeared*, but..."

Ezra tucked in the hem of his shirt, paused, and untucked it. "Do you happen to know how many people you found like Trevor?"

"Most of the houses were unoccupied, just like the grocery store," Taisha said. "And if they all went somewhere else, I can't imagine where it would be. There's no way they all tried to leave town; their cars are still here. We found... maybe ten like Trevor."

"And you just left them?" I asked.

"They aren't any use to anyone," Molly said. "This is a matter of survival."

Ezra made a noise in his throat. "It figures you'd jump at the chance to play out your prepper fantasies without first considering you could seek outside help."

"We did try! We sent two scouts out beyond town, and they didn't come back. Decided to ditch us."

"'Scouts'. Listen to yourself. This isn't some apocalypse video game. And you're accusing me of hoarding potato chips, but which one of us ordered another case of iodine tablets to add to her Shit-Hits-The-Fan closet after promising that would be the last of the prepper spending that month?"

She leveled her gaze at him, strawberry blonde hair hanging in her face. "It's called potassium *iodide*, it was only a couple more bottles, and I needed to use up the last of that Patriot Supply gift card from my dad. And don't go telling me I stocked up for the wrong kind of apocalypse. There could be radiation in those sandstorms for all we know."

My eyebrows shot up. "Wait. Are you two exes? That's great; my love life isn't complicated enough already."

I hadn't meant to say it so loud. Molly's mouth hung open as she stared at Ezra. "You and the Pie Professor?" Her piercing laugh echoed across the parking lot. "That is... wow. Well, he loves pie, and you have a weird whipped cream fetish, so it sounds like a perfect match between the two town rejects."

A vein pulsed in Ezra's forehead, and tendons strained in his jaw. He whirled on me, and I shirked against the stair railing, prepared to cup my ears if he started yelling.

His voice came out velvet soft. "Let's get out of here. We can go to my place."

I blinked in surprise. "I'm not leaving Trevor. I don't want him to hurt himself again."

"He can come too."

"But..." I rubbed my eyes until I saw stars. Ezra's hands closed over mine and gently pulled them away. Dark motes danced in my vision. I said, "Do you believe me then? That I didn't sleep with him?"

"I'm only into women," Trevor muttered.

Ezra searched my face, then nodded. "C'mon. All those pies are taking up room in my fridge. Let's go eat one."

The idea of sitting in Ezra's kitchen while I worked out a plan of action was a deep comfort against knowing that everyone in town was missing.

I changed my clothes and ran a brush through my hair, then snagged a pair of sweats for Trevor. I didn't want to think about where everyone had gone and if they'd ever come back. Those church missionaries who were eager to talk until I'd asked them too many questions about their scriptures that they couldn't answer. That elderly teacher with the cane who held the stop sign every day at the crosswalk as school was getting out – I'd asked her why she was stuck with that job, having to walk all the way out to the street, and she'd just sighed. The bag girl who'd burst into tears after I complained that she dumped jars of condiments on top of my bread. The manager had yelled at her, not me, but somehow I still ended up as the asshole. Charla had forcefully suggested that for everyone's sake, I place my orders online from then on, even though that did nothing to eliminate the risk of mayo jars on my bread again.

If I'd been more percipient earlier on, asked the right questions, and wasn't the town eccentric, I could have formed a plan with others before something so devastating happened. But it was their fault too, for keeping me at arm's length, always irritated by my presence and refusing to use my name. This town had been screwed up long before a UFO flew over.

A nasty part of me said I should be like Molly, uncaring, only invested in my survival and Ezra's. Even he'd said the town wouldn't give a thought about us in return.

But I did care. I couldn't turn off that instinctual part of me that wanted to help others, nor did I want the weight of guilt that would come with not trying.

As I stopped at the base of the stairs, Molly said to Ezra, "I'm coming with you. If Professor Pie is making plans, I want to be a part of them."

I plucked the daisy from Ezra's grip and poked it behind my ear. "My name is Denver, and I'm sure an expert prepper like you doesn't need help from a reject."

"I'm serious. I want to know what this UFO looked like, what these little seashell things are that you were talking about. All of it."

"Now you care."

"We need to work together!"

"What's this 'we' you speak of? Ezra and I have been just fine without anyone else's help." That was a lie – I hadn't been fine since Friday.

Ezra's mouth pulled into a tight line, and he leaned toward my ear. "Maybe we should let her come. There aren't many of us left. And I'm not fine."

"And she's going to help with that with her anti-radiation tablets? I can't believe you dated her. She's horrible."

"I have a feeling most of that hostility is coming out because I'm here. It was a really ugly breakup."

I wasn't sure that was true because she was rude whenever I went to the post office, but I wasn't going to push the subject.

"Can I come with y'all?" Taisha asked. "I don't want to go back to the rec center with those doomsday boys. I'll help you keep Trevor company."

Trevor's eyes lit up and he grinned.

"Let us help," Molly called. "You're not the only one who's good at planning."

More gazes hung on me than I liked. I stared at grains of orange sand in the creases of the asphalt. "Tell you what, if you apologize to me, Ezra, Trevor, and Taisha, you can come."

"What do I need to apologize to Taisha for?"

"I don't know, but I'm sure there's something."

Molly drew in a deep breath and tapped her bat against the ground. "I'm sorry for saying it isn't worth the effort to patch up your brain-dead friend. I'm sorry for telling Ezra that he got fat, even though he did. And I'm sorry for saying you're the town reject, even though you are. If Taisha's mad, I'm sorry for that too. Okay?"

"That was terrible." Shaking my head, I strode down the street, a light grip on Trevor's elbow so he didn't wander away. Molly could either come with us or not, but I had better things to do than stand here and talk about it any longer.

A car sat halfway in a drive, the back end hanging in the street. The doors stood open, drifts of sand buttressing the tires. Curtains fluttered out of the home's ajar window, and a sprinkler attached to a hose soaked a wilting flower bed.

Trevor rubbed his eyes. "What day is it?"

"Tuesday," I said.

"Shit. I gotta go to work." He pulled away, then stopped as Taisha approached him. She was several inches taller than him, her afro adding even more height, and the expression on his face was one of dazed awe.

"Um, you don't work today," she said. "Holiday."

"Really?" Trevor pumped his fist. "Sweet. What did you say your name was again?"

I tuned out his muddled efforts at flirting, but couldn't ignore the clomping of Molly's boots.

We walked in front of Ms Pierce's yard. Her door stood open, sand covering the entryway. Her hose lay in the grass, and I could still hear the sound of it whistling through the air before it struck my face. I shuddered and clutched my elbows. What did aliens want with a sixty year-old woman? Or Trevor, even? It was hard to imagine experimentation being a top priority after their craft had exploded. Maybe the aliens ate some of them. Or they were mental vampires, draining knowledge and function from people's brains, then dropping them back at their houses as confused husks.

Our footsteps echoed off quiet ranch houses, the sound of our breathing uncomfortably loud. Reaching Ezra's and being enveloped in the soft spice of his living room was a welcome change from the eerie, empty streets. Molly made a circuit around the leather furniture, poking at books and cameras with an awkward unfamiliarity. I thought of asking how long it had been since they broke up, but it hardly seemed appropriate.

She slapped the stone globe on the coffee table, sending it spinning. "How much did this thing cost? It looks hella expensive. Actually, you probably don't know since you stole–"

"You finish that sentence and I'll help you out the door," I said.

She put up her hands, but her lips twitched in a smirk. "Okay. Sorry."

I collapsed into a kitchen chair and set my hat on the table. Ezra cleared off his microscope and glass slides, then handed me a spiral notebook and a pencil. Physically writing down each event from my spreadsheet was soothing, as was crossing off theories that I was certain were no longer correct. I startled as Ezra set a slice of coconut cream pie before me. Vanilla custard, chewy coconut flakes, and buttery crust melted in my mouth as I took a bite. I groaned and sagged into the chair. I'd lost my focus on the spreadsheet, but I could hardly be mad at Ezra for handing me pie.

Trevor ignored his slice, his gaze roaming Taisha's face.

I said, "Don't do that."

He ducked his head and whispered. "Do what?"

"You're being totally straight, and it's grossing me out."

His face scrunched in confusion so exaggerated it was comical. I said, "I'm teasing. Giving you a hard time because you're so afraid of someone perceiving you as gay."

"You have to be a man to be gay, right? But you're non-binary. So…"

I could almost see his brain melting like his toaster, but at least he was carrying a train of thought. "Gay is a fine catch-all for me. So is queer. I like guys and some other non-binary people. People can use whatever labels feel right for them. Or no labels."

Taisha licked whipped cream off the tines of her fork. "Looks like you're the minority in this group, Trevor."

"You're gay too? Lesbian?" He deflated.

"I'm only attracted to men." She hesitated and glanced at me, maybe for moral support. "But in case you missed the conversation earlier, I'm a trans woman. So if I check you out the same as you're checking me out and you say that's gay, we're going to have a problem."

"Why would that be gay? Trans women are women."

Maybe Trevor wasn't as dense as I assumed. I stuffed a heaping bite of coconut cream in my mouth and pressed my fingers to my temples. Words stood out to me from my list of events as I chewed. I circled them hard until graphite dusted the paper.

Incipient alien terrain, which had defied our digital photographic efforts.

Accordion landscapes that wouldn't let us leave but were capable of being digitally recorded.

UFO explosion, raining down brain-weakening particles.

Trevor turned to Ezra, who stood beside the counter, staring at the pie with an empty plate in front of him. "If you like Professor Pie, that makes you what?"

"I'm pan." Ezra put the cover on the pie without serving himself a slice, then stuck it in the fridge. "I like all genders. Though I swore off cishetero people after Molly."

Molly leaned against the counter with her arms folded, a slice of pie beside her. "Don't mind me. I'm not in the room or anything."

"Isn't that straightphobic?" Trevor asked.

I threw down my pencil. Chatter and company while I was trying to think wasn't something I was used to, and I was never going to form a plan with so much distraction.

"There's no such thing as heterophobia," I said. "Not in the same sense as homo or transphobia. *That* prejudice comes with power because being cis and straight is still the default, even with the progress that's been made in the past twenty-odd years. Just like there's no such thing as reverse racism. Being prejudiced against straight people happens, certainly, but Ezra not wanting to date them anymore doesn't equate to massive, targeted hatred for one's sexuality or identity. Now can we please talk about–" I couldn't address the topic in a straightforward way. Trevor seemed nearly back to normal, and I didn't want to put him in a state where he was going to hurt himself or be unable to form a complete thought.

He hadn't glazed over when I spoke of everyone in town being gone. It was only when I mentioned UFOs and aliens that his mind seized up. That meant I was on the right track. It might be possible to test ideas depending on his reaction. Deflecting the subject would mean I was correct; engaging with it like normal meant I was wrong.

I scribbled down keywords I already knew, then looked up at him. "Trevor, we lied when we said today was a holiday. An event is happening in town."

"What kind of event?"

My pencil pointed to one of the ideas I'd crossed out: Ezra's mind control conspiracy. It was close enough to what I knew of the truth to work as an explanation, and would either rule it out or confirm it as a theory in case I was wrong.

"Remember when I told you everyone was gone?" I dropped my voice and looked over my shoulder at the empty living room. "The government is making guinea pigs of us."

He chuckled, then turned to the others, but they all humored me and nodded in confirmation.

"You serious?" He poked at the bandages on his arm. "I guess that makes sense. I'm having a real hard time remembering things."

"We know. People are being kidnapped and taken to Washington for research."

"Shit. How are you sure?"

I wrote, *Not kidnapped = not abducted?* "Everyone who's still here knows at this point. But you and a handful of others have already been tested on and don't remember."

Trevor's nose wrinkled, his breath shallow. "Do I have a tracking device in me? Can they hear me right now?" He raked a hand through his dark hair. "My dad *knew* it. Used to talk about this shit all the time. Tracking chips in vaccines. Brain-destroying cell towers. Turbines that would blow wind full of memory-erasing… memory…" He blinked lethargically, then jolted up. "Do you think people really went to Mars or was it filmed in a studio?"

I jotted down, *Memory-erasing wind.* That went with my particulate distribution idea. I scribbled *Confirmation that an outside element is making people complacent so they won't fight back,* then tilted the notebook to Ezra.

Molly peered around his shoulder with a frown. He took the book from me and wrote, *If people aren't being abducted, where are they going? Wandering off on accident?*

All of them? I replied. *People walking into the repeating highway like moths into a flame?*

He scratched his head and shrugged.

"What are you writing down?" Trevor tried to peek at the notebook, and I tilted it away.

"We think this place might be bugged. Ezra's checked, but we can't be too cautious. You can help us, though. I know you don't remember what happened, but your answers are important anyway."

"Okay. I don't want this shit going on here."

"Great. There are tiny seashells all over town with advanced tech. They're influencing people."

He frowned. "Seashells? We're nowhere near the ocean."

I wrote, *Not the shells.* "And the sand."

"You sure you know what you're talking about? That doesn't make sense."

Not the sand. But they were a byproduct of something else, or had some other purpose. Maybe I was thinking too small.

"An extraterrestrial environment is imposing itself on Muddy Gap."

He blinked slowly, eyelids out of sync. "I guess deserts have sand too. But Wyoming isn't a desert. Not like Arizona or something."

"This environment is from another dimension."

"Arizona..." He sat up with a start. "Hey, where'd this pie come from? You got some secret power, Professor? Pie outta nowhere."

I jotted down, *Alien environment from another dimension.*

"The sand populating, the storms – it's going to get worse. More frequent."

Molly squatted next to Trevor, her hands on her thighs. "Will it destroy buildings? Stop transportation? Is it going to spread beyond town and take over other ones?"

Trevor pawed at the pie with an open hand and whipped cream squeezed through his fingers.

My mind raced, dots connecting. "People are becoming complacent not to be abducted but so this environment can consume everything in its path, and no one will be lucid enough to stop it."

Trevor's head hit the table hard enough to rattle the forks on our plates, then he slid out of the chair. I gasped. Shit. I caught him under one arm, and Taisha grabbed his other.

She glared at me. "You're killing him."

"I'm not–"

"Some friend you are." She grunted, trying to heave him upright. When I tried to help, she shoved me back. Ezra pulled Trevor to his feet.

Trevor touched his forehead, leaving a smear of whipped cream. "I'm never drinking wine coolers again."

Molly shrugged. "See? He's okay."

But a bloody goose egg was already forming on his brow, his gaze unfocused. I hadn't wanted to hurt him. "Sorry. I got caught up in trying to piece this together. I was just– I was just thinking out loud. But I didn't expect my guess to be correct." Or maybe I had only *hoped* it wasn't correct.

Taisha huffed, brushing past me with Trevor's arm across her shoulder. She and Ezra helped him down the hall to Ezra's bedroom.

I sat and picked up my pencil, because it was that or stand awkwardly while I dwelled on the fact that if I ever actually had one of those DNA tests done, it would conclude that I was 100% asshole.

Molly took Trevor's vacated chair and chewed her lip. "Spell it out for me."

"Muddy Gap will be swallowed by an alien environment from another dimension unless those of us noncompliant figure out how to stop it." Goosebumps broke out on my arms. It was a devastating conclusion. This wasn't little green men abducting random people, then dropping them back off in their houses with no memory of the experience. This was much, much worse.

Molly stared, eyes wide. "Not just Muddy Gap. Everywhere." Her chair scraped across the linoleum as she stood. "If these sandstorms continue, I don't have enough gas masks for everyone. And Ezra probably threw away the one I bought him for his birthday."

I raised my eyebrows. "You got him a gas mask for his birthday?"

"Yes!" she snapped. A red flush tinged her pale cheeks. "It wasn't the only thing I got him that year, okay? Don't look at me like that. Especially not with all of this going on. I just... wanted him to be safe in case something ever happened." She strode out of the kitchen and pushed through the front door.

The words on my notebook made my skin itch. I scratched at my arms until Ezra pulled my hands away. His chest pressed into my back, arms wrapping around me. I stiffened. The temptation to relax against him, to press my nose to his neck and inhale his cologne was overwhelming, but I wasn't sure why he was holding me. I was nothing but a mistake, so I couldn't imagine that the action was romantic.

Maybe he thought I'd melt down if he didn't physically hold me together.

"You don't like that. Sorry." He slid away.

"I didn't mean to hurt Trevor." I rubbed at the red nail marks I'd left on my arms.

"He's okay. He's responding to questions and looked pretty excited when Taisha said she'd keep him company."

"Everyone hates me." And the notion that I'd have to face the monumental task of stopping the alien environment from spreading with only a couple of allies made me feel smaller and more vulnerable than the neon tetras that had been in my fish tank.

"I don't hate you. This is really bad, huh?"

"Aliens are trying to terraform Muddy Gap. And I bet you all the pie in the world that Molly's guess is correct. It'll spread to other towns."

Ezra clutched his elbows, his mouth a hard line. "Maybe that UFO was unmanned. Or... uncrabbed."

"You mean like they sent it first, and then when their environment grows, they'll show up in another one, ready to take over?"

"When an invasive species starts colonizing, the native populations are always decimated. They don't have any defenses against it. By which, I mean *we* don't. It's going to kill all of us."

"No, it isn't. If this plan was unstoppable, there'd be no reason to produce a brain-warping agent. They could just plop down their terraforming device and let it do its thing." I tapped the words with my pencil. "I think it's vulnerable to attack and they know it. We can destroy it before it consumes the town. We just have to find the source. We need to look for wreckage."

10

Brittle brush crunched under my boots. A jarringly cheery blue sky hung above, but walking around behind Gem's Market was no better than being inside it.

Molly's two brothers – in nearly identical ensembles – wandered across the street, checking abandoned vehicles. They both looked in their late teens or early twenties and seemed to do anything Molly told them to. She'd probably bullied them mercilessly when they were growing up. It was a struggle not to tell them I could still see them even with their jungle-camo outfits.

"We've already investigated the buildings in this area." Molly's bat cut furrows through the dirt. She clanged it against a shopping cart, and I winced. A gas mask hung around her neck. She'd chastised Ezra for no longer having his – he claimed it was probably still in a closet somewhere, and he hadn't purposely gotten rid of it. She'd handed us KN95 respirator masks instead.

"But you weren't looking for ship wreckage. You were focused on finding survivors and stockpiling food and tools," Ezra said.

Her chin jutted out, a gleam in her eye. "Yeah. That was important."

"Didn't say it wasn't."

We'd driven around, rolling through residential streets, past the baseball field, and beyond the skeezy motel at the edge of town, but aside from everywhere being unoccupied – the occasional buildup of sand here and there – there were no clues. No aliens, no hunks of metal, and no giant crabs. I couldn't shake the sense that I'd taken a mental wrong turn, and we were wasting our time. I'd set a timer in my contacts to see how long it would take Molly to call us morons and give up, but I was losing the bet I'd made with myself.

Maybe this was all wrong. I kept drawing off of my UFO books, thinking about Roswell crashes and Area 51. Little grays with big heads and big eyes. It was all pop culture stuff. We were probably closer to the truth with our interdimensional crab idea.

I should have asked Trevor about spacecraft wrecks, but Taisha wouldn't let me near him. She'd stayed behind, concerned that getting closer to the remains of the UFO would mess him up even more. I could appreciate her concern, and maybe she could smell the awkwardness baking off of all of us and wanted no part of it. But we had bigger things to worry about than Molly being Ezra's ex and how his mixed romantic signals were making me feel.

Wind shushed by, carrying away a grocery bag. Tumbleweeds quivered in an abandoned shopping cart. The void of sound created by the absence of cars and shoppers made hair stand up on my neck. Even the birds were silent.

Several knives and a hammer clinked together in my backpack, though I wasn't sure what I'd do with them if I actually met an alien. Ezra tromped over rabbitbrush populated by tiny yellow flowers, and I cupped my nose at the stench.

"God, I hate those bushes. They smell like cat piss."

He looked down, then veered around more of them. "You notice anything yet?"

I shut my eyes, trying to ignore the smell of the rabbitbrush and the smell of Ezra. Tried to concentrate on sounds other than his breathing, seeking a whine that pierced my brain, a hum that filled my teeth, any delicate sensory anomaly that might indicate extraterrestrial tech was nearby. But all I could think about was the way Ezra had curled an arm protectively around me when I talked about my mom, and how little moans had escaped his lips while I stroked him in the car.

Shaking my head, I blinked at the sky. "There's nothing. My autism isn't a superpower. Sorry. I wish it was."

Molly blew a deep breath through her nose. "I'm trying really hard to be nice, okay? But this feels pointless. We all want what's best for the remaining people in town, so I think–"

"Do we?" I plucked a stem of rabbitbrush from the hem of my jeans. "You abandoned all the affected people. Implied that it would be better to leave Trevor for dead."

"And I don't see you out helping them either. You only helped Trevor because you like him."

"I don't *like* him." I shot a glance at Ezra. "But he's my neighbor, and once I saw the state he was in, I couldn't leave him alone knowing he might die in the apartment right below me while I slept."

"So you helped him to alleviate any potential guilt, but you haven't seen the others with your own eyes, so they don't matter as much."

The scope of a town-wide search for all of those people would detract from our current objective. Stopping the terraforming – and hopefully whatever signal was jamming their brains – was arguably more beneficial than herding them all into Ezra's house for Taisha to babysit.

I wanted to tell her that, but the words tangled in my mouth, and I flapped my hands instead.

She stared at me, lips pursed. "All I'm trying to say is that we want to help the town, and this plan isn't working. The conclusions you came to based on Trevor's reactions made sense, I guess, but there's nothing to back it up. There's no sign of wreckage, and the evidence of alien terrain is… what exactly? Those little white pebbles that Ezra said are mind-control devices and some sandstorms?"

A gust of wind blasted me with debris as if Molly had summoned it by words alone. My hat tore from my head and orange grains stung my skin. Dust filled my nose and scratched my eyes. I pulled in a choking breath and shielded my face. My hair whipped around me in a vortex. Ezra coughed, and a clear chunk of something bounced off his back.

Molly grabbed a fistful of my shirt and yanked me forward, then pulled Ezra by his arm. I stumbled over bushes and ground squirrel holes. The shouts of Molly's brothers carried with the howling wind. Sand raked across me and filled my mouth. I remembered my respirator mask and pulled it over my face.

Orange haze swallowed the world. The rubbery flaps of a loading dock curtain slapped against my face as Molly hauled Ezra and me through. Angry light warped across the walls of the small warehouse, and papers tacked there flapped frantically. Sand caked Ezra's hair, tiny cuts oozing on his cheek.

Hard impacts drummed the roof, and I crammed in my earplugs. Dust billowed across the floor, the wind hurling branches and clear chunks of stone inside. Ezra soundlessly shouted and pointed toward the swinging double doors at the end of the room, but the wind hushed so quickly that I turned the other way. The rubber curtain flaps fell still, clear sun sparkling on the sand across the floor.

I shrugged off Ezra's attempt to stop me and parted the curtains. A faint haze hung in the air, blue sky burning through. Small dunes of orange sand rippled through the scrubby prairie.

Pulling out my earplugs, I uttered, "Where the hell is this coming from?" Did this mean we were close to the terraforming device? We couldn't see any wreckage, but maybe it had a cloaking device that was still in effect.

Only… this sandstorm was tiny compared to the one that had swallowed Ezra's car out on the highway and encompassed all of Muddy Gap. There'd been no clear indication of a source then either.

155

I was thinking about this wrong. I had to be. But then what was right?

Sand suddenly swelled in front of me, erupting across my boots and flowing between my legs. I shrieked and stumbled back into Ezra. He caught me by the shoulders, mouth agape. The dune grew, gushing sand from the center like a science fair volcano. Something moved in my peripheral vision. Tiny red plants with flocked leaves quivered amid the grasses.

Molly pushed up her gas mask, her eyes wide. "Did– did those plants just appear out of nowhere?"

My heart throbbed, and I wasn't sure if it was from fear or the idea that maybe we were in the right spot after all. That last sandstorm hadn't been localized. This one was.

I strode toward Gem's.

"Where are you going?" Ezra asked.

"To get a shovel. Xenoterrain is literally sprouting beneath our feet. I'm going to dig it up and see if there's any evidence of technology or ship wreckage below the surface."

"I'll help."

Molly hurried in front of us, her quickened breath fluttering the tangled hair hanging in her face. "Wait. So this is all... Your theory is right? It's really aliens, and the terrain is going to keep growing. It's going to spread beyond the town. Consume other ones." Her voice dropped to a halting whisper, and she scrubbed at her arms. "Commerce and communication will stop. Society will break down. It's the apocalypse. It really is, huh? This is it."

I frowned. "It won't happen. I'm going to stop it." Brushing past her, I strode into the warehouse, Ezra beside me.

Her brothers called from the street, and she shouted back to them. Hopefully they'd help, and it wouldn't just be me digging a hole while people stood around and watched.

Ezra shook sand from his hair. He pushed through the swinging doors, and I followed him into the garden area.

"You okay?" I asked. "You got hit with one of those rocks."

He reached behind him, fingers grazing his shoulder blade. "Stings." Wincing, he pulled up his shirt. "How bad is it?"

Muscles flexed in his back, light sliding across his skin. A lacy brown birthmark peeked out of the waistband of his jeans. He glanced back. "Denver?"

"Oh." Shallow scrapes and a red welt had formed between his shoulder blades. "There's gonna be a bruise, but I think you're fine."

He dropped his shirt and turned around. "I'm *fine*, huh?"

I rolled my eyes, but he must not have noticed, because he took my fidgeting fingers and laced them through his.

Pulling away, I said, "I don't– I don't know what you want from me. Why do you try to touch me, bring me flowers, get jealous when you think I slept with someone else? I'm not going to make a mistake with you twice."

His brows pushed up, and he stuffed his hands in his pockets like I was the one hurting him. He was still wearing my Cheyenne Pie Fight shirt, and it was too baggy and shapeless. It hid his belly and didn't suit him. "Are you saying you're not interested in me then?"

I tugged on my hair. "No, you said you weren't interested in *me*."

"I never said that."

Maybe we were on the right track toward finding aliens after all, because clearly Ezra was existing in a different dimension than I was. "You said I was a mistake–"

"I did not say that." He snarled something in Spanish, then clenched his jaw, his voice tight. "I said I made *a* mistake."

"Which was me! We're talking in circles here and wasting time. There's nothing between us now, so let's stop pretending that there is so we can figure out how the hell to save our town."

He swallowed and looked away. "Right. Sure."

I swiveled and strode through the garden area doors. A rack of shovels hung on the wall. I snatched two of them, then reached for a third, but one slipped through my arms and clattered against the floor.

Ezra picked it up and crossed through the room without a word, then shoved open the back door. It slammed closed behind him.

I waited a beat before following. Maybe I should apologize. But what was I supposed to say or be sorry for? All I'd stated was the truth, and *he* was the one who'd broken it off with me.

Sorry fancy tongue maneuvers aren't yet part of my repertoire.

Sorry I don't have the manual for social navigation that you do.

Sorry whatever you expected from me wasn't enough.

Molly's voice drifted as I struggled to carry my armload of shovels through the garden area. A thread of wind howled through the gap in the door, making it impossible to decipher her words, but Ezra's piercing reply wasn't reassuring.

Shovels clanged against the doorframe as I tried to push through.

"If Denver thinks we should be digging," Ezra said, "then that's what we should do. Xe's been right about many things so far, and I'm not going to start questioning xem now."

If only that applied to our romantic relationship too.

I shoved through the door and strode toward the group. Ezra stood stiffly, facing Molly and her camo-clad siblings. An orange dune studded in footprints divided them.

Dumping my armload on the ground, I shooed them all away from the spot and jammed a shovel into the ground. I hefted the scoop behind me.

Molly approached again, then spluttered as sand buffeted her face. "Stop it. We need to get out of here."

"Leave if you want. I'm staying here and getting to the bottom of this. Literally."

"You don't think you're going to find this terraforming device by digging in one spot, do you?"

"No," I said. "Hence the other shovels. If this doesn't work, I bet we could find a metal detector in someone's house."

Ezra dug up one of the red plants and flung dirt over his shoulder.

"There are metal detectors back at the rec center." Molly wiped grit from her mouth. "We could go get them right now."

"That sounds great." Maybe she wouldn't dig, but at least she was helping.

"Then let's go."

Before I could tell her that this errand wouldn't take all five of us, Ezra planted his shovel in the ground and scowled at Molly. "You always do this."

She stared at him, some barely restrained emotion trying to surface on her face. "Do what?"

"Change tactics as soon as persuasion isn't working. A moment ago you were arguing that digging was a bad idea and we needed to leave. You said you wouldn't help. Now you want us all to head to the rec center for metal detectors."

She folded her arms. "I'm not allowed to change my mind? It's illogical to dig random holes. That's a waste of time. But metal detectors will help us pinpoint where to focus, won't they? You're mad when I disagree, and now you're mad that I'm agreeing. Sheesh."

I opened my mouth, but Ezra said, "One or two people can go get them, then. We don't all need to go."

"And risk you and Professor Pie getting swallowed in another sandstorm out here behind Gem's? No, we need to stick together. All of us go to the rec center."

My shovel clanged against a rock, and I dislodged it. Orange sand and Wyoming soil slid into the hole left in its wake. Ezra knew her better than I did, and it was obvious she was struggling to maintain pleasantries with him, but discouraging her meant she'd turn her back on us. It would be less help and zero of the resources she'd gathered.

Digging my truck keys from my pocket, I said, "You and your brothers can drive over there quick, toss the detectors in the back, and be back here in no time. If the sand kicks up again, Ez and I can duck back into the store while we wait."

She took the keys but said, "I'm not going without you two."

"Flattering, but we don't–"

"It isn't an option. I said we need out of here. This place is dangerous." She nodded to the guy beside her. He slid a hunting knife from the sheath on his belt and aimed it at my throat.

"Whoa." I put up my hands. It was certainly dangerous *now*.

"What the hell are you doing? Get that knife away from xem!" Ezra's grip on his shovel tightened, and he took a step toward us. I had no doubt he intended to push between me and the knife, but the guy aimed the blade more forcefully at me and said to Ezra, "You stay where you are."

My mouth dried out, and I forced a swallow. "There are easier ways to persuade people to go to the rec center to play foosball with you." Too much glee danced in the guy's eyes. Ezra wasn't kidding that Molly's family had a hard-on for survival fantasy. I was surprised they wanted to take us back to the rec center and not some reinforced bunker stocked with Twinkies and hazmat suits.

"Was this your intent the entire time you've been with us?" Ezra growled. "What is this about?"

Molly folded her arms, her shoulders hunched. "I'm trying to help you! You threw your damn gas mask away, Ezra! And you don't know the difference between iodine and potassium *iodide*." Her voice broke, eyes glossy. "'Alien invasion' was never on my dad's lists of potential apocalypses, but it doesn't matter. I have everything we need to get through this, and if you don't come with me, you're both gonna die out here!"

Ezra opened his mouth, then sighed and shot me an apologetic look. He turned to Molly. "It's okay to be scared. We all are. And I can see how your dad filling your basement with Geiger counters and food storage and making you do duck-and-cover drills would make you–"

"I'm *not* scared!" Molly's eyes blazed, and a tear rolled down her cheek. "And everything Dad taught me is going to keep me *and* you two alive. The survivors need a leader."

There was clearly far more to Molly's prepper upbringing than I'd initially thought, but why she cared so much about my survival and Ezra's when she didn't even like us was beyond me. I distantly wondered if she'd actually abandoned other people in town or if her strong-arming had scared them away. "A good leader does more than boss people around. They need self-awareness and active listening," I said. "And you're not listening to me when I'm saying we might have found the terraforming source!"

"You two are going to get yourselves killed out here digging random holes," she said. "Can you blame me for wanting to make sure that doesn't happen on my watch? Now, I said I'd help, but not until we have proper equipment. And some protection like–"

"I don't have time for this Machiavellian game of yours, whatever it is." I slapped the hunting knife out of her brother's hand. It skittered away and disappeared into a dune of sand. He gaped at me, and I almost felt sorry for ruining his *Road Warrior* vision of himself. "You think *we're* going to get ourselves killed? Do you think those camo ensembles of yours are going to do you any good? Look around. You need outfits patterned in shopping carts and Boot Barns."

The guy's eyes blazed, and he lunged for me. Ezra gripped the collar of his shirt and hurled him backward. The handle of his shovel cracked into my ankle; I lost my balance and fell to one knee, crushing some of the alien plants.

The guy pawed at sand, searching for his knife. Ezra threw a fist and suddenly both of them were on the ground, swinging at each other as Molly screamed at them to stop.

Something white smeared the knee of my jeans, and I wiped at it. A jelly-like substance came away, and I stiffened. "Hey, y'all?"

Gelatinous blobs coated the leaves of the red plants, some now smashed. They looked like the hailshells, but a clear coating with a rainbow luster glazed them. "Stop fighting." I whirled on the others, and my voice broke. "*Stop fighting!*"

Ezra froze, his fist pulled back. Blood smeared his lip and there was a gash above Molly's brother's eye. Ezra shoved him away and staggered over to me. He wiped his mouth on the collar of his shirt. "What's wrong?"

There were a lot of things wrong, but either my expression or something in my voice must have told him that we had a brand-new thing to be worried about. I picked up one of the gooey blobs and pinched it between my fingers. It squished with little resistance, like a dissolving marshmallow. "Do you know what this is?"

Molly and her brothers seemed to have forgotten about our fight because they crowded around, staring at the thing in my hand.

I swallowed hard. "It's alien caviar."

Ezra's eyes bulged, and he stumbled back. "*Eggs?*"

The brothers blanched, both of their gazes scrambling over the dirt around us. Molly pulled down her gas mask like it would protect her.

After flicking away the egg, I wiped furiously at my pant leg until the material chaffed my hand. "We've seen the hailshells everywhere. What if they aren't seashells in a crustacean sense, but desiccated eggs? Ones that weren't viable in our terrain yet so they dried up and died? Or the things already crawled out of them and left the shells behind."

Ezra stared at the smear on my pant leg. "Do you think... Do you think they're part of the environment? They could be little creatures, rather than intelligent aliens. Like, if we were going to terraform a planet and we wanted it to look like Wyoming, we'd generate not just prairie but jackrabbits and snakes too, and this is kind of the same thing. Or maybe the intelligent aliens *come out* of the eggs?"

I crushed a cluster of the white blobs under my boot. Bile rose in my throat as I scraped the jelly off on a rock. "If there were space fish laying these things, we would have noticed."

"I'm serious."

"I don't know!" I thought of all the shells in Ms Pierce's yard, soaking up water. The idea of cat-sized crabs overrunning the town wasn't funny anymore. "I saw a monster invasion movie once, and everyone was afraid of the giant alien lizard, but what was really scary were the 'tiny' parasites that came with it. Whatever hatches out of these eggs could be worse than our new alien overlords." I turned to Molly. "This is serious. Not that it wasn't before, but we have no idea what will come out of these eggs and when. Now, more than ever, we need to work together."

"I agree."

"Good. Then you can get those metal detectors and–"

"I don't have any."

"But you said–"

"She was lying," Ezra said. "It's what she does when she's not getting her way."

"Oh, and you're so honest," she spat. "I bet he doesn't know yet that you're a criminal. Go on, tell the Pie Professor how you broke into someone's house, robbed them blind, and spent a year in jail."

I frowned and turned to Ezra. He shrank several inches. "It was six months."

My mouth parted. He couldn't get a good job with his degree and was forced to bartend at a dive. He didn't trust the police to help us. And he took all that food from Gem's with no hesitation.

Ezra pressed his hands to his belly like it was the source of all of his shame, robbery included. But he'd felt awful for buying into the rumors about me, and if I took what Molly said – who's details contradicted Ezra's – at face value, I'd be doing the same thing. I didn't have the full story and really...

"Who the hell cares? It doesn't matter if Ezra robbed Fort Knox. We might all die out here, and he's been a source of kindness and comfort to me in the face of that. You wanna drive a wedge between us, you'll have to try harder." Terrible liar that I was, it wasn't the complete truth. My mind was trying to calculate how bad the crime had been for a six-month sentence, and weigh that against whether I was willing to let that kind of man be support for me. But it was a distant concern, dwarfed by hunting knives, the egg smear on my knee, and that we had nothing but a couple of shovels at our disposal.

"Why did you say you had metal detectors?" I asked Molly.

Ezra sighed. "Just drop it. She's not going to tell you her plans. Although I have a pretty good–"

Sudden wind howled past, blasting us with sand and snatching all the air from my lungs. I pulled my shirt collar over my nose and turned for Gem's, but there was nothing but orange in every direction, and I was no longer certain where it was. Molly gripped my arm and pulled me forward.

"Ezra!" Hair tangled in my face, my voice snatched away in the wind and sand needling my eyes. I tried to keep up with Molly's pace, nearly rolling my ankle.

"Get in! Get in!" she yelled.

She pushed me ahead of her, but I whirled around, trying to shield my face as I peered through gusting sand. "Not without Ezra!"

"He's right here!" She took my hand and planted it on Ezra's chest. I bunched the fabric of his shirt in my fist, overcome with sudden relief. She urged both of us forward. "C'mon, get inside!"

I expected the rubber flaps of Gem's loading dock curtain, but was met with the passenger's side door of my truck. Before I could protest, I was shoved in the back, Ezra beside me. Molly hopped into the front and screamed out the open door for her brothers. They slid in beside her and barely had the door closed before she floored the accelerator.

11

When we reached the rec center, the sandstorm had died out, but my protestations had not. Ezra kept putting a hand on my arm and shaking his head. If trying to reason with Molly was a waste of time, maybe my constant voice behind her head would annoy her enough to let us out of the truck.

"Even without the metal detectors, if you have goggles or welding glasses, we can–"

"Will you stop!" She threw the truck into park, yanked out the keys, and turned around. "You two aren't going back there. Who the hell knows what will come out of those eggs–"

"All the more reason to go back *now* and try to find the terraforming source before they hatch."

Her face suddenly shifted to neutral. She reached into her bag and pulled out a thick zip tie, then turned to Ezra. "Put out your hands."

"What?" His question was almost a laugh, and that must have been the wrong move because Molly threw open the truck door and yanked me out by my hair.

I tried to pull away, but she kicked me in the back of the knee, and I lost my balance and fell. The nails in her bat scratched across the asphalt. "You hold out your hands, or I'm going to make a homerun into the side of the professor's head."

She wasn't going to do it. Probably. But that uncertainty made me hold my tongue. I refrained from standing up in case she decided I was resisting. From this vantage, I couldn't see

Ezra in the truck, but a moment later his shoes scraped on sand. He stopped beside us, flanked by Molly's brothers, wrists bound in front of him and his face the color of a cherry tomato.

"You don't need to zip tie me," I said. "I'll walk in with–"

One of the brothers yanked me up and jerked my arms behind me. Hard plastic looped tight around my wrists. They pushed us toward the rec center. It was a small brick building with a false façade and a mural of questionable artistic talent painted on the side, depicting grazing pronghorns. The only thing sinister looking about it was the amount of red plants and sand that had cropped up around the front doors, but I didn't at all like the idea of going inside.

Before I could warn them that the red plants might have eggs on them that needed to be crushed, I was hauled forward and through the doors. With arms restrained, my usual stims were impossible, and my fingers beat against my backside like caged birds.

Trying to access the internet resulted in nothing, but that didn't stop me from refreshing my blog over and over in my vision until I ran into a chair in the lobby. I had no way of knowing if my last cached post had published during a momentary clear signal, and maybe it didn't matter. Authorities probably didn't know how to address what was going on in town any more than I did, and sending details about the erupting alien terrain and gooey eggs was likely information that brought them no closer to solving this problem.

Ezra walked alongside me in fuming silence. Veins stood out in relief at his temples, his jaw a rock. The smell of burnt coffee hung in the air. On a ping pong table near the door sat the cardboard packaging of several "healthy" microwave dinners – the kind that always left you hungrier than before you ate them.

A woman sat in a metal folding chair, her legs propped up on a table. She got up when she spotted Molly, and stood at attention like this was the goddamned Army.

Molly started to say something, then gave me a onceover and glared at one of her brothers. "Why didn't you confiscate Professor Pie's backpack?"

The brother tried to pull it from my shoulders. The inner contents jangled as the straps of the pack caught against my wrists. I grunted in pain. "You'll have to cut my zip ties to pull off the bag, genius."

He looked at Molly, who sighed, then rooted through the bag. She pulled out a hammer, two kitchen knives, and a flashlight with a crumpled receipt stuck to the handle. She shoved me toward the other woman, and my tangled backpack slapped against my backside. "Stick Bonnie and Clyde here in a cell."

I huffed. "This is asinine. Those eggs could hatch at any moment. We could find a backhoe and dig up whatever is creating this. I don't 'get' people a lot of the time, but you are on a whole other level."

Molly strode from the room without a word. More protests bubbled up my throat, but Ezra and I were pushed down a hall of dingy white tile. I squinted and turned my head from a spasming overhead fluorescent. Several closed doors greeted us. Molly's lackey opened one and pushed us inside. The addition of homey furnishings and toiletries to what appeared to have been an office made my stomach clench. It meant this was premeditated. They set this up with the intention of capturing us, or at least capturing someone.

Cold metal slid between my wrists and the zip tie sprung away. The woman snipped off Ezra's, then spun from the room before he could turn around. She slammed the door and the lock clicked.

I untangled my backpack from my arms, then pulled it back on properly, even though there was nothing of value left inside unless I could Houdini my way out of the room using a hair tie and ancient receipts from Gem's.

Ezra squatted, metal scraping on metal as he prodded something into the keyhole. I wanted to ask him if he'd learned how to pick locks with the sole intention of breaking into his neighbors' homes, but instead I said, "You said you had an idea about why she's doing this."

He straightened and turned around. "From what she's told me about her childhood, her dad was incredibly paranoid that some kind of end of the world event would happen someday, and he hammered that into his kids. I had no idea about her hoarding of survival supplies until months into us dating when she confessed that she was spending beyond her means and wanted me to help her create a budget. She has this huge closet of water purifiers and radiation tablets and God knows what else. It's probably all here in the rec center now." He rubbed his face and let out a weary sigh. "I should have seen this coming. Whenever something stressful happens she grasps for whatever she can control. Supplies. People."

That sounded like a terrible upbringing, but I had parental issues too and didn't capture people as a result. "Maybe she's trying to prove something now that she's in an actual apocalyptic situation. You think Daddy would be proud of her?"

Ezra huffed. "I bet you're right. She'd probably love to blow up the alien mothership herself like the final boss in a video game."

"I don't think there's a mothership."

"The point is that we're not doing things her way. She tried to use whatever ploy she could to get us to join her – metal detectors, pretending to care about our safety – but if we aren't going to play along, then she's going to ensure we don't get in her way. And if she can make me suffer in the process, then that's a bonus."

"Why does she hate you so much? Does it have to do with the robbery thing?"

"Yeah." He turned back to the door lock. "She used to live in Rawlins – so did I – and she was the UPS driver."

"I remember." I'd complained more than once about her stuffing boxes between the bars of the stair railings and dumping packages in the snow without knocking.

"My actions directly got her fired." He jammed an object into the keyhole, and when the doorknob didn't turn, he battered his shoulder against the wood. "It didn't happen like she said. I don't go around randomly robbing people."

"It's calculated?"

It was supposed to be a joke, but he turned to me, hurt in his eyes.

"Sorry," I said. "Look, I have questions, but they're not important right now. We need to get out of here."

"It *is* important. Maybe I can't do anything about your romantic feelings for me – or lack thereof – but I don't want you scared of me or thinking I'm a horrible person." He pulled a credit card from his wallet and slid it between the doorframe and the door. "My neighbor was stealing my mail for years. Packages would go missing; my abuela would send me birthday cards with cash inside that I never got. I knew it was him, but I couldn't prove it. I was dating Molly at the time and started asking her to bring the packages into my house, even if I wasn't home, so my neighbor wouldn't take them, but she wasn't always the driver. I had something important coming in the mail, so I set up porch cameras." He wiggled the credit card too hard, and it snapped in half. He swore in Spanish and threw it on the ground. "I caught my neighbor red-handed on video, picking up a package from my steps. But when I went to the police, they said it looked like he was only 'moving it' so it wouldn't be hit by sprinklers. I insisted they question him, but they brushed me off. I was so mad that the next day, when my neighbor was at work, I took *his* mail."

His Adam's apple bobbed. "He had cameras too."

"Shit." I realized I was hovering over him, so I sat on the cot and dug my fingers into the thin mattress. "Let me guess. This time the police cared."

"Of course they did. I was a brown man stealing from my white neighbor, and there was video proof and mail with his name on it in my possession." He slumped onto the cot and it groaned, the legs sagging. "They pulled my own video evidence to half-heartedly see my side, but all it proved was that the UPS driver was walking into my house without knocking – sometimes staying for an hour, on the clock. UPS fired her."

I cringed, imagining what a sensory hell jail would be, on top of all the other horrors that went on there. "That sucks so bad. What about your leather armchairs and the globe sitting on your coffee table."

"What about them?"

"Did the country club press charges?"

This time, Ezra laughed. "Nah, I got away clean."

"Okay, but I don't want you to risk more jail time for swiping the whipped cream from your job. That canned shit is not worth it."

"We're already in a jail. And I doubt I have a job to go back to."

A shadow drifted, and I waited, expecting Molly. When the door didn't open, I pounded on it. "Hey!"

Ezra pushed through objects on a tiny desk in the corner, producing paperclips and a nail file. He strode to the door and kicked it. "Let us out!" He tried poking the nail file into the keyhole, but it was too big.

"I sort of wish you really were a thief who excelled at breaking into houses."

He snorted. "Thanks, by the way, for not immediately believing her exaggerations. And for trying to defend me." After bending a paperclip open, he jiggled it in the lock. "I moved to Muddy Gap to start over somewhere new. Thought a small town where no one knew me would be great. I had a work-from-home job for a bit, but the company went under, and I started bartending. It is true that it pays better than real estate, but I couldn't get hired on as an agent again. I tried.

Anyway, everything was okay until I realized that Molly had moved here too. I think her situation was the same as mine – needing a fresh start and a new job – but as soon as she spotted me in the post office, things got ugly. Apparently she thought I moved here on purpose to, like, follow her or something. Gossip was rampant." He shook his head. "I am so tired of small-town drama."

"Same here." I peered through the filmy door glass. "Swear I saw someone walking around out there."

"I'm sure you did." Ezra grunted and threw down his paperclip. "Open this damn door!"

"I bet these jerkoffs have a secret handshake." There could be objects in the room we hadn't utilized, but all I could think of was egg sacs bursting open, interdimensional crabs or insects bristling with fangs skittering out and growing. Their environment spreading, consuming the town as they consumed the survivors. Tiny creatures invading my nostrils, my mouth, my eyes. Flesh picked from my bones until they were clean and shiny, eventually buried under drifts of orange sand.

Ezra's arms wrapped around me, and he guided me to the cot. "It's okay." He pulled a blanket – one of those pilly felt ones with ribbon edging – from the top of the filing cabinet and wrapped it around me. I wanted to tell him I wasn't trembling from cold, but I pressed my nose into his neck instead.

A soft groan escaped him, and his arms contracted tighter around me. He clearly wanted my affection, but I thought he'd wanted it before too. I followed the contours of his profile, the outcropping of his nose and cliff of lips. That dramatic mustache that said he probably knew how to make drinks far fancier than his dive bar patrons wanted. His lashes were so beautifully long, the scent of him filling my lungs. I couldn't stop my mouth from moving. "I'm not disposable."

His arms slipped away from me. "Of course you're not. Oh, Jesus. I really screwed up."

"So you've been saying."

"You aren't a mistake. You're not just a quick fuck." He raked a hand through his curls, and I could see him fighting for the words he was looking for. "I wanted to do the whole romance bit with you. Wanted to take you on a date somewhere nice where we could talk, have some drinks. I wanted more flirty texts. Things I'd think about to propel me through the week until I saw you again. Wanted to buy you little gifts so you'd think about me the same way. When we were sitting on the trunk of the car and you invited me to kiss you, that was great. But I got carried away. I was thinking, 'We might die out here. I need to seize the moment'."

"And we did. And now you regret it."

"Only because I wish I'd waited so we could take our time. I like you a lot, and I instantly regretted getting hot and heavy with you so fast. Then you mentioned being inexperienced, and that made it worse. Maybe you don't feel bad for how it happened, but that doesn't help me because I have this silly romantic fantasy built up in my mind. Which you keep managing to crush."

"Really?" Having someone want to savor each little interaction with me, to have me at the center of their daydreams, was such a foreign concept that I was waiting for a punchline.

I was never allowed to call Aunt Georgina "Mom" because my mother was going to get her life together and come back for me. She was going to be the mom she was supposed to be. Aunt Georgina had believed that, and so had I. No matter how much I loved Auntie, it hadn't taken away the pain of my mother's actions and the realization that I'd been raised on a lie.

After that, entertaining fantasies about how I wanted things to happen – romantic or otherwise – wasn't something I indulged in the way Ezra did. I couldn't, because reality never turned out the way you expected it to. People let you down. They lied to you and pretended they cared. That always felt much worse than having them be nasty to you from the get-go.

But it was so tempting to believe Ezra, to fall into his words. "I want that all to be true."

"It is true." He reached for my hand. I let his fingers slide over my knuckles and across my palm. My heart throbbed as he leaned closer, the heat of his skin and sugared scent of his cologne trying to push out the hesitation in my head.

Standing abruptly, I shook out my fingers, then walked to the tiny window inset in the door. "I don't want to be thrown away."

"I won't do that."

"I don't know how to believe you."

His voice came out slightly strained, not quite a plea. "Let me prove it to you. Let's have our date."

"What?"

"I'd still love to go to *The Lounge* with you, but I'm not sure that's going to happen, you know? So let's make this our date. We'll pretend. What are you ordering?"

"Um..." I wasn't sure if I'd say yes to an actual date with Ezra anymore – my head and heart were telling me completely different things – but this was only pretend. "It's *The Lounge*, so definitely alphabet pie. They have others, but you have to have alphabet."

"You aren't going to have an entree first?"

"Oh. Well, they don't have bologna."

After waiting a beat, he said, "You don't eat other things? Just bologna sandwiches and pie?"

"Mostly. But we already had this conversation, and I don't want to talk about my weird eating habits."

"Let's pretend there's bologna on the menu then. The best bologna you can get. The softest bread."

My stomach groaned. "Okay. And aged gouda."

"Perfect. I'm ordering a steak, medium rare, a baked potato with sour cream, and a side salad. And a cocktail. You want one?"

"A couple two three of them." I sat beside him and tucked my hands between my knees. "Are you going to eat alphabet pie with me? You didn't eat any of that coconut cream earlier, and you looked like you wanted some. I don't like that you're feeling bad about how you look."

He shrugged. "I got over what Molly said by the time I pulled the pie out of the fridge – silly to let her comments hurt me when you say I have a better ass than Julio Manhammer – but if I'd eaten any, she probably would have made some snide remark, and then *you* would have gotten into an argument with her. I just didn't feel like dealing with that over a flavor of pie I don't even like that much."

"I would have kicked her out of the house. Should have done that anyway. So you're okay? Because there's nothing wrong with the way you are. I like your belly and that round, perky ass."

A smile crept onto his face. "I'm okay, but you can keep talking."

Oh no. This was becoming far less pretend now. I scratched at the smear of alien egg on the knee of my jeans. "How many cocktails have I had at this point?"

"I'd say one, unless you're pounding them."

"Well... when I get to three, I'll tell you that you look like you could crush my skull between your thighs, and I'm here for it."

He snorted.

"Now, you gonna have alphabet pie with me?"

"Sure. What flavor is it?"

"You never saw the article I wrote on it back in November."

"Should I have?"

I shrugged. "It went viral. It's what I became known for." Now I was going to be known for miserably stuffing my face with peanut butter pie that I scooped off the road. "Anyway, it's cinnamon flavored. The alphabet noodles are cooked with cinnamon candies, and they absorb the flavor. The syrup reduction is used to create a pudding, and the noodles and minced pears are folded in. It's a nice pink color. It comes in a pastry crust and is topped with whipped cream and more noodles. Sounds disgusting, and I have no idea what the original recipe tasted like, but *The Lounge*'s version is excellent."

His brow furrowed. "Hm. Well, considering this is hypothetical, I'll eat it with you."

"Okay, with that settled, now's the lull where we sip our cocktails and wait for the food to come because we can't think of anything to say."

"Speak for yourself. I have all kinds of things I want to know about you."

"Really?" I hadn't expected that, so used to everyone bristling at my opinions. And I was alone, isolated for much of the day, with only people on the internet to chat with. But I often pissed them off too, because every topic online somehow turned into an argument.

The guys I'd been with in the past hadn't wanted me for anything but my body once we'd been together in person. And here was Ezra, trying to woo me the classic way despite the fact that we were stuck in a cell and the town might be gone before we slept together again. Not that I was planning on sleeping with him again. Definitely not.

"What's your middle name?" he asked.

"Something really gendered."

"You should give yourself a new one. Are there parts of your body that bother you?"

"I hate the bags under my eyes, and my knees dimple weird, but I'm not self-conscious of my weight, even though I know there are people who feel bad about being too thin as well. I have lower muscle tone than I should, but it makes me more androgynous, which I like." I paused. "Or did you mean body dysphoria? Sometimes. I have a dress I love but never wear because it makes my shoulders look huge. People comment on how much they like my hair, but I get hung up on how thin it is at the temples. I don't know what I'm going to do when it starts to recede more." And it wasn't like I could refer to how my dad's hair looked to know how mine might turn out. I tucked my hands under my thighs. "Can we change the subject?"

"Of course. What do you want to do after this? I think we should hit a pet store and buy you some new fish."

"That would be a nice gift. I've always wanted some glass tetras. And ghost catfish. They're transparent. All their bones are visible. Just a whole tank of see-through fish."

"Sounds like an alien" – he rubbed his face and some of his words were lost – "would dream up."

I sat up straight. "What? Say that again."

"I said, sounds like an alien. Something a sci-fi writer would dream up."

When we'd been sitting on the back of Ezra's car, eating pie and salsa, I asked him if he thought we were stuck in a dream. I was joking, trying to avoid talking about my mom and my ninth birthday, but maybe the idea wasn't any more preposterous than little green men who used their flying saucer's tractor beam to levitate cows.

The library books were wrong. Men in Black arriving to wipe your memory; crocodile people appearing in your bedroom at night; spaceships that would suck up campers in the remote Idaho wilderness and never bring them back. Maybe not all of it was fake, but trying to apply any of those stories to this situation wouldn't help.

I emptied my mind of all childhood memories of borrowed books with dried jelly stuck to the pages and tablecloths that said *OUTTA THIS WORLD*.

The light in the sky wasn't necessarily a craft. It wasn't necessarily an explosion. It flashed, burst – a bubble, sending something down. A creature with psychic power that could make people forget to be concerned about invasion. A creature that could crumple reality and wish its native habitat into existence.

Goosebumps erupted across my body. One of my childhood memories *had* helped – thinking about vintage video game puzzles. There was another one of those *Legend of Zelda* games I'd played. A black and white one where the hero's ship wrecked.

"You ever play that old game where you're washed ashore on an island you can't get off of? And the residents tell you they're all part of this whale's dream? In order to escape, you have to fight through dungeons, get to the whale, and wake it up. But when you do, the island, all the people, everything, vanishes." I scrubbed my arms. "We can't find a saucer wreck because there isn't one. No mechanical hums that hurt my ears or laser guns vaporizing people. Everything has been organic so far. Environment is being generated, but it isn't futuristic housing. It's sand, rain, rocks." My mouth was running too fast. I wasn't sure he could even understand me. "What if there's one alien, and it used a lot of energy to get here. It's hiding in a building or underground, trying to psychically create its terrain, one ingredient at a time, but it's difficult because Wyoming isn't like home, wherever that is. God, I wish I had the same power right now. I'd generate myself a sandwich."

Ezra stared, his teeth pressing into his lip. "So what would we need to do? Wake the alien up?"

"No, we need to kill it. And fast."

12

I pulled open a desk drawer. After dumping the contents on the floor, I did the same with the next one. Packs of gum, paperclips, staple removers, and a Tupperware container of almonds dashed against the tile and skittered away. "There has to be something in here that can help us get out, because obviously no one is coming back to bring us food."

"I don't know if that lock can be picked. Not by a layman like me, anyway."

"Then we get a hammer and break off the knob, or we use one of the legs of the cot as a battering ram." They were nice ideas, but I wasn't sure they would work. Molly had taken my hammer and knives, and the cot legs had already threatened to give out under Ezra's and my combined weight.

Almonds crunched under my heels as I shook out more drawers. A ring of keys caught my eye. I snatched them up and stopped at the door. I couldn't imagine why an office in the rec center needed a double cylinder lock, unless it wasn't one and Molly had simply reversed the knob so she could lock us in at the press of a button, but keys were promising. My frustration built with each one I inserted into the lock, every prayer that the knob would turn going unanswered. I hurled them onto the floor, where they bounced once, then slid under the cot.

Ezra hovered over me. "Sunday morning, after I got off work at 2am, I almost stayed in Casper instead of driving home. My friend and I drink together sometimes, and I'll crash on her

177

couch. But I wasn't in the mood. If I'd stayed in Casper, you and I wouldn't have gotten together to look at the shells in the microscope, and I'd be alone in this cell with no idea what the hell is happening in town."

"If you'd stayed in Casper, you probably wouldn't have made it back here. Or you'd be trapped in bent reality out on the highway. And I'd be in the fetal position beneath my tank of dead fish."

Normally after a taxing day, I'd be ready to sleep for twelve hours to recoup all the energy I'd lost, but all I wanted was the damn cell door open so we could hunt for the alien, this Dreamer trying to take over Muddy Gap. When I was drained, I needed familiar comforts. My earplugs, my pie, my blog, and my alone time. The Dreamer probably needed the same. That didn't stir any amount of empathy, but the idea was something I could leverage. The more of its habitat it surrounded itself with – sand and shells and the clear stones full of rainbows – the more at home it would feel, and the more powerful it would get. We needed to find the largest concentration of xenoterrain, and we'd find the alien.

Shouts drifted from somewhere beyond the door, and I froze. "You think they're playing ping pong? Or being eaten by whatever came out of the eggs?"

Ezra grimaced. "Maybe we don't want to leave this room."

"If we don't, we'll be a tasty, stationary target."

There were screws on either side of the doorknob, but no screwdriver. I picked up his shattered credit card and stuck the corner into the head of a screw, trying to focus on something other than face-eating aliens. "This credit company is really bad. You shouldn't use them."

"I'll remember that if we make it out of here."

"I'm serious. Their interest rates are the worst. Hope you can pay off whatever you have on there." I twisted the card. It warped and popped from the screw's channel. I shoved it back in.

"It's maxed out," he said. "I used it to buy my living room furniture after I got out of jail. Still haven't paid it off."

"See? Exactly. Better to not use credit cards at all. Too much temptation. I was addicted to auction sites for a while, buying vintage clothes. Sometimes the bids would go much higher than the item was worth, but I wanted to win, so I'd keep bidding. Totally maxed out my card."

"Competitive, are you?"

"Maybe." The corner of the card snapped off and I threw it down in disgust. I searched through the mess on the floor and picked up the staple remover. It was pen-shaped, with a rounded metal end for scooping out staples. It fit perfectly into the screw, and I grinned. "Molly wants to be the hero in this alien-defeating business? She should know that I'm full of opinions, I'm always right, and I'm going to kick her ass in this scenario." I wasn't always right, but in this instance, I was certain I was. My gut felt it. The alien was out there, hiding, dreaming. "Taisha and Trevor can help us, though we'll have to invent some other ploy to get him to work with us without messing up his brain. Geocaching or something." The screw turned and thick chips of white paint flaked away from the knob.

Ezra pushed up the cot and unscrewed one of the wobbly legs, hefting it like a club. "I don't want to hurt my ex-girlfriend, but–"

"She threatened to hit me in the face with a nail-studded baseball bat. If she attacks and you hesitate to smack her with an aluminum cot leg, I'm going to be really disappointed. Besides, it might not be her you need to hit." I twisted the screw until it popped out and chattered across the floor, then went to work on the next one. My fingers ached from turning the staple remover, and this screw didn't want to budge as easily. The metal head of the tool slipped from the channel, stripping away some of the X shape. I pushed harder, carefully turning the screw until it extended far enough for me to twist by hand. I flicked it away and wrenched on the doorknob. The assembly broke apart, and the other side of the knob clattered onto the hall floor. I peered through the hole at the flickering fluorescent lighting, then tried to shove the door open. It shuddered in its frame, but held fast.

Ezra nudged me away, then battered his shoulder against the wood. The door popped open just enough to see light through the cracks.

"Is there another lock?" I asked.

"I think it's a slide chain. A short one." He backed up, then rammed his full weight into the door. It flew open and slammed into the wall.

"Yes!" I handed him the cot leg and followed him into the hallway. The lights buzzed and flickered, the neighboring cell's door was closed.

I strained for voices. My contacts said it was seven-thirty, still light out. Molly was probably busy rationing out potassium *iodide* pills to her gang and deciding which one of them she would eat first if they had to resort to cannibalism.

We rounded the corner of the hall, and Ezra stopped so suddenly that I slammed into his back. A blank wall stood before us.

"I swear this is where they brought us in from," he said.

"I thought it was too, but my sense of direction is terrible." I turned back, passing our open cell and side-stepping the broken doorknob. I was met with another wall.

Twisting my hair around my fingers, I said, "We walked through the room with ping pong tables, down an open hallway, into a shorter hall with two doors. These are those two doors. Right?"

He slowly nodded, then pressed on the wall like it led to a hidden passage. "What's happening?"

I opened the door adjacent to our cell, met with another room of pilly blankets and toilet paper. "Where the hell is the exit?"

Eyes wide, Ezra peered inside, then strode the short distance to the other wall blocking our escape.

It was obvious now why we couldn't hear voices or antagonize anyone hard enough to get them to open the door. I bit my lip until pain blossomed. "It's like those hamster tubes. But some asshole kid put caps on each end and we're stuck in the middle." Did the alien know we'd caught on? Maybe it could sense our thoughts and plans and since it couldn't stop us mentally, it was stopping us physically. I wondered if it was mad that I called it the Dreamer and compared it to a flying whale from a video game.

A hairline blade of light cut through the darkness of the other cell. I walked in and squinted at it. At first glance, the room looked normal, but upon closer inspection there was a small gap in the wall, the paint pattern of the ninety-degree angle not joining up properly. Cool wind and the cat-piss scent of rabbitbrush buffeted my face. I pushed on the wall. Drywall cascaded onto my head, fragile and crumbly like a graham cracker pie crust. I shook it from my hair, took a step back and kicked the wall. The impact reverberated up my leg and knocked me off balance.

The thin veneer of drywall disintegrated, not revealing insulation or wooden studs, but a heart-lifting sunset sky, kissed in tangerine and candy pink.

"Ezra!"

He ran into the room, hesitated only a moment at the sight, then pulled me out into open space. Weeds snatched at our legs, chalky drywall flaking from my shoulders. I pulled in a deep breath, trying to get my bearings. A road wrapped around the rec center, the parking lot studded with an excessive amount of arc sodium lights. Or had. In its place were dunes of sand, a more glittering and vibrant orange from the cast of sunset. Pools of water punctuated the drifts, and those tiny red plants with frilly and flocked leaves sprouted here and there. My truck was nowhere in sight.

I turned back to the rec center and let out a squeal. As I hauled Ezra backward, I rolled my ankle and landed on my ass, pulling him down with me. The rec center now looked like a child's block house that had been kicked to shit. And a complete wall, along with some of the floor tiles, was *floating*, suspended in the air directly above where we'd been standing. Wind gusted, and something slid off the hovering chunk of building and sailed to the ground – the packaging from the "healthy" microwave dinner. It caught in a bush, then tumbled away in the breeze.

My chest heaved, heartbeat pounding in my ears. Whether it was coincidence, or the Dreamer really did know my plans, things were speeding up.

I pushed to my feet and shook away sand and drywall.

Ezra sat on the ground, still gaping at the Rubik's Cube mess of the rec center. "We're lucky our room wasn't a part of that. Just suddenly glitched, with us inside it." He clutched his belly like he was picturing his own body sliced in the same manner as the building, part of him on the ground and the other half floating in the sky.

The image was too vivid, the thought of bright red entrails spiraling up into space, that I doubled over, puking up stomach acid and coconut cream. Ezra held back my hair – a gentleman – and I groaned and wiped my mouth.

"Does this mean buildings are no longer safe?" I pulled a hair tie from my wrist and wound my hair into a bun, then turned in a circle. "Maybe nothing is. If we're standing out in the open, the environment could still shift and dump a house on top of us, or erupt with bigger dunes that swallow us whole."

My stomach dropped as soon as the realization did. "I thought finding the biggest accumulation of terrain would lead us to the alien. But if there's terrain everywhere, there will be no way to know."

The Dreamer could be right under our feet. It could be

existing partially in some other dimension, only visible when it turned a certain way. A constantly shifting foreign landscape would prevent us from gathering any clues.

My idea of digging random holes now sounded as pointless and foolish as Molly said it was. We were tiny specks in a growing alien desert, and there was nothing we could do.

"Ezra… We're not going to make it." Something tickled my leg. Little translucent creatures – crabs or scorpion-like things – teemed around my boots and sped across the cuffs of my jeans. I stumbled back and swiped them away. "Oh. Ew!"

Ezra stomped on them, teeth bared, then gripped me by the shoulders and hauled me down a dune. I tripped over stones, splashed through briny water, and trampled budding plants. The ground evened out, giving way to Wyoming prairie and segments of sidewalk. Foothills sat in the distance, silhouetted by the setting sun, and cottonwood trees and rooftops welcomed us back to town.

We cut down a side street and passed my complex, but following the road didn't lead us to Ezra's. Huge gaps spanned between the houses, sand built up in the creases. I spied Ms Pierce's house, her door still standing open and hose lying in the grass, but it wasn't in the right location, sitting at the twisted end of a cul-de-sac instead of three homes down from Ezra's street.

I swallowed. "At least nothing over here is floating."

Ezra kicked a red plant, and it lifted easily out of the sand. "And no more crabs. I bet they came out of the gooey eggs."

A portion of a parking lot, Gem's judging by the shopping carts, sat beside Ms Pierce's house. Twilight bled into sunset tones, but the shade wasn't right. A strange green cast – akin to the light flaring from the UFO – hung across the sky like a veil.

A hard lump formed in my throat. I found Ezra's hand and squeezed. Despite the fresh air and open space, this felt more like a cell than the rec center room had. We couldn't flee town, and even if we did, the alien's influence would surely keep spreading. Or it would chop off one of its limbs, which would grow into a new alien that would take up residence somewhere else. Maybe it had some other kind of asexual reproduction, like budding, or maybe it had come ripe with eggs, which had all hatched into those little crabs that Ezra smashed.

I thought of myself as a tiny fish again, a tetra in my tank, sensitive and weak. Only this time I was belly up, bobbing in the current with my dead eyes staring out at nothing.

My breath was coming too fast, chest a frantic bellows. Ezra pulled me through a sand-filled alley, back toward my complex. I wanted my trappings of home: my pies in the freezer, my fish, the internet. But only one of those things was still there, and filling my stomach with honey-lavender would only give me something new to puke up.

A chunk of Main Street sat askew, like someone had torn off a piece of a pop-up book about small towns and dropped it onto a sandy beach. The streetlights still worked, and a neon "OPEN" sign glowed from the front window of the saloon that had been across from the thrift store.

I tugged Ezra in its direction. "Want to go to work? I was promised cocktails."

"You want to drink?"

"I'm starting to freak out. A drink or two will help calm me down. I try to avoid using it as a coping mechanism. Seems like a great time, though."

"You're out of ideas." His shoulders dropped, the hope waning in his eyes.

I couldn't let him down. There had to be some other solution to all of this, but too much worry was getting in the way for me to see it. "Just for the moment. I just want one drink."

"Okay. Let's go drink then."

The door chimed as we pushed inside, and we were met with a dim ambiance that smelled like cigarette smoke and beer-soaked wood. The jukebox slowly strobed in the corner, and sticky tables and intimate booths filled the space between.

Ezra rounded the bar and rummaged through bottles. "What do you want?"

"Something sweet."

"Sex on the Beach?"

"I'll take the sex, but I've had my fill of beaches."

He snatched a glass from the back counter. I put my head in my hands and shut my eyes. The nerves inside me were lit up as much as the beckoning neon sign, and plans, gut feelings, and memories of dreaming video game whales all jumbled together into a knot I couldn't untangle.

Muddy Gap would be swallowed within a number of days, and if Ezra and I didn't disappear like the rest of the inhabitants, we'd probably get poisoned and die trying to eat those little red plants.

Something thudded on the bar, and I opened my eyes. A gradient of orange and crimson filled the tall shot glass, but chartreuse bled into it – a miniature of the invading alien sky outside – with a top layer of inky black.

He pointed to it. "No beaches. Sex With an Alligator instead."

"That sounds… highly unpleasant."

Ezra had made himself one too. We clinked them together without toasting to our future or health, and I tipped it to my lips. A bitter kick dissolved into citrus tang, soothed with sugary sweetness. Fire raced into my stomach and sudden lightheadedness threatened to sever me from my body.

I leaned my elbows against the bar. "The aggressive spice of anise, a burst of mouth-puckering lemon, and cloying raspberry ripe on the vine. This drink is a slap, balmed by a kiss. Seven stars."

"You can review cocktails too, huh?" He held up a finger. "I have an idea."

"At least someone does." I shut my eyes and massaged my temples, my thoughts trying to scatter, but the *whoosh* of canned whipped cream yanked me back to the bar.

He squirted a dollop on top of a creamy, buff-colored drink. "Try this."

I sipped it. Vanilla, fiery cinnamon, and crisp apple warmed my throat.

"Does it taste like alphabet pie?"

"No. Tastes like spiced cider."

He pouted.

"It's good though."

"How many stars?"

"You can have all my stars. I bet your regulars love your drinks. Was that your idea? Not something to stop the alien?"

His face fell, and he held out his arms in a helpless gesture. "I'm not as clever as you are."

I wasn't as clever as he thought I was, clearly. I took a long draft of the drink, which was reminiscent of biting Autumn days, the promise of food spreads, distant relatives, and the first flakes of snow. "I think understanding and a big heart are better qualities."

He poured himself a shot of whiskey and pounded it, then thudded the glass back onto the bar. "Those aren't doing us any good."

"I disagree. Arguing won't change my mind, so don't try."

"It's okay to not know what to do."

There was a finality to the words, like he was giving me permission to lie down in the sand and die. That thought held the weight of our failure, but the pressure it relieved was tempting. *Stop fighting. Close your eyes. It'll be over soon.*

There was no solution. No dungeons to fight through, no puzzles to solve, no final boss battle. This wasn't a video game or a library book story about flying saucers, or fodder to make my blog popular. It was me and Ezra, in an hourglass filling with sand.

I picked at a rip in the seat of my vinyl stool, pulling out a clot of stuffing.

"Take a breath," he said.

"I'm not panicking. If anything, I feel too composed right now. Too resigned."

"No, no. I mean..." He gestured to the hazy darkness around us. "I can see you fighting for a way to fix this, but take a breather. We're okay at the moment. Right?"

"No! We're not okay." I tore another chunk of stuffing from my seat. "And *no one* is going to be okay if we can't stop this. Not the people in Casper. Or my family in Rapid City." Aunt Georgina and Uncle Joe would die, their home and my familiar spaces of childhood bisected and suspended in the air. Elizabeth and her baby would be gone. Billie and her fashion. Abraham and whatever was important in his life.

Ezra gently gripped my biceps and looked into my eyes. I glanced away, focusing on the hoop ring in his earlobe instead. He said, "Right now in this bar. You and me. We are okay. Yes?"

If I looked out the front door at the deepening green sky and dunes of sand, it would prove otherwise, so I concentrated on his earring and the neon signs glowing in my peripheral vision. The bar below my elbow was sturdy. The wood planking beneath my feet was solid. Physically I was fine, and so was Ezra.

I swallowed. "We're okay."

He gave a satisfied nod. "Let's sit in a booth and listen to the jukebox. Or play pool."

There were a dozen reasons I could think of to argue against it, but the one that came out of my mouth was, "I don't know how to play."

He walked to the wall and pulled down two cues. When he rolled them across the green felt of a pool table, one of them wobbled slightly, and he frowned and put it back. After handing me a cue, he set a rack on the table and arranged the billiard balls inside.

Carefully pulling the rack away, he nudged a wayward ball back into formation, then aligned his stick with the cue ball. "I'll break." He took his shot, and the balls clacked and scattered across the table. One thudded into a pocket.

He pulled it out. "I'm stripes. You're solids." He took another turn, then stepped back, gesturing for me to try.

It looked so easy, but I was going to mess it up and embarrass myself. "You're going to wipe the floor with me."

Sliding his arm around my waist, he gently bent me forward over the pool table. I made a small noise in my throat. He wrapped his hand around mine on the stick, angling it at the ball. "I'll help you. Do you see the circle of light on the cue ball from the fixture over the table? Try to strike it there."

With his crotch pressed against my ass, his lips beside my ear, it was difficult to concentrate. "Which one do I hit?"

His mustache tickled my neck. "Any of them but the eight ball." As I lined up my shot, he said, "Give me the best stroke you can."

The stick scratched across the table, missing the cue ball entirely. I straightened and glared at Ezra, who blinked back innocently. "Is that really what it's called?"

His mouth twitched in a smile. "Yes. Would you rather I tell you to thrust your stick?"

The innuendo and the way he was holding me would have been playful and sexy in some other situation, but my nerves were misfiring like I had a terrible hangover, and the lights from the jukebox were jabbing a soft spot in my brain.

I squeezed the cue stick, the billiard balls blurring in my vision. "I can't do this."

Something in my voice made Ezra release me. His footsteps receded, and a glass thudded against the bar. If I couldn't figure out how to stop the alien, there might not be a tomorrow to wake up to. But I had no idea what to do, and I was ruining what little time I had left. Ezra was the only good thing going for me, and he was trying to give me room for comfort.

The grating noise of a whipped cream can filled the room, and I winced. Ezra sat at the bar, hunched over a new drink. He pounded it back, then put his face in his hands.

I stopped beside him. "Hey..."

He glanced at me, his cheeks flushed from the alcohol, then turned back to his drink.

"I'm glad you're here with me," I said.

He twisted his glass, his nostrils flaring and lips bunched, and I'd made him upset without meaning to and wasn't that such a *me* thing to do?

"Ezra, I–I want your comfort. I want your dates and your gifts and... One thing I know is no matter what happens, I don't want to be alone for it. Do you want to spend the night in my bed?"

His eyes widened. "Yes."

I cupped his cheeks and kissed him deeply, filling it with all my desires and all my fears. He moaned, returning my volley with the same intensity, an aggressive dance that left my lips aching, my tongue lingering with the taste of spice and cream.

We were kissing like the world was ending. Because it was.

I panted and wiped my wet chin on my sleeve, my skin chafed from his mustache.

Ezra's lips were glossy and reddened, his breath whistling through his nose. "I wish we could have more dates, though. More courtship."

I glanced out the door at the eerie green tint on the pavement and buildings. "I don't think there's time for that. Not when neither of us has a plan for how to stop this. I don't want to give up. But what choice do I have?" My chest tightened, guilt and obligation pulling me down onto my stool. "It shouldn't be my sole responsibility to save the world! No one would choose me to be an action hero. No one even wants me as their neighbor!"

"That isn't true. Sam seems to like you. Trevor does." Ezra held up his hands. "I don't mean romantically."

"It doesn't matter if they do. We're going to die, and we won't even have marked graves."

Ezra stared into his glass, his fingernail digging into a nick in the bar. "All I was suggesting is that we take a breather to play pool, but when you put it like that..."

A breather. Maybe our last breath. "Come home with me?"

He cupped my cheek, his thumb rasping across the stubble on my jaw. "Can I still take it slow?"

"Definitely."

I slid off the stool, then gripped the bar to steady myself. It had been a long time since I'd had alcohol, and drinking it on an empty stomach probably didn't help. I downed the rest of Ezra's failed attempt at making something taste like alphabet pie. Clinging to his arm, I pushed through the door.

A lime-green sky hung above, and I took small comfort that at least the constellations peeking through were still our own. Tiny crab-things scuttled away from our feet.

"Do you think Taisha and Trevor are still in your house?" I asked.

"I hope so. Hope they're safe."

None of us were safe. "I like the idea of Molly trapped in one of those rooms in the rec center. That's mean, huh? I'm always mean."

"You're not. You're a good person."

Tears burned in my eyes. I thought of Aunt Georgina, wooden spoon in her hand, glasses slipping down her nose. Uncle Joe, snoozing on the couch. He'd probably fallen asleep watching video compilations of people failing at simple tasks. Or exceling with ease at something unbelievably difficult. He liked them both equally.

I'd been an exhausting child, there was no denying it. But Uncle and Auntie didn't love me less for it. Didn't love me less for being dumped on them, for not looking or acting like their other kids.

There was no way to get a message out to them now, and I desperately wanted to tell them I loved them. "I should have messaged my family more. Should have tried harder to find out who my dad is, even if it meant talking to my mom. Wish I'd worn more lipstick. Eaten more pie. Had more sex. I've never even had a boyfriend. Not really. How sad is that?"

Ezra turned to me. "You have one now, if that's what you want me to be."

My heart swelled. I pressed my face to his shoulder. "What do you wish you'd done differently?"

"Wish I hadn't wasted six months of my life in jail," he muttered. "Wish I'd gotten more tattoos. My mom always had the best garden, and it seemed so big when I was a kid. Full of poppies and bees. I wanted to get that as a full sleeve. Wish I'd gone to more movies. More museums. Been able to be more romantic with you."

"You know what? Even if there's no town to wake up to tomorrow – even if there's no waking up – we can do some of those things tonight. C'mon."

13

I wasn't sure how Ezra had gone his whole life without watching *Right Side Down*. I'd figured he owned a copy of it just like me. He sat on the bed with his slice of pistachio pie practically untouched, gaze glued to the screen. It was difficult to concentrate, not because I'd seen this movie a hundred times, but I kept glancing out the window, expecting the streetlights and distant bar sign to suddenly shift, or half of my apartment to break off and shoot into the air.

Setting down my plate, I leaned over and twisted the blinds closed.

"Oh my god." Ezra took a bite of pie, then spoke with his mouth full. "Did you see that coming the first time you watched this?"

"No. It's trippy, huh?" It seemed absurd to feel any awe or surprise at a movie when something much more unfathomable was happening directly to us. But it was telling someone else's impossible story, one in which we were only along for the ride and didn't suffer any consequences.

More movies. More pie. Check. I couldn't do anything about Ezra wanting to visit museums, unless one was dropped directly onto us. Pastry flaked onto my plate as I took my final bite. After carrying it to the sink, I rummaged through a drawer and found a permanent marker.

Sitting back on the bed, I pushed up the sleeve of Ezra's

shirt, pulled off the marker cap with my teeth, and drew two poppies on his bicep. He watched, smiling, then turned back to the TV.

"If you think you'll pass out, let me know. Not sure how much of a wuss you are when it comes to pain. A full sleeve in one sitting is a lot." I drew bees darting through petals, twisting vines, and dewdrops hanging from buds. It was no masterpiece, and by the time I reached his elbow, I was lightheaded from marker fumes. But it was the best I could give him.

He took the marker, admiring his arm, then pushed me back on the bed. "Can I give you one too?"

"Sure."

After unbuttoning my jeans, he nudged down the waistband of my briefs. I pulled in a breath. Below my navel, he drew a heart, then wrote his name in the center.

"'Property of Ezra?'" I asked.

He capped the marker and unbuttoned my shirt. "No. Giving you my heart."

It was cheesy, but his pleased expression made me hold my tongue. Let him have his romance the way he wanted it, even if that meant him standing in the grass below my window, singing me a ballad.

He slid my shirt off my shoulders, kissing each spot he revealed. I melted into the mattress, helping him shed his own clothing. He caught my wrists, pushed them over my head, and continued his agonizingly slow mission of kissing every inch of me. His stiff cock pressed into my stomach; I squirmed, my whole body vibrating with desire.

"Stop teasing." I tried to pull my arms away, but he clamped down on my wrists, pushing them into the pillow.

A growl rumbled in his throat as he nibbled at my neck. "Pretty sure you like it." His teeth pressed lightly into my flesh, and I groaned. The noise must have been encouraging, because he did it again, leaving soft love bites along my neck. I whimpered and arched my back.

He suddenly released his grip and sat back. "You're fidgeting. Your hands are trembling. Am I stressing you out?"

"No. I was enjoying it."

He reached for me again, but I pushed him back into the sheets. "Too late." I ran my fingers through the carpet on his chest, then squeezed his love handles, admiring all his curves. "You are so hot. You smell fantastic. And your ass always looks like it's two seconds away from bursting the seams of your pants – which I've thought about, in great detail."

He chuckled, then pulled me down on top of him. The salt of his skin stung my tongue as I left pecks along his jaw. I worked my way down his body, but before I could put my mouth on him, he reached into his crumpled jeans on the floor. He produced his wallet and pulled out a condom. "Do you want it? It's grape flavored."

My effort to maintain a neutral face must have failed, because he frowned and said, "What?"

"Molly was right. You like food-based stuff during sex. Whipped cream. Grape condoms. You have a thong made of licorice back at your house?"

A red flush crept up his neck. "I did, but by the time I went to use it, it was hard and brittle."

"Definitely don't want sharp shards of candy near your junk."

He set the condom on the carpet. "I never thought it was weird to like those things. If it makes sex more fun, why not?"

"It's probably not weird. What do I know?" I tore open the packaging and rolled the condom onto him as he settled back into the pillows. It tasted terrible, like stale bubblegum, but I wasn't going to complain. He tolerated my quirks, and I was going to tolerate his.

Ezra moaned and held my hair back from my face. Light flickered through the blinds and my stomach clenched. Maybe this was it – the Dreamer choosing to eliminate my apartment complex next. Well, I was an easy target and no longer a threat. Who was I kidding? I'd never been a threat. My ideas were nice in theory, but meant nothing in the long run. It was probably too late for anyone to rescue us, but my hope was that the authorities took as much stock in what I said as my fans, and the National Guard was waiting on the other side of the distorted highway to blow any new alien offspring straight to Hell.

I wasn't sure I could die with dignity – not in this position – but I preferred to die with my mouth full of Ezra than full of sand.

He gasped my name and drew me back to the present. I took him deeper; his hips moved under me, fists clenched in the sheets. I focused on his quickened breaths, intent to stay here and not let my mind continue to sink. This was our moment and ours alone.

He pulled me up and kissed me deeply, making no comment about the awful grape taste still lingering in my mouth. "I want to make you feel good. Tell me what you want."

I hesitated. "Okay, but if you make a probing joke, we're stopping."

"I swear I won't."

Items rattled as I pulled a box out from under the bed. I retrieved a bottle of lube from within, and a little silver vibrator rolled into a corner. "See that? I had that when I met you the second time. The review company sent it to me and I thought it was lipstick. I was so embarrassed to talk to you, knowing it was in my pocket." The laugh that came up my throat fractured on its way out.

Lines formed around Ezra's mouth. "Are you nervous? I won't do anything you don't want me to."

"No, I just…" It was almost like having "Happy Birthday" sung to me. Attention riveted just to me, someone depending on me to give the right reactions when all I did was get them wrong. "I'm self-conscious having you focused on me now. I'm constantly messing up social situations, and this is a really intimate one. What if I don't– What if I don't moan loud enough or seem excited enou–"

"You're fine." He squirted lube into his hand. "And I'm certain that if I do something wrong, you'll tell me. Such a critic."

I chuckled, and it was steadier than before. "That's right." My heartbeat quickened as he slid his hand between my thighs. "I don't want to think. I don't want to worry. All I want is you right now."

"You have me." He gently slipped a finger inside me. I pressed my forehead to his neck and gripped his back.

His warm breath buffeted my skin as his hand worked. "Relax."

The tightness in my chest eased as I sank back into the pillows. My world had always been one of constant unpleasant sensory bombardment – flickering lights and grating noises and scratchy seams in clothing. And everything in general was actively getting worse out there.

Blades of deepening peridot light cut through the blind slats and across the ceiling. That wasn't my world anymore. It was the Dreamer's. But right now I had soft sheets, a comforting presence, and motivated hands.

My world was this bed. My world was Ezra.

I whispered my desires, but now without the hesitation. Ezra took his time, and when he entered me, it was as slow and romantic as I knew it would be. He thrusted gently, dark eyes half-lidded. My moans were lost against his mouth.

Ezra was the dream I only allowed myself to have in fleeting moments when my guard was down. Someone who wanted me. Someone who would stay.

"You're doing it right," I gasped. "Just thought you should know."

He let out a surprised laugh. "Glad to hear it." He brushed hair from my face, and I held his gaze for as long as I could.

"Promise you're not going to throw me away. Not going to abandon me."

He kissed my temple. "I promise. Here until the end."

The end was taking longer than expected. Early sun streamed through the curtains, washing the wall in a strange shade of chartreuse. I ran a hand across my front, double-checking that I was still here and intact. Ezra's body was hot and heavy, his arm across my throat constricting. I tugged on it. He pulled away and started to roll over, but I caught his arm and draped it over my waist instead.

"Go back to sleep," he murmured. "I'll keep guard."

The muzziness in his voice made me doubt that. "You gonna physically guard me with your body?"

"Mm-hmm. Big spoon protection."

I tried to slide away, and his grip on me tightened. I said, "I'll come back. Just have to pee."

He let me go; I slipped out of bed to the window beside it, stretching my legs. If death was imminent, I wished it would have happened last night, falling asleep in Ezra's arms, more content and secure than I could remember being in ages.

I glanced down at the marker heart below my navel. No matter what happened, I'd cling to last night, to pistachio pie, Ezra's teasing kisses, and the ridiculous image of him trying to put on a licorice thong and the thing shattering.

Poking a finger through the blind slats, I pulled them down and squinted in the glare. Suburban homes and streetlights stretched away from the complex in a bizarre configuration. They'd shifted again, fewer of them than the night before, and a lake had formed in the area where I was fairly certain the post office used to be.

My stomach cramped and I dug my nails into the sill. Don't freak out.

Ezra pawed at my hip from beneath the sheets, and I

snatched his fingers and said, "Maybe the sand will preserve us. We could be mummified together."

"You're romantic too."

I refrained from asking him if he'd been a goth as a teen. Instead, I crossed to the bathroom and relieved myself. On the way back, I stopped and stared at the space where the front door had been. A wall of shelves loaded with junk sat in its place. Stacks of chipped dishes, jumbles of computer cable, and hideous teddy bears missing their eyes. There was even another one of those mini instant cameras I'd tried out in the thrift store.

At least that depressed Christmas tree hadn't appeared in the living room.

Our exit was blocked. The pulse in my neck jittered, blood pounding loud enough to wash out other sounds. Don't freak out. Don't think about it.

I promised Ezra I'd come right back to bed, and that didn't include a detour into panicking. My world was the bed. It was Ezra. And I was going to hold onto that for as long as I needed.

I slid in beside him. He scooped me into a tight embrace and mumbled into my hair. "You were gone forever."

His scent coiled around me, the warmth of his skin soaking into my bones, but it wasn't enough to make me forget about the shelves fused with my wall. Riding with Ezra to the thrift store for instant film to test on the hailshells seemed like an eternity ago. We hadn't even carried out that experiment, too preoccupied by the irate shop owner and all the people in Gem's disappearing. I distantly wondered what the photos would have shown. If I took a picture out the window at the broken puzzle landscape, maybe it would be one giant void. A blackhole, hungry to swallow us.

Ezra had been so freaked out by the photos I took in the store – convinced the rainbow light dancing across the shots meant something – that he hadn't gone to work that night.

I squinted at the edge of shelves visible from my position on the bed. Ezra snored softly. Carefully slipping from his hold, I walked back to the shelf and picked up the camera box. I shook the little instant deal out and checked the film indicator. This one was full and appeared to be unused.

Heading back to the window, I pulled up the blinds, aimed the camera, and clicked. A photo ejected. I tore it from the strip and fanned it back and forth like I'd seen people do in movies. The image slowly resolved, rooftops and green sky and too much sand, but a long band of rainbow light stretched across the frame from some point in the distance. It wasn't a vague smear like the previous photos, but a beam. A line.

An arrow.

I shrieked, and Ezra jerked up in bed, eyes wide. "What? What is it? More crab-things?"

"Ezra!"

"*What?* Is something coming? Is it time?" He leapt up, taking half the sheets with him, and pulled me into his arms. He yanked down the blinds even as I protested, and hauled me back into the bed so quickly I dropped the camera.

Folding himself over me, he pressed his face into my neck. "Don't think about it. Shut your eyes. I'm here with you."

I gasped and struggled to push him away. "Nothing's coming. I got excited. I know what to do now!"

"What to do about what?" His hair was mussed, and a bit of his marker poppies had rubbed away. His arms still circled me protectively, and my heart swelled at the idea that he was willing to use his nude, vulnerable flesh as a shield against whatever horrifying creature was attacking.

"I think I love you," I blurted, then bit down on my tongue. "No, sorry. I shouldn't have said that. Haven't even known you a week."

He gaped, looking more confused than ever, so I smoothed out the instant photo and filled the space with more words. "Xenoterrain appeared in the thrift shop before we got there. There was sand on the floor and those clear chunks of stone.

I took photos, and there was a smeary rainbow on them. You thought it meant something." I held out the photo.

"Can you see this rainbow with your naked eye if you look out the window?"

"No. My UFO books may have let me down, but that one on hauntings is delivering. The light is leading to something. And not a pot of gold."

"The alien. This is a photo of its psychic energy or something." He slapped the bed. "I *knew* it. I knew I was right to be freaked out about those photos. But you said it was nothing, and you're so clever I figured that meant I didn't need to worry about it."

"I shouldn't have discarded evidence so easily. If I'd believed you, maybe we could have found the Dreamer before things got this–"

"All that matters is we know now, and that means we still have a chance."

"I want to do more tests. I could be wrong. I'll try photos in different directions and compare them to this one." And I'd pray I wasn't getting our hopes up for nothing. If the light didn't lead to anything, it would have been better if we'd stayed in bed until the end came. As it was, not knowing what the alien even was made it impossible to know what weapons to bring – not that we had many choices.

Ezra cupped my cheeks and gave me a hard kiss. "Let's get dressed and we'll go test it out."

I glanced at the corner of thrift store shelves blocking our exit. "There's a small problem."

He stopped at the shelves and put his fists on his bare hips. I retrieved the camera from the floor, then walked behind him and squeezed his ass. He startled, then smiled at me.

Even though we needed to test my new theory to see if it actually worked, I couldn't help the surge of joy coursing through me. "Let's just put a foot through the wall like I did before."

He prodded the shelf. "Feels pretty solid."

I dressed and grabbed my earplugs in case the stack of dishes came crashing down. Ezra pulled on his clothes and knocked on the wall in different spots, but each time, he shook his head.

It was a long way to ground level. We didn't have a ladder, and reaching the stair railing while hanging out the window seemed impossible. But I couldn't give up now. Not while there was still a chance.

Heading into the bathroom, I took stock of the room, then yanked back the shower curtain. A rolling desk chair with a split in the seat sat in the tub. Behind it, the office door was embedded into the wall, no doorknob or hinges to indicate it could be pushed open. But a small gap of open space sat between the doorframe and broken-toothed chunks of bath tile. I picked up the toilet plunger and jabbed at the wall. Tile crashed into the tub and across the vinyl chair.

Cringing, I pushed in my earplugs and hammered at the wall. The noise drew Ezra, and he wrapped his fist around a towel and helped me break out the tiles. Chalky dust drifted, my cowboy boots crunching on bits of ceramic and grout. The thrift store lay beyond.

Ezra tapped my shoulder and pointed to his ear. I pulled out my earplug and he said, "We should pack everything we need, because I don't expect us to come back here."

He was right. The place was a mess, and there was no telling whether the apartment would be completely destroyed the next time the landscape shifted.

There wasn't much food to pack – Trevor's bread, half a stick of butter, and a couple slices of pie. Ezra and I chugged the last of the milk and I refilled the jug with water. We gathered a couple other containers, changes of clothes, and knives. With my backpack and a reusable shopping bag stuffed full, I stepped past the tub and ducked into the thrift store.

Pieces of the ceiling were missing, revealing furls of kitchen laminate from the apartment above. The Christmas tree drooped over a shelf, and a rack of clothes floated against the ceiling.

I set down my backpack and stared at the black casters on the bottom of the rack.

Ezra eyed me. "Don't do it."

"I'm curious."

"Don't."

I leapt and snatched the bottom of the clothes rack. It didn't budge, holding my weight like I was a kid swinging from monkey bars. I tugged on it, kicking my feet, and the clothing swayed.

After dropping to the ground, I picked up the backpack. "That's interesting."

Ezra scowled. "That whole thing could have fallen down on your head."

"But it didn't. And I think it's important to test these physics. At least we know now that floating pieces aren't going to fall on us if we're under them."

"I wouldn't base that off of just one test."

"You want me to hang off of something else so we have more data?"

"No. Let's get out of here."

Green light shone through the front door, part of the street visible beyond. A sedan was parked at the curb, close enough to a fire hydrant that it would have gotten a ticket.

The sleigh bells shrieked as I pushed open the door. "See? This sidewalk is obviously floating. If I hadn't tried that with the clothes rack, we wouldn't have known this was safe."

I walked outside, the camera tight in my hand. We still needed to get down, but being higher up might give me a better photographic vantage. As I stepped on the sidewalk, the sedan beside me groaned. The back end slammed into the asphalt, and the ground beneath me heaved. My stomach flipped as I lost my balance. I reached for the fire hydrant, but it sagged into the car and the whole road gave out.

Ezra yanked me back before I fell into the disintegrating pavement. The awful screech of crumpling metal and shattering glass came from below.

I gripped him with one hand and the thrift store door with the other, my chest heaving and adrenaline jittering my fingers. The shop's dirty white tile still seemed intact, thank God.

"I told you." Ezra's light brown complexion had grown ashen, his eyes wide. "We shouldn't be playing around with this stuff."

"I wasn't playing! We need to get down from here."

"You're not being careful."

"Okay, okay." I tried to walk through the door, but he pushed me back and poked his head outside. I huffed. "We're equal here, Mr Big Spoon Protection. I don't want any of that chivalrous shit."

"You don't want any of it, huh? This is the same person who told me xe loved me not fifteen minutes ago because I was trying to protect xem, right?"

"Wait. I shouldn't have– It's not the same–" I clamped my jaw and flapped my hands, the words damming up behind my teeth.

He turned to me, and his face softened. "I could fall too, and your life isn't worth more than mine. That what you're trying to say?"

"Yes!"

"I'm sorry for teasing. I want us both to be cautious. That's all." After stepping past the doorframe, he inched along the remaining crust of sidewalk and disappeared from view.

I followed him, my back pressed to the exterior wall, and my backpack clamped tightly in my hand. The stair railing leading down from my complex appeared intact and where it was supposed to be. Ezra stretched out and gripped it, then pulled himself over. He leaned toward me, hand outstretched. I leapt over the gap and braced myself against the opposite rail to stop my momentum. We hurried down the steps before they decided to disintegrate too, and reached the pavement below.

I shut my eyes and blew out a breath. Sand ground beneath my heels, but at least we weren't standing on anything that might fall apart. The twisted wreck of the sedan sat a yard away, and the fire hydrant had gone straight through the windshield.

Holding up the instant photo, I turned until I lined up the view. A hard point of multicolored light extended beyond the post office lake, arching and fading into the sky. I pointed. "What direction is this?"

"North... I think."

Turning northeast, I aimed the camera and clicked. When the photo developed, it featured the same rainbow, but it was now in the far-left corner of the frame. Taking a photo of the south only produced a soft wash of color, akin to what we'd seen on the thrift store photos.

"It's right!" I bounced on the balls of my feet, then attacked Ezra in a hug. He laughed and squeezed me back. "We're not going to die. We'll be able to leave this dreadful town, go on dates, and I can visit my aunt and uncle..." This wasn't over yet, though. We had to kill the Dreamer.

Ezra studied my face. "If it catches on to us, do you think it can hurt us with its psychic powers? Make our heads explode like watermelons?"

I cringed. "I'm going to say no, partly because I don't want to consider that, but I think if it could, it would have done that to everyone in town. Likely its defenses are preemptive and passive... unless it's building its strength in order to do something like that. This definitely isn't the first place its species has attempted to terraform. It's too calculated. Maybe it's done it on other planets or in different locations on its own. Sends itself over a new area to claim and emits a mental block that will fall over any potential organisms that might resist or try to hurt it. I don't think it's bloodthirsty. We just happen to be in the way."

Backing up, I pointed to a large concentration of sand collecting against a truck in the parking lot. "Stand in front of that for a moment. But make sure there aren't any of those crab-scorpion things. They need a better name. Dreamlings?"

He walked in front of the truck. "This alien could be the mother crab and have massive pincers to snap us in half. Not sure how we're supposed to hurt it with a couple two three kitchen knives."

I took a picture and fanned it as I walked to him. "The good news is that it never stormed down Main, smashing things, so either it isn't that big or it isn't moving."

An absurd image popped into my mind – finding the localized source of psychic energy, but the Dreamer being one of the little crabs, indistinguishable from the others. I pictured us madly stomping on the scurrying little bastards, not knowing which was which.

Ezra developed on the photo, wearing another of my too-baggy shirts tucked into his jeans, a troubled look on his face.

"Damn, you're cute even when poorly dressed and frowning." I handed him the photo.

"I should be offended, but your resting face constantly broadcasts a look of high annoyance, and I still find you cute too. I like that crop top."

"That's not my resting face. I'm always annoyed." I pointed to the rainbow haze surrounding his body on the image. "Notice anything?"

He slid a hand around my bare midriff and traced the marker edges of the heart peeking from the waistband of my jeans. I assumed he wasn't paying attention, but he said, "The colored lights aren't overlaid on top of me. They're flowing around me."

"I bet if you took a picture of me, it would be the same. But if you took one of Trevor, he'd be covered in them." I held up the camera and squinted at the film count. There were eleven photos left inside. Muddy Gap was only four miles across, but if the landscape shifted, we might lose our bearings and need to take more photos.

"Hopefully that means we can't be split apart like the buildings or disappear into thin air," he said. "I still don't understand where all the people went. And the buildings. Teleported away to some other place? Trapped in another dimension?"

"The second one is my guess."

We checked the truck for keys, but came up empty. I hefted my backpack and we headed out of the parking lot, walking north. Discovering that we still had a chance to defeat the alien dumped a sour cocktail in my gut that made my hands tremble. The possibility of surviving this whole ordeal filled me with elation, but I ran even from tiny barking chihuahuas on the sidewalk. The idea of facing an extraterrestrial creature of immense power without any battle plan was terrifying. What if we made it all the way there only for the Dreamer to erupt from a lake of briny water and smash Ezra with one massive claw? Witnessing that would be the worst five seconds of my life before it used its other claw to snip me in half.

My throat clenched, and I forced down the urge to dry heave. I could say I was wrong, that the light meant nothing and we should crawl back into bed and await the end in each other's arms. But I couldn't. I had to try. For Ezra. For Trevor and Taisha, if they were still here somewhere. For Aunt Georgina and Uncle Joe and all my cousins. I had the chance to save people's lives. To not be a burden. To subvert people's expectations of me.

But my confidence diminished with each step.

14

I paused and stretched out my sore legs. "We had too much sex last night to go trekking across town this morning."

"You're complaining? Besides, we didn't think there was going to *be* a morning." Ezra hooked his fingers through mine. "We should have grabbed weapons from the thrift store."

"Like what? HDMI cables and that net with a hole in it?"

"I'm just saying that these knives aren't going to cut it. Pun intended. We should stop in any intact houses and see if there's food or weapons. Hammers, baseball bats, guns–"

"Crab crackers? Little meat forks? Tea candles for keeping the butter melted?"

He grinned, but the smile didn't reach his eyes. "Yes. We'll kill this thing and have a feast."

"Are you scared too?"

"Yeah, but the jokes are helping."

"Well, I hope you know how to fight. I saw a video once of a crab armed with a steak knife, and that thing wasn't playing around."

Ezra's face grew grim. "I know enough. Kind of have to learn that when you're in jail."

"That must have been terrifying."

"I don't want to talk about it."

"Sorry." I sucked in my bottom lip like it might help me take this line of conversation back, then dropped his hand. One of the cookie-cutter houses from the new subdivision passed

by on our right. Sand invaded the manicured lawn. The front
door was shut but a window stood open, curtains floating in
the breeze. "Let's check inside."

Ezra snatched my fingers. "Don't pull away. It's my fault for
bringing it up. But that conversation is off the table for now.
Same as you being uncomfortable talking about your mom."

"I understand."

My thoughts tried to escape to viral blog posts, eager fans,
national news stations, and government agencies. I checked
my connectivity, but there was nothing. Maybe I'd never be
able to access the blog again.

If everyone's focus was on Muddy Gap and the idea of the
alien threat spreading, they probably had bigger concerns
than who was still alive here in town. That probably meant
we still couldn't bank on outside rescue. My readers and my
family knew where I was – or had been; maybe they thought
I was dead now. I didn't want Aunt Georgina crying over
me. I didn't want my cousins standing around an unoccupied
casket.

And I didn't want to consider what my mom might be feeling
toward me, in any scenario, whether I was dead or alive.

I cinched the loose threads in my brain as Ezra and I headed
for the house. "I hope we have a future where there's room to
talk about hurty things, even if we never do it."

He planted a gentle kiss on my lips. "So do I."

The door squealed open, and Molly's voice cut between us.
"You two look like you've been having fun."

My stomach clenched and angry heat flooded my face. This
town was a maze but we still managed to run into the one
person I would have been happy to never see again.

She stood in the doorway in a tattered tank top and tall
western boots. In addition to her knee pads and gardening
gloves, she was wearing a pauldron made of tire rubber and an
eye patch over one eye. At first glance it was easy to assume
she'd been hurt when the rec center shifted, but she didn't

have any other injuries, and the wear-and-tear on her shirt looked deliberate.

Molly swung her nail-studded bat toward the steps in a macho display, and the blood on it didn't look as fake as her clothes. "Gave yourselves some cute 'tattoos', huh?"

"And you're in a cosplay outfit."

Her lip curled. "Don't bother trying this house. There's nothing in there worth stealing."

"It's unfortunate that your gang hideout turned into origami, huh?"

Ezra strode forward. "You could have killed us! You think it's funny, tossing us in a cell?"

She stiffened, her knuckles white on her bat. "You should be used to it by now."

"You bi–"

I shoved between them. "This isn't doing anyone any good. You don't want my theories, you don't want Ezra breathing your air, and we don't want you and your weird end-of-the-world kinks getting in our way. I'd say this town is big enough for all of us, but that is rapidly becoming untrue. We're running out of time. We need weapons. We need supplies–"

"I have all of those things," Molly said.

"Good for you. Wish we could say the same, but you shut us up in a room and left us to die."

"I would have come back once you were acting more agreeable, but we were a little busy trying to get Tara out from under a wall that materialized on top of her. She didn't make it."

That could have easily been us, and it was Molly's fault we were all there in the first place. "What happened to your brothers?"

"I don't know." Her voice wavered. "You probably don't believe this, but I did go back looking for you two later. But you weren't there so I figured you either escaped or disappeared like the others."

"That doesn't excuse your behavior in the first place," Ezra snarled.

"I'm taking charge! I'm trying to do what's best for all of us and if the Pie Professor hadn't been such an asshole and you two had agreed to come with me to the–"

"That's enough!" I cupped my ears. "We are running out of time and none of us want to die, so we need to get our shit together. *Together*. This situation is bigger than our petty differences. I don't like you, you don't like us, but we all have skills we can contribute. Not all of my theories have been right, but it's been a high enough percentage to help us stay alive and understand what's going on."

"You're smart. Is that what you're offering? Ingenuity?"

"Xe's more clever than you'll ever be," Ezra muttered.

Molly's nostrils flared. "And what skill are *you* bringing to the table? Stealing mail and paying for gym memberships but never going aren't exactly desirable traits."

Ezra opened his mouth, but I said, "He has good instincts. And a good heart. He's patient and protective–"

"Maybe with you."

"–and I would have given up days ago if I didn't have his support. And you…" She'd left us for dead, and I didn't like the idea of working with her, but if anyone looked eager to be a *Road Warrior* extra, it was Molly. If she was fantasizing about being the one to kill the Dreamer, whether to prove something to herself or gain control of the situation, she obviously had a fearlessness I didn't possess. It would be easy to give her a direction, help her find the thing, and let her deal the killing blows.

I cleared my throat. "You're prepared, know how to take control, and have guts. Which is exactly what this situation needs. It's… it's admirable."

Ezra gaped. Molly chewed on the edge of her thumbnail, then spit out a piece of skin. "I'm glad we're understanding each other. In these situations, the natural leaders rise to the top. In the old world, I was just a postal worker. Had to make money to pay the bills like everyone else. Circumstances and society put you in a place that you don't necessarily belong."

"I can agree with that."

"Ezra just sold houses. And you just... What did you do?"

"I'm a food critic. I blogged about pie."

"Right." She tapped her bat against the stairs, staring thoughtfully at the green sky. "None of those skills are useful now." I wanted to interject that my blog was the only thing that may have alerted authorities to the situation, but she kept talking. "Now is when we need our core human traits. Like you pointed out, you're smart. I'm ready to lead and not afraid to get my hands dirty in the process. And Ezra..." She looked away and drew in a deep breath. "He's always been a good sounding board."

Ezra tugged at the waxed end of his mustache, his jaw clenched like if he didn't hold it closed he might say something he'd regret. I couldn't guess what was going on in his head, but this was working. Miraculously, instead of pissing someone off when I started talking, I was swaying them.

I grinned. "Great. We ought to forgive each other for being nasty and agree to work together."

Ezra shook his head. "Wait–"

"Excellent idea," she said. "Glad you're seeing things my way. We can all agree that *I'm* leading this outfit?"

"Yes." I glanced at Ezra. When he didn't say anything, I pulled him aside and whispered. "I hate her too, but I have no confidence in my ability to kill a terrifying alien. She's wearing that costume like it's her resume. We let her tag along and when we find the Dreamer, she can lead the charge to kill the thing."

"Do you want to use her as bait?"

"No." I sighed. "I'm not being clear enough–"

"You are." He glanced over my shoulder. "I just want to call her 'bait'."

"I think 'tank' is a more accurate term, but call her whatever you want. Just don't say it to her face." I squeezed his marker-doodled bicep. "We only have to put up with her for a day, tops. She helps us kill the alien – or hell, she can do it all alone and be the hero – the barrier around town falls, the government swoops in, and we can have romantic dates at a therapist for all the mental anguish this has put us through."

He rubbed his scruffy cheek. "I don't like it. Look at her. This survivalist stuff has gone to her head."

"So let's leverage it. A paranoid, semi-feral postal worker who's eager to bury that spiked baseball bat into something is exactly what we need right now."

"I guess... If you think it's best." He raised his voice. "Fine."

Molly grinned. "I want you two to write up a list of what we need. I have supplies, but your input will help. The more we've prepared, the better."

"Perfect." I crossed the steps and held out my hand.

She gripped it and shook, then glanced at my other. "What's the camera for?"

"It's going to lead us to the alien. I discovered– well, actually Ezra was the one who first noticed that–"

Molly slapped the little instant out of my hand. She swung her bat and the nails whined past my face, then smashed into the camera. The casing exploded and undeveloped sheets of film spiraled out.

I yanked on my hair until stars of pain burst across my scalp. *"What the fuck did you do that for?"*

She kicked the shattered pieces into the grass. "We aren't going after the alien."

I shoved her into the doorframe. The bat clattered across the ground. "We *needed* that! There are no other instant cameras. We can't find the alien without it! Oh Christ."

I stumbled away. The landscape was a blur and pressure pulsed behind my eyes. Ezra reached for me, then his attention snapped to Molly. He gripped my arm and started to yank me sideways. Something slammed into my shoulder. Searing pain raked across my skin. I pitched forward and tripped over Ezra's foot; grass scraped across my hands as I hit the ground.

Ezra roared, shoes scratching on sand. Molly cried out and the bat clattered against the pavement. I tried to push myself up, but hot pain lanced my shoulder, and I collapsed. Bits of camera casing littered the grass in front of my face.

A hand – Ezra's – snatched the bat. I managed to roll over. He brandished it at Molly and his voice broke. "What the hell is wrong with you? Xe had no ill intention! Xe shook your hand, and you attacked xem!"

"He attacked me!" Molly's pretend eye patch had flipped up, her eyes blazing and hair a frazzled mess. "Over a stupid camera."

"That camera was our last chance." I groaned and sat up, too afraid to look at my arm in case it was hanging on by a ragged strip. "You've killed us all."

"I thought I made it clear that I'm in charge." She jabbed a finger at me. "We aren't going to look for the alien. It's creating a new world. A world where those of us meant for this time will survive. We'll start over. No more post offices or suburban houses. Or pies."

I let out a whimper.

Ezra bared his teeth. "You're sick. We thought you locked us up so you could get to the alien before we did. But that isn't enough for your twisted prepper fantasies. You *want* the apocalypse to come, and you're actively making it happen. This isn't a game!"

I felt along my arm, then instantly regretted it as my fingers sank into a wet channel in my flesh. My stomach reared, but I kept my hand pressed to the wound.

Ezra pointed the bat at Molly. "You stay away from us."

She gripped her throat. "You're going to regret not aligning with me. In a couple days, this town will be gone. The alien will spread its desert across the US and absorb everything.

People – the ones who are left – will panic. They'll kill each other. Starve to death. But I won't. I'm prepared."

"Sick." Ezra grabbed my backpack, then scooped his arm under me and helped me up, his gaze trained on Molly. I stifled a cry and leaned against him.

We staggered away from the house, and I wanted to turn back to ensure she wasn't following us, but twisting even a little triggered pain.

Ezra looked over his shoulder without slowing. "I knew trying to side with her was a bad idea."

"Then why didn't you tell me that?"

"I did!" he hissed. "But you're insistent and clever enough–"

"I'm obviously not clever."

"You are. But you have poor social judgment."

"Did you know that's what she was planning? Preventing us from reaching the alien so she can be a part of some new world order?"

"No. She's obviously had some kind of breakdown. Dressing up like she's a character straight out of *Fallout*..."

None of us were coping with this situation well, but at some point, Molly had crossed the line from control fantasy to straight-up delusion. I said, "She needs help."

"Yep, she sure does." He glared back at the house, mouth pulled into a grim line. "But it's obviously not safe to be with her. We need to get out of here and treat your wound. You have any first aid in the bag?"

"Kitty bandages."

He grunted. I clung to him as he pulled me down the street past spliced trees, chunks of floating streetlights, and a house without a roof. The elementary school blocked our path, one side merged with an apartment complex. After trying the doors, he picked up a rock and smashed it against the window until it shattered.

I cringed, blood oozing through my fingers. He popped open the door and led me inside, then shoved a metal bench against the entrance. Overhead lights flickered on at our presence. We passed a reception counter and a bank of photocopiers, then turned into a small room with cots and pillows in paper cases.

He flung open cabinets, pawing at cotton earbuds, sanitary pads, and rubber gloves.

I pointed at an upper shelf. "There. That package."

He pulled down a pack of *Kaolin Clotting Gauze* and tore it open. I sat on a cot and he pressed a spongy sheet to the back of my shoulder. A whimper escaped my lips.

"Tell me about the best pie you've ever had." He pushed hair away from my shoulder. "Every detail. What kind. The crust. The... hm."

"Spices? Texture? Presentation?"

"Yeah. All of it."

"We should be talking about how to proceed. We can still get to the general area of where the alien is. Or if we go back to the thrift store and grab the film for your Polaroid... but that involves finding your house to get the camera, and we don't know where it is."

"Later. We're not leaving until you're bandaged up. Tell me about the pie."

I drew in a labored breath. "There are so many. But *Brother's Pancake Shack—*"

"In Rawlins?"

"Yeah. Has the best lemon meringue. Have you had it?"

He pressed another sheet of gauze to my shoulder. "No. I think I had their brownie mountain thing once, though."

"The lemon is tart, but tempered with just enough sweetness for a bright, sunny flavor. Airy meringue with perfect, golden-brown peaks. And the crust is buttery shortbread with bits of Marcona almond. Such a gourmet addition, and for Rawlins. The fluff of meringue with smooth lemon curd and that crunchy crust is orgasmic."

"I think I gained ten pounds just listening to you describe it.

Sounds delicious. Should have tried it when I lived there." He crossed back to the cabinets, retrieving ointment and bandages. After washing his hands, he pulled on a pair of gloves that looked a size too small, then sat back down. "How come you never moved to New York City or San Francisco or Las Vegas? Some place where there are a ton of fancy restaurants with weird pie flavors for you to critique?"

"Too expensive. I barely made enough money to survive here, especially after my online writing gigs dried up. And I like the quiet and the space. Don't want to live in a packed city that's hard on my senses. Cars honking, people partying, the smells in a subway or a bus. Being stuck in a crowd on a sidewalk. There's no way. It would hurt so bad I'd turn to dust." I paused, painful heat throbbing in my shoulder. I had no idea how long it had been since I'd had a tetanus shot, and there'd already been blood on that bat. If Molly gave me Hepatitis or HIV, I would never forgive her, no matter how much I hoped her actions stemmed from a mental breakdown and not some violence that had always been in her soul. "I renewed my will to live this morning, and Molly destroyed it."

"Don't say that. If anything, it's given me the drive to defeat the alien out of spite."

"Did you love her?"

Ezra peeled back a corner of the gauze, then pressed it back down. "Yeah."

"Do you wish you hadn't?"

He sighed, and I said, "Sorry. You don't need to answer that. I've never had an ex so I don't know. Seems complicated. But we can throw that into the vault of hurty things not to talk about."

"I think it's possible to still love who someone was to you. You'd think when your feelings for each other change that it would taint those memories, but it doesn't have to. They're separate."

"I'm sorry for telling you I love you. I don't know how you're supposed to know or what it feels like. I just blurt things out."

His lips grazed my earlobe, voice gentle. "We might still die, so don't take it back. Not right now."

I tried to turn to kiss him, then winced as pain zagged through my shoulder. "You have good memories of the past with Molly, but awful ones now. Do you think it can work the other way? Layering a good memory on top of a bad one? Like maybe you go to a haunted house and are terrified and swear them off, but years later you go with a friend and it's cheesy and fun."

He peeled away the gauze, then cut through my crop top and folded it away from my back. "Is this hypothetical, or are you inviting me to hold your hand at a funhouse?"

"Hypothetical. I can't deal with the lights and jumpscare noises in those places. You can hold my hand on a Ferris wheel, though."

"I'm a little scared of heights but I've always thought Ferris wheels are romantic." His gaze fell to my arm. "Looks like the bat grazed you. None of the nails made deep punctures, but they shredded your skin and there's some bits of debris in the wounds. I need to flush it out."

I sucked in a breath, involuntarily shying away as he squirted water over the area. He patted it dry, then wiped ointment across the top. The pungent scent made my eyes water – or maybe it was the pain – and I pulled the collar of my ruined shirt over my nose. I drew in the metallic tang of blood and sugared petal scent of Ezra's cologne, still clinging to my skin from the night before.

I didn't know whether to define my life in Muddy Gap as a good memory or a bad one. The good must have outweighed the bad at least until the alien arrived, though there was a chance I'd simply become complacent in my loneliness and lack of connection.

Amid the awful things that had happened in the past few days, there were good memories too. Maybe they couldn't be stacked as a sandwich of good and bad, but both were woven into the same fabric, inseparable.

I thought of chocolate cream pie, nine birthday candles, and the UFO-patterned tablecloth. Blue cake frosting between the webs of my fingers and the words *creature, burden,* and *it* hurled into me like Molly's bat. That memory would always be there, and it was difficult to picture any scenario that would be similar enough and happy enough to layer on top. Trying to meet my mom halfway was out of the question.

Ezra smoothed bandage tape over my shoulder, then a piece down my arm. His gloved fingers slid over my jaw, and he pressed a soft kiss to my lips. "You okay?"

"I guess. Are you done? We need to keep going. If we can find a truck or an ATV, we'll get to the location of the Dreamer quicker."

He stood, gathering up medical supplies and stuffing them into his shopping bag. "You don't want to walk because we had too much fun last night, and now you're whiny and sore. Watching Julio Manhammer videos didn't prepare you for that, huh?"

I swatted his ass with the package of gauze. Gripping the edges of the cot, I tried to stand, then groaned as pain seared through my shoulder.

Ezra scooped an arm around me and hauled me up. I sagged against him, sweat breaking out on my brow. We paused in the front office, and he scouted out several classrooms, but an elementary school wasn't an ideal place to find alien-slaying weapons.

Leaving the waxy crayon smell of the school behind, we headed north under a deepening green sky.

"We should have found another baseball bat. Do you think elementary school gym teaches baseball?" I asked.

"Maybe with plastic bats and those big wiffle balls. And you don't look in any shape to be wielding a weapon."

"I can hold a torch and you can hold a pitchfork."

"It would help if we had a mob and weren't just two people."

I stared at the unsettling sky, the two of us still tiny neon tetras in a huge tank. One weapon, a shaky heading, and absolutely no plan.

The roar of an engine cut through the sound of my labored breathing, and an SUV appeared ahead, bouncing over chunks of sidewalk and dunes of sand. It splashed through a puddle, spraying briny water, and skidded to a stop in front of us.

Taisha leaned out the window. "You two look like you could use a ride."

15

A pair of fuzzy dice that looked like they were trying hard to overcompensate for something swung from the rearview mirror of the SUV. I pulled them off and flung them out the window.

Taisha glanced at me, and I said, "They were in the way. I need to see where we're going."

"Fuzzy dice are the uncool kind of retro, anyway." Trevor, visible in my visor mirror, sat beside Ezra in the back. The goose egg on his forehead was gone, but it had drained downward, giving him a puffy purple crescent beneath his eye and a ring of blood around his iris. A pair of ear-cupping headphones with the cords cut off sat around his neck. He leaned forward. "Hey, if you need to talk about *the thing*, let me know so I can cover my ears."

"'The thing?'"

"The thing you can't mention around me or my brain turns to mush. I know it's not a government experiment because if it were, I wouldn't be able to think about it. But if I concentrate on other possibilities, I'm going to figure out the correct one and mess up my brain again. So I'm pretending super intelligent chickens have risen up to claim us as their slaves, mostly because it's ridiculous, but also because I saw it in a cartoon once when I was high."

I tried to twist around in the seat, then winced and gripped the armrest. "Ezra and I were pretending crabs were to blame, but– Shit. Sorry."

"For what? It's crabs? Can't be. My brain's not getting fuzzy."

I figured it was close enough to the truth that Trevor wouldn't be able to process it. Just like "UFO" and "memory-erasing wind" were approximate enough terms to do damage. But the Dreamer either looked nothing like the tiny crustacean-things teeming in the sand, or it didn't think of itself as similar. I took small comfort in the hope that I wouldn't have to fight off giant snapping claws.

"I'm sorry for hurting you before," I said to Trevor. "I didn't mean to, but I'm still a dick for pushing you too far with my questions."

"You're not a dick," he replied. "In fact, you're the nicest person I've met here in town."

I scoffed. "Well, you haven't lived here long so..."

"Yeah, but you can tell a lot about someone from your first interactions with them."

"We argued about milk."

"A friendly argument while you helped me clean up all the groceries that had spilled out of my bag onto the stairs. You didn't need to do that. You didn't even know me. And you definitely didn't have to offer me the milk in your fridge to replace my own. Just because I didn't want it doesn't mean I don't appreciate the thought."

I frowned. "But... no one here likes me."

"I like you." He shot a glance at Ezra, then put up his hands. "As a friend. And I don't want to get mushy, Denver, but I'm glad you're here while we fight back against our chicken oppressors."

I stared at Trevor's reflection in the visor mirror. "You called me Denver." And he called me his friend.

"Well that's your name, isn't it?"

A weird mixture of joy and confusion filled my chest. Trevor alone was hardly the whole town showering me with affection, but it still felt like I deserved an "I told you so" from someone.

I glanced at Taisha, thinking of her casual invitation for us to practice our liquid eyeliner skills together... before she got angry at me for hurting Trevor. "What about you? Do you find me blunt and opinionated and obnoxious?"

She adjusted the side mirror, then swerved around half of a bathtub in our path. "Yes." Before I could chalk that up as more evidence of what I'd always known about people's dislike of me, she said, "But only in the best way. You seem like the friend I'd go to when I need someone to stand up for me. Or when I need the brutal truth about how my outfit looks."

I stared at a dusty shoe print on the glove compartment. It was so easy to take the negative to heart – and I'd been the recipient of plenty both in Muddy Gap and while growing up. But just because the opinions of people like Molly, failed lovers, and my mother were the loudest, it didn't make them more *right*.

"Well, fuck." I sniffled and cleared my throat. "Alright then."

Silence filled the cab, and I kept my gaze fixed on the dusty shoe print, because if I accidentally made eye contact with any of them, I was going to lose it.

"Where are we going?" Taisha asked. "North, but– Are you okay?"

"Yep. Fine." Holding up the instant photo of our path of psychic light, I compared it to the view through the windshield. The light's vanishing point was so vague – in the direction of foothills but no way to tell how close; beside some buildings but unclear which ones – that we could drive right by and never know. If Molly hadn't smashed our damn camera, this wouldn't feel like such an impossible task.

I squinted harder at the photo. Another object, barely a silhouette, sat near the termination of the rainbow. Something with a bulbous top and narrow base. "The water tower!"

"I'm on it." Taisha veered around a hovering diner booth. The tires squealed on sand, and dust drifted through the window.

High cottonwood trees, part of my apartment complex, and the fire department obscured our view, but barring a completely clogged path, staying on this heading would lead us straight there.

"Trevor, put your headphones on." I waited until they were securely on his ears, then glanced at Taisha. "Please tell me you have an alien-destroying bazooka in the back. Or sticks of dynamite."

Clusters of eggs dotted a bank of sand in front of us, huddled near water, and she swerved to run them over. "Not quite that badass, but I do have a compound bow and a bunch of arrows."

"Whoa. Do you think you can use it?"

"I hope so, since it's mine. Molly took it from me and stuck it in the rec center. Said we needed to keep our 'stash' safe. Know what she gave me to use instead? Pepper spray. How the hell was I supposed to kill an alien with that?"

"You weren't." I caught Ezra's gaze in the mirror, then looked away. "I'm glad you and Trevor are safe. Glad you were looking out for him."

She smiled. "He's cute. We–"

The back wall of Gem's Market blinked into existence directly in our path. *Oh shi–*

Pain exploded in my face and sawed across my neck. Glass shattered and metal screeched. A high-pitched whine and cotton fuzz filled my head. I pulled back and moaned, nose throbbing. An airbag filled my vision and my seatbelt locked tight against my throat. Groans and murmurs filled the cab.

Bits of blue-green glass dusted the dashboard, and the lid of a convenience store cup had popped off, soaking the center console in pop. With fumbling hands, I managed to unlock the belt. Taisha sniffed, blood dribbling from her nostrils. Smaller airbags filled the spaces in the back, and Ezra pushed them out of the way. Trevor held his head.

"Is everyone okay?" Ezra's voice shook, his expression dazed. He tried to open his door. When it didn't budge, he climbed out the window, then fought with Taisha's door. Trevor's cheek was an angry pink where the airbag had hit him.

Trevor helped me out, careful of my shoulder, though it was now a background pain compared to my face. I blinked black motes from my vision. Sparkling water heavy with the scent of salt stretched to the right, reflecting mint clouds and submerging homes. My apartment complex and the fire department were no longer behind us, replaced with high dunes and the park's tennis court. The tiny, fuzzy red plants had taken on a sinister quality, meaty leaves like serrated tongues, with clumps of dreamling eggs pearling on the top. The creatures swarmed across the plants, some of them big enough to see a rope of blue digestive tract running through their translucent bodies.

Ezra pulled me into a gentle hug. "Are you okay?"

"None of us are okay! Look at this place. There's an ocean forming, our vehicle is wrecked, and all the landmarks are gone. The water tower isn't going to be in the right place now, if it's even here at all. We don't have any way of knowing which way to head."

A breeze whipped past us, and I distantly wondered if our air composition would change too. Maybe all of the oxygen would disappear and we'd asphyxiate.

I thought of layering good memories over bad – ensuring the world where going to *The Lounge* with Ezra, where visiting Aunt Georgina and Uncle Joe, and where owning pet fish, wearing lipstick, and writing up pie reviews was still a possibility. Then I pictured Molly, with her stupid fake eyepatch and tire armor, and the world of death and despair she wanted.

I wasn't going to let that happen. Pulling away, I rooted through the wreckage of the SUV for my backpack, slung it over my good shoulder, and shoved open the garden center door of Gem's. Ezra caught up with me, his expression still a bit stunned.

"Are you hurt?" I asked.

"I hit my head on the seat in front of me."

"Do you think you have a concussion?"

He hesitated, blinking. "Ask me again in a few minutes."

I carefully brushed curls from his forehead. His pupils weren't dilated, and he seemed to focus on me okay once I was looking at him. "What's your name?"

"Ezra Gómez Miramontes."

"Where are you?"

"Hell, clearly."

"What about you two?" I asked Trevor and Taisha.

"My face hurts from the airbag..." Trevor looked down at himself. Fresh blood had blossomed through the bandages on his forearm, and the ring of red around his eye from the goose egg was unsettling, but he didn't seem to be nursing any new injuries. "Good thing we were all wearing seatbelts and in a big-ass SUV, huh?" he said.

A bit of blood still slicked Taisha's upper lip, but she rested her compound bow across her shoulder, jaw set, and looked much more the epitome of strength and tenacity than Molly had. But when she headed past us, she limped slightly and stifled a groan.

"Taisha?" I asked.

"I'm fine. I don't think it's broken."

"Maybe you should sit down so I can take a look at–"

"No. Let's go find supplies while we're here."

I thought of arguing, but I would have given her the same response if she'd insisted I sit down and have my shoulder looked at again. Different parts of my body were battling over which hurt the most. My cells were too full of static charge to want to take a breather right now, but if anyone showed signs of feeling worse instead of better, we were going to stop and rest for a while.

Stacks of terracotta pots and dusty trowels greeted us as we headed through the garden area. Bags of soil had split open at the sides, and some of the little red plants had sprouted in them, though they seemed to be struggling more than those outside.

Several onions lay on the tile in the produce section. The misters kicked on, even though there was nothing to hydrate beyond some stray spinach leaves and an abandoned stalk of celery. Everything else was probably wilting in the rec center.

Though I doubted I'd find anything, I said, "I want to check behind the service counter and see if they have any instant cameras before we go. You never know."

Ezra nodded. "The sporting goods section sucks, but there might be something useful. Come find me when you're done."

"Okay." I weaved around abandoned shopping carts and ducked behind the counter. Some of the cabinets were locked, but I found a set of keys by the register and opened the doors.

Trevor leaned over the counter. "Pass me a pack of Badger Reds. The shorts."

All of the cigarettes looked the same, and I wasn't sure what "shorts" meant. I tossed him a package of disposable lighters. "It'll be faster if you find them yourself."

I pawed through USB charging cables, earbuds, pregnancy tests, and lighter fluid, but there weren't any cameras or accessories. A pack of cigarettes fell on my head as Trevor snatched his favorites.

"Sorry. I am so ready for one of these." He picked it up and peeled away the cellophane wrapper, then repeatedly smacked the butt of the pack against his palm.

Cringing, I said, "Go have one. I'll be there in a second." Boxes of contact solution – the extra strength version used for oxidative degradation – caught my eye. I unlocked the case and rummaged through, but that seemed to be the extent of anything even distantly camera related.

Trevor had left, though I could smell cigarette smoke from somewhere nearby. I strode down an aisle and stopped in front of the first aid, wondering if I should just grab one of everything in case we needed it. Sniffles and a muffled sob drifted. I frowned and peered down the adjacent aisle. Taisha sat on the floor, elbows on her knees and her compound bow beside her.

I hurried past displays of nail polish and foundation and stopped beside her. Tears rolled down her cheeks. She drew in a wet breath and avoided my gaze. I squatted down and began to undo the purple laces on her Doc Martens. "Let me see how bad it is."

She batted my hands away, speaking through ragged breaths. "It's not that. I felt something pop in my knee when we crashed, and it kind of feels like it's going to give out when I walk on it, but it doesn't really hurt. I..." She wiped her eyes, smearing mascara across her cheeks. "I've been trying hard to hold it together ever since things started getting weird. And I thought I was doing a pretty damn good job, but–" She laughed and fanned her face. "Fuck. I haven't been on estrogen long, and I cry for no reason now."

"I'm pretty sure an alien invasion is a perfectly good reason to cry."

Taisha gestured to the candy-colored eyeshadows and liners on the pegboard hooks across from us. "I saw all this makeup and broke down." Tears welled in her eyes, and her chest hitched. "I don't want to die when I've only just started to live."

A lump welled in my throat, and I struggled to swallow it down. This had been Ezra and I just last night, and filling the time with pie, movies, Sharpie tattoos, and romantic sex had been enough to at least crowd out my panic for a while. I reached for a package of makeup removal wipes and gently rubbed one over Taisha's face. Turning to the eyeshadows on the shelf, I selected a bright sapphire that would look incredible on her dark skin. "Makeover time, girlfriend. Shut your eyes."

"This doesn't seem like the time for that."

"It's the perfect time." I opened the compact, coated the sponge brush with eyeshadow, and swiped it over her lids. "Who says you can't slay an alien and look beautiful while doing it?"

She snorted, then her expression grew somber. "Moving here meant that no one knew my deadname. They wouldn't have to struggle to use my new pronouns like people who know me do. But I still don't pass very well–"

"I think our cishet gamer bro would beg to differ." I ripped open a package of liquid eyeliner, then shook the tube. "There was no mistaking the 'damn, you're fine' look on his face when he first met you."

Her mouth pulled into a small smile. "He's asked me a lot of questions about being trans. Some of them were silly, but they were all in good faith and not invasive. You definitely can't say that about every guy."

"No, you cannot." I carefully drew the liquid eyeliner along her lash line, flicking it up at the edges.

"I thought about moving long before I did. Had it all planned out. I'd even found people here to form a band already."

"Punk music?"

She chuckled. "*Cow*punk, to be exact. And I was getting a chapbook published... And I'm already talking about it in past tense. Like everything is already over."

"I want to tell you everything is going to be okay, but I'm nothing if not offensively honest, and I have no idea what's going to happen when we find the Dreamer. But no matter what, at least you'll be yourself." I stood and offered her a handheld mirror. "A gorgeous badass who absolutely needs to say something if her knee starts hurting."

"Alright." She tilted her face in the mirror. "I think you got my eyeliner pretty symmetrical. I get to practice on you next time."

"Deal." I helped her up, wondering if she was playing down her injury as she limped slightly to the end of the aisle.

Trevor nearly ran into us. His gaze lingered on Taisha, circuiting her face before landing on me. "Hey. Ezra was wondering where y'all went. He found some shovels and aluminum bats." He lifted a grocery bag full of spray paint cans. "Also, I know how to make flamethrowers."

I eyed the cigarette dangling from his lips. "Why don't you let me hold that bag for you, and we can talk about it in a moment. I'm going to grab some first aid from the next aisle over. I'll catch up with you. Don't let Taisha fall."

Trevor turned back to her, and I managed to take the bag of paint cans from his hand without resistance. His questions to Taisha drifted as I rounded the aisle. I dumped out the cans and what looked to be supplies for making Molotov cocktails. None of us were getting blown up on my watch, especially since I didn't know how Trevor's brain would be affected once he was near the Dreamer.

I filled the emptied bag with first aid, then headed through the store. As I rounded the side of the frozen foods aisle, I slowed to read the packages. There weren't many: plain New York cheesecake, a tub of mini cream puffs, and Smith brand key lime pie.

"Lies," I muttered, but pulled out the box and pried off the top.

The door to the cooler had been left ajar and the pie had thawed, giving it the perfect consistency. Which is about all it had going for it, considering that Smith brand used Persian limes in their recipe, not key, and I avoided buying anything of theirs as a result. If they were willing to fib about their limes, there could be any number of problems with their other pies.

I took large bites of the slice, the flavor too mellow and whipped cream too greasy. Dropping the box on the ground, I brushed off my hands. Hopefully Trevor's vice was more satisfying for him.

A whisper of wind tickled my bare back, and I shivered. As I turned around, a shriek caught in my throat, tangling into a hard knot I couldn't swallow.

The service counter, the checkout islands, and the front half of frozen goods were gone. Chartreuse sun filtered down on high crests of sand, and hailshells bobbed in dimples of water.

I drew in a deep enough breath to force my throat to work. "Ezra!" I slipped on the box of pie, staggered up, and ran down what remained of the aisles before sprinting out of the severed store. "Ezra!"

An endless ocean of sand stretched into the distance, Muddy Gap only a dream that fades upon waking.

Orange grains coated the smashed lime pie stuck to my boots. My skull vibrated, my nerves live wires burning through my skin. I ran, stumbling, away from Gem's, and turned in a circle. The newborn sea twinkled nearby, the only landmark.

A section of shelving appeared overhead, then winked out of existence. A carton of heavy cream tumbled out of the sky and plunged into the sand.

I slapped my cheeks until they stung with pain, screamed Ezra's name until my throat was raw, and kicked the carton of cream until it exploded open. Warmth cradled my throbbing face as I collapsed. I shut my eyes, trying to cling to the scent of him, but the brine from the ocean invaded my senses.

He said he wouldn't abandon me. He said he'd stay until the end.

He promised.

Sand sugared my dry lips. Two dreamlings, each about the size of my hand, fought over the smashed carton of cream. It was hard to count their legs because they kept moving, but they clearly had pincers for gripping because they'd turned their grocery store find into a tug-of-war death match.

They scuttled, yanking at the paper carton. Their segmented tails – thoraxes? – arched over their heads in an aggressive display. What the hell would the winner do with the carton? Wear it like a shell?

I thought of Ezra, jabbing his finger in the air and saying, *Interdimensional hermit crabs.*

A little one, its dewdrop eyestalks clearly trained on a juicier prize, snipped at my arm. I slapped it and it skidded away on its back.

I was going to be eaten by these things, or buried in sand, and I wasn't sure I cared. Everyone was gone, including the friends I hadn't realized I'd had. I could get up and search for them, but I had no way of knowing if they'd been transported along with the front of Gem's to somewhere else in town, or snatched out of existence, the atoms of their bodies rent into some unrecoverable shape in a different dimension.

Grains stuck to my cheeks in damp channels, though I couldn't remember crying. I blinked grit from my eyes. There was no way to find Ezra now. And no way to find the Dreamer.

I distantly wondered if Molly was still here somewhere, building a sandcastle fortress.

After scraping pie from the heel of my boot, I flicked it at the fighting dreamlings. One stopped to inspect the glob, then resumed its battle.

"Yeah, it wasn't very good." Archer brand was great if you could find it. My cousins always asked for it when we were kids. They didn't care about the pie so much, but it came with jellied candy slices poked into the whipped cream. The little segments of each lime slice looked like stained glass when held up to the light.

My cousins would fight over the candy pieces, then abandon the pie, leaving me to eat most of it. Which was fine.

I dropped back into the sand and stared at the sky, which didn't need anything held up to it for it to be tinted green. My least favorite color.

Dragging over the backpack before the dreamlings stole it, I rummaged through and found my too-big Cheyenne Pie Fight shirt that Ezra had worn. I pressed it to my nose and inhaled. Something tumbled from the folds and snicked across my ankle. I winced and turned over the object. It was one of those clear pieces of glass or stone I'd picked up after arriving back into town with Ezra.

It was hard to say now why I'd put it in the backpack when the things were everywhere, but my pack always ended up with random artifacts from my life. And the stone had seemed pretty with the way the colored light bent through–

My mouth fell open. I held the stone to the sky, one eye squeezed shut. The scattered prism within honed into a rainbow beam.

Shoving to my feet, I turned in place. The light moved like a compass needle, still pointing north.

"Oh my god."

Snatching the backpack and terrifying the dreamlings, I ran in the direction of the beam. My shoulder throbbed, bandages crinkling as I slipped over dunes and crushed plants underfoot.

There was still a chance. If I killed the alien, maybe the sand, the ocean, and the glitched buildings would vanish, the dream destroyed. Muddy Gap would be back. Ezra would be leaning over his porch railing in a gaping robe, drinking hazelnut coffee. Trevor would be playing his first-person shooter, disappointed that the nudity was only a man's bare ass in a cutscene. Molly would be scowling at customers in the post office. Charla would be smoking outside of Gem's, thinking about Sam.

I'd be sitting lonely at my computer desk, writing up a post on my unpopular blog and talking to the dwarf frogs in my fish tank.

But if it didn't reset things back to normal, at least the rest of the world would be safe from it happening to them.

The beam shifted in the clear stone. I skidded down the side of a dune and splashed through a pool of water. Sand stuck to the creases of my mouth, the crooks of my elbows, and I was pretty sure there was some in my underwear. I paused and took a long pull from the water jug in the pack. It tasted faintly of milk and I gagged, but forced myself to soothe my parched throat.

Pulling out one of the kitchen knives, I continued my pace, keeping my route trained to the direction of my cosmic compass. The light's vanishing point widened until a kaleidoscope of color filled the stone. I turned, aiming it in every direction, until I realized that the biggest, brightest concentration was immediately below my feet.

This area of terrain was indistinguishable from any other. I wasn't sure whether to be relieved or terrified that some nasty creature wasn't tromping across the sand toward me or erupting from a pool of water.

I strode in the circumference of the concentration of light, then tucked the stone in my pocket and dropped my pack. "I'm here! I'm here and I'm mad as hell. Show yourself, you crabby bastard."

Serrated plants wavered in the breeze and gnats dove past my face. A magpie, likely very confused, landed nearby then took off as soon as a dreamling scurried toward it.

Doubts prickled the back of my mind. Maybe I'd never been right. Ezra thought I was so clever, but maybe *he'd* been the correct one and this was a government experiment with tiny mind control devices that were making me hallucinate. Or maybe Trevor's chicken overlords were to blame.

Nearby, something shifted under the ground. I froze and squeezed the knife. When it didn't happen again, I crept over, heartbeat thudding in my ears, and toed the spot. Something shrank away, leaving a channel in its absence.

Squatting, I pawed at the sand, revealing what looked like a twisted plastic bag. It tapered to a point, terminating in clear filaments that branched like veins. I poked the transparent bag-thing with the tip of my knife and it contracted, wrinkling, then slowly plumped, expanding with air. It snaked toward my feet, extending into a long tube, like a tree root. Or a tentacle.

We'd only gone to the ocean once when I was a kid. The car ride had been agonizingly long, but I'd brought my favorite library books and a handful of toys, tuning out Uncle Joe's efforts to sing classic rock. The chalet we stayed in had been cramped for six people. I had to sleep with Beth, who hogged all the sheets and got mad when I woke her up to tell her one of her boobs had fallen out of the side of her camisole.

When we went down to the beach, I busied myself plucking up broken seashells and colorful stones, and played with the shiny strands of kelp that had washed ashore. I stopped at a rubbery crumpled thing coated in gray-brown sand and stared until Abraham kicked it and said it was a giant condom. Billie smacked him, hissing that I didn't know what a condom was and wasn't supposed to. She'd told me it was a dead jellyfish, and that it could still sting me if I touched it.

I hadn't gone on a family vacation in decades. If Aunt Georgina had invited me on one during our last conversation, I'm not sure if I would have accepted. But I couldn't stand the thought of a future where there were no more awkward family get-togethers. No more birthday parties and kitchen-counter confessions.

I plunged my knife into the alien tentacle and easily sliced through. Iridescent liquid wept from the amputation, and the limb writhed. The severed piece wriggled away from its body, then deflated and lay still. I uncovered more of the tentacle, which tried to contract away from me.

"You took everything from me. *Everything*. My town." I stabbed through layers of jellied flesh. "My boyfriend." Ichor sprayed as I sawed through a thick vein. "My fish."

A groan rumbled from somewhere underground. I raked the knife across the thickening limb, and air whistled from the inflated sacs within.

This fucking extraterrestrial used-condom jellyfish had dropped into Muddy Gap like it owned the place and started dreaming up a world none of us had asked for.

"Nightmare." I slashed the limb into ribbons.

The ground rumbled and a massive tentacle snapped out of the sand, revealing a portion of a convex central body with a bubbled surface that reminded me of the inside of an orange. The limb momentarily blocked the sun, scattering light rays through the inflated sacs and fringes of branching cilia. I gasped, the enormity of what I was witnessing filling me with a terrible reverence. This creature robbed me of everything I loved, and I couldn't allow its power to spread, but I was frozen in full-bodied awe. It was beautiful and gruesome and *gigantic* and oh fuck–

The tentacle hurtled toward me, slamming into my back before I could dive out of the way. I plowed into the ground, diaphragm spasming, and gasped for breath. The tentacle whipped from side to side like I was an irritating fly it was trying to shoo.

I wheezed, clutching my chest. Another tentacle tip emerged yards away. It arced over me, pushing sand against the one I'd hacked into calamari. Most of the Dreamer's body and likely the rest of its spoke-like limbs were still hiding underground. Chopping off one tentacle wasn't going to do any good. I needed to find its heart, or its brain, or its central nervous system. I'd even stab its giant eye if it had one. Something to get the message across that it wasn't welcome.

Scrambling up, I veered around the tentacles, heading for the core of the alien. The lash across my back throbbed, and my shoulder ached. Pebbles rolled in my boots and sticky sweat dried against my forehead.

Soap-bubble air sacs bloomed across the Dreamer's body. I climbed on top of the largest exposed one, toward its core, but before I could plunge my knife in, my foot ripped through and I fell into the hole. Rubbery, deflating walls pressed around me, and I flailed, tearing through them. My knife slipped from my ichor-coated hand. Membrane rippled, the sun and clouds distorted. The metallic scent of ozone and rotten tuna enveloped me. My stomach roiled. Slender veins burst, coating my face in fluid.

A rumbling moan vibrated the tissues and penetrated my bones. I was hurting it. Instead of trying to claw my way out, I thrashed harder, punching through gelatinous flesh. Foul air gushed from a burst sac, and the walls contracted around me, squeezing, trying to expel me.

I dove deeper.

16

Think about pie:

Tart lime.

Creamy peanut butter.

Squeaky pecans.

Ripe cherries.

My stomach revolts, face plastered with gore and the stink of rotting fish.

Faint, watery light filters through layers of destroyed tissue, and I don't know which way is up. I'm in the center of the Dreamer's bubbled, citrus-flesh body, but I can't tell how deep. I draw in a breath, lungs starving. Oxygen-heavy air rushes out when I plow through a sac wall. I draw in quick breaths, taking in all I can before the tissue collapses against me. My arms slip against membrane, jeans wet and chafing as I kick like a diver, no heading whatsoever but I'm going to do as much damage as possible while I'm here.

Colors dance in my vision, the same pearlescent sapphire I swiped over Taisha's eyelids.

I don't want to die when I've only just started to live.

I've lived more in the past week than I did in my whole ten years of being in Muddy Gap. Or maybe my awareness of my life only became noticeable by virtue of everything I lost.

The Silvas had a Saint Bernard named Rosa with sad eyes and an unbelievable amount of drool that would lie in their front yard like one of the taxidermal animals in Gem's Market.

If I was having a rough day, I'd stop and pet that dog, and neither she nor the Silvas minded how long I was there.

The general store on Main Street had the best coffee, and sometimes I'd buy a couple squares of their novelty fudge. Cheddar cheese fudge seemed like a blasphemous flavor combination, but the sweet creaminess paired with the distinct tang of aged cheddar was intriguing enough for me to buy it again.

Black stars teem at the edges of my sight, and I can't tell if I'm floating or falling.

There's a knock at the door. Whose door? Where am I? A fifty-something Arapaho man in beaded moccasins and a Gem's Market T-shirt – Sam – holds up my bags of groceries and smiles. "Hey. I was on my way home, so I thought I'd drop off your order myself. Sweet potato pie this week, huh? That's my favorite kind. Do you like beer?"

"Beer... pie?"

He laughs. "No. The kind that comes in a bottle. I'm gonna have a couple and set up my telescope. Saturn is really bright right now. And I just thought, y'know, maybe you'd want to see too."

My head pounds, nostrils gummed with rank alien blood.

Egg yolks run through the grating of the stairs, and Trevor's skim milk makes a steady *pat pat* against the concrete below. There's a deep channel between his brows, but it softens as I help him gather his spilled groceries.

I stuff marinated pork chops and boxes of shredded wheat back into his unripped bag. "Skim milk is disgusting anyway. You're paying over five dollars for a jug of white water."

My knuckles smart as I plow my fist into a hard knot of tissue. A screech vibrates through the collapsed walls and everything tilts.

Ezra brushes strands of hair away from my face as sweat cools on my brow. Emerald shadows slide across my bedroom ceiling, a sinister replacement for the amethyst fish tank light that used to dance there. I roll toward him, tucking my face into his neck and inhaling deeply. His bare warmth envelopes me, broad chest rising and falling in a satisfied cadence.

My voice is barely a whisper. "I don't want to fall asleep." He pulls back slightly, running his thumb over my sandpapery stubble as I say, "If I close my eyes, you might be gone when I open them again."

"I'm not going anywhere. I'm not a figment of the Dreamer's imagination."

"Are you a figment of mine?" He's not here. I'm not sure if we even had this conversation.

"No. I'm real." He pulls back the covers, then jiggles his hairy belly. "Look how rock solid I am." When I laugh, he says, "You can't prove that I don't have a six-pack hiding under here."

Flaps of flesh slap against my arms, and I scramble to hold on before I'm shaken away from whatever it is that I punched: the Dreamer's brain stem, its gonads, I don't care. The pulse of it beats into my arms, hot and urgent. I pummel the ropy organ and tear at it until goop sticks under my broken nails and my hands are slippery. The Dreamer roars, convulsing. Something strikes the ground above – below? – me and jars my teeth.

Horse hooves clomping on asphalt. Hand-rolled candles at the craft market. Christmas lights twinkling against window panes. The slick greasy vinyl of diner booths. The scent of sage on the breeze.

With a yank, I rip a bundle of tissue free, then dig for more. I gasp, every breath an effort. A blizzard of static fuzzes through my mind and white dots dance in my vision.

Getting packages in the mail. Falling snow illuminated in the glow of an arc sodium light. Neon tetras darting through plants. Carving into a fresh slice of pie.

Beams of lavender and mint scatter through the ichor-smeared walls. The ropy organ is frayed, and its throbbing pulse weak and uncertain. This is working. I'm killing it.

But my head is floating away.

My feet plunge into wet sand on the beach, and I laugh, salt spray misting my skin as my cousins chase me with slimy kelp.

Apple cider spice and cool whipped cream fill my mouth as Ezra kisses me, his calloused and gentle hand cupping my jaw.

Airy meringue.

Decadent salted caramel.

Herbaceous honey-lavender.

Cinnamon alphabet noodles.

Rubbery flesh slides across my cheek, and I'm sinking, drowning, dreaming. The last shred of me is screaming to get up, to keep fighting.

Molly said if aliens ever arrived in Muddy Gap, they'd be here to take me home. But I don't belong with them.

I belong with Ezra.

I belong with my friends.

I want people to stop leaving me.

I want my damn town back.

My fist tears through the final threads of bundled tissue and the walls spring apart, slamming me through an air sac. I gasp, gulping putrid air. Sunlight flits through the gauzy gore above me, and I kick my feet and claw for it, trying to break through the surface of this sea of horror.

A breeze chills my slicked hand, and goosebumps erupt across my arm. I pull through the opening, chest heaving and shoulder searing with pain. I fight my way out of the Dreamer's body and roll into the sand.

Pushing unsteadily to my feet, I stare at the glistening ocean, trying to unstick the lump from my throat. Dunes roll away in all directions under a key lime sky. Dreamlings teem across serrated plants. Far in the distance sits the severed half of Gem's Market.

I turn back to the alien. It's thrashed hard enough to reveal most of it, looking like a translucent bouncy house that someone took a machete to. Limp tentacles spread away from its ravaged core. I stomp on one, tears blurring my vision. There's no reaction, the Dreamer as lifeless as the sand-coated jellyfish Bram kicked away when we were kids.

It's dead, but I haven't fixed anything. This isn't a dream, and the xenoterrain hasn't vanished.

Gore dries to a flaky film on my face, my hair stiff and crunchy as I stumble away. Not sure where I'm going. What does it matter anymore? I stopped the Dreamer, but it hasn't brought back Muddy Gap, and it hasn't brought back Ezra. All traces of the life I've lived have been dragged out to sea, dissolving in the brine until they may as well never have existed. But I still exist.

I don't know if I want to.

My arm tingles with numbness, my fingernails rent to the bloody quick. I double over and vomit lime pie into the sand.

A sudden ream of notifications appears in my contacts.

mammas_apple: DENVER WHERE ARE YOU
sayhellotomydog: Yo are you okay?
burnt_nugget: A National Guard unit tried to enter your town and disappeared. Wyoming Triangle!
hippie69: Xe's probably dead. I hate this.
   jonjon: We're all gunna die!
unlimitedcorndogs: I'm escaping to Canada like everyone else.
    elvis_lives34: Seriously dude? Like an alien can't come to Canada because it doesn't have a passport or what?
grandmaZ: Someone should come up with a new pie to honor Denver's memory.

I type, "I'd love that," then collapse in the sand.

A distant beeping pulls me from the depths of sleep, and I swear it's Trevor's smoke alarm, but that can't be right.

My eyes flutter open. I'm met with a low ceiling and confining walls, and it takes a moment to register that it's an ambulance. Paper crinkles beneath me and tubes snaking from my arm clack against the metal railing of a gurney. Someone in a white hazmat suit swabs oil slick ichor from my arm with a long cotton bud, then pops it into a clear tube, caps the end, and writes on the label with a marker.

I clear my cobwebbed throat then lick my lips, dislodging grains of sand. "How did… you get in here?"

They hold up a badge hanging around their neck like that explains everything. I can't focus on the low-resolution photo or tiny letters. Not sure what the holographic seal in the corner stands for.

Their voice comes out muffled. "You're Denver Bryant, right?"

I nod. "The highway–"

"What are your pronouns and honorific?"

"Any. How did you get through the repeating highway? Did you solve the puzzle?"

"Mx Bryant, I'm afraid you've gone through something very traumatic. All I want you to do is reorient yourself right now while I tend to your injuries."

I groan, and my fingers clang against the gurney railing. "How far does the sand extend past Muddy Gap? You need to kill the dreamlings – the, the crab-scorpions before they reproduce. I'm not sure–"

"There is no sand. No crab-scorpions."

Wiping a crust of gore from my face, I stare into the person's reflective visor, but all I see is myself, looking like an extra in a horror movie. "They're gone?"

I push up, elbows weak. Beyond the open doors of the ambulance, Wyoming prairie rolls away beneath a vibrant blue sky. My chest heaves, and the repetitious beeping of the nearby machine speeds up.

"You're okay." The person puts a gloved hand on my shoulder. "I understand this is very confusing for you. Please relax."

"You found the alien, right?" I shove stringy hair away from my face. "Big destroyed jellyfish-looking thing? Or like an anemone, maybe. It couldn't have been far from wherever I was."

The person pauses, their hand heavy on my arm. "Mx Bryant, there's no alien. We haven't found anything but you."

Tape holds down the IV needles in my arm. I rip it off and one of the needles goes with it. Bright blood dots my arm. I pull out the second one and the person snatches my hand.

"You're going to give yourself a hematoma!" They press a wad of cotton to the IV sites and wrap a tight band of elastic gauze around my arm.

I expect them to push me back on the gurney, but maybe they think I'll hurt myself if they interfere. My joints protest, shoulder and back aching. My heartbeat throbs in my raw fingertips. I hop out of the ambulance and squint in the glare. Pebbles and prairie grass poke my bare soles. I still reek like tuna and brine, but fragrant sage carries on the breeze. The remnants of a building foundation sit to my right, rebar jutting through the concrete. Military trucks are parked in clusters, and a pop-up tent buzzes with more people in hazmat suits.

I clutch my elbows and walk away, expecting the ocean, but it's the view beyond the rec center – snaggle-toothed hills flocked in sagebrush, faded yellow graffiti on one high peak.

My toe stubs something, and I hiss. A dome of colored stones curves from the ground. Squatting, I brush away dust, then frantically dig around it with my aching hands.

"Mx Bryant." My hazmat-clad caretaker stops beside me. "You need to come back. You can get cleaned up and rest. We've quarantined this whole area, but whatever you can–"

The words fade to background fuzz. I grip Ezra's globe by its metal meridian and haul it out of the dirt. I wanted to tilt and spin it when I sat in his living room, but was too afraid my fidgeting and quirks would be repellant. He'd gently taken my hands when I was stimming too hard or hurting myself. He'd made sure I sat down, drew a breath, and wasn't ready to explode.

I hug the dusty globe and press my cheek to the inlaid serpentine stone of Russia.

Hazmat person scoops me up by my good arm, and I squeeze the globe to my chest. "If you try to take this away from me, I'll fight you."

They put up their hands. "I won't take it." They click something on their helmet and the polarized sheen on their visor disappears to reveal a middle-aged white woman with close cropped red hair. "I'm Amelia Foster, she/her–"

"Are you a doctor?"

"Yes. Please come back."

AL HESS   245

She leads me back to the ambulance. I curl myself over the
globe the way Ezra curled himself over me. Dr Foster peels away
the bandages on my shoulder, and I want to protest, because it
was Ezra's work – bandaging my foolish wounds while I talked
about *Brother's* lemon meringue pie with Marcona almond
shortbread crust.

Instead, I wince and grit my teeth, pressing my face to the
slick lapis lazuli ocean in my arms. Sample vials fill up the little
plastic holder beside me: test tubes of my blood, tissue samples
from my wounds, stuff combed from my hair. Dr Foster scrapes
gunk out from under my broken nails; my nostrils flare, my
other hand clenched around the globe's meridian.

Someone new arrives and shows me another badge I can't
read, because Dr Foster has swabbed my eye and it's cloudy
when I blink. Blog notifications pop up endlessly on my
contacts until I shut them off.

"Mr Bryant," the new person says, "did you hear me?"

"What was the question?"

"No question. We're leaving." I get the sense that they're
smiling behind their helmet. "Have you ridden in a helicopter
before?"

Maybe I'm supposed to be excited. But it's going to be
loud and I've lost my earplugs, and no one has told me
where I'm going. Before I can protest, I'm pulled to my feet
and led out of the ambulance in crinkly clothing that chafes
my thighs.

Beyond the pop-up tent and military vehicles, a black
helicopter swirls prairie dirt into a frenzy. It spirals into the
blue sky. I squeeze my eyes shut against the *WHUMP-WHUMP-
WHUMP* of the blades and try to ask where they're taking me,
but my voice is lost to the noise.

A gloved hand grips my globe, trying to pull it from my
arms. I snarl and plow my fist into a hazmat visor. Someone
wrestles me away. People shout, snatching at my arms, and
I thrash. I scream, and I'm nine years old again, and I don't

want to be taken away. Not by drug addict mothers, or UFOs, or military people in hazmat suits.

Every cell in my body is electrified, my hands possessed with so much frantic energy that I drop the globe. People back away, looking at each other like they don't know how to store this sample, this petri dish of grieving alien evidence.

Arms envelope me, and I start to resist, but the heady scent of honey and flowers spirals up. Ezra's mustache tickles my neck, his firm chest pressed against mine.

"Sit down. You're going to shake yourself apart." He tries to tug me into the dirt, but I clamp my arms around him.

He isn't real. All of the alien's ichor filling my nose and mouth and eyes has given me its power, and I've dreamed up Ezra to comfort me when I most need him. But now that I'm thinking about it, he's going to disappear, and I'll be alone.

"Don't leave." I sob, digging my sore fingers into his back. "Don't go away."

"I won't. I promise."

"You said that last time."

He leads me away from the noise of the helicopter, then cups my cheeks and stares into my face. Grains of orange sand dust his eyebrows, his dark eyes searching. I can't hold his gaze, but he keeps it trained on me. "Don't blame me. You're the one who just *had* to go look at the pie selection. Distractible weirdo."

I chuckle, but my voice breaks, and Ezra pulls me to him before I collapse. I say, "I thought you were dead."

"With the way Trevor kept going on about football and shoot 'em up games and chicken overlords, I started to wish I was." He pulls back, then peers down the collar of my paper shirt. "What the hell happened to you? You killed it, huh? All by yourself." There's awe in his eyes, the edges of his lips curling in a smile. "Molly would be seething mad."

"She isn't here, is she?"

"No. No idea where she's at. Me, Taisha, and Trevor got

teleported so far away. We figured you were still near the ocean, but it was just a little shimmer in the distance, and it was going to take us hours to get to. Those National Guard people intercepted us before we got to you. They don't believe what happened."

I frown, eyeing the scientists carrying things to the helicopter. A couple of them still stand by, apparently waiting for me to calm down enough to go with them.

"Did you consent to have samples of your blood taken?" Ezra asks. "Swabs from your cheek?"

"No. They just did it."

"Dammit. We aren't going to become some science experiment in a lab, and we have no obligation to go with them. I'm not going to let you get dissected."

I'm not sure that fear is justified, but it makes me glad I haven't answered any questions yet. "Well–"

A scientist approaches and tries to grab my arm. Ezra bares his teeth and pulls me away. "We're not getting on that helicopter or going anywhere with you."

"Sir, we're under strict orders to–"

"We're not doing it! We'll sit in a tent and answer questions here. *After* we've been able to clean up and rest. You can't throw Denver into an evidence locker in Area 51 and forget about xem. I won't let you."

"That isn't our intention."

"Good." He tries to lead me away, but people step in our path, and one of them has a rifle slung over one shoulder.

They say, "You need to board the helicopter."

This isn't a fair fight. The grainy image of alien corpses from the 1947 Roswell incident surface in my mind. Dr Foster said there was no alien. I thought she meant it had disappeared, dried up, blew away, but maybe she was trying to convince me. *You didn't see anything. It was in your head.*

There's nothing stopping the government from spinning this however they want. And if they kill us, no one will know. Except...

I pull up my blog, tapping out of urgent notification bubbles telling me I have two-thousand-plus new comments. On a fresh post, I write: *I'm alive. I hope you never need to find out firsthand what extraterrestrial bowels smell like. The military is here, gathering evidence, and they want to take me and my boyfriend away. I'm not going. If something happens, I need you all to be my voice. Tell the news. Tell the world. Don't let the government cover this up.*

My boyfriend's name is Ezra Gómez Miramontes. (Yes, he's the same man from my very awkward previous video.) My friends' names are Taisha Williams and Trevor Scott.

Hazmat person unslings their rifle. They gesture toward the helicopter with the barrel. "Get on. Now."

I write: *I'm Denver Bryant, and I killed the alien.*

After hitting publish, I check my subscriber count and Ezra catches me as my knees buckle. "I just sent a message to my" – I unstick the number from my throat – "twenty-six point eight million blog subscribers, that you're holding us hostage here."

The person stiffens. They lean in to one of their associates, then say, "It would be a bad idea to tell anyone what you think you experienced. You'll cause mass hysteria over your hallucinations."

"Hallucinations? What the hell are you talking about?" I nearly suffocated within the innards of a horrible, awe-inspiring extraterrestrial, and this asshole has the nerve to call what happened to me a hallucination. "We experienced an alien invasion! And I'll keep posting details the longer you threaten us at gunpoint to get on a helicopter."

They march toward me, fingers pinched like they plan to rip the contacts out of my eyes.

I clutch Ezra's arm and hit record, sending it to a new post. "I'm recording this! I'm streaming it live!" Panning across the clusters of scientists, the helicopter, Ezra, then switching to mirror mode, I stare at my own crusty, gore-coated face. Ezra jerks me backward, and I can't see what's happening. Maybe I don't want to. My words come out in a rush, but the recording software still manages to lip-read and transcribe what I'm saying fairly accurately. "The alien was massive. It had a bubbled, central body with radial spokes, like a starfish or an anemone. The tentacles were yards across and inflated with air sacs. It had the ability to psychically generate its native terrain into existence, and it completely destroyed the town of Muddy Gap, Wyoming. I ripped out its heart with my bare hands. No one is going to tell me what I saw was a fucking weather balloon."

I close mirror mode and let out a squeak. The person with the rifle is inches away from me, and Ezra's ashen face is reflected in their visor. They say, "Muddy Gap, Wyoming isn't a town. It doesn't exist."

Ice sleets through me. They don't want to only erase me and Ezra, they want to erase the entire town.

Dr Foster draws the person away, then approaches with a tight smile. "The labs in our secure facility are much more ideal, but we have all we need to conduct interviews here if this is where you would rather stay."

"I don't want to stay anywhere. I want to go" – I almost say *home*, but the word has no meaning now – "with family."

"That's understandable. And we will make those arrangements as soon as possible. Please come back with me. All I want you to do is answer some questions."

"If that were all, you wouldn't need guns."

"It isn't personal. We weren't sure how you would react once we found you. We'd like to make sure there aren't lingering effects to whatever you were exposed to. I want to take a few more swabs if you'll let me." She glances at Ezra. "Your friend can stay with you, and you can keep your contacts in."

All of this sounds okay, but I thought my arrangement with Molly sounded okay too until she smashed my camera and raked all the skin off my shoulder with her nail-studded bat. Ezra has more sense than I do when it comes to social situations, so I make a mental note not to agree to anything until I consult with him first.

Completely walking away to let the military and government handle the mess is tempting, but not if they're going to cover it up, make me look crazy, and make assumptions about an event they didn't witness firsthand. And even though they aren't forcing me on a helicopter, I'm not confident they'll let me out of their sight.

Leaning to Ezra's ear, I whisper, "I want to see this through to make sure it's being handled correctly, but I need *your* brand of cleverness and insight."

His cheeks flush, and I wonder if Molly made him feel stupid for their entire relationship. He raises his voice. "We stay together – no questioning us individually – and that includes Taisha and Trevor. No taking swabs or samples without our explicit consent. When we tell you all we know, you let us go."

"That sounds reasonable."

"And if Denver is feeling overwhelmed at *any* point, xe gets a break."

Dr Foster nods. "Is it too much to ask that you not record everything?"

"Yes." I know full well that they can throw up privacy shields, which won't stop my livestream, but it will block any video from getting through. Even if that's the case, the feed going and people watching is a comforting failsafe against being made to disappear and no one knowing what happened to me.

"I'm only trying to keep you from embarrassing yourself," Dr Foster says.

I scoff. We're ushered into a tent with a couple of tables, a plastic cooler, and boxes of equipment that haven't been unpacked. I stand in the middle of the space and rock on my heels. The promise of being able to bathe and rest, or even having a place to sit, no longer seems like something they're interested in granting me, but at least I'm not being stuffed in an evidence locker.

Light wavers through the gap in the tent flaps, and even though there's no locked door, I'm certain that trying to leave will put us face-to-face with someone with a rifle.

Ezra draws in a breath and opens his mouth, but the door flaps swing away and Taisha and Trevor duck inside.

Raising her eyebrows, she pulls me into a sudden hug. "I'm so glad you're okay."

I hesitantly give her a return squeeze. "I'm glad you're okay too." Glancing at Trevor, I say, "And you. How are you feeling?"

He plucks a cigarette from one of his pilfered packs and pokes it in his mouth, squinting. "You know, whenever I fantasized about alien invasions, it was green women in metal bikinis. Not a giant starfish. That's not sexy."

"It certainly wasn't." I realize he's acknowledging what happened and not pretending chickens are to blame. "You can think about it then without it hurting you?"

He lights the cigarette and takes a drag. "Yep. I'm disappointed I didn't get to help you kill it."

"It was disgusting."

"I can tell. Still, though." He claps me on the shoulder, smoke spiraling past his face. "That's so badass, Denver."

I smile. "I'd give you a hug, but I know how not-gay you are."

"Pssht." He gives me a side-squeeze, then pulls away. "God, you stink."

"I know."

Something scratches and stutters across the ground outside the tent. I cringe. One of the hazmat people drags two folding chairs inside and dumps them by a table. They slap down a notepad hard enough that the pen clipped to the top pops off and rolls into the dirt. At least I can't see their expression.

Dr Foster ducks inside and perches on one of the chairs. I reach for the other, but the angry scientist claims it and spreads their legs like they're at home on the couch. That's fine, since there are plenty of boxes of what is likely expensive equipment stacked around us. I drag one to the table and drop onto it. It's too bad I don't weigh more.

Ezra, Taisha, and Trevor park on other boxes.

Dr Foster sighs. She retrieves her pen and clicks the end. "Although quite rare, there are documented cases throughout history of group hallucinations–"

Everyone exclaims at once, and I cup my ears.

"Hallucination?" Ezra scowls. "You have no idea what we've been through."

She puts up her hands. "I can appreciate that. I'm sure everything you experienced seemed quite real and harrowing, but please hear me out."

"No." I rub the crinkly paper on my thighs, trying to smooth the texture, until Ezra takes my hand. "This was *real*. An alien arrived in Muddy Gap."

"Muddy Gap is not a town. There's nothing here. One only needs to look around. It used to be marked on maps as an unincorporated township with one service station, but that was decades ago." She levels her gaze through her visor. "Look it up, if you don't believe me."

It's a challenge, and I have a feeling my odds of winning aren't good. It's been a week since I started blogging about strange occurrences, and the government could have manipulated or erased things during that time.

Pulling up a satellite map, I locate Muddy Gap, but it's only a point on the highway. No neat rows of houses, no cul-de-sacs, no cottonwood trees or green rectangle of the baseball field. That either meant that when the xenoterrain disappeared, our reality got stitched back together wrong… or someone changed the map.

I scratch at my paper pants. "You can't erase a town of eight hundred people!"

She leans back. "What people? No one lives here. If they did, what happened to them? The 'alien' ate them?"

"No. They… they disappeared into what I believe is another dimension." My theories sound weak in the face of the map floating in my contact view.

"I realize this is frustrating for you. I was hoping that by removing you from this environment, it might help bring your memories back. Since you refuse to leave, that makes it more challenging. But I assure you all that there is no alien. No one has died that we are aware of. And you're safe–"

"Then why are you wearing hazmat suits?" Taisha asks.

"Merely a precaution. Since group hallucinations are so rare, we aren't sure what we're dealing with. A viral or fungal infection, something in Casper's drinking water, or drugs that you consumed together." She smiles like she's trying to explain something complicated to a toddler. "Let me ask you something. How long do you believe, Mx Bryant, that you've lived in Muddy Gap."

"Ten years."

"Has family ever visited you there?"

I hesitate. "No."

She turns to Ezra. "And you were only recently released from a correctional facility. Less than a year ago, correct?"

He shrinks in his chair, brows furrowed.

"What about you two?" She turns to Taisha and Trevor. "Have family or friends visited you here? People we could contact to confirm that they've also been to this town you believe existed?"

Trevor scratches his head. His gaze darts to me, then around the room, and the poor guy has already been so confused that Dr Foster making him more so when he's finally recovered makes me want to flip the table. Trevor says, "I only just moved here. Taisha too."

Dr Foster nods gravely. "As I suspected. Something caused the four of you to travel into the middle of nowhere and believe an alien attacked a town that doesn't exist."

She said I was only going to embarrass myself by keeping my livestream going, and it certainly seems that way, except that I have video evidence of the repeating highway and photos of the black voids left by the hailshells. But if she doesn't know that, I'm not going to tell her because they might hack my blog and erase it.

I switch to mirror mode so the recording can read my lips and transcribe it for the video. "I'm covered in alien gore and injuries. All of us saw the crab-scorpions and the sand. We watched buildings disappear and reappear in different configurations. You're gaslighting us. You're trying to remove the impact of everything that happened to me!" My voice breaks. I stand and flap my hands. "I saw unimaginable things. I was lost in folded reality and made it back. I was captured and imprisoned. I had a spiked baseball bat driven into my shoulder. I swam into an alien's heart and destroyed it from the inside out. I made friends. I... I fell in love. And you aren't going to take that away!"

The boxes of equipment tumble over with a crash as I kick them. "I hope to God that for everyone's sake you've combed the area and made sure there aren't polyps or buds or eggs hiding in the dirt or underground. Because I am *not* diving into another tuna-smelling monster to save all your asses. Now someone let me take a damn bath!"

Angry scientist stands so suddenly their chair clatters over and folds up. They start to round the table, but Dr Foster cuts in front of them. "It's alright. This is difficult to process. I understand."

"Do they train you how to lie with such a straight face?" I shove through the tent flaps and march outside, into a town that doesn't exist.

17

Ezra tugs me closer on the cot, his arm circling my waist and nothing between us but flimsy disposable clothes. Wan light filters through the seams of the large military tent they've housed us in.

"Are you awake?" I whisper.

He mumbles and nuzzles my neck. I should be able to relax after a shower and a night in bed with Ezra, but it still feels like I'm covered in the Dreamer's insides, like its fluids have leeched into my skin despite how hard I scrubbed myself under the scalding water. And it's impossible to sleep when there's a hard cinder smoldering in my chest, because I can't decide whether I'm upset at these government agents for trying to trivialize my experience by calling it a hallucination, or upset at myself for wishing that's all it had been.

"Do you think there's a possibility Dr Foster is right?" I ask, trying to keep the hopefulness out of my voice. "That it really was all a dream? I keep thinking of the UFO books I read as a kid, and how obsessed I was with them–"

"No. It's complete bullshit. Don't let her lies get to you. I saw sand dunes disappear right before my eyes. Plants shriveled. One moment the ocean was there, then it was gone."

I decide not to tell him that most people would agree that could only happen in a dream.

He continues, "The alien terrain disappeared, but none of the buildings or people came back–"

"I know." I don't mean for it to sound so harsh. My nose stings, and I clench my jaw. "They're all gone. Killing the Dreamer didn't help them."

He pauses for a long moment, and I can't see his expression, but his arms clamp harder around me. "That's not your fault."

"I could have done more."

"You saved the world."

"But I didn't save our town."

"I think you're amazing. For stopping the Dreamer, for figuring out what was even going on in the first place. Don't let these government assholes' words get under your skin." His mustache tickles my neck, lips finding my earlobe. "With the town gone, it makes it easy for them to spin the narrative however they want. Muddy Gap was so small, and most people haven't heard of it, so the easiest way to cover this up is to pretend like it never existed. They want everyone to believe we're four people who traveled into the middle of nowhere, did some bath salts, and started posting our hallucinations on the internet. It'll stay sensational for a week at most, then everyone will go back to celebrity drama and the latest memes, while the government can put pickled alien tentacles on the shelves in their top-secret labs."

"Other places did business with Muddy Gap. Delivery trucks came out."

"And if they tried to this past week, they probably got stuck on the highway and died. Or they'll be paid off to pretend there was never a town here. I wouldn't underestimate the length they'll go to in order to cover up what happened."

"Why? People deserve to know."

He sighs. "I don't know how to fight this. Or even if we should. I'm an ex-con and they know–"

"You swiped your neighbor's junk mail in frustrated retaliation."

"I don't want people in authority ruining my life again. And

I don't want them to ruin yours. You have millions of people on your blog who believe, and that might have to be good enough."

My body tenses and I clench my teeth, not because I'm angry at him but because he's probably right. No one in town believed me while it was happening, and convincing the world would be exponentially harder.

But at least the world is still here. Someone else's small town with all its flaws and idiosyncrasies and comforts is still here. And maybe I couldn't save Muddy Gap, maybe I didn't appreciate what was there when I had it, but the memories of it were the only thing giving me strength to keep fighting through the Dreamer when all I wanted to do was close my eyes and dream myself, never to wake up again.

I'd grumbled to myself about the new cookie-cutter subdivision and how creepy the identical houses looked as they stretched down the street. I'd complained to more than one person in town about what a waste of money the shiny new gateway sign was, arguing that nearly one hundred grand could have been put to better use. But maybe what I'd disliked so much was what those things represented – change. The town had been growing, expanding all around me, and if it had continued, I would have been even smaller, even more lonely. I was never Denver to anyone, but I wouldn't even have been Professor Pie. Just another face on a crowded sidewalk.

If we manage to make it out of here, it's unlikely I'll ever be an anonymous face in a crowd again. I'm not sure what to do with that thought.

Ezra kisses my ear and kneads my uninjured shoulder. Thumbs dig into my knotted muscles, and I groan.

"Too hard?"

"No way." I relax as he works the tension from my back. It's too bad this isn't happening in a more enjoyable place like his house or a hotel room.

"Don't think I didn't notice how you took back your takeback," he says. "You told that doctor you fell in love. I assumed you were talking about me and not a pie flavor."

"I hate to tell you this, but you'll always play second fiddle to pie. I was referring to you, though, yeah. We've been through so much. We spent together what we thought might be our last night on Earth, and it was comforting in the face of something so terrifying. I wasn't going to die alone because I had you. Not sure how to keep myself from loving you after that."

"I think I love you too."

My immediate urge is to be surprised and disbelieve it, but I cram the feelings down and let joy fill the space instead. Why shouldn't someone love me?

I roll over and hiss as my injured arm presses into the mattress. Ezra runs his thumb across my bottom lip, then kisses me softly. I bury my face against his chest, and he whispers through my hair. "Let's run away together."

It would be more tantalizing if we had a choice in the matter, but I don't say it, because it would ruin his romantic musings. And running – from the military, from this empty town, from my thoughts – sounds appealing right now. "Where are you going to whisk me away to?"

He makes a contented noise. "Where do you want to go?"

Muddy Gap was my home, and now the government is trying to tell me it never existed. "I want to see my aunt and uncle. That isn't romantic, though."

"I can make anything romantic. Uh, that came out wrong. No PDA in front of your family."

"Pretty sure my aunt would be excited to know I have a 'new boy' in my life." And the idea of bringing my first actual partner home for family to meet fills me with delight and terror. "Rapid City is four hours away from here."

"Let's go. We'll make the military drop us off in Casper and we can rent a car. My parents are in California, so that would be a far longer drive than to visit yours. Gonna call them as soon as I can, though."

"You're assuming the military will let us leave. And what if there are more aliens? What if the Dreamer isn't dead, and it recovers? I should be here to..."

"To be told it's a hallucination? I don't think the military is going to be negligent with this. They don't want aliens here either. They just don't want anyone to *know* it's aliens." He yawns. "Go back to sleep, babe. We can talk more in the morning."

I shut my eyes and burrow into the sheets. Ezra's breathing grows slow and measured. I start to sink into twilight, but his groin rubs against my ass and prospects of sleep evaporate. I check my blog instead. I have a feeling I've lost subscribers based on Dr Foster's gaslighting, but it's hard to tell because the number is still greater than it was yesterday – now up to twenty-nine point two million.

It's baffling that less than half of the comments are about the alien and how the government is trying to spin my story as a group hallucination. People comment on my avoidance of eye contact, speculate on Taisha and Trevor's relationship, and create side-by-side comparison photos of Ezra and Julio Manhammer. I haven't told him.

News outlets are going wild, but it's only regurgitated info from my blog and vague mentions of the Mandela Effect being responsible for people believing Muddy Gap was a real town.

Urgent voices cut through the tent walls. I open my eyes. Ezra's grip on me tightens as I try to slide from bed.

"Let go," I whisper, but he snores. Unconsciously protecting me with his big spoon. It would be cute if there wasn't a commotion going on outside. I pry his arm loose and he rolls over. A plasticky strawberry scent emanates from my washed hair, but at least it's no longer crusted in alien entrails. After gathering it into a ponytail and climbing out of bed, I start up the livestream again.

In the dim light, everything is vague shapes, and it takes a moment to realize Taisha's cot is empty. My heart clenches. Maybe she tried to make a break for it, or maybe they've decided we're all being too disagreeable and need to be executed.

I turn in a circle; there has to be something to use as a weapon. Trevor is asleep in his cot. An arm, darker in complexion than his fair skin, peeks out of the sheets. I dash my gaze away, but it's too late. All my subscribers who are theorizing that Trevor and Taisha are a couple will be clogging the livestream with comments all day. I can't blame the two for finding solace in each other, but I don't want to announce their business all over the internet.

Creeping out of the tent, I check for a guard, but the people are yards away, shouting and pointing at a chunk of the thrift store hovering ten feet off the ground.

Proof! Solid evidence not only for the outside world, but I'd like to see Dr Foster explain it away as a hallucination when she's staring right at it.

The realization hits me: something came back.

My fingers tingle, pulse throbbing as I stare up at the vibrant blue sky, searching for any tinge of green. The Wyoming landscape is unmolested by sand and dreamlings. Thank God. But a house, intact and complete with yard and driveway, sits beyond the tents. Someone in a pink shirt and shorts moves past the front door. I jog toward them, my mind racing and paper pants making an irritating *whisk-whisk*.

Ms Pierce steps into her grass, a bewildered look on her face. She's missing one of her crocs, silver hair frazzled, but otherwise intact. Her gaze latches onto me, and I shrink into myself. That hose is still attached to a spigot and snaking through the hailshells in the yard.

"Professor Pie?" She clutches her chest, soaking in the barren terrain beyond me. "I–I was standing in my kitchen, wondering why there was sand in the sink, then realized I didn't know how long I'd been there or what I'd been doing before. Where is…"

"Everything? It's a long story. Are you okay?"

"I don't know. Are you?"

The question reminds me of my injuries – tight bandages across my shoulder and arm, tender bruises on my back, fingertips with torn nails throbbing, and my bicep sore from a tetanus shot. I touch the steriglue-coated gash on my cheek. "I guess."

Hazmat people dash our way. Ms Pierce's eyes bloom, and she clutches my arm. They bombard her with questions even I don't have the answers to.

I push her behind me. "Do you believe me now? Or are you still going to try to spin this as being in my head? Because if her house and part of the thrift store have reappeared, so could other buildings, and there's no telling where they'll arrive. There's no time for pretending I'm crazy. We need to get out of here. *Now*. Before we end up like the wicked witch in The Wizard of Oz."

One of the agents reaches for my arm. A photocopier suddenly appears in the air to our left, then slams into Ms Pierce's yard.

"You see! It's going to be a bus next or an entire hair salon."

Scientists scatter like kicked marbles, scrambling for their equipment, their tents, and their trucks.

Ms Pierce scrapes sand from her arm. "The wizard was kind of a jackass."

"We need to go."

She stumbles, trying to keep up with my pace with her one shoe, but I don't want any of us sliced in half by a wall. Ezra rushes toward us, his hair smushed to one side. He pauses for half of a second when he spots Ms Pierce, then beckons frantically for Taisha and Trevor to follow. The tent we slept in lies collapsed on the ground, a chunk of the rec center sitting on half of it. Inside the section of hallway is the room Molly trapped Ezra and me in. A cell sitting on a cell.

"Everyone intact?" I ask no one in particular. "No one's foot got severed?"

"We're okay."

I have blog notifications shut off, but someone must have leaked my personal email, because urgent messages from random people pop up in my contacts, layering over the top of each other. All of them have subject lines screaming various flavors of *OMG DENVER GET OUT OF THERE*. Like I need to be told more than once.

Dust plumes as military vehicles roar away from the area. I wave my arms, trying to flag one down, but it blows past us, then swerves to avoid clipping the corner of the post office that appears in its path.

Trevor gapes. "It's like there's so much lag that the town is slowly generating one piece at a time."

There's nothing slow about this. I zag past a stop sign and a cottonwood tree, pulling Ms Pierce with me. We're never going to make it to the edge of town, but hiding seems like a poor idea when there's no telling if a new structure will appear on top of or within an existing one.

"My house!" Ezra snatches my hand and hauls me in a new direction. His driveway and garage are missing, and his leather armchairs, coffee table, and bookshelves sit in a perfect arrangement in the center of the yard.

I start to protest that familiar doesn't mean safe, but I made a point to trust in his cleverness too, so I usher everyone through the door.

A person in a hazmat suit stands alone in Ezra's yard, head tipped back toward a single fluorescent light panel flickering in empty space. They pull off their helmet, revealing familiar eyes and a strained mouth.

"Dr Foster!" I beckon frantically.

It breaks her from her trance, and she follows us into Ezra's. His living room is empty, geometric dimples in the carpet from the displaced furniture. Past the kitchen is a door I assumed led to a pantry. Ezra flings it open and pushes us down a dark stairwell. Lights sputter on, revealing a basement with more leather seating and a flat screen mounted on the wall.

The floor chills my bare feet, and the hair tie has given up on holding my ponytail. Ms Pierce has lost her other croc somewhere.

The sound of our labored breathing fills the space as we all stare at each other. A thunderous crash shakes the floor above, and Taisha screams.

"Over here." Ezra leads us beneath the stairs, and we huddle in silence.

I cup my ears, expecting another crash. When it doesn't come, I scoot far enough out to monitor the room in case something new materializes. There's a chance something could block our only exit, and I should have mentioned that to Ezra before he pulled us all down here. Muddy Gap has fewer underground structures than surface level, but that hasn't stopped ground-level walls and shelving from appearing several stories up. There's no telling how much might generate below ground.

Dr Foster's face is pallid, her features taut as she twists her gloved hands together.

"I deserve an apology now," I say. "We all do."

"I'm just doing my job."

I scoff and flip to mirror mode, letting the recording transcribe my speech. "Tell me this at least, and don't lie or I'm going to push you out of this basement to fend for yourself: is the alien dead? For certain?"

Switching back, I stare at her hesitant face. She nods. My contacts explode with more email notifications.

"Have you found more?" I ask. "Little offspring underground or stuck in sagebrush?"

"No. We've combed the area with ground-penetrating radar and not found anything else."

"You should set the remains on fire, just to be safe. I think it needed special conditions to survive. Unable to take hold without surrounding itself with its environment. And not great at defending itself except for its initial burst of psychic power. Those tentacles still hurt, though."

She chews her lip. "Maybe we have more to talk about."

"I'd say so."

Ezra peeks out from under the stairs. "I'd like to be certain we're not going to be fused with a chunk of Main Street first."

I lean against him, waiting for thuds and praying that the Christmas tree from the thrift store doesn't impale one of us. My inbox is filling with emails, many of them lamenting that the blog is down for them. My stream is still going, people are watching, but I'm not surprised with as much traffic as I've been getting.

Despite Dr Foster's affirmation that the Dreamer isn't coming back, I imagine curtains of orange sand falling through the seams of the stairs, the sky turning a ghastly green, and dreamlings fighting over the milk in the fridge.

Ezra absently toys with my hair, running his fingers through over and over. The repetition is so soothing that my frantic thoughts slow, and I shut my eyes. Eventually Trevor mutters that he has a leg cramp and climbs out around us.

He stops at the couch, picks up the remote, and turns on the TV. Some daytime talk show with a jeering audience splashes across the screen. I expect him to sit down on the couch, but he rounds the corner and the stairs creak with his ascent. Taisha's mouth pulls tight, then she slides past us and follows him.

I would have sent Dr Foster as the disposable scout instead.

Ms Pierce frowns. "Aliens caused this?"

"Just one. I killed it."

"Oh." She pats my arm. "Thank you."

Footsteps thud down the stairs. Taisha says, "We think it's safe."

I'm not sure how anyone can tell at this point, but I help

everyone out and we head back into the kitchen. Bits of glittering glass and drywall litter the kitchen floor. Ezra's battered car sits halfway into the living room, the beams from the roof on top of it. It seems strange it would cause damage when other things phased through each other without destruction, but when I'd tried walking across the floating asphalt beyond the thrift store, it disintegrated. Maybe a magpie landed on the roof, and it was enough disturbance to destroy the compromised wall.

It seems a shame that the government wants to cover everything up, when physicists and biologists would have the time of their lives studying what's happened. The idea of a cover up seems incredibly weak now, though, and I wonder if Dr Foster will face repercussions for admitting there's a dead alien.

The door hangs open, Trevor standing on the porch with his hands on his hips. I consider knocking on the doorframe to ensure it isn't going to collapse on us, then think better of it and insist everyone walk through without touching the framing.

The wind carries familiar scents – road tar, mowed grass, laundry soap. But there's nothing familiar beyond Ezra's yard. Pieces of buildings sit at odd angles, houses face the wrong direction with trees jutting from the roofs, and a flowerbed of snapdragons – sans dirt – hovers over my head, the root system a bit too reminiscent of the Dreamer's tentacles.

Ezra plucks a pink one out of the air, then tucks it behind my ear.

"Hey!" A gravelly voice drifts. A white woman with bottle-blonde hair stands on a portion of street, waving her arms over her head.

I jog her direction. It's Charla, wearing a nightie that I wish I and the whole internet didn't see.

I focus on her red toenail polish. "You okay?"

"Professor Pie! What... I don't understand."

"I know. Glad you're back, though."

She pats herself like she doesn't believe me, then makes a beckoning motion. "Hey young man, I could really use one of those."

Trevor stops beside me and offers Charla a cigarette from his pack. Sam stumbles from his trailer in his skivvies, then gapes at a toilet hovering in the air. I stop beside him. "I bet it will still work if you flush it. The water will drain, then fill up again."

"But... it's not attached to anything."

"Probably all kinds of things you can see with your telescope now. Although, I think we should get out of here."

People collect in the street in various states of dress and confusion. A woman stares at a cast-iron pan in her hand, then drops it. A naked kid rubs his eyes, bubble bath clinging to his legs like barnacles, and someone pulls an oversized shirt over his head and scoops him up.

It isn't the whole town – not by a long shot – but seeing some of Muddy Gap return fills my heart. "Someone call Edgar at Public Works. This place is a mess."

Chuckles ripple through the crowd. Trevor takes a drag and exhales smoke. "Mrs Mumford better give me a discount off next month's rent. You too, Denver. Actually, you killed the alien, so you better get free rent for life."

Gazes rivet to me. People whisper, and I hunch my shoulders and stare at my dirty feet. I wait for someone to say, *Well, of course he killed it. It takes an alien to know one.*

Charla squeezes my arm. "I don't know what happened exactly, but that sounds frightening. Thank you for doing that, hon."

Sam crushes me in a sweaty hug and pain flares in my shoulder. "Thanks, Professor Pie."

"Yeah, thank you, Professor." I can't tell who says it because everyone is talking at once, all of them telling me I'm a badass.

I shake my head, not sure whether to laugh or cry. "I kill a monstrous alien and save the planet, and I'm still just Professor Pie. The local weirdo with only a nickname."

"I always thought of it as a term of affection for you," Charla says, "but intent doesn't matter if it comes across as hurtful. That charity potluck at the church had a couple of amazing pies. I was going to invite you, but I know how much noise and crowds bother you. You had such a hard time in the store that one day, literally shaking while you tried to pay for your groceries." Her brows push up, and she blinks away the glossiness in her eyes. "It broke my heart, and I haven't invited you to anything since then. I should have anyway. I'm sorry."

"Really?"

Sam pulls his attention from the floating toilet. "I'm always out with my telescope when the weather is nice. I couldn't really tell if you liked it last time, but you're free to hang out with me whenever you want."

"Thank you." I pause, glancing at Ezra. "Sam... Do you stick extra things in my grocery orders on purpose? Extra bologna, shampoo, kitty bandages."

He lowers his voice. "Sometimes, yeah, if it's on clearance. Or we'll have a buy-one-get-one special. It's only supposed to be for in-store purchases, not online orders, but that's ableist so I make sure you get it anyway."

Ezra was right.

So many times unbagging groceries, wondering why I'd been given two half gallons of milk instead of one, or tubes of sunscreen, or little fruit pies in paper wrappers that didn't taste great but I ate them because there was nothing left in the pantry.

"I... I thought those were mistakes. Mix-ups."

"Nah, just looking out for you." Sam makes a fist like he wants to give me a friendly punch on the shoulder, then thinks better of it. "And I'll call you Denver if you don't want to be called Professor Pie."

I smile at Sam and the other gazes pinned to me. My town. My neighbors. Friends. "Maybe it's a fine nickname. Thank you for your kindness. I'm glad you're safe. I wish there were more of you here who were."

Some of the people still stare with dazed expressions, but panic flashes on others as they scan the faces in the crowds. This isn't even a tenth of the population, and though it's likely there are many more confused residents in other areas of town, there will be a lot of mourning going on, and I don't have the energy to stick around for it. My only consolation is that the families I recognize seem to be intact, children and spouses accounted for.

A piercing crash breaks through the chatter, and I flinch. Dust gushes from the collapsed front wall of Ezra's house. The roof awning sags, then smashes into the car below. I poke my fingers in my ears. Thank God we got out of there when we did.

"We should move everyone somewhere safer," I say. "This place isn't structurally–"

A figure rounds the house and marches through the dust. They cut an imposing silhouette with their spiked mohawk and high shoulder padding. A baseball bat hangs from their hand, and even before the haze clears, I know who it is.

Molly's hair is a hackjob, shaven on the sides with a messily-chopped strip down the center. Greasy black makeup streaks her eyes, and the translucent shells of unsettling large dreamlings are mounted on the shoulders of her football chest pad armor.

"I've been thinking about you a lot." Her bat scrapes across the ground as she nears me, and I tense, prepared to take cover if she starts swinging. Ezra outstretches his hands, then takes a hesitant step toward her. When he wraps his fingers around the bat and tugs, she doesn't resist.

She keeps her gaze trained on me, even as a tear escapes her eye, dragging a line of eyeliner down her cheek. "When the environment disappeared, I realized you succeeded in killing the alien. And I didn't understand why you did it. You were an outcast, but in the alien's world, you didn't have to be. It was our chance to rise to the top. To make something of ourselves and prove to people that we were better than how they judged us."

That's bullshit. If we'd followed her, the only thing that would have changed was who the judgment was coming from, and I didn't want to live in Mollyland.

I flap my hands, trying to get out the words, but she says, "How fucked is that thought? That I grew up learning to prepare for an apocalypse, and when one finally came, I was such a useless coward that I decided the only way to prove I was a good leader was if I was the only one left to lead?"

I raise my eyebrows and glance at Ezra. His expression is as bewildered as mine probably is. Molly shoves me, but there's no force behind it as she says, "Go on, Pie Professor. You have an opinion for everything. You think I deserve to lead anyone after hitting you with a nail-studded baseball bat?"

That's probably as close to an apology as I'm going to get, and I'm not sure I'd forgive her if she asked me to. But when I search for anger inside myself, all I find is a bone-deep exhaustion. "I... I think we all went through something very traumatic. And I hope you wouldn't have done those things under normal circumstances. I think you need some help."

Her nostrils flare, tears running down her face. She pulls off her apocalypse chest-pad armor and throws it on the ground. One of the dreamling shells on the shoulder crunches, scattering translucent shards that look like ice under the bright Wyoming sun.

Ezra shuffles his feet, mouth pinched and hands stuffed firmly in his pockets. He suddenly disappears into the gathering crowd and comes back with two young men. Without their head-to-toe camo, it takes me a minute to recognize them as Molly's brothers. They rush forward and crush her in hugs, talking animatedly. Her father seems like a piece of work, but hopefully her brothers can give her some comfort to process what she's going through. I don't have the energy.

I drop onto a set of steps that I think belonged to the library. Ezra sits beside me, and I rest my head on his shoulder and say, "This has been a very strange morning in a series of very strange mornings."

"I think now would be the perfect time to run away together."

"I'm tired. Let's drive away instead."

He kisses my temple. "Deal."

18

There are things about Trevor that simply don't fit together. Trevor as a gamer makes sense. Trevor happily talking to everyone who asks about what happened in Muddy Gap makes sense. He insists he's doing it to shield the brunt of attention from me – and while I need it – there's no reason for him to lie about his motives. He enjoys his new fame, and there's nothing wrong with that.

What doesn't make sense is why a smoker is concerned enough about his recent carb intake to go jogging around our hotel every morning. I tried to tell him lung cancer was far more serious than the risk of him gaining a few pounds from all the diner food we've been eating, but maybe it's not actually about the carbs.

His voice drifts from the hall, and they simply don't make hotel doors thick enough, even in the four-star *Blackwood Lodge* in Casper.

"No, xe's not talking to anyone right now. You think you'd want to have conversations with strangers after being inside the bowels of an alien?"

Someone replies, but it's too faint to make out.

Trevor says, "Sure, but that's because I'm xyr liaison, and also I didn't– Okay, well, if it's a gift basket or something, I can take it. I know why you want to give it to Denver in person, and please understand that xe's not ungrateful. None of us are. You should have seen the dump the government put us up

271

in earlier this week before people here got word we were in town, then they chipped in to pay for–"

Ezra grumbles into his pillow, and the only pieces I understand are *ay dios mío* and *pendejo*. Ezra is not a morning person.

Trevor's voice fades, and I drift into a half-awareness: a beam of sunlight warming my chest, the deepening rhythm of Ezra's breathing. I roll over, trying to get comfortable, but the pillow is too firm, the comforter not heavy enough, my thoughts swarming like dreamlings.

Every evening, Ezra has moaned loudly about how incredible the water pressure is in the walk-in shower in our suite. Afterward, he'll pull on one of the fluffy complimentary robes, raid the mini bar, then flop on our California king-size bed to watch a free movie on the gigantic TV.

But the bath towels are thin and scratchy, there isn't enough space to set my laptop on the fireplace to charge, and I can't even enjoy the hot tub due to my wounded shoulder. Trying to go outside is even worse when I don't know what reporters or fanatics or religious extremists will be waiting for me.

I don't want to be ungrateful. The motel we stayed in the first two nights had cigarette burns in the bedspread, mold stains on the ceiling, and a large kitchen knife inexplicably propped in the bathroom window.

I should be wearing one of those fuzzy robes, have Ezra mix me cocktails from the selection in the fridge, and relax on the faux fur in front of the faux fire. When we get hungry, we can order room service or go to the diner down the block, where a different random patron has taken care of our bill each time. Live it up as much as we can since this is only temporary. In two days, a team of scientists will pick us up and take us back to Muddy Gap to help them collect xenoterrain and record accounts of our experiences. All my waking energy – and all my nightmares – have been spent on the Dreamer and what happened to the town, and thinking about *anything* else is preferable. But the government already tried to fuck this up once, so how am I going to turn down the opportunity to ensure this is done right?

After that... I don't know what happens. This hotel room isn't home. Nowhere is. Aunt Georgina and Uncle Joe insisted I could live with them for as long as I'd like, but I'd rather not alarm them by waking up screaming in my childhood bunkbed.

There's a loud rap at the door, and I jolt awake. "Denver?"

"Damn it, Trevor, go away!" Ezra flings a pillow at the door, where it makes a soft impact then flops to the floor.

"Sorry, but I really think you two should see this." There's a giddiness I haven't heard in Trevor's voice since he first set eyes on Taisha.

"The only thing I want to see is the inside of my eyelids for the next two hours." Ezra snatches another pillow and crams it under his head.

I squint at the farmhouse-chic alarm clock on the nightstand. "It's already nine."

"Time has no meaning when you work nights as a bartender."

"Tell you what" – Trevor's voice lilts even more – "take a look out your window, and if you don't like what you see, you can go back to bed."

"We should have run further away." It's not the first time Ezra has muttered that this week, but as much as he's liked to complain, he wasn't ready for Taisha and Trevor to go their separate ways just yet either. When plans of leaving Muddy Gap came up, we'd all stared at each other in some unspoken agreement to keep our backs pressed together a little longer. And having Trevor act as publicity liaison and my media assistant has given me time to process, decompress... and melt down a couple of times. I plan on paying him even though he insists I saved his life several times over, so he should do it for free. But he already thwarted the blog subscriber "mammas_ apple" from coercing me into her car, so I'd say we're even.

"Are you looking?" Trevor asks.

I throw back the sheets and slide out of bed. A blade of light cuts through the heavy mesa-patterned curtains. Ezra groans as I part them, and I half-expect him to throw a pillow at me too, but he rolls toward me and rubs the sleep from his eyes.

If someone has spelled out their undying love for me with red Solo cups again, I'm going to be unhappy. But Trevor knows by now not to bother me with that kind of unwanted attention.

I blink in the light, waiting for my eyes to adjust, but there's a severe glare coming off someone's Airstream in the parking lot below. The thing looks like a UFO, a big chrome cigar reflecting parked cars and blue sky. Someone in a hot pink cowboy hat stands in front of it, and when they tilt their face toward my window, I realize it's the drag queen from the local RV dealership commercials.

I slide open the window, leaning toward the musty screen, and she shouts, "Howdy! Sorry to disturb you, but I'd love to have some moments of your time, if that's not too much to ask from the person who saved the world."

It might be a lot to ask, depending on what she wants, and I wish people would stop referring to me that way, even if it's true. "Give me a sec." I pull on a pair of pants, pass Ezra, who is scooping hazelnut coffee into the machine on the counter, and cross to the door of our suite. When I open it, Trevor grins and waggles his eyebrows.

"Does she want me to be in a commercial?"

He hesitates. "Yes, but I don't think Wanda will take back her gift if you tell her you can't do it."

"What gift?"

"The Airstream. She gave me a tour of it and damn. All I could think about was how trashed the cabinets were in our apartment complex, and when the place was closed up for too long it smelled like cat piss even though Mumford claimed she shampooed the carpets before I–"

I flap my hands until he stops talking. People online have

been offering me things since my livestream: money, gourmet dessert boxes, blowjobs, their firstborn child. Companies wanting me to wear their shoes, use their shampoo, endorse their pies. We set up a relief fund for the displaced residents of Muddy Gap, and Trevor has been directing people there. It surpassed $500,000 in the first twenty-four hours.

"Just tell Wanda to donate to the relief fund."

His eyes bulge. "You're kidding, right? She wants to give you a motorhome worth over a hundred grand."

"Imagine how much that would help our fund."

Ezra says to Trevor, "We'll meet you down there in a moment." I protest, but Ezra shuts the door and turns to me. Some of the grumpiness has been wiped from his face, and I don't think the coffee can take credit. He clutches his mug and thumbs toward the window. "If you won't be in a commercial in exchange for it, I will. Hell, I'll dance naked in the street for it."

"Great. You should suggest that to her."

"Why are you declining the thing before even seeing it? Is it out of guilt? Because you've done enough. You deserve good things too."

"I..." I sigh and clutch my elbows. "I don't know. How do you just accept a gift like that?"

Trevor is right. The cabinets in our complex were gouged to hell, and the pee smell was never quite shampooed out or covered up by the overpowering *Vanilla Escape* air freshener in my bathroom. My front door lock was obstinate, the medicine cabinet shelves were rusty, and it took all my strength to twist on the knob in the shower. But I'd had a cozy weighted blanket on my bed, my desk chair was molded perfectly to my backside from so much use, and I knew every creak in the floorboards by heart, every shadow animal formed by the craggy popcorn ceiling.

No matter how fancy the Airstream looked inside, it would be as foreign to me as this hotel room was.

Ezra finishes his coffee in one draft and pulls on a shirt. "C'mon. Let's at least go check it out."

Either I go willingly, or Trevor comes up here to badger me further, so I begrudgingly dress and follow Ezra down the woodsy-patterned hallway. I turn on my contacts camera and wedge in my newly purchased earbud. I have plenty of material for my blog now, and whether I want the Airstream or not, any video of the tour I upload will do far more for Wanda's marketing than a local TV commercial. Trevor said using my phone to pick up my voice while I recorded was far less convenient than getting an earbud, and I needed better tech. He'd called me a Philistine, and I was so impressed he even knew the word that I hadn't argued.

Ezra and I take the elevator to the first floor. Two foil balloons shaped like alien heads are staked in the grass out front, and the sky reflected in their bulbous foreheads is a little too green for my liking. A battered pickup truck sits at the curb, the sides covered in aggressively painted Bible scriptures. Mounted on the back is a sign that proclaims: DO NOT WORSHIP FALSE PROPHETS. JESUS IS HERE AND ONLY HE CAN SAVE YOU!!!

Jesus is parked in the fire lane.

Trevor appears beside me and thumbs at the truck. "Don't worry. I already told the front desk."

"I'll be sure to bestow my false prophet blessings on the hotel clerks for all the weirdos they've had to run off this week."

We follow Trevor to the Airstream, which looks far larger up-close. So does Wanda. She towers over us in Holstein-patterned platform cowboy boots and a denim mini skirt, waves of banana-yellow hair cascading out from beneath her hat.

"So nice to meet you, Denver. And Ezra, yes?" She shakes our hands, long acrylic nails curling around my fingers. "I'm Wanda Lust."

"With a name like that, I guess your choices were to sell motorhomes or become a hobo, huh?" I say.

Ezra starts to correct me, then closes his mouth. Wanda beams me a cherry red grin and says, "You can save the world *and* be funny. The talent."

My smile feels like it's dried to my face, tight and cracking. "I can't always pull it off. Being funny, I mean. I'd rather not have to save the world again." Trevor will probably tell me to edit that line out of my recording so I don't sound like a downer to my millions of subscribers, but I don't possess the histrionics someone like Wanda Lust has. All I am is myself, take it or leave it. "I'm recording this, by the way. For my blog. Can you tell me what this big silver cigar is all about?"

Her smile grows bigger. "Absolutely! Please come inside."

Ezra and I follow her up the metal steps. Wanda rattles off dimensions and features, and I breathe in the factory-new scent, passing seafoam Ultraleather seating and recycled-aluminum countertops. This aerodynamic classic boasts panoramic windows to let in natural light and a grand vista of whatever adventure destination you're parked in.

Beyond the window, a tow truck pulls up to the fire lane in front of the Jesus pickup, then lowers the underlift. I draw the blackout curtains closed.

Wanda ushers me to the dinette, demonstrating the convertible capabilities like a gameshow assistant. She pushes down the table, then folds the seat cushions over the top and voila! It's now a bed.

Trevor and Taisha step inside, eating those little blueberry muffins from the continental breakfast. Before I can tell them getting crumbs all over the woven vinyl flooring is a terrible idea, I spot a clear acrylic bubble mounted on the wall in the bedroom nook. Black aquarium gravel sits at the bottom, and ribbons of light bend through the water, refracted into blurry rainbows on the wood laminate. A male betta fish with a turquoise body darts through the water, his gauzy red fins flowing spectacularly around him.

"Wanda?"

She pauses in the middle of a sentence, expressive hands frozen. I say, "This betta would do better with an air pump. And he needs some plants to hide and rest in. Plastic are okay, but an aquatic variety like Anubias is a good choice. I have a feeling having the tank this close to a window will encourage too much algae growth." I survey the walls, then head back to the dinette. "This would be a better spot. Not too much light but still far enough away from any grease coming from the stove. A good view while you sit here on the computer or while you're eating."

Wanda blinks at me. "Um, the fish is just for display. Adds a bit of a personal touch when I'm giving tours. It goes back to the dealership when I'm done."

"Ah."

I'm guided into the bathroom, but I don't hear any of what she's saying. I imagine sitting at the dinette with a slice of rhubarb custard, typing up a blog post while the betta keeps me company. No. I can do better than that. Ezra and I sitting in a restaurant I've never ventured to in some other state, trying their fare so I can write a review, *then* retiring to the Airstream with its betta and its outlets in appropriate places. A weighted blanket on the bed, my own pillows, Ezra and I cuddled up beneath the panoramic windows... That would be my speed of adventure.

"How's the water pressure in the shower?" I ask.

Something shifts in Wanda's face, and she clasps her hands together. "I'm so glad you asked! Many models of detachable handheld showerheads have low water pressure due to the water having to travel a greater length through the hose, but this baby here has a flow rate of two point five GPM, which is the highest allowed in the US. You can toggle between power rain, pulsating massage, bubbling water–"

Ezra leans his head inside the shower, then gives me two thumbs up.

He doesn't have a home any more than I do. Not a physical

one. And we haven't known each other long in the grand scheme of things, but he's already told me the idea of us heading off on different trajectories would take the bottom out of his world as much as it would mine. Whatever future adventure awaits, I'm confident we'll do it together.

Wanda trails off and stares at me. "Do you care about the water pressure at all? Or any of this? I feel like you've been somewhere else this whole time."

I'm being ungrateful again, but all that knowledge does is make me want to dig harder into my defenses. "I have a lot on my mind."

"Of course you do. And off the record – or leave it in, your call – I *was* hoping for some promo out of all this. But that's not why I want to give you the Airstream. I'll save you my 'you stopped the apocalypse and tangentially saved my life' speech. I've been to your blog, though. Seen your videos, and I just... want you to have it." She bounces her shoulders in a shrug as exaggerated as the rest of her. "What do I have to do, give you the fish too?"

"Yes," I say immediately. "I'd take just the fish, honestly." Before any of them can tell me not to turn down a one hundred grand motorhome for a five-dollar fish, I continue, "But if you really want me to have all this, I'll take it. Thank you for your generosity."

I head back to the acrylic bubble tank mounted on the wall. The betta shimmies to the surface, taking in air. "Feels like it could be home."

19

Fourth try – I can do it this time.

I shake the nerves from my hands and stop in front of the mirror again. The studio makeup is ghastly, airbrushed foundation so thick I look like I'm wearing a facial mask, and there's a bit too much purple in my lipstick to match my floral-patterned suit.

They've told me to simply ignore the cameras, but that's what everyone said the last three times too, and it didn't stop me from freezing up and being unable to follow through on the interviews.

It should have been easier last time, with Ezra, Taisha, and Trevor there, shouldering the brunt of the attention, except no one mentioned that there was a live audience in addition to cameras. I'd at least made an appearance, but the experience was so overwhelming that every question directed at me hung in the air for an awkward few seconds before Ezra or someone else answered.

For whatever reason, my selective mutism and reputation for denying or canceling interviews only increased my popularity, and Trevor mentioned that the online consensus for me following through with this interview was seventy percent against.

"Mx Bryant?"

I squeeze the fidget toy in my pocket and press the quiet clicker side, even though it isn't as satisfying as the one that makes noise. The assistant leads me to a small room with muted colors and two chairs. They lean toward my ear. "You're going on in ten. Remember, it's not live, so if you need to stop, say so. They hid the cameras. Just face Bennett."

I walk inside. The host, Bennett Carter, is a slender Black man with a thousand-watt smile. He's intimidatingly attractive with a confident air, but as he holds out his hand and we shake, I sense there's genuine friendliness beyond his veneer. He says, "So glad to have you here. Welcome."

My thumb rakes back and forth across the toy's clicker. "Thanks."

That one word is more than I've been able to say in any other interview. I sit and blow out a slow breath.

"That is a handsome suit. I can't pull off florals. Makes me look like wallpaper." He picks up a coffee mug with the show's logo and takes a sip. "I heard you were offered a modeling contract."

"I've been offered quite a few things. The majority of which would make my boyfriend leave me."

"You mean the marriage proposals?"

I snort. "Among other things. If anyone should be modeling, it should be Ezra. I mean, have you seen him?"

"You've been focused on more serious matters. Have all of the residents of Muddy Gap been able to relocate with the money you raised?"

"A lot of people left to stay with family. We've reached out to those we could find and were able to give them enough of a windfall to take care of some bills, buy food, and put a deposit on rental. That sort of thing. Taisha has been in charge of that, and she's doing an amazing job." She's already talked about it herself in interviews, and even though this interview is going to be about something else entirely, everyone likes to bring up the fundraising at least once. They need that little slice of feel-good before digging into discussion of eldritch space horrors.

"I'm glad you have other people to help divide up the work, since you've been quite busy with other things. Your name is in scientific journals now, and academic papers on extraterrestrial biology."

"Yes, but I'm not a scientist any more than I'm a model." I click the toy in my pocket. "I helped with descriptions of the alien, its composition and behavior. Went back to Muddy Gap with a research team and found evidence of the xenoterrain for them to study."

There wasn't much. Combing through the entire town, we came up with enough sand and hailshells to fill a five-gallon bucket, a couple of the dried-up red plants, and three dreamling remains. One of them had been inside the carton of heavy cream, and I wasn't sure if that made it the winner or the loser.

Bennett drags a box from around the chair and pulls out the large dreamling shell I provided the studio with before the show. His lip curls even as he tries to maintain his smile – he's trying to count the legs, just like everyone else does.

"There are thirteen," I say.

"An odd number? Why do you think that is?"

"No idea. I'm not the scientist. I learned enough about the Dreamer to stop it. Anything after that is not my forte."

Bennett sets the dreamling back in the box and nudges it away. "But your experience was also instrumental in helping scientists create a theory of how the alien manipulated spacetime. Deducing where the foreign environment came from and where all the people went. Can you demonstrate?"

The two sheets of paper I requested sit behind the coffee mugs, and it's a relief to hold something physical that might convey my thoughts better than my words.

I pick up the white one. "This paper is Muddy Gap's plane of existence. It's flat, smooth. We can travel across it in a straight line." I set it back on the table, then pick up the orange paper and crumple it into a tight ball. "This is the alien's environment. Imagine it's condensed much more than this.

"We argued over its origin. Did the alien generate it with its mind? Did it carry the environment with it from some other place? Is this dimension existing in the same physical space as our own at all times but can only be pulled through under certain conditions or with a great amount of psychic power? We can't confirm unless – God help us – another alien appears. But this is what we think happened afterward.

"When the alien arrived, it started to unfurl its environment" – I open the orange paper slightly and place it on the white one – "on top of ours. These opening folds exposed sand, stone, shells, and several instances of odd-smelling rain. When Ezra and I tried to take pictures of the hailshells through our contacts, they didn't show up properly because they were still partially inside these proverbial folds. The alien struggled to keep the paper open, so sometimes it would close again, taking most of the environment with it. As it gained strength, this happened–"

I partially unball the orange paper, then start wrinkling the white one. "At the same time, the Dreamer was crushing Muddy Gap. The edges accordioned and people got lost in creases. Ez and I tried to leave town and got stuck, driving over and over within the same complex wrinkle." I smash the white paper into a ball. "Buildings folded into others, pieces went missing, stuff got stuck in the air."

Bennett takes the white paper and opens it, trying to smooth it over his knee. "And when you killed the alien, the reverse happened? The orange paper crumpled back up and the white one opened. Things returned to normal."

"Sort of. People and things came back, but look at that paper. No matter how much you try, it's always going to be kind of wrinkled. It will never be smooth and perfect the way it was before. And there are still people and buildings missing. Some of the folds in that white paper are sealed closed. They never opened, and I doubt they ever will."

I pick up the balled orange paper and flick it into the box containing the dreamling shell.

"Thank you for that explanation," Bennett says. "I'm not sure having that knowledge brings any amount of comfort, but it's better than lying awake at night wondering about it, huh?"

I picture him without his studio makeup, staring at his bedroom ceiling in the dark. There's probably a lot of that still going on. At least I have Ezra to comfort me when nightmares come.

"Let's talk about the 'Dreamer'." He sets the wrinkled white paper in the box. "You've described the alien as many things on your blog: akin to a jellyfish, an anemone, a sea star. But a government team dissecting the remains has drawn up sketches and determined it most resembles a diatom, correct?"

A panel flashes on behind him, displaying a 3D generated model of the Dreamer. Memories of iridescent light warping through inflated tentacles rise in my mind, and I can almost smell the ozone-and-tuna scent of its insides.

I thumb the fidget toy, but it's the noisy side and clicks fill the room.

Bennett looks past me, intensity in his eyes, and the screen shuts off. "Sorry about that."

"A diatom is what they're comparing it to as far as looks go, yes. But honestly, after seeing the drawings and models and thinking back to when I was there... to me it looks like a brain cell. And sometimes I wonder if it had reproduced, if the aliens would connect through synapses, forming a network across the Earth."

Bennett's makeup maintains his rich bister glow, but some of the cheer falls from his face. "That's a frightening thought."

"It is. And I'm under no belief that what happened in Muddy Gap can't happen in another place. There's no way to stop another alien from arriving if one has the means and desire. But with as much exposure as the incident has had, my hope is that if someone eventually sees a light flaring green in the night sky, or strange sand inexplicably built up in the streets, they'll be knowledgeable enough to take action before it's too late." I cross my legs and take a sip of water from my coffee cup. "But hopefully there'll be no need to go diving into alien guts."

Smile strained, he says, "Let's change the subject, shall we? I want to be able to sleep tonight."

"I'd like that too. Do you want to hear about the book I'm writing?"

He hesitates. "Is it about the alien?"

"Not at all. It's about pie."

Two clamshell containers holding *The Lounge*'s alphabet pie sit in the fridge next to a can of whipped cream. I scoop up the cartons and set them on the Airstream's compact counter.

Ezra grabs the sacks of sandwiches on the shelf below, then tilts his head. "Are you going to make them all eat one of these? *And* the pie?"

I purse my lips. "Who is the food critic here? *The Lounge*'s alphabet is excellent, and yes, I'm going to make you try some."

He lifts the sacks. "And sandwiches you haven't taste-tested? Just bought enough for everyone upon hearing the name?"

I lean against the seafoam dinette booth and peer out the window at the house up the drive. "I'm not going to have a sandwich named after me and not force my family to eat it. And if they don't like The Denver Special, well, more for me. Uncle Joe is barbequing, so there will be plenty to eat."

Cars line the drive, and most of them I don't recognize because I haven't seen my cousins in so long.

Wrapping his arms around my waist, Ezra tugs me back and purrs. "Nothing will be more delicious than the original Denver, and I'm not sharing."

"This is family so you have no competition here. You don't have competition anywhere."

He smooths his shirt over his belly, then smooths his mustache, then smooths his hair. "Do I look okay?"

His form-fitting tee with a deep V-neck is one salvaged from his Muddy Gap house, and tight jeans hug his round ass. He's sporting a fresh fade, his cologne more saccharine and spicy than any pie.

"You're too sexy. One of my cousins will steal you."

"Want me to do some laps around the trailer?"

"Then you'll be sweaty and sexy."

"I could pop the hood of the truck and check the oil."

"Then you'll be dirty and sexy." I tug his hips to mine and grind against him. "You're making it worse."

He lets out a breath and picks up the sack of sandwiches. "I don't want to meet your family all hot and bothered."

I follow him to the door, then hesitate. I'm wearing nearly the same thing as him, jeans and tee, but it suddenly feels far too sloppy for this reunion. "What about me? How do I look?"

"Everything pales in comparison to you. The stars lose their light, the flowers look like ash."

"What book did you steal that from?"

He chuckles. "It was a movie, actually. But I still mean it."

We twine our fingers together and walk up the drive, past the dandelion-riddled yard and a rock garden teeming with succulents. The trim on the two-story house is different, but familiar curtains hang in the picture window, and windchimes Aunt Georgina has had since the beginning of time tinkle merrily in the breeze. Voices drift beyond the gate to the backyard. I lead Ezra that way and push through into savory barbecue smoke and familiar laughter.

Long folding tables that have assisted every party and holiday in the household are burdened with snacks, drinks, and disposable plates. Bram stands beside one, clutching a fruity wine cooler, his hand in a bag of potato chips.

He glances my way, then does a double-take. "There you are! How the hell are you?"

"Hi. I'm doing great. How are you?"

"You wouldn't have to ask if you kept in touch."

I suck in my lip, but he pulls me into a hug and says, "I'm just giving you a hard time. You going to introduce me to your other half?"

"This is Ezra, he/him. Ezra, this is Abraham, he/him. When I was a kid, Bram would make up all kinds of wild stories because I was gullible and he knew I'd believe them."

"Denver!" Aunt Georgina rushes toward us, tears spilling down her face, and scoops me into a hard squeeze. She sobs into my chest, snatches Ezra's shirt, and pulls him into her embrace too. Frizzy hair that's escaped her updo tickles my cheek. She's lost weight, less substance to her than there used to be, and I can't help thinking it's my fault.

I frown and pat her back. "Are you mad at me? Have I been causing you stress?"

Pulling back, she smacks my arm. "I haven't seen you in so long, and your whole town got turned inside out! Of course I've been stressed. You killed an alien, and TV interviewers have talked to you more than I have."

"That's not true. I only did one interview." And I won't be doing more. I have nothing else to say.

She gives me the look she always does when I'm being pedantic, so I point to Ezra. "This is–"

"Ezra. I know. I do read your blog. And I watched a recording of your livestream about twenty times." She pats Ezra's chest like she wrinkled him. "It's nice to meet you. Thank you for being so good to Denver. I can tell you're a huge comfort to him. I insist you call me Auntie."

His cheeks redden. He takes the cartons from my hands and sets them and the sacks on a table. "We brought food. Denver's weird pie, and Denver's weird sandwiches."

"That sounds about right." Abraham reaches into the bag and pops open a carton. "What kind of sandwiches?"

"Bologna."

"Definitely sounds right."

Uncle Joe strides over with a greasy spatula, followed by my other cousins. His mustache is whiter than I remember, and time has lined his face. "Hey, kid."

We exchange more introductions, more hugs, and more jabs dug up from the vault of things to tease each other about, until I insist we sit down so I can eat one of my namesake sandwiches.

I pop open a container and pull one out. Though I haven't had one, I did look up the ingredients once I heard about it. It's hefty, thick slices of smoked and fried bologna, melty white cheddar, caramelized red onion, butter lettuce, and zesty gherkin mayo between grilled wedges of seeded Texas toast. I take a bite, and the medley of savory and salty flavors makes me moan loud enough that everyone glances at me.

"Oh my god. A masterpiece. Ten stars."

Ezra's plate is stacked high with ribs and potato salad, but he slides over one of the sandwiches and gamely tries it. His eyebrows shoot up and he nods, speaking around his bite. "That is good. I would never know it was bologna. Actually, I've never had bologna. It always looks so gross in those yellow packages."

"Wait until you try the pie."

Aunt Georgina pours a wine cooler into a cup, and the drink fizzes. "I want to know everything that's going on with you. What are you working on? How's your life? How serious is this relationship?"

"You did say you read my blog." I take another bite of glorious sandwich.

Lines form around her mouth. "Yes, but I want to hear it from you."

There's so much food and diningware on the table that I don't notice the pattern of the tablecloth until I push away the bowl of potato salad and reach for a napkin. Bright pink letters proclaim OUTTA THIS WORLD above cartoon flying saucers. A blue glob of something crusts over the pattern.

My fingers jitter, and I drop the napkin.

Ezra tucks it under my plate and leans toward my ear. "You okay?"

"Sure. Yeah." It's just a tablecloth. Auntie has probably used it for dozens of get-togethers since my ninth birthday. And that blue smear isn't necessarily birthday cake frosting.

Billie swallows a bite of ribs and wipes her mouth. "I heard your town is a tourist attraction now."

"Huh?" I look up. "I guess. Haven't been back there after the research team got what they needed, though I did see some pictures. They're letting people walk through the structurally sound building arrangements on the outskirts, and someone mounted spy glasses on a platform so you can look through and see the things that are floating, but the inner part of town is fenced off."

"I'm still paying off the furniture in that house," Ezra mutters.

"It's so wild." Beth shakes her head. "I want to hear the whole story. All the weird details."

I sigh. "Well–"

"Not now." Uncle Joe wipes a drip of barbeque sauce from his white shirt. "He's probably sick to death of telling it."

A car door slams beyond the fence, and Aunt Georgina sets down her drink. She draws in a slow breath. "Okay, honey, I know you don't like surprises, and I know you don't want to see your mom, but–"

"What?" Ice water pours through my veins, and I grip the seat of my chair. The tablecloth, my cousins, even the placement of the table under the walnut tree, it's all the same. My mom is going to push through the squeaky gate, high as a kite, drawling "Happy Birthday", and this was all a mistake. We should have kept driving to Chamberlain. I want to be anywhere but in this seat facing the gate, having my mom ruin what is supposed to be a gathering where I belong and am wanted.

The gate squeals, and a man takes a tentative step inside. "Am I in the right place?"

"Yes!" Aunt Georgina hops up and leads him through the grass.

His black hair is pulled into a low ponytail, and freckles dust his light brown skin. My heart throbs as I soak in his long nose and prominent cheekbones, the curve of his chin, and the way his fingers fidget at his sides.

He doesn't need an introduction.

I push out of my chair and round the table. "Should I call you James, or Dad?"

His fingers curl through the belt loops on his jeans. "Maybe James, for now. And you're Denver. I like that name."

"Aunt Georgina gave it to me after I came out as non-binary. I didn't like my original one. I've been looking for you. Wanted to meet you but there are too many James Bryants, and I wasn't sure which one was right. I look just like you. Did you want to meet me too? How much Cherokee am I?"

He blinks, face blank, and I've said too much at once, my anxious mouth running unattended.

"You're a fourth Cherokee," he says. "And yes, I did want to meet you. Long before this. But the name I had for you wasn't the one you have now. Your mom was no help except to provide the number of your aunt. I was too nervous to reach out to her. But I saw you in that TV interview and realized how foolish I've been not to meet my kid."

"Do you have others?"

"Yeah. Two. And a wife. But I thought it would be best to come by myself this time." He tugs on his ponytail. "I feel like I'm intruding here."

"Not at all." Auntie ushers him toward the table. "Come eat."

"Do you like pie?" I ask.

"Who doesn't?" He takes a seat, and Uncle Joe passes him a plate.

"I know I'm asking too many questions, but can I ask another? It's slightly more important than if you like pie, but not by much."

James gives me a tense grin. "Go ahead."

"I asked Auntie and Uncle Joe to give me a new first name, but will you give me a new middle one? I know my middle name is *your* name, and that's why I haven't changed it, but I want something gender neutral."

His gaze scrambles across the yard and the walnut tree. "Um."

"I don't mean right now. You look overwhelmed. Just at some point."

"Sure. I'd be honored."

I sit beside Ezra. He kisses the side of my head and squeezes my hand.

We stuff our faces with food, and I break out the pie before anyone has had time to digest their ribs and bologna sandwiches, because if my mouth is occupied, I can't keep asking my dad questions he's not yet prepared to answer.

I thought it was impossible to layer a good experience over the top of my ninth birthday memories, but the UFO tablecloth, the overhanging tree, and my view of the gate no longer seem like harbingers of renewed trauma, but puzzle pieces sliding into place. Things are where they belong, and so am I.

"I'm writing a book." I glance at Auntie then at my dad. "Oh, but you saw my interview so you already know."

"Tell me about it anyway," James says. "I want to hear."

"Ezra and I are traveling the country, trying pies in diners and bakeries. It's like my blog, but will only feature the very best ones. No negative reviews. And Ez is the photographer. He has these amazing vintage cameras and is using them to do TTVs. That's 'through-the-viewfinder'. Instead of using film for his Brownie and Argus Seventy-Five, he looks through the viewfinder and takes the photo with his contacts. It gives the pictures a nice retro feel that often matches the diners we're in."

"That sounds like a lot of fun." James pulls one of the sandwich cartons toward himself. "That your Airstream out there?"

"Yeah. And I'm enjoying it a lot. The whole experience." Much more than I expected, and I hope directing business to Wanda Lust's RV dealership has earned her many sales. My out-of-town pie excursions used to be the highlight of my week, but they were also lonely. I ate by myself, no one to share in my joy or disgust, and I only had a handful of readers who cared about my opinion.

Being able to sit beside Ezra and offer him forkfuls of pie – heavy on the whipped cream – in between his photo shoots, made the experience much more fun. We'd tour the city and window shop, then curl up in bed in the trailer. Several times, I woke in a cold sweat, certain I heard hailshells drumming against the Airstream's roof. Another time I thought I was suffocating inside the Dreamer's rubbery flesh. But each time, Ezra was there, his big spoon folding around me.

Whorls of whipped cream cover the pie, and bright red alphabet noodles decorate the top. Whenever I've ordered it from *The Lounge* in the past, it's been a random scattering of letters. But some cheeky pastry chef has spelled out *HELLO DENVER*.

I slice into it, revealing a layer of pink pudding embedded with more noodles and bits of diced pear. After dishing everyone a slice, I carve into mine and take a bite. The playful zing of cinnamon candy and creamy pudding melds in my mouth.

Ezra's face scrunches like I'm making him eat worms. He takes a tentative bite, then relaxes. "Definitely not the worst of the pies we've tried so far. I like it, actually. I thought it would be horrible."

"Thanks for that vote of confidence in my pie critiques."

"So where are you going next?" James asks. "Do you have specific restaurants in mind to hit? Places you've researched? Or do you just randomly choose them?"

"It used to be random when it was only for my blog. But since we're looking for the very best pies for this book, we're researching them ahead of time. There are a couple of places in Sioux Falls to stop at, and then we're heading down to a little town outside of Omaha. One of my original blog subscribers owns a diner called *Grandma Z's,* and she made a pie in my honor. Cherry and star anise in a hazelnut crust. It's called the Denver Deep Dish." I thread a stray alphabet noodle through the tines of my fork and smile. "I can't wait to try it."

ACKNOWLEDGEMENTS

I grew up in Boise, Idaho, down a long desert road that had only a few houses and the state prison. My bus ride was an hour; I was the first one on in the morning and the last one off in the afternoon.

Being the awkward autistic kid I was, I had more books than friends and would fill my long rides reading. My favorite library books were an unwieldy book on the paranormal, and a tome of Greek mythology with a topless Medusa illustration on the cover that was apparently appropriate in an elementary library back in 1991.

At the time, I knew only one kid on my street - Jared - and I would often move seats to sit with him. One morning, shortly after getting on the bus, he tapped me on the shoulder and pointed out the window, up into the bruised sky and said, "What's that?"

It took me a moment of searching before I spotted what Jared was pointing at. Hovering high up in the air, framed between the telephone lines, was something black and triangular. I had no idea what I was looking at. It wasn't a plane or jet. The object was static, a geometric void puncturing the canvas of the sky. A kite? Much too far away and much too big. A balloon? Too angular and not shrinking into a pinpoint as it floated away.

Grainy color photos in my library book on the paranormal came rushing back to me, and I shrieked, "It's a UFO!"

Jared scoffed. "No it's not."

"Then what is it?"

He stared back out the window uncertainly, and his silence told me all I needed. If neither of us knew what we were looking at, very logically that made the inverted triangle an unidentified flying object.

As the bus made its slow route toward town, I kept my gaze fixed on the object in the sky. Each time we turned a corner, I would hop seats, pressing my face to the smeary windows, intent not to lose sight of the UFO. I tried to tell other kids what was out there, if they'd only look.

They made fun of me.

An older kid chimed up and said he believed me one hundred percent. For just that morning while he was waiting for the bus, a giant flying saucer had descended on him, blasting laser beams, and he'd rolled into the bushes just in time to avoid being disintegrated.

No one believed me, not even Jared who'd been the first one to see it. But it didn't sway me from being convinced I was seeing something I had no explanation for.

As we neared town and the sun peeked over the horizon, the UFO hovered beneath a bank of pink frosted clouds in the distance. A sudden beam of white light exploded from the tip of the object, spreading over the rooftops of the suburban houses below. Then it shot into the sky, disappearing into the clouds. I searched frantically, trying to catch sight of it again, but it was gone.

I look back on this in disbelief. There's no way it actually happened. I'm misremembering what I saw. But after getting to school that day and settling into my desk, I distinctly remember pulling out a piece of paper and drawing an inverted triangle with a beam of light coming out of the tip. My mom remembers me talking about it. Time hasn't skewed my memory.

Is it possible my childhood imagination and love of paranormal library books convinced me I was seeing something that defied description, when in reality it had a perfectly normal explanation? Sure. I don't know if aliens exist, and I'm not claiming I saw a spacecraft piloted by one. But that event has stuck with me through the years, and it heavily influenced *Key Lime Sky*.

I'm incredibly grateful for all the believers - not necessarily in aliens, but in me. *Key Lime Sky* would not have been possible without the following people:

My fantastic agent, Ren Balcombe, and everyone at Janklow & Nesbit.

Gemma Creffield, who fell in love with this book from the very first pitch line. Desola Coker, Caroline Lambe, Amy Portsmouth, Eleanor Teasdale, Karen Smith, and the entirety of Angry Robot.

My critique partners: Keshe Chow, Bria Fournier, Essa Hansen, Darby Harn, and Jennifer Lane.

My friends and family, who may not all read my books but have always encouraged my creativity and success.

And Mom, for believing me all those years ago.

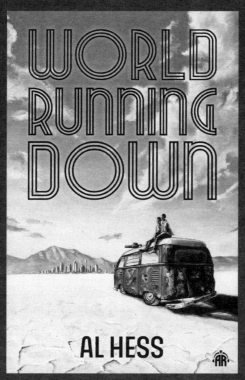

1

A Good Deed in a Weary World
Valentine

This was not a dignified place to die. Sepia hills sat beneath a chalky sky, salt flats and barren desert rolling away in all directions like a crappy abandoned landscape painting. Hexagonal ridges of salt crunched beneath Valentine's boots as he stepped around the body, glittering grains rasping against his legs as the wind picked up. The otherworldliness of so much white sucked all the warmth from what would be this pirate's final resting place.

Valentine crouched in front of her, his likeness peering back at him from her tinted shades. Blood and dirt crusted the hole in her forehead, and whatever weapons or valuables she'd had were already gone. Feathers were woven into her ratty hair, and they fluttered against her mouth, still open in a silent scream.

He tried to push her jaw closed, but it was stiff from rigor. Ugh. It didn't matter how many bodies he encountered; he would never get used to dealing with them.

Footsteps neared, but he didn't look up. Ace nudged the woman's temple with a steel-toed boot. "She probably deserved it. Put on some act about how she's trying to feed her family. They do that, y'know." She knit her brows in mock supplication, then clasped her hands beneath her chin and raised her pitch. *"Please, mister. I got starving kids at home.'"*

Valentine scowled. Maybe it was spending practically every moment of the past year together that made Ace so adept at pressing his buttons. Or maybe it was natural talent. Either way, it was tiresome. The pirates were their enemies, sure, but whatever thoughts had gone through this woman's brain before the bullet did were likely no different than what he or Ace would think so close to the end.

"You need to pick up knitting or tarot card reading. Making fun of the dead is not a distinguished hobby."

"And burying random corpses is not a productive one!"

"Just because it's not–"

"You can't stand out here in the sun for hours and dig a four-foot-deep hole for some woman who would have lodged an arrow right through your eyeball without a second's hesitation. There are too many people in the world to worry about. And salt pirates should be particularly low on that list."

Valentine picked up the shovel and jammed it into the ground, then hefted the dirt behind him. His concern didn't work that way.

"Jesus, Val." Ace sighed. "Stop it, will you?"

The shovel clanked against a rock, and he struggled to dislodge it.

Ace pinched the bridge of her nose and blew out a slow breath. "I don't want us to waste time when we have a delivery to make. Plus, it's dangerous. I shouldn't have stopped at all, but I thought she might have something good on her that we could grab quick."

It was *his* van, but Ace was always the one who ended up driving.

He flung dirt over his shoulder, continuing to ignore her.

"Val..." Ace stepped back toward the van.

They were supposed to be a team, but the only time they got along was when they did things her way, and he didn't have the energy to fight about every decision.

"Val, c'mon!" she repeated.

Sighing, he dropped the shovel. "Fine, then let's go." Hopefully the pirate's kin would look for her when she didn't come home. They could give her a proper pirate burial, whatever that entailed.

Trying to keep his voice level was difficult. "We gotta be in Festerchapel by nightfall, anyway." He pursed his lips. "Such a gross name. Sounds like a church full of zombies."

Ace squinted, sun-bleached hair fluttering in the wind. "Dog Teats is worse and always will be."

"Don't make fun of Dog Teats. Only bar that sells the mead I like." It was also the biggest queer community this side of Las Vegas. He knew everyone there; a couch, food, and friends were always available. Unfortunately, the road there was near non-existent, and Ace argued they could pick up work in places more easily accessible.

"You should just drink whiskey neat like every other salvager. Put hair on your chest."

"Is that what I've been doing wrong?" He looked down at the pirate one last time and pulled her scarf up over her face, tucking it beneath her head so the wind didn't blow it away.

Brittle brush whisked at their boots as they headed back for the van.

Ace hopped into the driver's seat. The old beast was looking a little worse for wear with every passing month, but Valentine supposed that made it more intimidating. They'd had to replace the passenger's side of the windshield with a metal vent cover last month. It had previously withstood three years of pirate arrows, rocks, and birds, but was apparently no match for Valentine sitting on it when drunk. His ass had gone right through the pane.

He tested the sliding door, laced in rust and studded with welded staple steps. The damn thing had a habit of flying open when they were driving if the lock wasn't secure. They'd lost half a shipment of copper piping before, but that wasn't close to what a disaster it would be to lose any of the fuel barrels stacked in the back right now. The tank batteries within two hundred miles were already tapped dry, but traveling the extra distance to an oil field with a partially full one had earned them more barrels than Festerchapel had asked for.

An unwanted visual of them exploding open on the highway entered his mind, and he checked the lock again.

He climbed the steps to the top of the van and collapsed in the scalding vinyl seat behind the static-gat. He much preferred driving to sitting up here. Driving gave him an active task, all his thoughts cinched down like they were supposed to be. But Ace complained the gat was too hard to wind up. It was, which is why they'd gotten such a good deal on it.

Valentine hooked his boots into the stirrups of the gun stand as Ace drove them south. Hot wind buffeted his face, the torn shoulder of his blazer flapping. The gatling squeaked as it swiveled on its stand, and the dead pirate disappeared into the distance.

He couldn't shake the image of his reflection in her glasses – strong cheekbones, heavy brows, all his shortcomings indistinct. Dress him in the perfect suit, a city suit, with wide lapels and broad shoulders and a silver collar clip. Scrub the dirt from his face and slick back his hair. Give him shiny shoes without a speck of blood or shit so he could look like one of the apathetic jerks in his magazines.

Reaching into his back pocket, he pulled out his slim billfold and removed a magazine page from within. The edges were creased, and the fold lines had become soft and fuzzy with age. He opened it and smoothed it over his knee, shielding it from the wind.

The heaviness in his heart grew as he stared at the spread. A model stood casually, his gaze on something in the distance, like the fact that he had the world's squarest jaw and a thousand-dollar outfit weren't worth his time to consider.

He was a man who had probably never spared a thought for his Adam's apple, for his height, his narrow hips, or his dick… Well, he probably thought about that last one a lot, but never the idea of *lacking* one.

Valentine would never have any of those things, but once he had a city visa, he could relieve some of this anguish. Residents of Salt Lake City had free medical care, which meant he could go back on testosterone and get chest surgery. And after that, yes – hell yes – he was going to buy a sexy suit. Permanent citizenship felt like a delusion – he'd already failed the practice test several times – but there were so many more resources in the city. Once he had a visa, he could get better textbooks, watch tutorial videos, or hire an actual tutor to help him. Memorizing historical figures and writing grammatically correct sentences was easy, but doing algebra made his brain melt.

It was hard to stay optimistic about eventual residency though, when he was up here roasting his ass with sand raking his face; when every day meant heading into dangerous territory for materials needed by places called *Festerchapel.*

Dark forms crested a nearby hill, speeding toward them at an alarming rate. Shit! Not again. Ace would be livid if she knew how much he daydreamed up here.

Heart throbbing, he folded up the magazine page and stuffed it in his back pocket.

Dust billowed behind two motorcycles, weaving effortlessly across the white salt. Something whined past Valentine's head and he ducked behind the gun stand.

He swiveled the gat toward the riders and struggled to wind the handle. The obstinate thing took too much time to warm up, but once it got going, it turned everything it touched into toast three shades too dark.

Static crackled, purple arcs of electricity snapping between the barrels. An arrow pinged off the van. Ace screamed something that was mostly his name and a handful of obscenities. He cranked faster.

His chest and arm ached in protest and his hand slipped from the handle. The hum within the gun became a disappointed sigh, and the electricity died.

"Asswrench!" Heaving his weight against the crankshaft, muscles straining, he wound it with both hands until it screamed with sparks.

The van lurched violently, throwing Valentine from the seat. He slid across the scalding roof, scrabbling for the gun stand. Sharp bolts scratched across his fingers as he clawed his way back. He snatched the spade grips, hauled himself upright, and hit the trigger.

Lightning blasted from the whirring barrels, snapping against the salt and leaving black scorch marks in its wake.

"Back off!" Valentine shouted, but his voice was snatched away by the wind.

One of the riders veered toward the van; Valentine swung the gat their way and the tires on their motorcycle exploded. The rider vaulted over the front and slammed into the ground. Smoke wound from their clothes, and they didn't get back up.

The second cycle raced closer, the two riders coming into focus. The one on the back was tiny, swimming in their oversized helmet. A junior pirate.

Valentine curled his hand away from the trigger. He couldn't fry a kid or fling them off a speeding bike. Why in the hell had they been allowed to come on a raid?

He aimed the gat in front of the motorcycle and squeezed off a warning shot, but the rider simply weaved around the blasted earth and kept pace with the van.

The junior pirate pointed a pipe gun and fired. Something shattered against the gat's seat in a puff of red smoke. A fiery itch raced down Valentine's throat and into his lungs. He coughed violently and gulped a painful breath, batting at the haze through teary eyes. That little shit.

We are Angry Robot, your favourite independent, genre-fluid publisher, bringing you the very best in sci-fi, fantasy, horror and everything in between!

Check out our website at www.angryrobotbooks.com to see our entire catalogue.

Follow us on social media:
Twitter @angryrobotbooks
Instagram @angryrobotbooks
TikTok @angryrobotbooks

Sign up to our mailing list now: